THE ATTACK

He crouched in the alleyway, listening with all his senses to the night as it surrounded him. Once more he was picking up those hideous thoughts, the chanting of a thousand condemned souls crying out in desperate supplication.

And so they came for him.

There was a clanking sound, like a manhole lid being forced open from below. There were no other sounds save the pounding of Philip's heart. There were no cars, no pedestrians.

Only Philip and that thing from the sewer.

It waited there, its glaring red eyes searching, searching. It had an odor, both foul and sweet, like perfume-covered excrement. Then it moved down the street toward the alley.

The thing that had been stalking him lunged out. He felt a claw rake his shin. Then came sharp pain, the warmth of dripping blood. He continued to run. Another thrust—the claw dug into his back, scraping away nuggets of flesh. Philip cried out, his screams high as those of the thing that was attacking him. He could feel the breath of the creature as its mouth found his neck, the hungry teeth digging into his skin.

For the first time, he saw clearly what it was . . .

Also by William Schoell:

SPAWN OF HELL

SHIVERS

William Schoell

LEISURE BOOKS ∞ NEW YORK CITY

A LEISURE BOOK

Published by

Dorchester Publishing Co., Inc.
6 East 39th Street
New York, NY 10016

Copyright©1985 by William Schoell

Printed in the United States of America

PROLOGUE

IN A SMALL room in an old hotel, an elderly man wrote feverishly. Sitting at a desk and scribbling in a notebook, he would stop now and then to pull his sweater more tightly around his shoulders. Cold. He was cold.

Mr. Peterson got up and crossed to the window. Sighing heavily, shivering, he closed the window and shut out the draft. No good—his weary old bones were still chilled. He was still shivering. He knew what *that* implied. *So little time,* he thought, *so little time.* He went back to his desk and continued writing:

The change was slow at first, subtle. We didn't even realize it was happening. A few of us seemed to act . . . peculiar. But then the oddest thing—after awhile we thought their behavior was perfectly normal, because we were behaving that way too.

Something shuffled out in the hall. There was a knock on the door. "Peterson—you in?"

It was another tenant, Mr. Baloos. Mr. *Blues*, they called him. *Not now*, Peterson groaned. He dared not be disturbed before this was finished. He didn't know how long he might have left.

The knocking was more insistent. Blues wanted to chat, play poker, or borrow money. It was always one or the other. "Go away!" Peterson yelled. "Not *now!* I must have my rest."

Offended, Mr. Baloos didn't answer. The shuffling resumed, fading away down the hall. Peterson, eagerly embracing the quiet, concentrated and began writing again.

At first they thought it was primeval in origin. Primeval, ha!—Prime Evil is more like it. They discovered the capsule by chance, while building the foundation for a new chemical plant. No one could have guessed what they'd find inside. Instead of something to study and dissect and probe, it studied and probed and dissected them. It took over their minds. It took over our minds. God help me, it took over mine.

It wasn't long before everyone was under its spell, under the control of our "visitor." And we knew—for it had planted the information in our minds—that we dare not rebel against it. Those of us who had seen it, been ... touched ... by it, had been treated. If our actions, our thoughts, were in any way interpreted as being a threat to its survival, a threat to its mission, we would ...

Peterson was shaking now, his arms and legs trembling so badly it was all he could do to stay in his chair and hold on to the pen. He forced himself to write.

It's happening. I've fought successfully against it for as long as I could, kept my thoughts from reaching it. But—I knew I could only do this for so long.

He had to rest. Sweat poured down his face,

mingling with tears. He must write, he had to get it all down—before . . . The world must know. The city must be warned. He knew what was going to happen. The creature's control had a side effect—the minds of it and its victims were inextricably linked. It knew what they were doing and thinking, but *they* knew what it was doing and thinking too. They knew, Peterson knew, its monstrous plan.

So little time.

He struggled against the fear and the shivering and wielded his pen like a dagger, wedging words into paper. He saw spots in front of his eyes. The thing was making a last-ditch attempt to dissuade him from his task—soon the hallucinations would come. With the hallucinations would come death—unless he stopped, relaxed, let down his guard, and let his mind be taken once again.

He wrote: *On the surface everything seemed normal. It knew that we could not hurt it or stop it. When it came time for my retirement, I even got the de rigueur gold watch and reception. It let us go off on our vacations, have our sick days, and except for one of us—the most important one—carry on our lives as if nothing untoward had happened. Oh, how we wanted to scream and cry when we were with our friends and family. How we wanted to tell them what had happened. But it wouldn't let us. And even when we were able for moments to wrest free of its control, the shivering would start—it would send us a warning—desist or die. Die horribly. The shivering would start, and we would stop.*

Those of us who retired, who left the firm, thought we'd gotten away. That we could forget the past and go on with our lives and never feel its influence again. But no one ever escaped. None of us ever went far. It saw to that. We all knew its influence could only extend so far, that it had limits, geographical limits. So it made sure that our desires were subtly altered, that we stayed close by. Only the most meek among us were allowed our distance.

The one who suffered the most was Everson. He was the strongest—psychologically, physically, in every way—and hence the one who most needed to be watched.

And now, poor Everson . . .the creature has gone too far.

He underlined the words with a stroke so deep and bold that it literally tore into the paper.

He was getting tired. He was getting weak. The spots were getting bigger. He could no longer see the paper. He could no longer hold the pen. He sobbed, miserably. He lifted his hands to his head and tried to keep himself from screaming.

What does it matter? part of him asked. What was he but a dried-up old man struggling by on a pension, a brilliant scientist reduced to a pitiful existence in a dreadful hotel. He had never known the value of a dollar, never saved his money, never seen the warning signs—when you're old and without money, you might just as well be dead. Why hadn't he seen the warnings?

But the rents had been so high. And he'd had

gambling debts to pay, debts which wiped out his savings. Everything he and his late wife Doris had worked so hard for. What does it matter? he asked himself again. *Doris never lived to take that trip we'd planned anyway.*

He only hoped that somebody would find his memoirs. Writing them would literally be the death of him. Had he gotten it all down? Could they piece the rest together?

Would they *believe* what he had written?

He was still shivering, only it was worse than before. Much worse.

For a moment he almost screamed that he was sorry and would never do it again, he almost screamed that he would burn the notebook and spend the rest of his miserable life in atonement if only he'd be spared. Anything, he'd do anything to save himself from *that*. But it was too late. This time he had gone too far. The process was irreversible and he knew it. He was shaking like a junkie undergoing withdrawal. He was sweating like a pig, trembling and jerking like a palsied epileptic. He managed to get up from his chair, knocking it to the floor. He took one step.

"No!"

With horror he realized it had regained complete control of his mind. Something compelled him to grab the notebook in his hand, to tear it into shreds.

No. My sacrifice will have been worthless.
"Damn you!" he screamed.

He was jerked over to the window like a puppet on strings. The pages were in crumpled pieces. His hands shot out and crashed bloodily through the glass. He did not cry out. He felt no pain. His mind was filled with utter despair as the papers flew out of his hands to trickle away with the breeze, floating down down into the alleyway to mingle with the trash. Now there really was no hope. Everyone was doomed. All was lost. Lost in a sea of refuse.

The walls were coming closer. The damned thing had picked his brain and discovered his deadliest fear. *Claustrophobia*. The room was closing in. Peterson, still shivering with maniacal fury, reached out his arms to push the walls away.

No! Keep away. Help me!

His heart was pounding wildly. The four walls were pressing against him and his arms were too weak to keep them away. The spots before his eyes were bigger. His arms flailed in every direction, helplessly, as the room became the size of a closet, a trunk, a suitcase.

The size of a *shoebox*.

With disbelief, Peterson saw the stuff of his body crumbling, dissolving, running down his legs. Blood and flesh intermingling. Even his clothes were beginning to burn, shred, drip into the stream of gore. How could *hallucination* have done this to him, have squashed him? No, it was not the hallucination that was killing him. He was suffering the fate he'd been *warned* against.

Peterson tottered, slipped, fell back against the wall beside the shattered window. Somehow from his shoebox he saw his blood still sticking to the cracked glass, until it too began to sizzle and dissolve, dropping to nothingness on the floor. As Peterson lay against the wall, his arms raised up in the air, and his legs spread outward, his entire body *melted*.

Until he was a mere smear upon the wall.

PART I

Wednesday, October 16th

ONE

"MY BROTHER IS missing."

Steven Everson sat on a bench in the police station, waiting to speak to someone in the Department of Missing Persons. He was unshaven, and his clothes were disheveled. He had not slept for hours. Though normally a good-looking man of thirty-one, he now looked unattractive and on the verge of forty-five. He kept rubbing his eyes, trying to clear away the persistent cloudiness. He sighed and wiped his mouth with the back of his hand.

Thirty minutes later a young woman ushered him into an office for his appointment with one of the detectives on the Missing Persons Squad. He sat down in a chair next to a cluttered desk. The desk was full of papers and the remains of a half-eaten breakfast. The big man at the desk introduced himself as Detective John Albright. He looked like he drank too much beer and ate too much pasta. He was broad-shouldered and big-boned, so his excess weight didn't look quite as bad on him as it could have. During the conversation he kept scratching his crewcut and rubbing his puffy cheeks with his fingers.

The whole thing seemed unreal to Steven. Thinking back on it later, he would hardly remember what either of them had said. He simply explained what had happened, and asked what could be done to locate his brother Joey. The officer listened to him patiently, now and then asking a pertinent question.

"How old is your brother?" the detective asked.

His brother had disappeared on October 15th, sometime between two-thirty and three-thirty in the afternoon. He had gone out jogging, like he did every day, wearing red shorts and a white T-shirt. He had been in his usual good humor. He'd refused a cup of coffee from the pot Steven had just made. Rushing out the door, he'd promised to return within the hour.

He had never come back.

Steven hadn't started to worry until after a quarter to five. Unable to concentrate on his latest mangled manuscript, he had turned on the television to watch a couple of mindless game shows and sitcom reruns, finally switching to an old science-fiction film at four-thirty. He got up at the first commercial and went to raid the refrigerator. He had glanced up at the wall clock in the kitchen. Joey was only about an hour late, but he was usually so punctual that Steven couldn't help but feel a bit uneasy. After all, everyone knew that Central Park wasn't the safest place in New York City, even in the daytime.

"My brother is twenty-one."

"Does he have any friends in the city?"

"Not really. He's only been living with me a few weeks. He graduated from UVM—that's University of Vermont—last June, spent the summer bumming around with some classmates."

At six o'clock he'd finally gone out to look for Joey. He'd followed in the boy's footsteps; he knew which path his brother took. He had walked down along Central Park West until he reached the entrance to the Park at 72nd Street. He had stood across from it, on the other side of the road, watching as cars passed by, looking absently at the pedestrians gliding through the shadowy dusk. The park had nearly been deserted at that hour.

Briskly, he made his way toward the jogging path that Joey liked to use. To his left there had been a big, wide-open field that stretched almost all the way to the east side of the city. Only one of the several baseball diamonds had been in use —by a small group of teenagers who seemed oblivious to the darkening sky. Steven had seen the skyline of the East Side buildings. They'd been all lit up, as mysterious and beautiful as a city of the gods. Monuments of loneliness.

"There is a woman," Steven said.

Albright raised his eyebrows.

"Nothing too serious. Someone he met in a singles bar one night." He saw a funny look on the detective's face and added: "Joey didn't spend all his time in bars. He spent most of his time looking for work, going out on interviews—"

"What sort of work?"

"Something in the sociopolitical field. He had a BA in—" he stopped short. "He was something of an activist."

"Tell me about this woman."

"I never met her. He saw her two, three nights a week. Name's Vivian." Steven scrunched up his face trying to remember the last name. "Vivian something—I forget. He told me very little about her. She was really the only person Joey knew in the city—aside from me, of course."

Albright leaned back in his chair, took a sip of coffee, and said: "Mr. Everson, there are some things I have to be very blunt about. Your brother is the—let's see," he checked some papers in front of him, "the 315th person to disappear this week."

"What did you say?"

"You heard right. I said the *315th* person to be reported missing this week. *So far.*"

"That's unbelievable."

"Nobody *ever* realizes. But in a city this size, well, you can imagine." He took anther sip of coffee. "Most of the cases are solved pretty quickly. Kids run away from home. Fathers chuck it all and leave the family. Stuff like that. In fact, you might get a phone call, or find your brother waiting for you, when you go back to your apartment."

"You mean, there's nothing else we can do?"

"About 15,000 people a year disappear, Mr. Everson. There's not much more we can do. When some people still don't turn up after a long absence, the family often hires a private detective who can give his whole attention to a case. We can't do that. We haven't got the manpower. We circulate pictures, ask around, the usual. But that's all we *can* do."

"But . . . my brother. What about him?"

"Don't start worrying yet, Mr. Everson. Believe me. We got people like you who have been waiting *years* for their loved ones to come home. For you it's barely been over a day. I'm sure your brother will turn up if you give it time. He did the singles bars? He might just have wound up at somebody's place last night. You ask me, he's shackin' up with this girlfriend of his. You get in touch with her?"

"I don't have her number. Can't remember her name, as I said. He would have called me by now, in any case."

Albright sighed. "Mr. Everson, we'll do the best we can. Let's see. You've given us a picture, right? We'll check with hospitals and morgues. Give it time. He'll show up."

"What if he shows up *dead?*"

Albright just looked at him. "Have faith, Mr. Everson. Kids—young guys on the make on the loose in the big city—you know how they are."

Steven tried to control his anger, his frustration. "He was wearing *jogging shorts*. He never came home to change. How can I make you understand? He never did a thing without telling me! He went into Central Park and never came back."

"Mr. Everson, if something happened to your brother in the park, we'd know about it by now."

A thought flashed through Steven's mind. The acres of woods and grass and rocks in Central Park—no-man's-land. Bodies that could be buried, hidden, lost without a trace if no one was looking for them.

"You remember the last name of this Vivian gal, you tell us. Or call her yourself. That's where your brother is, you can bet. Kids aren't very responsible to their elders these days."

"But—" What was the use?

Albright's demeanor seemed to soften a bit. He was studying the picture of Joey—fair-haired, a lightly freckled face, blue eyes, a *handsome* boy—staring at it as if some secret place inside him had been touched and a vague memory stirred. "Good-looking kid." He looked up, all business again. "He'll be all right."

"Isn't there *anything* you can do?"

"Please, Mr. Everson. Keep in mind the enormous workload we have. If we were to spend so much time and effort on every individual case, especially in this instance, when a boy has only been missing a little over a day—well, you can imagine how much work we'd get done. We'll just have to wait."

Steven almost laughed. *We'll* have to wait. Who was he kidding? He'd spent the night calling hospitals, going from one Third Avenue singles bar—Joey's haunts—to another asking if anyone had seen him, spent a sleepless night tossing and turning. And he says, *we'll* have to wait.

New York was so huge—when someone disappeared it was like they'd jumped into a slimy ocean of uncaring rabble.

Steven got up and shook the detective's hand. Neither of them had anything more to say.

Harriet MacGruder waddled into the elevator of the Berkley Arms Hotel, pressed number nine, and dropped her shopping bags onto the floor. Like the hotel, she'd seen better days. She was a short, squat woman with big, fleshy arms, an imposing bosom, and a homely—but pleasant enough—face. She wore a weather-beaten straw hat at a cock-eyed angle. While the elevator wheezed its way up to the ninth floor, she hummed a tune she had heard in the super-market.

When the elevator stopped, she got out and walked down the grimy pink hallway until she arrived at her room: Number 917, completely furnished with a hot plate and a tiny refrig-erator. The bathroom—which she shared with three other people of both sexes—was further down the corridor. Now and then she would get down on her hands and knees and scrub it like crazy with detergents and cleansers, but within a week it was just as dirty and smelly as before.

She couldn't understand it, as her neighbors appeared to be clean. Especially Mr. Peterson, the man who occupied the cubicle—they called it a room—to the immediate right of her own. Most of her neighbors were old people like her-self—spinsters, bachelors, widows and widowers left alone to die by their uncaring children and relatives. It made no difference. Whatever their lives had been like once upon a time, they were all living the same life now. The single-room-occupancy hotels contained so much loneliness and despair they had developed their own special odor. And it was a foul one.

Mrs. MacGruder entered her room and placed the two shopping bags on her bed. She hadn't much space to move around in. Most of her clothes were crammed into the wardrobe, and her other possessions were in and on top of the desk in the corner. Little mementoes of seventy eight years. Toys. Old love letters. Souvenirs from trips with her late husband. Trips all over the world, she said, though she had really never been out of the country.

She opened a can of soup and sat down to read the paper while it heated on the hot plate. She skipped to the movie section. Now and then she and Mr. Peterson would go to see a film together. They had to budget carefully to make their small checks last throughout the month, but they could afford to see a film if the price was right and the theater nearby. One particular movie caught her attention. She took the paper out into the hall with her and rapped on Mr. Peterson's door. There was no answer, which surprised her. Perhaps he was asleep.

She went back to check on the soup, glad to see that it had not yet started to boil; she hated the way boiling made it taste. She remembered then that she had not seen her neighbor for quite some time now, and began to worry. She turned off the hot plate, opened her door, and went out to check on him again.

His door was not locked; a suspicious sign.

She gave no thought to what she might find, but opened it abruptly and entered. It was hard to see, as the lights were out and very little sunshine filtered through the windows at this time of day on their side of the building. Everything seemed to be in order, except there was an odd, fruity smell in the air. The room was colder than it should have been—no wonder. The window was broken. *Now how did* that *happen?* she wondered.

Mr. Peterson was definitely not there. She snapped on the lights, looked around more thoroughly, including a peek under the bed and in the wardrobe, then went back to her soup and the newspaper. Strange, very strange. Perhaps Mr. Baloos had seen him; she would have to ask him later.

She ate the rapidly cooling soup, finished digesting the grim news of the day, and took a nap.

She'd meant only to sleep for a little while, but when she finally awoke it was four hours later. She felt quite refreshed; in the mood for a good movie. She went back out into the hall, opened Peterson's door once more, and stepped again into his room. Now the sunlight was coming in so brightly through the shattered window that she didn't need to turn on the lamp.

Her eyes were attracted to a strange splotch on the wall near the window. When she'd first noticed it before, she had assumed the reddish stain was simply the result of dripping water running down the pink wallpaper. It happened all the time, what with the lousy plumbing in the hotel.

But now she could see the stain more clearly, more distinctly. She went over to it, and saw that it was actually composed of a rather sticky, dripping substance not unlike blood, but with the consistency of jelly. She reached out to touch it, but drew back, suddenly frightened. She stepped back a few feet, staring at the wall, and it was then that it hit her. The shape on the wall had a very familiar outline.

Mrs. MacGruder could have sworn that it was shaped just like a man.

Joey, where the hell are you?

I was supposed to take care of you, that's what Dad said. In case anything happened, I was to take care of you. I've done a lousy job, huh?

Steven sat in the living room of his apartment, a converted brownstone, staring at the couch his brother had been using for a bed. They hadn't had much time to talk. Joey was always on the run—an interview, a date, a night on the town. He'd saved up a lot of money by working part-time while he'd been in college. He'd even intended to pay Steven back the money he'd lent him for tuition as soon as he got a job.

Only twenty one. Twenty one years old. What a time to die.

But he wasn't dead. He couldn't be! He had to stop thinking that way. Joey would walk in the next morning, bright and smiling, with some story, some sensible, if infuriating, excuse. And Steven *wanted* to be infuriated tomorrow. He'd take anger over sorrow anytime.

He couldn't sleep. He knew that. He sat down on the sofa and thought about his brother for what seemed like hours. His brother was missing and nobody cared. He'd learned so much from Joey. The boy had taught him to open his eyes about so many things. Joey was so much more *involved* in everything—so much more of a political person, a realist—while Steven was the impractical dreamer. Steven had been caught up in himself all the time, while Joey often seemed to be carrying the woes of the world on his back. That's why Steven had been glad to see Joey gallivanting around the city like a kid in a candy store; he'd been such a *serious* youngster, concerned that every person be given a fair deal. In contrast, Steven had thought of almost nothing but what he could get out of life—he could see that now—as if he was the center of all existence. He had spent his time embroiled in a writer's fantasies. Joey could have offered so much more to the world, given half a chance. It just wasn't fair. Not fair at all.

Damn it. He had to stop thinking about his brother as if he was dead. Save the eulogies for later.

Steven wished there was somebody he could talk to about this. Andrea—his girlfriend? lover? combatant? What could he call her these days seeing as how their relationship was crumbling? Anyway, she was out of town and, if she knew when she planned to return, had kept it a secret. He'd taken a well-deserved two weeks off from work—he was Senior Editor of *NightLife* Magazine—and wasn't really all that close to any of the people he worked with, not enough to call them up at home just to burden them with his problems. At least he was free to give Joey's disappearance his undivided attention.

Of course there was always his old buddy, Harry Faulkin, the weatherman. Harry and he had grown up together, gone to school together, built snowmen together as children. But Harry's best friend was Harry, of that there was no doubt. He was not the shoulder-to-cry-on type, no sir. Steven was fond of the fellow, but only to a point. No, Harry was not the one to turn to when in need of comfort. Still, he *did* work for a TV station. Maybe later, if Joey had still not returned, Harry could pull some strings, get the boy's picture on the air.

The house was so empty without Joey. Steven hadn't realized how lonely he'd been.

It was six o'clock. He realized that he hadn't had a bite to eat all day. He got up, went into the kitchen, and opened the refrigerator. He looked through the shelves carefully, searching for something bland but with substance. He had no real appetite. All he wanted was something to keep up his energy.

The phone rang? Police? *Joey?*

It was a woman. She said her name was Vivian Jessup.

Vivian? Joey's Vivian?

"I just wanted to know if Joey is okay. He *is* all right, isn't he?"

How did she know that Joey was missing? Or did she mean something else?

"He hasn't come back yet," Steven said, wondering exactly how close this woman had been to his brother, and what part she might have played in the boy's disappearance.

"Come back? You mean you don't know where he is?"

Steven quickly told her what had happened.

"Oh my God," she said. "Then they've done it."

"Pardon me?"

She didn't explain, so Steven continued. "I filed an official report earlier today at the precinct. They just told me to wait and see, they'd do all they could."

"What *are* they doing?"

"Not much." He told her what Albright had said.

"I'm so sorry. I was . . . very fond . . . of Joseph. I . . ."

"Vivian," he interrupted. "Have you seen my brother? Did you see him yesterday or any time last night? Do you know where he is now? You're about the only person he knows in New York."

She didn't answer at first. Then she said, very quickly: "No, I haven't seen him. I—look, I can't talk on the phone. Please understand. I *would* like to talk to you privately. Could you come see me this evening about nine o'clock?"

"Yes, I guess so. But what is this about? Do

you know something about Joey's disappearance?"

"I'm not sure." She paused, as if trying to get her breath. "I really can't talk now, not on the phone. Come by tonight." She gave him her address.

Steven scribbled quickly in a note pad by the phone. *Madison and 68th.*

"You will come?"

"I will. But can't you tell me what this is all about?"

"Tonight. Nine o'clock. Goodbye."

She hung up.

Eric Thorne left the Institute at 8:15 P.M. and headed towards Broadway. His "friend" was missing tonight. His "friend" was an old drunkard who each night sprawled outside the entrance to a shuttered restaurant, and had done so at one spot or another for several years. Eric wondered what the hell had happened to the guy. He was *always* there.

He walked on toward the subway thinking about the nice dinner he'd be consuming in approximately an hour, but his thoughts kept returning to the derelict. Now that he thought about it, most of the bums who had hung out in this section of the city had disappeared. Other people might have assumed it was the advent of cold weather that had driven them elsewhere, but Eric knew better. He had worked in this area long enough to know that that wasn't true. When winter came, they would just huddle up with a bottle somewhere, the alcohol warming them and pickling their brains to beyond the point where they could distinguish heat from cold. Of course many of them died. But not all. Not this many. And they were almost *all* gone now. Poor souls.

He was about to descend to the subway when an old sot approached him from behind the darkness of an abandoned car in the alleyway. "Fifty cents, mister? Got fifty cents?"

Was this the last remaining tramp? Eric wondered. He almost laughed at his own suspicious mentality.

He was almost sure that he had seen other figures back there in the shadows, nestled in alcoves, hiding next to garbage cans. But they'd darted out of sight—with a speed too fast for any derelict—before he could make certain. Perhaps they'd been figments of his imagination, products of his worsening eyesight. Well, at least this one was real.

"Fifty cents, please?"

Eric dug into his pocket for change. A quarter and two dimes. Well, it would have to do. Even as he handed the money to the man he knew it was more an act of futility than of kindness.

"Thank you, mister. God bless ya. God bless ya."

There was something odd about the man. Beneath the smelly rags he wore for clothes, behind his dead, almost unseeing eyes, there was something *there*. Instead of the blank expression, the vacuous gaze of the typical drunk, there was a palpable *feeling*, an emotion made up of equal parts confusion, loneliness, and terror. They stood there at the top of the stairs staring at each other, both waiting for the other to speak. The drunk wanting and needing explanations; Eric waiting to hear the man before him give voice to the unspeakable horrors he had witnessed. Why could neither of them speak?

Eric turned away and started down the steps. Before he had gone even halfway, the drunk called out.

"Where are they?" he said. "Where have my friends gone?"

Eric turned back, saw the look of horror on the old drunk's face, read his feelings and emotions, and almost *reeled*. He started back down the stairs again, practically running toward the token booth. He quickly bought a token, raced through the turnstile, and just made it onto an uptown train.

He found a seat. He glanced out the window behind him as the train left the station, and saw that the drunk had followed him down the stairs, and was even now staring at him from the other side of the turnstile. The sight chilled Thorne's blood. He pressed his hands over his eyes and did not remove them until the train had arrived at the next stop.

Amid the bustle of people who boarded and departed, he felt more secure. He tried to determine why that old man had so unsettled him. Certainly he'd dealt with derelicts before. Why such distress?

Because the man had read his mind.

It was usually the opposite. Thorne could pick up thoughts and feelings from other people, had been able to do it all his life. He had picked up frightening thoughts from that man, horrible images of living nightmares, of death and decay. That man had *seen* things, seen repulsive things done to other people. And though Thorne had caught only glimpses of the horror, that had been more than enough.

But it was not the images that had left him so shaken, but rather the fact that the man had willingly transferred those images to Eric's mind, had even, in fact, picked up Eric's thoughts as he'd walked by. He had *known* that Thorne had been wondering where the other derelicts had disappeared to! He had approached Eric not for money, but for the exchange of information.

Damn it! Thorne swore to himself. *This is what my life has been devoted to. Why did I run away? Why didn't I stay there with him, learn what he had to say?*

Because the implications were just too horrible. The images he had picked up were too unreal, the product of a crazed consciousness. He would have learned nothing from a man whose mind had long since abandoned him. Surely he had not been sane. He couldn't have been.

But nevertheless, he had definitely been a *sensitive.* Thorne could not ignore that. He would have to find him again.

And God help him when he did.

* * *

Steven left for Vivian's apartment at 8:35. He walked down to Lincoln Center to catch the crosstown bus at 66th Street. The bus cut through Central Park and would stop not far from Ms. Jessup's apartment house. He boarded, paid his fare, and sat down in the back. There were only a few other passengers.

As the bus turned into the road through Central Park, he stared out the window, trying to see past his reflection, to catch a glimpse of the darkness outside and whatever it might have been hiding. He felt chilled—not just by the cold weather, but by the eerie quality of the park at night. Was his brother in there some-where—in pain, crying, bleeding to death—or dead? Last night he'd looked all over the area where Joey had gone jogging, and again this morning before he'd gone to the police. *Nothing.*

The bus went through a tunnel, and the moon-light was blocked. Steven thought for a moment that he had seen someone walking through the tunnel, someone hunched over, tired or ill. *Joey?* He turned his head and stared into the tunnel as the bus pulled out, but the figure was gone, if it had ever been there at all. *Stop seeing Joey in every shadow,* he told himself. *It won't do any good.*

He got off at Madison and 65th Street, walked up three blocks, and turned right at 68th. The woman's home was located in the middle of the block. It was an old, but swanky, apartment house, with an aging doorman and a big, mirrored lobby full of plants and cushioned chairs. The doorman checked with Vivian

Jessup via intercom, and Steven was allowed to proceed to the elevator. He stepped into the car, pushed the correct button, and tried to summon up a mental image of the woman he was about to meet. Her voice on the phone had been sultry, husky, sensual even, and she'd sounded older than he'd expected. Wasn't that the rage these days—older women, younger men? He'd never really known what type of women his brother had gone for, but there was no reason to assume he stuck to women his own age. Maybe the two of them had had some kind of crisis—like he and Andrea had had. *They'd* spent plenty of nights staying up discussing their future, hadn't they? Couldn't Joey and Vivian have been doing the same?

There were only two apartments on each floor. He pressed the buzzer outside 14A and listened as soft, delicate footsteps approached from within. *Please be there, Joey. Be inside "shacked up" with Vivian.*

The door opened. A cautious face looked out. Pretty, soft. Tense.

"Are you Mr. Everson?" the woman asked.

"Yes. Ms. Jessup, I presume?"

She nodded. "*Mrs.* Jessup. Come in, please."

She was a beautiful woman, but even more "mature" than Steven had expected. She appeared to be at least in her mid-forties, maybe older. There was a glamorous aura about her, a sort of fading loveliness recaptured in part by paint and powder. She had an upswept hairstyle and wore vivid red lipstick. Golden earrings dangled from her creamy lobes. Her face was narrow, small, with hazel eyes, high model's cheekbones, and a slightly longish—but attractive—nose. Her lips and eyes were small—made larger by the lipstick and mascara. The eyelashes may have been false. She was about five-foot-five, and slender. Her outfit—though a casual one—was chic and expensive, not the thing one wore to the supermarket.

As she ushered him into the living room, Steven wondered how she and Joey had ever managed to connect. He couldn't imagine her sitting with the "chicks" in the East Side singles bars. Cocktail lounges and hotel bars were more her speed. She had to be quite wealthy, judging from the apartment. The living room was exquisite, with soft lights, mahogany furniture, and a rolling bar. There was a thick blue rug on the floor. The view from the panoramic window was stunning; one could see most of Central Park. The enormous Gulf and Western building, so brightly lit, was in the distance.

"You look a great deal like your brother, you know. Very handsome boys, I'll tell you."

"Thank you." He didn't feel particularly handsome. Something was wrong with Vivian. She was too composed, trying too hard to be casual—he found it hard matching her with the worried, nervous voice he had heard on the phone, although he was sure it was the same voice.

"Can I get you a drink?" she asked, flashing her lovely, warm eyes in his direction. She motioned for him to sit on the couch.

"Yes, I'd like that. I could certainly use one."

"All right." She smiled. It was out of place, considering. "What do you take?"

"Bourbon on the rocks, if you have it."

"Of course, I'll just take a moment." She went to the bar, selected a glass, and poured a great deal of liquor into it. "What do you do for a living, Mr. Everson?"

"I'm a magazine editor. And occasional free-lance writer."

"Oh? That's interesting. Are you working on anything now?"

Why was she bothering with small talk? He wanted to get on with it. "Nothing in particular," he lied. He was in the middle of a free-lance celebrity profile, but there was no need for her to know that. He cleared his throat. "Mrs. Jessup—just what is it that you wanted to talk to me about?" The significance of the *Mrs.* finally hit him. Was she a widow, a divorcee— or was Joey fooling around with a married woman?

"Oh *that*," she said. "I'm so—I'm sorry if I alarmed you before." Just for a second, her smile had faded; Steven had caught it. She was hiding behind a facade; she was deeply disturbed and trying to hide it. But why? Why not come out with it?

She walked over to the couch with his drink. He sat there staring at her, a study in impatience. Their eyes met briefly as the drink passed from her hand to his, but she turned away before he could peer too deeply.

She remained standing. "It's just—it's just

that I . . . Well, to be frank, I had someone here at the time and I . . . Look, let me make myself a drink and we'll talk."

"All right," Steven said. He wondered why she had called him in the first place if, as she claimed, she had had someone with her?

While she made her drink, he watched her. She sensed it too, though she wasn't looking in his direction. She spilled some of the gin she was pouring, and an ice cube tumbled onto the rug. When she was ready, she came over to the couch and sat beside him. He got a strong whiff of her perfume and noted that she smelled rather nice. Her smile was gone. She wore a tense look that was occasionally punctuated by a quick nervous grin, almost a twitch. "Is your drink all right?"

"It's fine." He looked around the room as if to emphasize what he was going to say. "Mrs. Jessup. Is my brother here?"

"No, I don't know where he is."

Steven just sat there and looked at her. "Well, I was under the impression that you wanted me to cover over because you had something to say about his disappearance. You asked me if he was all right when we talked on the phone, as if you knew something, as if you knew that he was missing." Steven remembered that she'd said something else that was funny—"they've done it" or "he's done it"—but it had happened so fast he couldn't be sure.

She touched her lower lip. "No—I-I didn't know. I was just afraid . . ." She held her forehead with her fingertips, grimacing. The strain on her face made her look sixty. "Mr. Everson, I don't know where Joey is. I didn't know he was missing. When you told me what had happened I just thought that I could—console you—tell you a little about myself and Joey. Maybe explain a few things that might help you to understand why Joey—"

"Why Joey what?"

"Why Joey might have . . . done away with himself."

"*What?*" Steven jumped out of his seat and turned to face her. "Done away with himself! You think Joey committed suicide?"

"I'm not sure, mind you. I just thought it might be possible. That's why I called to make sure he was all right. Don't look at me like that." She shivered. "God, I don't *want* him to be dead. I just wanted to *prepare* you."

"Why? Why would he have killed himself?"

"Please sit down," she said. "You're making me nervous." Pulling his arm she got him back down on the sofa. "Sit down and I'll tell you everything.

"How much did he tell you about our relationship?" she asked.

"Virtually nothing. I didn't even see the kid that much." For a moment Steven regretted his use of the word "kid," not because Joey was in fact a grown man, but because it accentuated the age difference between his brother and Vivian. He didn't know how sensitive she might be on the subject.

"We were quite close," she said. "I met him . . . at a party . . . a few weeks ago. Not long after he came to New York. He said he was staying with you until he could . . . afford his own place. He thought very highly of you.

"I found him quite charming and clever. And very attractive. But still, he was a child. I was forty-two and he was—obscenely younger, as I'm sure you're aware. I thought it would be foolish of me to think otherwise. It's kind of unfair. Old men go everywhere with their little-girl lovers, and no one gives a damn. But when the situation is reversed—well, let me tell you, everyone seems to care. In spite of what you see on the soaps."

She took more of her drink, sat back on the couch, a little more relaxed now. "It feels so good to talk about it."

"Then you and Joey were having an affair. Is that how we put it these days?"

"I can tell. You think I'm disgusting."

Steven shook his head. "I'm neither a prude nor a hypocrite. You're right about the double standard. Anyway, Joey's—social life—was his own business. And yours, I suppose." He stared into his bourbon. "My brother was ahead of his time in many ways. Mature for his age. I can understand why the age difference wouldn't have mattered to him."

"No, no, that's just it. It didn't! It didn't. *I* was the one. *I* was the one who couldn't take it. I listened too much to my friends, to other women my age. I told Joey just last week that it was over between us. He was extremely upset."

Steven didn't know what to say. Was Vivian implying that Joey killed himself due to unrequited love? That he threw away a lifetime because—let's face it—a woman literally old enough to have carried him in her womb no longer cared for him? He knew all about "strange bedfellows" and "unlikely partners" and all that, but this was stretching credibility to the limit. Joey was only twenty one, after all.

Vivian picked up on his disbelief. "I know it must sound strange to you. But in the brief time I knew your brother, I could tell that he was sensitive, that he held in his feelings. He'd sit and listen for hours while you told him your troubles, but he'd never burden you with his own."

That much was true. Joey was like that. "And you think he was upset enough to want to *die?*"

"I hadn't thought it hit him that badly. But then there was the phone call."

"What phone call?"

"He called me up two nights ago and told me that if I didn't take him back he'd kill himself. Drown himself in the river, he said. He sounded drunk, out of his head. I assumed it was just childish bellowing. I didn't take it seriously. Now I wish that I had."

Vivian leaned over and put her hand on top of Steven's. "I didn't want to tell you any of this. I know you loved him. But when you told me he was missing . . . I couldn't see you spending hours looking for him, never knowing if he was alive or dead. You had to know the truth, no matter how painful. I couldn't let you go on wondering what had happened, when I knew what had happened, that he was dead."

Steven got out of his seat so suddenly that the woman almost spilled her drink. "*No!* It just doesn't make sense, lady." Leaning over her, he put a constraining hand on her shoulder. "I don't mean to sound rude or unkind. I realize that you're possibly as worried as I am. But I don't believe that Joey's lying at the bottom of the river. He was not the suicidal type."

"Of course, I can't be positive," she said, shrugging off his hand with irritation. "But I thought you should be aware of the *possibility*, at least."

Steven stood up straight. "I understand that and I appreciate it. But Joey was in good spirits yesterday afternoon. I know he hides his feelings, but I don't have to be an expert in psychology to know that people don't run off and kill themselves—for whatever reason—unless they're horribly depressed, practically on the verge of despair. I'm his *brother*. Don't you think I would have seen it, would have known that something was wrong?"

"Perhaps he was afraid to tell you. I'm sure I'm not the kind of woman he usually associated with. He was afraid you might object, or laugh at him. That's why he never told you much about me. He figured—it was over. Why bother?"

"If he was suicidal, over you or anything else, he couldn't have hidden it from me. Yesterday he was downright jovial."

Vivian seemed not to have heard him. "We saw each other at least three or four times a week. Sometimes we'd go out. Other times he just came over and spent the night. He was kind and tender. Passionate in that way of youth." She spoke as if she was entranced. "Such a sweet boy."

Steven spoke more forcefully, trying to break the spell she was under. "Look, it doesn't matter whether Joey told me about you, or his breakup with you, or not. The fact remains that I am his brother, and I would have known if he was that distraught. For Pete's sake, he was living with me. I could tell his moods, what kind of changes he was going through. And I'm telling you that yesterday he was in great spirits. He went out in the afternoon without giving me the slightest indication that he was upset about anything. I'm sorry if that bothers your ego, Mrs. Jessup. I'm sure you cared for him a great deal, and he probably cared—*cares*—for you. But my brother, who had his whole life ahead of him, would not put on his shorts and his sweatshirt and go galloping out of the house in the middle of the day with a smile on his face and then go commit suicide. It just doesn't fit."

Vivian just sat there and looked up at him, her face completely expressionless.

"At least you can take *comfort* in the fact that he didn't kill himself," Steven said. "Not because of anything you may have said."

Vivian got up and moved slowly toward the bar. "Care for another drink, Mr. Everson?"

"No. I've hardly touched the first. Look, I'm sorry if I've hurt your feelings. I didn't mean to."

"Do you think I *want* him to be dead? I only did what I thought was best. I could have kept silent, left you totally unprepared for the worst. Well, I hope you're right. I hope he didn't kill himself. Over me. Over anyone. I hope he's safe and sound. Somewhere."

"I'm sure he is." Steven downed his bourbon in one gulp—it burned but it felt good—and moved toward her as she added more ice to her own unfinished drink. "But damn it! Why do I have this feeling that *you know* where?"

"*What?* How would I know where he is? What kind of accusation is that supposed to be?"

Embarrassed, Steven backed away and hoped the correct response would occur to him. "It's just that you still seem to be hiding something. On the phone. Tonight. Right now. I keep getting this feeling that you're only giving me half-truths."

Vivian slammed the lid down on the ice bucket. "Well, I'm sorry if you don't trust me. I'm sorry if you think I'm a crazy, disgusting old woman who dared to fool around with your precious younger brother. You're just angry at me because you think you failed. You think that you failed somehow, that you were a lousy babysitter. But it's not your fault and it's not mine."

A manic look came into Vivian's eyes. She shuddered violently. "This city chews people up, did you know that?" She ran a hand over her shoulder. "It just swallows them whole. Don't waste time looking for your brother. He's been swallowed up, consumed by the city. We'll never see him again, so don't bother looking. Just go on with your life and *forget him*. For both our sakes."

"What on earth are you talking about? Are you *crazy?*"

"Your brother is *dead* and you must accept it!"

"How can you be so sure of that, God damn it!"

"Because I know it, I feel it. *Please*. Don't ask me any more questions!"

"What kind of perverse—"

"Go ahead and call me names. It won't change anything." Vivian walked to the opposite end of the room and pointed down the hall toward the door. "Now do me a favor and get out of here. You've made me very upset."

Steven walked over to her and grabbed her by the shoulders.

"Leave me alone," she said.

"I'll leave you alone. After you tell me how you can be so positive that Joey is dead. He's my brother. A *young man*. I love my brother and I want to know where he is. I want you to tell me everything you know, and I want you to tell me *now!*"

Vivian stared at him, a look of utter horror on her face. That first flash of panic that he'd noticed when he'd grabbed her had been washed away and replaced by livid terror. She started to shake uncontrollably. "I don't know anything. I don't know anything. I just wanted to prepare you, Mr. Everson. I just wanted to help you. I can't tell you a thing, I swear. It would . . ." It was as if she was giving a performance for an unseen spectator. "I don't know where your brother is. I don't know if he's dead or alive. And I don't care. Just leave me alone. Please, *please*, leave me alone!" She was screaming now, her voice hoarse and her visage twisted into a hideous mask. Startled by the sudden change, Steven removed his arms and stepped back; he couldn't take his eyes off her. She kept shaking, continuing to scream about how she knew nothing and wanted to be left alone.

"All right! All right!" Steven held out his arm imploringly, waiting for her to calm down. It took a couple of minutes for her to return to normal, for her face to relax. When she regained her composure, Steven found his anger returning. He tried to stay in control. Getting upset would clearly do no good.

"Look, Vivian, I don't know what's wrong. And I don't want you to have another fit. But I do want you to have a little talk with the police. Strictly routine. Will you be agreeable to that?"

"No police," she said quickly, the panic welling up in her voice again.

"They just have to ask you a few questions. Not tonight, if you're upset. But tomorrow. Any time you're ready. You'll have to do it."

"No. No police."

"I won't leave until you agree."

"I *can't*."

"Just say yes. I'll take care of the details. They'll be in touch with you."

"It's not necessary. I've told you everything."

44

"Yes. I'm sure you have. But the police will want to, will *have* to, speak to you anyway. Please say you'll agree."

She looked at him miserably. "I have no choice, do I?"

"No."

"Then you can give them my name. I'll talk to them, I promise. But I'll only do it if you leave now. It was a mistake to have you here tonight."

"All right. I'm going. But the police will be in touch, I can promise you that. There's a lot you have to answer for."

They said good night at the door. Steven gave her an imploring look, a silent prayer that she'd break down and tell him what had happened to his brother. She turned away and closed the door.

As Steven walked to the elevator, he could hear her crying. Real waterworks. She was sobbing so strenuously that the sound of it came through the door she'd collapsed against and drifted down the hallway. Who was she crying for? Steven wondered. Herself or Joey?

The elevator came. Vivian would have to comfort herself tonight.

Steven wasn't up to it.

TWO

PHILIP REGINALD HAUPSTER had been born over fifty years ago in a small Pennsylvania town, son of the richest man in the state. When the family's considerable assets were wiped out during the Depression, his mother ran off with a philandering married neighbor and his father blew his brains out with a pistol. From then on things went steadily downhill.

He'd stayed with his Aunt Sarah until he'd reached manhood, upon which he was cast out to have his way with the world. The world fought back. He made a reasonably secure living as a door-to-door salesman in New York, but found himself unable to sustain personal relationships. He had always been thought of as a "creepy kid," and in adult years continued to upset people by his presence. This was not due to his appearance, but to his manner, the odd way he had of "psyching" people out. Of knowing their innermost thoughts before they did. Of suddenly going into trances in the middle of a dance or conversation. He didn't realize that he had a *gift*, and neither did his acquaintances. Those who did suspect stayed away from him completely.

He met a young woman while still in his thirties, and they fell in love. They seemed to understand each other perfectly. She died in a horrible bus accident, and Philip lost his reason for living. His work suffered, what few friends he had shunned him. He found himself utterly unable to deal with life, to take care of himself. His appetite for alcohol subsequently increased.

He had always been an alcoholic, but had somehow been able to keep it under control, until the death of his lover gave him the excuse to drink that he'd been searching for all his life. He was haunted by strange dreams and ambiguous visions. He heard ghostly voices and picked up people's thoughts with such frequency and clarity that it was enough to drive him mad. His mind finally went, and he consumed more and more quantities of alcohol. It was only a matter of time before he was making the street his home.

Had he been born later in the century, people would have more easily understood what the man was all about. He could have received help, met people who were willing to show him how to control his gift, how to deal with the realities of being extra-sensitive, having perceptions beyond his comprehension. Though there were those among his contemporaries who had known of and experimented with ESP, the belief in the "sixth sense" was not as prevalent as it is today. In some ways, Philip Reginald Haupster was a victim of his time.

He had been a nice-looking man in his youth. He hardly had a face anymore, it was so lined and shriveled and hollow. He survived by going now and then to shelters for food and warmth, but when people tried to reach out to him their disgust would emanate from their minds and envelop him, forcing him to cry out in despair, to ultimately run away from any form of salvation. He had been down in the Lower East Side for some time now, taking comfort in the fact that there were others like him all around, their minds too numb to invade his consciousness, and their thoughts too scrambled and inwardly directed to disturb his sleep. They did not find him disgusting; they could hardly have cared less.

He'd made friends with some of them—if you could call what they had friendship—knew them by name. Randy, the defrocked minister. Eddie, the deaf-mute. Paul, the artist who couldn't pay his rent. His favorite was Ronnie, who'd once sung with Philip's favorite swing band. Drunks, deadbeats all.

But then they started leaving—no—being *taken away* by the things, those creatures that lived in the sewer. He had wanted to run away before they came for him, but something had compelled him to stay. It hurt just to think of the desolation, the cold, paralyzing fear that enveloped him now that he was alone. There was no one he could explain it to.

Until tonight.

That man's thought had sliced into his as clearly as the high-pitched scream of a siren cleaves the night. The stranger had been wondering about the disappearances, blindly offering his thoughts to anyone who had the power to perceive them. Philip had sensed that this man could read *his* thoughts too, with great clarity; so he had run after him, explosed himself to the merciless eyes of another—something he normally *never* did.

But though the man had been like him in that special, uncanny way, he had not responded favorably. Philip had watched the train depart, thinking then and there that his last hope had gone with it, his last chance to find true peace and solace, to understand himself. His last chance to determine where the others had all been taken.

Now he crouched in the alleyway, on top of a discarded mattress, listening with all his senses to the night as it surrounded him. Once more he was picking up those hideous thoughts, the chanting of a thousand condemned souls crying out in desperate supplication. The words he heard and the images he saw were too mind-boggling for him to bear. It took all his power to suffocate the anguish. That left him no strength to resist the strange force that had forbidden him to leave the area.

And so they came for him.

First there was a clanking sound, like a manhole lid being forced open from below. It clattered against the pavement. The noise was so loud it filled the streets. There were no other sounds, save the pounding of Philip's heart. There were no cars at this hour, no pedestrians.

Only Philip and that thing from the sewer.

It had pulled itself up completely from the

49

hole, and it waited there, sniffing the air, its glaring red eyes searching, searching. It had an odor, both foul and sweet, like perfume-covered excrement. It moved away from the spot where it had surfaced and moved down the street toward the alley where Haupster was hiding.

Haupster sensed the thing's approach, and knew that it was *his* turn to be carried away into oblivion. He heard more noises now, and trembled with fear. The thing was not alone. There were others of its kind even now emerging from the underground. No matter where he ran, one of them would *pounce*.

He was overwhelmed. The psychic emanations were repulsive and his quivering body was drenched in his own sweat. He got up and bolted out of the alley, darting past broken chairs and scattered bottles. He almost tripped on a torn box spring, but managed to stay upright until he was again in control of his movements. Somehow he was able to operate despite the alcoholic haze that forever permeated his being. It was as if he possessed a new strength which allowed him to clear his mind and shake off the deadening effects of countless quantities of booze. His brain had a new opponent to conquer—sheer, paralyzing fright.

The thing that had been stalking him lunged out as he neared the exit from the alley. He felt a claw rake his skin. Then came sharp pain, the warmth of dripping blood. He continued to run, overturning a garbage can filled with jars and newspapers.

Another thrust—the claw dug into his back, scraping away nuggets of flesh. Philip cried out, his screams as high as those of the thing that was attacking him. He kept on running, crossing the street and heading for the relative safety of the subway.

Hunched over awkwardly on all of its four appendages, the creature pursued. Haupster grabbed another garbage can. Surprised at the ease with which he lifted it, he almost dropped it back on the ground. Regaining his grip on it, he held the can in front of him. A smelly goop dripped out of the top and plopped down onto his feet. The thing battered at the can with its claws and teeth, trying to get at him. For the first time, Haupster saw clearly what it was.

"Ronnnieeee!" Haupster cried.

Haupster dropped the can and shielded his eyes with his hands. Within seconds a row of teeth had grabbed his arm, biting the flesh nearly down to the bone. Haupster cried out. Something—another one of his pursuers—came up from behind and lunged at him, knocking Haupster's body to the ground. The odor was unbearably fetid. Haupster could feel the breath of the creature as its mouth found his neck, the hungry teeth digging into his skin.

Pummeled into near insensibility by a rain of heavy blows, Haupster felt himself being dragged back down the street. Slowly the things were making their way back to their hole with their burden. Haupster's chin was scraping against the sidewalk painfully, so he twisted his head and let his cheek absorb the impact of the concrete. As they crossed the street, his face and body swept up all the dirt and dust and urine, the discarded cigarette butts coating the roadway. He was pulled up onto the curb on the other side, and taken down the block with nary a struggle.

Soon they reached the manhole. Haupster was thrown down into the yawning abyss.

By the time he hit bottom he had died of fright.

Steven made himself some scrambled eggs when he got home. Anything more elaborate would have been indigestible. Still, it might soak up the bourbon he'd consumed—not that he'd had that much. He didn't know where his appetite had suddenly come from; maybe from seeing how the other half lived—namely the wealthy and crazy Vivian Jessup. Joey—killing himself over *her*? Ridiculous! He quickly drank a cup of strong coffee, following it with two more. Drinking liquor too fast always gave him a headache.

Well, tomorrow the police would question Mrs. Jessup, and they would find out about any mysteries she might have in her closet. The rich, neurotic lady would certainly break down in front of the stern, no-nonsense Detective Albright if she had to face *him*. She would crack into a million pieces. It would all come tumbling out of her mouth, and his brother would be saved.

What if she was telling the truth? he

wondered. What if she really knew nothing? What if she was really just a poor, deluded creature whose hold on her own self-worth was so tenuous she'd had to cast herself in the role of heartbreaker, a middle-aged temptress driving boys to suicide?

Or what if she was *right?*

He piled the cup and dishes in the sink, and went soberly into the living room. He had lived in this place for seven years, moving here when his marriage to Denise had dissolved after two. He'd been too young and immature; she'd been too disillusioned with the realities of marriage. Both had wanted freedom. They were still friends, but Denise had moved to the West Coast and they didn't see much of each other. She would not appreciate his bothering her with this. She barely knew Joey and, in any case, he hadn't the right to ask her to be concerned. Joey had—as Albright kept repeating—only been missing a little over a day.

He picked up the phone and dialed Andrea's number, even though he had promised himself he would not give in. He'd planned to let her make the first move, let her call him if she was of a mind to.

The phone rang and rang without answer. She was probably still out of town at that booksellers' conference.

Joey, where are you?

When his "little brother" had asked if he could stay with him until he got settled in New York, Steven had hesitated before saying yes, feeling a bit guilty that he hadn't suggested it himself in the first place. He did need his privacy. But after a week or so, he'd started to relish Joey's company, even missed him when he went out and didn't return till the following day. His kid brother. They'd always been friends.

He sat down in the easy chair, with the lights out. The light from the full moon and from the streetlamps outside came into the room and provided illumination. It was a warm and cozy room, cluttered with books and magazines that were on shelves, the floor, and a small rectangular coffeetable in front of the couch. The wallpaper was dark, with a green leaf design. The carpeting, though old and graying, was soft and comfortable for naked feet. The black-and-white TV had belonged to his parents —a very old set, but it still worked perfectly. There were a couple of plants around the place, mostly ones that Andrea had given him. He really didn't care for plants.

He thought about his parents again. They had both died while Joey was in college; the memory still hurt. Mrs. Everson had died of cancer, theoretically. Steven was the only one alive who knew that she had really killed herself not long after hearing the diagnosis, preferring an artificial descent into unending sleep to months of agony and torment. He had never blamed her. Her kind of cancer hadn't been treatable then as it was today. He could not have stood to see her wither away, locked up alone in a hospital ward waiting to die.

Steven's father had successfully circulated the story that her illness had been bothering her for years—which was not quite true—and that it had been a miracle she'd lasted as long as she did. Of course, some people wondered about it, and others knew outright that the fabricated story didn't quite hold up, but no one was tactless enough to confront him with it. She died in her sleep, a painless death—that much was true.

Joey was confused, like everyone else who'd been close to her. There had been no inkling, until perhaps right before her death, that anything had been wrong with her. Just some minor complaints, which she usually kept to herself. But he accepted his father's story. Mr. Everson had figured, however, that Steven could deal with the truth. Steven often wondered if his father had really forgiven his wife for leaving him and the boys. He seemed to understand why she had taken her life; she had told him about the illness. But perhaps he had expected her to be "stronger," to hang on until the finish, to never give up hope. To look after Joey while he was still too young to go out in the world.

It didn't matter now. Their father was killed in a blazing automobile accident a year later, leaving behind a charred, unrecognizable corpse that no mortician could prettify with makeup. The coffin had been closed.

Both deaths had devastated Joey. Steven had had it easier only because he was no longer under their wing. When they died, they simply hadn't been as big a part of his life as they were of Joey's.

But if Joey was dead, it would hit him harder

than both of his parents' deaths combined. Joey was young. Joey could be an important person someday. Joey had everything going for him, everything to live for. It just wasn't fair.

Steven was exhausted. He couldn't keep his eyes open any longer. He fell asleep in the easy chair and didn't wake up for hours.

Vivian Jessup wanted to drink herself into oblivion.

It was the only way she could handle it, the only way she could keep the anguish from overwhelming her.

Joey Everson.

She hadn't intended to go to bed with him, to do *any* of the things she'd done. She'd only planned to watch him, to warn him, to keep him from his dire fate.

What a fool she'd been. As if anyone could have saved him.

She knew what Joey was going to be used for. Just as Peterson had known. In her lucid moments, when it didn't have control of her, she knew she had to try and save him, so she'd formulated a plan.

A plan that hadn't worked.

To think it had been Gerald, her late husband, who'd betrayed her back at the beginning.

She had resigned from the firm several years ago, before the *nightmare* started. She found the subtle discrimination against women exhibited by the firm to be a barrier and a burden. She could hardly control her frustration at watching her husband rise on her accomplishments while she remained only his assistant. Never an equal, always a slave. She had almost gotten her first nervous breakdown.

So she had quit—both husband and job—and moved to New York to live luxuriously on her dead father's legacy.

But then one night Gerald came, muttering obscenities and dripping tears, with a story so incredible . . .

He'd nearly died that night, nearly been killed —as a penalty for talking. It had almost given her her "second" nervous breakdown.

Vivian had wanted to reject the whole business out of hand, but she'd taken it upon herself to drive out to the lab one day and see for herself . . .

That had been the beginning of the end.

They'd taken her into their confidence, so she knew *everything*. At first she'd felt terror. And then—most terribly—indifference. It did to her what it had done to the others—even now she didn't quite remember what the process consisted of—and made her one of the *damned*.

She'd wanted to tell Steven everything—but she'd start shaking, shivering—and she knew, she *knew* that it was listening and would not hesitate to destroy her if she dared to go too far.

Poor Joey. She hadn't intended to care for him. But the only way she could protect him— short of warning him outright and dooming herself—was to make the boy her lover. She was still attractive. Many young men were flattered by the attentions of sophisticated women. She'd known where to find him, which place to look.

At first she had felt out of place—until she looked more closely at some of the women under the low amber lights and realized that their youth was more artifice than reality. One night she'd seen him, approached him—made messy, rapturous love in her bedroom, enjoying his fine strong boy-flesh as it filled her up to her soul.

She'd never known she'd had such feelings.

She'd tried to live her life as a normal person, as a normal widow—Gerald had died a natural death, a heart attack, some months ago, the lucky bastard—but it was no use. Always she could feel it *listening*, almost *lusting*—God help them—along with her as she kissed and touched and stroked every inch of her handsome, wonderful young man.

She'd only made matters worse. She'd only managed to make Joey more *appealing* in its eyes.

Time and again she'd tried to warn him, only to stop before she could finish.

So yesterday they'd gone ahead and snatched him. He was as good as dead. She hadn't really known they'd go through wth it until she'd called the boy's brother . . .

How did she ever get into such an impossible situation? Why *her?* There seemed to be no way out of it. The warning she had received tonight might have been *more* than just a warning. How horrible that would be. She'd spend the night sleeplessly, waiting for it to happen, and then, once she'd dozed off . . . well, she wouldn't, couldn't, let it happen to her. She would get away tonight! As for the police, what could she possibly have said to them?

She ran into the bedroom, grabbed a suitcase from the closet, and started to pack. The creature's influence couldn't extend everywhere, could it? Surely it had limits. She threw in only the essentials. She extracted several hundred dollars from a wall safe behind a painting over the bed, and changed into a more nondescript outfit. She left the lights in the bedroom on, but switched all the others off. She locked up behind her, went down in the elevator, and walked out of the building.

Around the block was the garage where she parked her car. She hurried there, trying to keep her face hidden from passersby. She might be spotted, might be watched, by another of the creature's conscripts. They would tell on her just to save themselves. At the garage she asked the attendant to get her car, a blue sedan, up from the lower level.

The attendant was taking forever. She tapped her handbag restlessly, picked at her hair. What was keeping him?

Finally her car was driven up the ramp, and she got inside. She turned right onto Lexington Avenue. Then down to 59th Street. She hadn't the slightest idea where she was going, only that she had to get out of the city as soon as possible. She swerved around pedestrians and raced dangerously through stoplights. A cabbie hollered after her.

There was some sort of traffic jam near 63rd

Street. An accident? She turned the wheel and jumped the curb, almost smashing into several panicking strollers. She drove along the sidewalk until she reached 62nd Street. She turned right and headed toward the river, leaving a dozen startled pedestrians in her wake.

Something started happening to her vision. At first it was just specks. Then large dots. Then a terrible throbbing ache in her head that made her blink furiously. She couldn't see anything in the road ahead. She felt like she was on fire, and started to tug at her collar. A dizzy feeling began overtaking her system. She stomped on the brake.

She was getting the shivers. *Bad,* this time.

Almost blinded, sick with nausea, Vivian was thrust forward in her seat as the car crunched sickeningly into something in the road. The impact served to jar her into a temporary remission. Her fender had smashed into the back of a double-parked truck. There was no way she could handle the arguments, the shouting, the exchange of phone numbers and data. She got out of her vehicle, and started running down the street, ignoring those pedestrians who had witnessed the accident. Luckily, the truck's driver was somewhere indoors, unaware of what had transpired.

She almost hailed a taxi at the corner, but was dismayed at the number of people standing on the curb up and down the street with the same idea in mind. What should she do? She couldn't think straight. She started to run down Lexington toward the subway at 59th, bumping into people, almost knocking some of them down. She accidentally tore a package right out of someone's arms and sent it crashing to the sidewalk. She ignored the yelling, the curses. She hadn't time.

She decided to take the subway to Grand Central. Surely she'd be safe right out there in the open. It wouldn't do to have witnesses, after all. At Grand Central she would take any train to *anywhere*, just so long as it took her out of the city. Hopefully the sick feeling, the shivering, she'd experienced before would not reoccur. She tried hard to close her mind, to keep her thoughts of escape from floating . . .

Finally she saw the stairway down to the IRT. Only a few short stops and she'd be there. No one was going to hurt her. No one.

After an infuriating delay, she'd managed to acquire a token. The clerk on duty had rejected her hundred-dollar bill. She'd scrounged around in her purse until she found the right change.

She went through the turnstile, and waited there with about fifteen other people for the downtown train to arrive. She realized that she was on the local platform. Perhaps the express would get her there faster. She looked around until she saw a sign that read *Take Escalator for Downtown Express*. She walked to the middle of the platform, stepped onto the escalator, and let it carry her down to the platform below.

She was still shivering. Her fingers wouldn't stop shaking. She was finally having that nervous breakdown. She just knew she was.

She started gasping for air. Something told her it was a mistake to go too far below the ground. Her heart pounding inside her, she absurdly tried to climb back up the motorized metal stairs. In her breathless, panicky state she was certainly unable to perform the maneuver. She could only ride down helplessly.

She stepped off the escalator when she reached the lower section. There were fewer people here than there had been on the platform above. Only four or five, most of them congregated around a bench down on the other end of the platform. Vivian felt all alone again. Terrified.

She heard the train. She was in luck—the express had arrived before the local. Staring down into the tunnel with impatience, she could see the widening twin lights of the first car as it approached.

Then the pounding started. Not just her heart. Not just her blood. But every cell of her body—every bone, artery, vessel, muscle—was starting to throb, to *vibrate*. Vivian's eyes started to bulge out of their sockets, almost bursting from demoniacal pressure.

Not like this, Vivian gasped. *Not like this. I won't let it kill me. I'll do it myself first!*

The train was about to enter the station. Her face a mask of horror and determination. Vivian stepped over to the rim of the platform—

The tracks were full of writhing, twisting shapes, men and women in straitjackets, screaming and cursing and weaving baskets, urinating upon each other. It was a crazy house.

A crazy house. *Her nervous breakdown had arrived and* she was crazy . . .

—and hurled herself onto the tracks.

Vivian's body was spread-eagled across the sizzling third rail. Sparks erupted from beneath her as her body began to smoulder.

The train roared into the station, its massive wheels grinding along the tracks.

Vivian's body was neatly sliced into several uneven parts.

Eric Thorne got off the train and walked along the downtown twin of the platform he had been on earlier that evening. If he looked across the tracks to the other side he could see the turnstile that the derelict had watched him from before. He went through the turning exit gate, walked up the stairs, and crossed the street so that he stood precisely at the spot where the man had first approached him. There was no one around.

It was quite cold this evening. His long gray jacket was missing the top button, so Thorne pulled the sides of the coat together with his fingers. He wondered if he'd be needing gloves. He didn't know how long it would take for him to find the man. But he must find him. It was an opportunity not to be missed.

He felt no psychic emanations, saw nothing, heard no voices in his subconscious. Not a trace. He was afraid that the man might have moved into another section of the city. Thorne *had* been gone over four hours. He had gone home, made and eaten the elaborate feast he'd been planning, then relieved himself and headed back to the subway. Fortified thusly, he felt able to take on this rather grim assignment. And a dangerous one too, perhaps.

During the day it may have been desolate enough, but the area was empty beyond belief in the evening. The night intensified its bleak open spaces and hollow shadows. Most of the buildings were large warehouses or plants. Several of them in the immediate area housed printing presses. A few buildings contained offices for obscure organizations which thrived on cheap rent. The liquor store on the corner was closed at this hour, as was the sleazy, greasy coffeeshop across the street. Thorne decided to walk down to the Institute.

The building where he worked was a large, brown, unattractive structure that had at one time been a home for—depending on the decade —the elderly and infirm, unwed mothers, or orphans. Sometimes he picked up thoughts, desperate feelings, that had been trapped within the walls for many years. He had learned to deal with them.

He opened the front door with his keys, peeking in through the large rectangular panes of glass to see if anyone was about. There shouldn't be. No one had been there when he'd left two hours previously. He stepped into the hall, pulled the door shut, and snapped on the light. The corridor was long and in need of a paint job. More of the pale green coat on the walls was chipping off each day. He walked down the hallway, and turned to the right into a tiny kitchen. He'd make himself a nice cup of coffee, then resume his search. He went to the sink, extracted a cup from the cabinet above, and filled a pot with water from the faucet. Putting the pot on the hot plate, he switched on the current.

He got the jar of coffee from the cupboard and spooned it into the cup. Then he sat down at the little table in the corner and waited.

Who was he kidding? He really wasn't up to walking the streets in this godforsaken area at this hour in search of some drunk who had probably long since disappeared. And yet, it was something by all rights he should do. The man had had "talent," that was undeniable. But how could Mr. Proper, always sober Eric Thorne, manage to deal with a disgusting drunk, sensitive or not? He looked at the coffee jar, rolling back and forth in his hands, and had to smile.

He had been with the Institute for ten years. They did everything from testing people for extrasensory perception to holding seminars on out-of-the-body sexual encounters. Their job was to explore the paranormal, and to investigate the vast, unspoken possibilities of life beyond mortal ken. The spirit world. Alternate realities and dimensions. Telepathy. Telekinesis. Under one roof there were many experts in the field of psychic research. As well as volunteers. Quite a few were genuine "sensitives"—those with certain abilities which separated them from "ordinary" men and women. Eric Thorne's specialty was extra-sensory awareness—any ability which indicated that one was sensitive to stimuli not included in the five normal senses. Mind reading. Thought transference. It was a fascinating field, and one that Thorne would forever be a part of. For he himself was one of the greatest "mind readers" in the world.

The thought of it used to scare him. No longer. Now he was proud. Fiercely proud. And dedicated to discovering the reasons for his having such special gifts. Dedicated to seeking out and helping those who were like him. That's why he had to find that derelict, that drunkard, who had so far abused his power instead of *using* it. Thorne felt new determination. No matter what the risk, he must find him. He would just have to guard against the powerful, *evil* thoughts that he'd picked up before. Thoughts which he now assumed had not come directly from the man, but rather from other sources which had *affected him*. Thorne was anxious to find the answers to the mysteries that his chance—or had it been a chance?—encounter had revealed.

He poured the boiling water into the cup, where it dissolved the crystals of freeze-dried instant coffee. He added some cream from the refrigerator, and one teaspoon of sugar from a bowl on the table. He stirred it all slowly, waiting for it to cool. He was still hesitant about going out there again, out into the unfriendly darkness. He started to drink, trying to overcome his apprehension. It wasn't easy.

Finally the cup was drained. He got up, made sure that the hot plate had been turned off, then switched out the light and went back into the hallway. He walked down the corridor, flicking its light off.

And stepped out into the night.

Lina Hobler rolled over in bed and blinked furiously, trying to adjust to the lack of light. She got up, dragging the blanket with her, and turned on the lightswitch. Her mouth was dry, her tongue coated with a smelly paste. She looked in the mirror and cringed. Her hair was flying out in all directions, and the bags under her eyes were more pronounced than ever. Her face was so lined it looked like a map of Europe. She opened a bottle of mouthwash, gargled, and spit out a thick mixture of saliva and mint.

She was still a bit woozy from the afternoon's drinking. It was happening more and more these days, these desperate plunges into the bottle. It was half empty now—on the kitchen table, a cheap brand of whiskey. The glass had been discarded after the first two drinks. It was lying on the floor, cracked in two places.

Her boyfriend hadn't been home for days. It often happened. He'd go off somewhere—she never knew where—and then return with plenty of money and a small bouquet of flowers. She was always charmed enough not to scold. Normally these periods when she was left alone rarely lasted more than a day or so. But this period had gone on much too long. Lina could usually control her drinking, though she'd always been at it heavily. Left to her own devices, however, she could sometimes go overboard.

It was too much to deal with. Never knowing if Brock was alive or dead, coming back or gone for good. They'd been living together now for almost five years, and she should have been used to these episodes. But it was tough, real tough. Like never knowing when you're coming or going. She called these periods her "upside-down" phases.

Often she wondered if Brock had left her for another woman. Sure, he was nothing much to look at either. But he *was* a big, well-hung hunk of man, and he took good care of her when he had the dough. A far cry from a feminist, Lina was positive the only way a woman could live was to let a man support her. Even twenty years ago, when she had had enough money to buy New York, she'd let men handle her business affairs. That's why she was now living in a shithole in the borough of Queens, which might just as well have been Outer Mongolia as far as she was concerned.

The main man in her life when she had been *Miss* Lina Hobler, songstress supreme, singing star of America, Grand Diva of the night clubs and the air waves and the record shops, was Arnie Molleran, her manager, accountant, advisor, and live-in lover. Arnie took care of her, all right. The "investments" that he made with her money went straight to the race track and the gambling tables, never to the stockbroker.

When Lina's career plummeted in 1962—the lowest spot in her life—she turned to Arnie and asked him for some of that financial security that he had always told her she could count on when things got rough. Alas, there wasn't any. First it was Lina's jewelry, then her furs, then her cottage in the Hamptons, then her sailboat, then her townhouse, and finally it was Arnie. All of it gone. When the money went, when the job offers stopped, when Lina was too plastered to even perform, when everything she owned was in hock, she felt that she could at least count on Molleran's love. No dice. She woke up one morning to find a note on the pillow next to hers:

Goodbye, babe. It's been nice. But we got to make it on our own now. Love, Arnie.

She had cried for three days straight. Drunk for three weeks. Then her life turned into a *real* Grade-B movie. She managed to live on loans from former fans and friends. Once she even tried a comeback, but muffed it when she showed up for a TV appearance two weeks after the show had been taped—bombed, of course. She fled from her apartment in New York late one night, owing seven months' back rent. A friend of hers paid the first three months rent for an inexpensive flat in Woodside, with a warning that there would be no more handouts forthcoming. Lina gave up the bottle for awhile, got a job as a waitress in a burger joint around the corner, and responded to remarks such as "Do you know who you look just like?" with a weary "Everyone says so," or "I used to be Rin

69

Tin Tin." Of course, she used an assumed name: Rona Wordsworth. She had figured that she'd cash her checks by flirting, and eventually fucking, with the man who worked behind the sinister grilled counter in the check-cashing joint. But it turned out she was paid off the books, so there was no problem; she was always paid in cash.

She met Brock in a bar late one Wednesday evening and it was lust at first sight. Their first time in bed together she told him who she really was, and he said that he had known it all along. He offered to take care of her. Poor Lina should have known better by then. But she let him move in with her, and he took care of the rent and everything else. She quit her waitress job and thought she finally had it made.

The first time Brock pulled his disappearing act she really panicked. Her drinking got so bad that one night at Barney's Bar and Grill she did an impromptu striptease, slapped around another woman who made fun of her body, and even threw a bottle at the barman. She wound up sleeping it off in the can. Brock later explained that he needed periods away to get extra money, but wouldn't volunteer more information. Lina knew that he worked at a facotry, and already had a steady paycheck, but she was so glad for the gifts and conveniences that the "extra" money brought her, she never particularly cared where it came from. She figured maybe Brock was mixed up in a mild way with the rackets, that he needed time away from his clinging parmour now and then just to have some breathing room. But he'd always come back.

Until now.

Lina sat down in front of the mirror and cried, sure that he had left her due to her fading sex appeal. She was fifty years old, much too heavy, and what had once been her beautiful blond hair was now pale and stringy. She hated to go outdoors during the daytime. The super's ugly children and their neighborhood friends always laughed at her, taunted her, called her disgusting names. Little brats. Kids had always made fun of her, even when she'd been a child herself. They'd been jealous of her angelic face and silken hair and the way the adults treated her. They were cruel and sinister, evil little midget monsters. She often had nightmares of being totally at their mercy. The bastards.

What would become of her? she wondered. What would become of her?

Her excursion into self-pity land was shattered by a knock on the door. Brock? It had to be! *Silly thing, crying your heart out all for nothing.* She wiped her eyes and ran to open the door, not caring that she was only dressed in a torn and filthy slip.

It wasn't Brock. Two rough-looking characters forced their way into the room before she could close the door on them.

"Where is he?" the shorter man said, a nasty-looking character with a rodent's face and a cigar jutting out of his mouth.

"Brock?" she asked. "Is that who you're looking for?"

"That's right!" the other fellow said, a tall, rather handsome blond man with a well-built body and thick-lensed glasses.

"He's not around. He hasn't been here for days." She wished she had taken the time to put on a robe. She felt so ugly in front of these two strangers, both of them looking her up and down as if she was naked.

The little guy laughed. "What did I tell ya?"

"How long has he been away *this* time?" the blond man asked.

"For *days*, I told you. Why? What is it? Is something wrong?"

"No. If he comes by just tell him that Jake and Eddie were here to see him."

"Do you know where he is?" Lina asked, grabbing her robe from off the closet doorknob.

"If we did, we wouldn't be here, lady."

"All right!" she shouted, pissed that these two creeps who had invaded her privacy had no word from her man. "Then get out of here. There's nothing I can do for you."

"Watch your mouth, puss," the ratman said, holding out his hand toward her face as if he was planning to squeeze it. "You just tell your boyfriend that we were here. Then forget it, okay?"

"I will. Now get out!"

The two men glared at her for a few seconds, then started to laugh. They left, slamming the door behind them. Lina muttered "shit-faces" and threw the robe on the floor. She took off the slip and went into the bathroom. She stepped into the shower and turned on the water, letting it cover her body, soak through her hair, slosh around inside her mouth. Wonderful, *wonderful*, warm water. She got out, toweled herself dry, and changed into fresh clothes. She brushed her teeth, properly this time, and applied a thick coat of make up. She couldn't stay here alone anymore. She grabbed her purse, checked to make sure that she had enough money, and left the apartment.

She hoped the super's kids were in school—or dead, preferably. She had triumphed over her evil playmates once before—they'd had to see her mug on record albums and TV shows and know that *she*, the pretty little girl they'd all made fun of, had grown up to be somebody while they were nowhere rotting. But now? Now, she thought, the little monsters had it all over her. They'd dance on her grave when she was dead and never know that once she'd been a star.

She was out in the hall waiting for the elevator when the phone rang. She was back inside on the fourth ring.

"Hello."

The voice that answered gave her the absolute ever-lovin' creeps. A man's voice. A frightened voice in spite of its scary resonance.

"Is this Lina?" he asked.

"Yes. Yes, I'm Lina. Who is this?"

"Never mind. I have information. About Brock."

"*What?* Where is he?"

"No. Not on the phone. You'll have to meet me." He paused. "Someone might be watching you."

"Who? Who's watching me?" Those two men?

73

she wondered. No. They looked too dumb to be keeping an eye on anyone.

"I said not on the phone. I'll give you an address."

She got paper and pen. She jotted down the location.

"I'll come right now," she said.

"No. Not now. Tomorrow evening. Nine o'clock. And not before."

"Why can't I see you tonight?" she said, wanting to plead, wanting to get down on her knees and beg.

"I can't explain. Tomorrow. Don't be late."

"But . . ."

He hung up.

She put down the receiver and let out an exasperated sigh.

Boy, she sure could use a drink now.

THREE

ERIC THORNE HAD arrived home at his apartment on the Upper East Side at one o'clock in the morning. Exhausted, he had gulped down a glass of juice and two aspirins, raised the heat five degrees, and collapsed into bed.

His search had been fruitless. Walking up and down deserted streets, turning abruptly at the slightest sound, trying to see if someone was following him. At times he'd felt as if he was being tracked, hunted down, by some unseen presence walking behind him a step out of sync. He'd whirl around to face his invisible pursuer, only to see nothing, no one there at all. It was a terribly disquieting feeling, that uneasy suspicion that something was constantly stepping out of his sightline just as he revolved to confront it. Insane, but real. Frighteningly real.

He had tried to relax and let whatever emanations might be about flow smoothly and easily into his consciousness, but nothing had come. He'd tried to hone in on the powerful mental force that the derelict had exhibited earlier in the night. But it was gone. Missing. It and he had disappeared along with all the other pathetic denizens of the area. Gone to some secret place.

Eric had been trying to get to sleep for over an hour now. Nothing worked. Sometimes it was tough for him to close his mind entirely; he was too susceptible to communications, both from those around him—behind the walls in the other apartments—and from the mystic other side, the many worlds of alternate reality. Tonight, intensified by his unnerving experience, was one of those times. He could not drop off into slumber and sublimate all the messages he received into his dreams as he usually did. Instead, he was inundated by bizarre but incomplete images, like pieces of a hideous jigsaw puzzle floating from the ether into his mind. The puzzle was all jumbled up so that no one could see the actual horror as it was —only a torturous *hint* of what was being depicted in the illustration. Fragments of waking nightmares. Mere glimpses of a totality so repulsive and terrifying that Thorne wondered if it was his own mind which refused to put the pieces together for the sake of protecting his sanity. Perhaps if he managed to mentally fit the fragments together, it would be too much for his mortal mind to bear. Or perhaps his power was simply not strong enough to form the complete picture.

There was a great deal of anguish. Crying, wailing, hysteria. Death, much death. Incredible pain. He started to descend into the images, the sounds, letting himself give in to their persuasive spell, letting his mind be carried away, overwhelmed by the sights and smells and sounds of this strange netherworld, going down, down, exploring. Afraid, so afraid, and yet too fascinated to resist.

Below.

There were people all around him, packed together, naked, crammed into one tiny space. They were of all different ages, with nothing in common that mattered except for their fear, their utter despair. Everything was blurred, too hazy. He couldn't make out any of their features, only the general impression of their bulk, their height. So many, too many, to look over. Where were they? He tried to hold onto this image, grab onto it before it was replaced by a different, equally brief and furtive scene. Hold it, lock onto it like a camera, capture it so that it could be re-examined later when he returned to true consciousness. He did it. He *did it:* he was still there, in that room or cubicle, that space—trapped with all the others.

He was vibrating, both literally and figuratively. He started to moan out loud. But it wasn't his body that was shaking, it was the very *enclosure,* the space they were crammed into. It swayed erratically, almost hypnotically. *What did it remind him of?* He raised an astral head and "looked" in what he sensed was a forward direction. There was something like . . . a window. There was only blackness beyond it. Then—*what could it be?*—a stark, brilliant white rectangle that loomed larger and larger, growing and growing and growing until there

77

was nothing but white.

Then he saw a big steel door with writing on it. A *massive* door.

He came out of the trance screaming for his very life.

He sat upright in bed, breathing hard and covered with droplets of perspiration. He reached over and snapped on the night-table lamp. Not enough light. He got up, went to the wall switch, and turned on the brighter overhead lights. Better, much better.

He went back to the bed and sat down. He looked around the room. It was blue, all blue. No black open spaces or white rectangles. Just blue. Calm, comforting blue. Blue rug, blue wallpaper, blue bed covers, and light blue sheets. Blue.

He went into the kitchen with its brighter lights and polished wood and sleek formica surfaces. He got a glass and turned on the tap. He drank three full glasses of water in rapid succession. He put the glass in the sink. He turned around suddenly. The wood counter was right behind him. Too close, too close. He needed more space, much more room.

He went into the living room. It had never looked so tiny before. The sofa and the two easy chairs and the new color TV and the stereo console and the bookshelves all seemed right *on top* of one another. Why had he never noticed it before? How could he have put so many things into one tiny room? Space, not enough space.

He started to leave the living room, heading for . . . where? There was nowhere left to go! He looked into the bathroom. The door was wide open, for all the world resembling a *maw*. It was waiting for him to step inside, waiting for him to commit that one little error. He averted his eyes. He couldn't bear the thought of walking into such a tiny little room. He started turning in circles, helpless, not knowing where to go. He realized he'd been crying without even being aware of it. He sat down on the couch and buried his face in his hands. He sobbed, suddenly hating his pathetic little apartment, feeling tragically hemmed in by the very walls, locked away with useless pieces of furniture that would dare to exist when his dismal life was over. He looked up again. It was all so clear, so pathetically clear.

He got up and switched on the television, turning the volume up higher than usual. He needed to hear other voices, see other people. He knelt down in front of the set, staring so hard into the picture tube that his eyes began to squint. It took a moment for the picture to come in. He felt a chill, reminded of something—but it dissipated as soon as he could make out the images on the screen. An old western. Lots of noise. Shooting, hollering. He made the volume louder. He relished it, not really paying attention to the action or the dialogue. Just losing himself in the noises and images. Lots of images. Sane, familiar images. Comforting. Like blue.

He had no idea how long he'd been in front of the set like that when he heard someone in the next apartment banging on the wall. It snapped

him out of his condition. He quickly lowered
the sound. The banging stopped. He continued
to look at the screen for another ten minutes,
but by then was back to normal, able to face
reality again. He shut the TV off. He hated
westerns.

Eric got up and stood there awhile rubbing
the bridge of his nose. What a trip! He must
have gone crazy, all because of that trance he'd
been subjected to. He'd have to get himself
together, be prepared to deal with any other
psychic attacks that might occur. He had
tapped into a *conscious force* so powerful that it
had twisted his emotions, causing him to dive
into a fit of depression that was senseless and
unecessary. Worse, it had been draining. He
seemed to ache all over.

He was all right now. He went into the bathroom without pause. He splashed water all over
his face and looked in the mirror. His normally
rosy complexion was cadaverously pale. He
looked like he'd been through the wars. His
thick, mussed-up black hair and thin black
mustache stood out startlingly against the
pallid flesh. He looked much older than thirty-
seven. The heavy eyes from lack of sleep.
Cheeks too fleshy; someday they'd be jowls. Not
handsome. Not ugly. He had a professional face.
Competent. Almost mousy—until he opened his
mouth and spoke to you. His authoritative voice
always made it clear that he knew what he was
talking about, that no one could push him
around.

He was a small man, thin-boned. He would

80

never have a weight problem. He would have had a nice body had he worked at it. He was divorced. Sometimes lonely. Mostly not—due to a large collection of friends and acquaintances that he'd acquired over the years. Fascinating people. Many of them in his own line of work.

He drank two more glasses of water, then went back into the bathroom to urinate. He kept watching the door as he did so—*why?* he asked himself—almost splashing his piss on the floor. He felt quite tired now, reasonably sure that the worst was over and that he could sleep a normal sleep. He brought his pillow and blanket into the living room, and slept on the couch with the lights on. First thing in the morning he would talk to someone about his experience.

For now, he was content not to think about it at all.

Detective John Albright sat in the kitchen of his house stirring a cup of reheated coffee. He poured in some sugar—too much sugar—from a box on the table. He took a sip, cursed under his breath, then downed half the cup in one thirsty gulp. He heard a rustling noise behind him, turned, and saw his wife coming down the hall from their bedroom.

"It's three o'clock, dear," she said softly. "Is something the matter?"

John sighed heavily and sat back in the chair. "Just couldn't get to sleep. Sorry if I kept you up."

Gloria Albright sat down in the chair opposite him and fingered some stale donuts lying in a battered carton. "You didn't. I've been sleeping like a log. I just woke up a little while ago and wondered where you were." She was worried. She could tell that something was bothering her husband, and been bothering him for quite a few weeks. He always kept things bottled up, unable to express his feelings with the ease some people could. She put her hand on his, her fingers tiny against his big red knuckles. "Is something worrying you?"

"No, no. It's nothing, honey. I don't know—I just couldn't fall asleep."

"Did you get any sleep at all?"

"A little bit. Not much. Kept waking up again. My stomach didn't feel too good."

"You *had* to have a milkshake. You know what they do to you."

"I know, I know."

Milkshake, like hell. Gloria knew it was something far more serious than stomach distress. Was he feeling the same tensions and stress of middle age that she sometimes felt? One kid married, another in college, the little one at home. Thought a third child would keep them young. It hadn't worked. Looking at the little fellow, feeling more tired taking care of him and cleaning up after him and running after him, only reminded her of how old she was getting. It had been so much easier with the other children. *Stupid,* she often called herself. *Stupid. You could have done things, gone places with the money you'd saved. You and Johnny.*

You alone. You could have done something more with your life.

"What are you thinking about?" John asked her.

"I was just wondering what you were thinking about."

"Why don't you have a cup of coffee?"

"I might as well." She got up and went to the stove. When she came back with the cup of coffee, he hadn't shifted position; his countenance was just as morose as before.

"John, honey," she said sweetly. "What's the matter? I can tell that something's bothering you. Tell me what it is."

"It's that damn milkshake. I told ya."

"I told *you*, but that's not the point. Now don't change the subject on me like you usually do." She put her hand on top of his again, looked into his eyes, trying to read them.

How could he tell her what he couldn't quite put into words?

"Is it the job? Is that what's bothering you?"

"I don't know," he said, trying to suppress a yawn, failing.

"Don't go to sleep on me now."

"Something funny's goin' on Gloria. I'm told not to worry, but I do. I do."

"What's funny?"

"Gloria, today I was given fifteen cases to look into. In one day."

"Was somebody sick? You always get a bigger workload when somebody's out sick, you know—"

He cut her off, not wanting to *rationalize* any

longer. "No one was sick. It wasn't that. Nobody was laid off. It's just that—we get more cases."

"So you had more reports today than usual."

"It's been like this for a long time."

"But Johnny, you've been through this before. The runaways, the missing daddies, the wives who run off and leave their kids. All that sadness. It's bound to get to you now and then. But you guys find just about everybody and bring them all back home, don't you?"

"Not anymore," he said grimly. "Not lately, Gloria. The number is rising. Higher each week. Not only are there more reports of missing persons, but we're not finding nearly as many of them as we used to."

"Somedays it's worse than others. Don't let it get you down."

"No, it's not that. I can deal with my job, with the sadness, and all the rest. I can't deal with this strange—epidemic we're having. The other guys on the squad talk the way you do. 'More people. Sicker society. More yoyos running away, dying, killing themselves.' But I've *looked* at the statistics. I went *through* the files and the charts and the papers. More and more people are poppin' outa sight each day, and I don't fuckin' know why. And we ain't findin' all that many of 'em."

"Johnny. It's a thankless job, a futile job, at times. You said so yourself."

"You're not listening to me. Within the past six months, our workload has tripled. Everybody says, 'So, that's life. Everybody wants to disappear all of a sudden, ha ha. Shut up and do your job.' So I shut up and I do my job but I still wonder: why? What's happening out there that so *many* people should just vanish all of a sudden? I checked the figures over and over and over one afternoon. I was terrified. If it keeps up, we're gonna have an empty city."

Gloria looked at him reproachfully. "Now Johnny. You're exaggerating and you know it. You have insomnia. That milkshake—your stomach ache is—magnifying—everything." She suddenly leaned over and put her hand on his forehead. "John, you're *shivering*. Are you getting the flu? You don't have a fever."

"That must be the milkshake too!" Albright snapped. "You asked me what was wrong; I told you. What do you have to bug me for?"

"I didn't mean to 'bug you.' I was concerned."

He got up, waving his arms around. The coffee cup overturned, spilling out what was left in its contents. "All right already. Forget I said anything. I'm crazy, okay?"

"Don't yell at me, Johnny. I just don't want you to get so upset. What do you think's going on—a conspiracy or something? There has to be a logical explanation. Things are tough all over these days. The world is crazy. Why don't you just accept that—for whatever reason—more people each week are reported missing now than were a few months ago."

"And fewer and fewer are being found."

"What are you going to do? Kill yourself over it? You have enough to worry about. Your health. Your weight. You're not the only one with problems; I have problems. Why don't you ever talk to me, find out what *I'm* feeling?"

"I talked to you tonight. What the hell good did it do? Huh?"

She didn't answer. She looked away from him, only looking up when she'd heard his footsteps retreat into the bedroom. She wiped her eyes, beginning to tear, and got a towel to clean up the spilled coffee. She put his cup and her own into the sink, put out the light, and checked in on little Bobby.

She was feeling sorry for herself and she knew it. But John had to be exaggerating the work situation; it just didn't make any sense. He'd been acting peculiar for days now, and it put even more of a strain on their already troubled marriage.

She'd swallowed it hook, line, and sinker, that was it, about how being a woman meant that you gave birth to lots of babies and stayed home to take care of them. She loved Bobby, loved all her children, but often wondered if she'd paid too high a price. She couldn't deal with all her continual disappointments. Instead she kept telling herself, *Be glad for what you have.* It worked most of the time. *Sure, you're no beauty queen, you look older every day,* she said, *but you're as happy, happier than those young sex queens in the movies, what with all their unhappy love affairs, their silicone boobies.* Still, she couldn't help but wonder if her life might have been more—exciting, rewarding, what-have-you. Couldn't she have—accomplished—something? Hell, she knew that going to work, having a career, wasn't all it was cracked up to be. Who says she would have been happy trudging off to work day after day—same faces, same hours, same routine. It always looked so glamorous for the career women with important, high-paying jobs, chic clothes, and slim figures running around in the commercials aimed at liberated women. Work all day. Play all night. But for a dumpy, plain-looking, untalented woman like her, the dog-eat-dog world would not have been kind. Or so she told herself.

She loved John. But sometimes she felt so alone.

She tried once to talk to her husband about the changing role of women, about "alternate lifestyles." He had listened uncomprehendingly, too much of the old school to be concerned. She believed with all her heart that the new, freer attitudes were right, were necessary. Not every woman had to marry and raise a family if she didn't want to. Why hadn't she realized that earlier, so at least she could have experimented? Maybe she'd have stuck to her old life, gone back to the housewifey routine after she'd had her fling. It was the not-knowing that bothered her. And her daughter, their first child, with so much talent—what had she done? Gotten married at nineteen. To a bum yet.

Bobby was fast asleep. Cute little kid. Looked more like her than like his father. Seven years old. Helpless. She went over to the bed and hugged him softly, tenderly. How many children had run away today, she wondered, so many of them unloved, running from unbearable home lives and horrible situations. How many kids would wake up to find a parent gone? What a sad, heartbreaking life it could be, this family life. How sad and unrewarding. She wanted things to be different for this child. *Different.*

She pushed the boy over slightly, careful not to wake him, and spent the night at his side.

One room away, her husband was drifting off to sleep. He would have been crying had he not been taught that men don't cry. He was scared. He felt so alone.

What a sad life, he thought.

So sad.

There was a wild party at Harry Faulkin's place that night. And it was still going strong at 3:30. It was his thirty-first birthday and he'd decided to throw himself a bash. Why not? No one could give a party for Harry Faulkin like Harry Faulkin could give himself. New York City's premiere weatherman would do it up BIG!

He had his multi-level apartment done up in weather motifs. Huge cotton wads were thrown all over the place to resemble clouds. He had special sprinklers installed so that it looked as if the walls were dripping rain. His stereo played a sound-effects recording that imitated thunder, and the lights were gimmicked so that they would flash on and off like lightning. Fans were situated throughout the room, making it windy, and giving the more scantily clad guests a hypochondriacal case of the sniffles. It was absolutely crass.

Everybody loved it.

Some people thought that Harry Faulkin was an obnoxious, conceited jackass, about as much a "meteorologist" as the bubble-brained anchorman were "journalists." He was pretty and young and helped the ratings, which is why he'd been installed as WNUC's latest weatherman. WNUC was the home of "FUNNEWS," the news program that was never boring. Airplane disasters, earthquakes, and mass murders were reported with the same plastic smiles used for "cute" spots about roller-skating nuns. Underneath this "funny" approach was a hardcore conservatism that would have embarrassed Joe McCarthy.

Faulkin avoided most of his colleagues and stayed in one corner with selected guests of the nubile variety. He had been putting the make on a bosomy redhead earlier that evening when someone called him to the phone. "It was ringing and ringing in the bedroom," a drunken executive said, "so I thought it might be important."

Faulkin shut the bedroom door and said, "Who's this?"

"Steven."

"Steven, baby! Where are ya? Tonight's the party!"

"I know. Look, I can't come. I completely forgot about your birthday. I'm kind of upset about something. I just woke up."

"What's wrong, pal?"

"Nothing. Look, you've got a party to throw. I just wanted to call, say Happy Birthday, and explain why I wouldn't be there."

"Well, *why?*" Faulkin listened for a few moments, nodding his head and going "uh hmm." "You ask me, buddy, your brother's shacked up with some chick." He listened again. "*Heeyy,* don't bite my head off. But the little bugger *is* quite a stud, isn't he?"

He listened for a few moments more, rubbing his chin with a fingertip. "Well, I'll see what I can do. But you know how it is. Little kids—everybody's soft on them. But it's hard to make a news story over a grown man who's only been gone one day. And besides, I'm only the weatherman."

"Do you think I'm being overprotective, Harry?" Steven asked him. "It was just that the circumstances . . ."

"Lots of sexy chicks go joggin' in Central Park, baby. Your brother *could* have connected with one, and they've been makin' like rabbits ever since. Give the kid a break. Listen, why don't you come on over? Lots of good booze. Lots of pretty broads. Have some fun. It'll get your mind off things."

"Believe me, I thought about it. But this thing has me concerned. I don't know why—I think Joey's in trouble. Anyway, the police may try to get in touch with me."

"Suit yourself. If you change your mind . . ."

"I know. We'll see."

They said goodnight and ended the conversation.

Much later as Harry walked back from the bathroom, an attractive, very tipsy brunette tiptoed over to him and planted a kiss on his chin. "Happy Birthday, Harry darling." She looked around stupidly and pouted. "But Harry, you forgot the snow."

"*What* did I forget?" he asked, wiping some onion dip off his shirt with a cocktail napkin.

"The snow. The *snow!* You've got thunder and lightning and wind and rain, but there isn't any snow."

"Oh, shit," Harry exclaimed, slapping a palm to his forehead. "You're right. Damn it all. I thought I had taken care of everything."

"Well, don't cry, lad," a bald-headed senior VP said heartily. "Here's some hail!" At that, he grabbed a few ice cubes from the bucket and threw them at the brunette. She squealed with laughter and pinched him in the ribs. "Stop that, Mr. Harderman!"

"Snow. God damn it!" Harry continued. "It would have been so easy too. Wait a minute!" He snapped his fingers and headed toward the kitchen, ducking arms full of drinks, turning away from the less attractive female faces. It took him ten minutes to cross the room.

He found two people necking in the darkness of the kitchen. When the light came on, they giggled and went back to the party. Someone had thrown up in the sink. He turned on the faucet to wash it away, and looked through the cupboard for some rice. Feeling quite giddy, he knocked over lots of packaged food in the effort.

Someone came up to him. The brunette.

Sylvia was her name.

"What you doin'?"

"Looking for some snow. We have to have some snow."

"Oh, Harry. You don't really have to bother. Too bad we can't have some *real* snow. Snowball fights and snowmen and igloos and snow angels and all that."

"Please. I *hate* snow. Messy and yuchhy."

The girl was offended. "How can anyone *hate* snow?"

"Blame my grandmother. She used to tell me horror stories when I was a kid to punish me. Once when I stayed out in the snow too long, she told me about the snow worms, these horrible bloodsuckers that live in the snow and sneak up on ya and eat ya—only you can't see 'em 'cause they're white. Until they fill up with blood, that is. *Your* blood."

"*Harry*. That's horrible."

"So was my grandmother."

"Uh." He knocked a box of macaroni to the floor. "I could have sworn I had some rice."

"Well, it won't snow tonight, that's for sure. I heard your weather report."

"I don't see how you could have missed it. You do work in the studio, baby."

She giggled again. "I remember that you said that tonight was to be 'not too cold and very clear.'' And that tomorrow was to be 'unseasonably warm, possibly signifying a freak heat spell on the way.'

"That's right, baby. You listened good. Heard every word."

"So it can't snow tonight."

His hand finally latched onto a box of rice. It tumbled out of the cupboard, and Harry swerved his body to grab it before it hit the floor. He would have gotten it, except that something outside the window suddenly caught his eye—something that was captured in the flashing lights from the living room.

"Baby. Do you see what I see?"

"What?" she asked.

"Look. Out the window."

Snow.

PART II

Thursday, October 17th

FOUR

STEVEN HAD INSISTED on seeing Detective Albright in person on Thursday morning. Both of them looked awful. Both were preoccupied, carrying personal burdens that made it hard for them to concentrate on what the other was saying. The detective had yet another half-eaten breakfast on his desk. As they rushed through the police formalities, the detective belched, excused himself, and questioned Steven unenthusiastically.

"So your—eh—brother is still missing?" he asked, his teeth crunching into a toasted buttered bagel.

"Yes, he is. Obviously he wasn't out gallivanting Tuesday night like everyone seems to think he was." The detective nodded. Steven added irritably, "Don't you ever eat breakfast at home, like most people?"

"If I ate at home my wife would make me a big breakfast, and I'd eat it, because my wife is a terrific cook. Omelets are her specialty. And I'm supposed to be on a diet, understand?" He chewed the piece of bagel thoughtfully, as if hoping Steven would go away.

"Well, now that we have that out of the way," Steven said, "I don't suppose you'd be interested in some additional information I have that may shed some light on the case?"

"Go ahead. What is it?"

Steven told him about Vivian Jessup, her story about Joey's suicidal threats, her fear of talking to the police.

"If someone from the police were to question her, perhaps we'd be able to get to the bottom of this."

"She sounds a little batty to me," Albright said. "But I suppose it wouldn't hurt to have a talk with her. Wanta come with me?"

"You mean, you'll go? You'll do it?"

Albright gave him a comical glare. "Don't look a gift horse in the mouth."

"Sure, I'll go with you. I could tell you if what she's saying corresponds to the story she gave me last night."

"As soon as I'm finished, we'll leave." He smiled at Steven. "Want a piece of bagel?"

Steven declined.

They drove over to Vivian's apartment in silence. Albright cursed a few times at the lousy drivers and the slow-moving traffic, but did not address himself to Steven. Steven couldn't find much to say either. He was still wondering why the detective had taken time from his busy schedule to check out what could not have been one of his major cases. Not that he was complaining.

They parked down the block from Vivian's building, disembarked, and asked the doorman —not the one who'd been on duty the night before—to ring the buzzer to the manager's office.

The manager was a middle-aged woman with a puffy face, bleached hair, and a fattening body squeezed into slacks that were excrutiatingly tight on her. "Yes?" she said nervously. "Can I help you gentlemen?"

Albright showed her his badge. Upon discovering that he was a representative of the law, she got even more nervous. "Is something wrong?"

Steven was surprised at the lazy detective's initiative. He extracted a picture of Joey from his wallet and asked the woman if she had ever seen him entering or leaving the building. When she responded negatively, he asked her a few simple questions about Mrs. Jessup.

"I don't know her too well. My husband fixed some things in her place last week sometime; said she had company. Male company. He might be able to tell you more. But I don't know much about the residents' comings and goings. It ain't none of my business." She offered to call the woman over the intercom.

"No thanks," Albright said. "We'd like to go up unannounced."

"Suit yourself, officer."

They went upstairs to her apartment and rang the bell. There was no answer.

"Can we get the key and look around?" Steven asked.

Albright gave him one of his exasperated looks. "I don't think it's warranted, sorry." Steven cursed under his breath.

"Let's go back down," Albright said impatiently.

They returned to the lobby. The door to the manager's apartment was open and emitted loud noises. Steven and the detective stepped inside and saw a grizzled old man in overalls, the bleached blonde's husband, holding a paper spread open in front of him. His wife looked up from the section he was showing her and placed her hand to her mouth. She looked from Albright to Steven and back again.

"You the police she tol' me about?"

Albright nodded. The old man held out the paper for the detective to take. "I'm afraid you won't be asking poor Missus Jessup nothin', if you're the ones wanted to talk to her."

On the third page of the paper there was a picture of the woman taken several years earlier. She was smiling, her hair long and framing her face attractively. In bold print the headline read: NOTED BIOLOGIST FALLS TO DEATH IN SUBWAY.

Steven grabbed the paper from Albright and read with disbelief.

The old man looked at the detective and said, "Happened just last night. They found her driver's license in her handbag. Otherwise, 'tweren't no way to tell who it was, all cut up like that. They're notifying relatives now. Probably come to close up the apartment later today or tomorrow."

Steven's eyes whirled through the story,

scanning the important details: *Vivian Jessup, a retired biologist, was killed in the subway... It is unclear at this point whether she fell accidentally, jumped of her own volition, or was pushed ... Witnesses did not notice her presence until she was falling onto the tracks at the 59th Street station... "There was no possible way we could have saved her," said one ... Mrs. Jessup was the widow of Gerald B. Jessup ... The couple became well-known in scientific circles when they worked together to shed new light on positive uses of bacteriological agents...*

"Did you know about this?" the manager asked, blinking away tears. "Is that why you came here?"

"No, I assure you," Albright told her. "I'm with the Missing Persons Squad. I came on an entirely different investigation."

"You must have known," the woman argued. "How could you not have known? You *are* with the police department."

Albright almost laughed. One hand didn't know what the other was doing.

"We honestly didn't know," Steven interrupted. "I had no idea this was going to happen. We are investigating my brother's disappearance."

"Your brother?" she asked. "You mean the young man in your picture?"

"Yes. He's been gone for two days. We thought that Vivian might have had some information."

"Alfie," the woman said to her husband. "Look at the picture for them."

Albright handed it to him. "Look familiar?"

"I can't be sure. Maybe. Maybe not. I might have seen him coming in with her once or twice when I was watering the plants out in the lobby —but I just can't be sure. You'll have to check the doormen."

"What do we do now?" his wife inquired. "Will we have to talk to more detectives? About that poor woman? Oh, what an awful way to die. Horrible. Horrible."

"Steady, Nancy, steady." Alfie gave the picture back and put his arm around her shoulder. "We'll talk to anyone we have to."

"Can I use your phone?" Albright asked, pointing to the push-button job on the table behind Alfie's back. The old man nodded. Albright took the entire phone off the table and walked with it to the other side of the room while he "punched."

Steven left Alfie alone to comfort his wife and walked out into the lobby. Mrs. Jessup had been far more than she'd seemed. Not just a rich lady looking for fun and excitement, but a scientist of some renown. Steven's concern over her hideous passing was overshadowed by the horror of its implications, the implications of these new insights into her life. Just yesterday she had been talking about suicide, his brother's suicide, and only an hour or so after he had left her . . .

Was he responsible? Was it his fault? His badgering, his insensitivity? Had his overwhelming concern for his brother caused him to overlook her very real anguish? But she had been so oblique, so uncooperative.

Albright had left the manager's apartment

102

and was walking over to Steven. "Well," he said, "maybe the lady couldn't stand the guilt. Killed herself 'cause she thought she made your brother do himself in."

"That might explain her death," Steven said, "but *not* my brother's disappearance. I still don't think he killed himself over her."

"Probably not. Just her delusion. Joey'll turn up, don't you worry."

"You can guarantee that?"

Albright ignored the remark. "Sad business, this. Did you know she was a biologist?"

"Hadn't the slightest clue."

"Surprised?"

"I suppose so. Look, can't we get into her apartment *now?* There might be something— some information—in there that we can use."

"Nope. That's not my job. If they find anything in there I'll hear about it and I'll let you know. Don't worry."

Steven's shoulders sank. "I can't help but think . . ."

"Think what?"

"Forget it."

"Go ahead. Tell me."

"My brother disappears. Vivian insists my brother is dead. And now, *she* gets killed the next day. What does that look like to you?"

Albright stared at Steven for a moment, weighing his response. It did not come with any great conviction.

"Coincidence."

"You don't really believe that, do you? Man, you cops can explain anything away."

Albright shook his head. It looked as if he had

something on his mind, something he had to get off his chest, but he remained silent.

"Are you all right, Detective Albright?"

The man's head was quivering and his face had reddened.

"Uh. Yeah. Sure, I'm all right." He was back to normal now. "Listen, I have things to do. Do you mind if we split up here? I'll call you if anything comes up."

"So that's the story," Steven said bitterly. "My brother was just a nobody. Let him disappear and who gives a damn. But her—she was somebody. Famous biologist. Wealthy widow. Everybody's going to try to get to the bottom of *this*, right? But my brother can get lost and stay lost."

"Now look, Everson," Albright said. "Your brother is missing, and that's all. Missing. But this woman was ground to pieces by an express train. When somebody falls in front of a train, there's gotta be a reason, and it's our job to find out what that reason is." Again his voice held no conviction. He was just reading lines.

"Not *your* job, remember? *Your* job is to look for my brother."

"And a million others. Look I've taken a personal interest—I don't even know why—and you oughta be glad. Because since your brother was reported missing, I've been given almost *fifty* new cases to look into. That's right—fifty! So shut your mouth, go home, and let me do my job. Y'know, the fact is that this woman's death may have been the best thing that could have happened. If your *brother's* mixed up in it, we'll find him, all right?"

"What's that supposed to mean?"

Albright's face curled up in a nasty sneer. "A young buck. A rich old lady. Ever heard words like 'hustler,' 'gigolo'? She kicks him out. The spending money is cut off and the young buck is angry. He broods about it, follows her, pushes her in front of a train. Ah, sweet vengeance."

"Joey would *never* have done something like that!"

Albright raised his hands defensively. "I'm only telling you how some people will see it. Don't get mad at me. At least they'll be out there lookin' for the kid. Let's just hope he *is* innocent."

"Of *course* he's innocent. He's the victim here, not—" Steven stopped suddenly, too tired to continue the argument. "I'm sorry. It's been such a strain. Believe it or not, I appreciate the time you've given me. It's all turning into such a mess."

"Go on home now," Albright said with concern. "Try and relax. You don't look so hot."

Steven caught a glimmer of a smile on the edges of Albright's mouth. He smiled back and the detective's beam widened. The man reached out and slapped Steven on the shoulder.

"It'll be okay."

"I hope so."

They separated. Albright stayed in the lobby. Steven went out into the street to hail a taxi.

Steven gave the cabby his address and sat back in the seat to relax. He was stunned by Vivian Jessup's death. What had driven her to it? Where had she been going at that hour? To see Joey? He rubbed his eyes, eyes that were red and full of crust. Aching eyes. Leaning back his head, he closed them and sighed. He did not open his eyes again until he'd arrived back home.

Back at the apartment building that Steven had just left, Detective John Albright fitted the manager's passkey into Vivian Jessup's lock and slowly opened the door.

Harry Faulkin woke up with a start, wondering what time it was and if he was late for work. He checked the clock on the night table. Plenty of time, although it was already past noon. He looked over at the other side of the bed, and was surprised to see no one lying there. He grumbled, got to his feet, and headed for the kitchen. His head hurt and his mouth was dry and fetid.

The living room looked like a grotesque combination of Halloween and Christmas. Thank God somebody had remembered to turn off the "rain water" or it might have overflowed the basins in the front of the baseboards. He mistrusted machinery when left to its own devices. The big puffy clouds were in pieces, scattered all over the room. He'd turned the phonograph off, but the "lightning" had been flashing all day. What an electric bill he'd have. He switched the light off, and turned on the regular lamps. It looked like all the guests had left; usually he found one or two of them behind the couch or in the bathtub.

He would have to give his maid Thelma an extra-special bonus for cleaning up this mess;

he sure wasn't going to touch it. Hors d' oeuvres had been ground into the carpet, and the table-cloth on the buffet table was stained with every-thing from cigar ashes to onion dip. Champagne glasses and beer mugs were lying on the sofa, and little plates dabbed with left-over delicacies had been deposited in every convenient nook and cranny.

He ignored all the sloppiness and entered the kitchen. It too was messy, but not as bad as the other room. Mostly there were empty liquor bottles all over the place. He had to clear them away from the counter so that he could make a pot of coffee. He sure wished it wasn't Thelma's day off; he would just have to let everything stay as it was until she returned on Friday. She'd raise unholy hell until he told her she'd get a much larger paycheck at the end of the week.

Something drew him to the window. He was about to look out into the brand-new, if slightly-used, day when he realized that it had inex-plicably started to snow earlier in the morning. He had first noticed it when Sylvia and he had been looking for rice to use for snowflakes. Dumb idea, he thought now. He forgot if he had thrown the rice around or not, but if he had, Thelma would surely find it.

He peered down into the street, wondering if it was coated with white. Nothing. If it had actually been snowing—and he remembered now that some of the other guests had seen it and kidded him about his inaccurate forecast—then it certainly couldn't have lasted too long. But there hadn't *been* any indication that it would snow. He put the coffee into the pot. Who cared? No one ever expected the weather forecasts to be right. Least of all his.

Finally, somewhere under his continuous preoccupation with endless hedonism and self-concern, Harry remembered the phone call he'd gotten from Steven. Something about his brother. The guy'd been pretty upset.

Steven was an okay fellow. They'd known each other an awfully long time. He picked up the kitchen extension and dialed his friend's number.

"Stevie baby! How's tricks?"

"Harry! How'd the party go?"

"Te*riff.* Te*riff.* I'm telling you." He was good as segues. "How's your brother? He come home yet?"

"No. Haven't heard a word. I might as well go back to work. I'm too upset to enjoy my time off."

"Still got a couple of weeks, right?"

"Yeah."

"Listen. Don't worry. The kid'll turn up. You know how they are. Let's get together for brunch today. Talk the whole thing over."

"Okay. Where'll I meet you?"

Harry gave him a name. A place conveniently located. For Harry, that is.

"See you then, Harry. It'll be good to talk to someone about this."

"You and Andrea still have problems?"

"She's out of town. I'll tell you all about it."

"Okay, pal. Coffee's boiling over. See you soon."

"Bye."

Harry poured himself a cup of coffee and sat down at the kitchen table. *Harry, my boy,* he thought, *you make a good friend.*

It was almost three o'clock in the afternoon when Eric Thorne was finally able to take a break and go have a talk with Emily. His day at the Institute for Psychic Research had been a hectic and unrewarding one. Perhaps it was because his mind was so preoccupied. All he could think about was getting away to talk to someone about the uncanny experience he'd had in his apartment the night before. It all seemed so distant now. Except for a brief moment when he'd first stepped off the train and started to walk toward the building, he hadn't succumbed to panic or fear once during the day. But he couldn't help but dwell on the incident. Just telling someone about it would be of enormous therapeutical value.

Dr. Emily Jannings was another young person on the staff, and her specialties were divided. She would occasionally assist Thorne in his ESP research, but her main thrust was toward the more physical manifestations of brain power. Mind over matter, for instance. Thorne would test a person's ability to pick up thought waves from another room, while Emily would see if—and to what degree—someone could use their mental abilities to make an object move.

Thorne decided to speak with Emily because

he was closer to her than to anyone else on the staff, and because he respected her opinion over everyone's. There might be others who were more knowledgeable, perhaps, but none who had her warmth and sympathy and understanding. She would listen with her heart as well as her mind.

He approached her office, hoping she was free at this hour, free long enough for them to discuss the matter in detail. He turned into the small room where Emily sat looking over some papers.

Eric rapped once on the open wood door. "Mind if I disturb you?"

"Eric! Come in," she said brightly, putting the papers together and placing them on top of a pile in the corner of the desk. "What can I do for you?" She was in her late thirties, with wavy brown hair cut short and curving away on either side of her forehead. Her eyes were light blue. She had a long graceful neck, and a pretty face with soft features and high cheekbones. She had a preference for dark suits; this afternoon was no exception. She handed Eric her pack of cigarettes as he spoke.

"I'd like to talk to you about something that happened to me last night. Something disturbing." He declined her offer of a smoke, but lit hers with his lighter.

"Thank you," she said. "Well, what happened exactly?"

"I believe it was either a psychic attack, or I accidentally—or purposefully, I should say—tapped into someone else's thoughts. Or someone else's reality. I'm not sure which."

"Well, that's not altogether unusual for you, Eric. Although I must say, this business about psychic *attacks* does sound interesting."

"I wish that's all it was. Interesting. Actually, the experience put me into a severe mental state —left me drained and panicky—and quite frightened the wits out of me."

"You'd better go over it. In detail," Emily said. He did.

By the time he was finished relating the events of the evening, Emily had started her third cigarette. She always smoked rapidly when something particularly intrigued her.

"And you think that the 'nightmare' you had last evening was somehow related to the drunk who approached you at the subway?"

"Yes. I'm sure of it," Eric replied. "The feelings I had were the same. The images I saw were similar."

"But it wasn't until *after* you went to bed that you saw anything especially . . . coherent?"

"That's true. I only picked up random bits and pieces from the derelict's mind, but they were the same as the bits and pieces I saw later at home in bed when I began to relax. Then I began to let the images *saturate* my mind so that I could see a clearer, yet more complex, picture."

"What's your explanation for it?"

"I don't know. I can't believe the drunkard was behind it all. It was all he could do to keep himself alive. If he *is* alive. At this point, who can tell?"

"Do you think someone deliberately fed you those images, *wanted* you to see what you saw?"

"No. No, I realize now that that wasn't the case. I would have had an easier time of it, for one thing. Even if I had been picking up the thoughts of someone who was unaware of my existence, it still wouldn't have been quite so hard to get a *fix*. No, I think instead that I tapped into an uncommonly powerful mental force or forces. Frighteningly powerful. I was susceptible because I had been thinking about the derelict all night, and I'm sure that what I saw had something to do with him. His mind, as insane as it was, was still very strong."

"Was it his mind you 'encountered?' Someone's nearby? A neighbor's, perhaps?"

"If the images had come from nearby, there would have been a residue, a presence, all about me in the morning. Besides, I would have known by now if another sensitive lived in my building."

"It's a big building."

He tapped his head playfully with his index finger. "I've got a big mind."

She laughed and got up from the seat. "Let me get us some coffee and we'll talk about this some more. I'll only be a moment."

"Fine. I could use a cup."

She returned five minutes later with two cups and some packets of sugar. They each finished preparing their coffee, then returned to the subject at hand.

"Well," Emily said cheerfully, "now that

we've determined the cause, let's discuss the effect. You suffered extreme paranoia, depression, abject loneliness, claustrophobia . . . let's see, did I leave anything out?"

"Yes. I subjected myself to an old western. Something I'd never do if I was in my right mind."

She giggled. "I *love* westerns. But to each his own. You craved companionship. You felt that the four walls were closing in on you. That the bathroom would devour you if you stepped inside. Trapped. Enclosed. Like inside a mouth."

He swallowed the coffee and nodded. "Yes. A singularly unpleasant sensation, I assure you."

"No doubt. Your feelings of terror started to subside only when you turned on the TV?"

Eric placed his hand on his cheek, trying to remember. "Yes. No—it was earlier, my blue bedroom. I couldn't stand anything dark or bright. The terror changed into a fear—of those extremes in color, or tight, cramped spaces. Then, I became horribly depressed. I felt pathetic, sad about my lot in life."

"We all get that way sometimes."

"Yes. Yes, we do. But this was intense. Remarkably intense. Not brought on by anything in particular."

"Subconscious memories of the images you saw. People crying out. Herded together in pain."

"Yes. That could be it. It had to be unconscious, though, because at that time, I wasn't even thinking about what I'd seen in the trance."

"And to counteract the despair, the emptiness, you turned on the TV."

"Yes." He was excited now, hoping that together they could help him understand his ordeal.

"And there was no more terror."

"No. Except for one moment."

"When? When did it happen?"

"I—I can't remember."

"Try. It could be important."

"I—uh. I can't. Yes. Yes, now I remember. It was when I first turned on the TV set. But it went away as soon as the picture came in."

"You mean it happened right after you switched on the set, right before there was any picture?"

"Yes. No. I mean it happened just *as* the picture came in. I think. Then it went away. For good."

"Hmmm. Interesting. Blackness and then harsh, bright white light."

"What's that?"

"What you told me you saw during your trance. Darkness, through an aperture. Then a rectangle of light getting larger and larger."

"That's right."

"Well, when you turn on a set, you're looking at a sort of window. At first it's dark, and then the picture comes in. A flash of light, getting bigger and bigger on the screen."

Eric sat back in the chair. "Yes. Exactly. That must have been a reaction to what I saw in the trance. Not really similar. But enough of a suggestion to recreate the fear I'd felt."

"Well, that explains it. You just accidentally hooked up with someone's TV reception, and with all the junk on the air these days, it's no wonder you had a nightmare."

Emily laughed. But Eric could only manage a weak smile. Talking with her had helped, but had brought him no closer to answering the questions that bothered him. But then, he hadn't really thought it would.

They conversed a short while longer, of innocuous things, minor things, relating to the job and the people they worked with. Then Eric left, thanking Emily for her time.

He knew as he walked down the corridor toward his office that Emily had only been trying to make him feel better; she certainly hadn't meant to laugh at his distress. Or had he communicated his distress eloquently enough? Whatever the case, he knew that he was far more worried about the past evening's experience than he had let on to Emily.

And he truly dreaded dusk.

At a quarter past one that afternoon, Henry Judson was looking through a microscope in the police laboratory, his face constricted with mounting horror. During his five years with the department, he had analyzed poisonous chemicals, determined blood types, and studied samples of skin and hair. But he had never seen anything quite as bizarre as what he was seeing now. He removed the smeared slide from the microscope and placed it on the table beside it.

Then, he quickly jotted down some notes on a white pad, labeled the paper carefully, and took it down the hall to his superior's office.

Ernest was taking a break, chatting by the water cooler with a young man and a middle-aged woman. Henry excused himself and asked Ernest if he could speak to him privately in his office. His superior complied.

Ernest lit one of his odorous cigars. "What is it, Henry? You don't look so good."

"Well, sir . . ." Henry said, hesitating. "I was analyzing a substance that was brought in after lunch." He consulted his paper. "Sample 81B. Unknown substance—uh—found on the wall of a hotel room."

"Yes, I recall that. Looked something like jelly, right?"

"Yes. But it isn't."

"What did you find, Henry?"

"Well, sir—it seems to be a solidified mixture of blood plasma and cell tissue and . . . well, I isolated all its components, and it appears to be a jellied paste made of flesh, blood, and bone—and clothing fibers—all mashed together, somehow transformed into a gelatinous form. I can't figure it. I've never seen anything like it."

"You mean, that stuff they scraped off the wall was from a human being?"

"I—I think it *is* a human being, somehow—compressed—into that jelly."

"Let me take a look at this." He reached over to his intercom and signaled his secretary. "Joan, I don't want to be disturbed by anyone until I get back to you, is that clear? I'll be in Lab 27."

116

"Yes, sir."

"All right, let's take a look at this stuff."

They walked out of the office and headed toward the lab.

It was way past two o'clock when Ernest had finished and compared his findings with Henry's. "Both organic and inorganic material, that's what threw me off," he said. "But you were right. Absolutely right. It's unbelievable. But what on earth could have turned a man into jelly like this?"

"I don't know, sir," Henry said, involuntarily shuddering.

Although Steven lived in an entirely different neighborhood, and the restaurant was around the corner from Harry's apartment, Steven arrived at the place first. He sat at a table nursing a bloody mary and waited for his friend to show up.

He liked Harry, had known him practically his whole life—though he had to admit the man was a living anachronism. It would always be 1960 for Harry Faulkin. His whole irresponsible attitude toward life and women—or "broads" and "chicks," as Harry called them—seemed to indicate arrested development. But for a man without any discernible talent—aside from bedmanship, to hear him talk—Harry had managed to go far.

He walked in half an hour late, mildly apologetic. "Stevie, my boy. Let's get me a drink and get down to business."

He ordered a martini, very dry, with a twist.

"Any new developments?" he asked Steven.

"Nothing. Harry—where can he *be?* This just isn't like him."

"My theory doesn't sound promising, huh?"

"That he's with some woman?" Steven paused, then figured he might as well go ahead and tell Harry about Vivian.

"I read about her, man," Harry said a few moments later. "The gal that took it in the subway. *She* was your brother's lady friend? No flies on that kid. You think her death and your brother's disappearance are connected?"

"I don't know what to think, Harry. Joey was just a kid looking for work and a little fun in the meantime. At least, that's what I thought. Now I find out this 'girl' he's seeing is a middle-aged widow, that she thinks he committed suicide— and then *she* falls in front of a train. There might be no connection at all. But it's the only thing I have to go on."

Harry was excited. "Look, Steve. You asked me last night if I could get Joey's picture on the news. You didn't tell me then he was shacking up with that dead woman. We covered Vivian Whatshername's death on the program. Maybe, just maybe, I can convince somebody there's a new angle here. Deaths, disappearances . . . sounds interesting already."

Steven wasn't sure he liked the sound of that. "Do you know if Vivian's death has been determined an accident, murder, or suicide yet?"

Harry shook his head. "Even the witnesses weren't sure. It all happened so fast, I guess. You know how those things are. Anyway, if they cover the broad's death on the news again tonight, maybe they can mention your brother's disappearance, flash his picture, y'know? Got one handy?"

Steven took one out of his wallet. "Here."

"Good. Let's order. I'm starving. Relax, buddy. It'll be okay. Has Harry ever let you down?"

Harry managed to make it to the studio only fifteen minutes late. He went into his dressing room and waited for the makeup lady to come and prepare him for the broadcast. In the meantime, he studied his copy.

While he was acquainted with basic techniques of meteorology, and knew what the terms that he used during his weather report meant, he was certainly no scientist. The facts about the upcoming weather were given to the news writers, typed up and spiced with snappy patter, and then handed to Faulkin for him to look over. There was no need for memorization, as everything he reported was written on cue cards that he could refer to from time to time. He was allowed to ad-lib in his own inimitable manner. But in spite of the fact that he did not actually predict the weather—scientifically or otherwise—he was still held accountable for it by his friends and coworkers. It was simply a tradition. Harass the weatherman when it rains, even if he was no more a weatherman than the entertainment reporter was a qualified critic.

Tonight's weather was to be the same as yesterday's. There was no mention of snow anywhere in the report—not even a *chance* of it. So where *was* this unseasonably warm weather, this "heat wave" they were supposed to be having? At least Harry could take comfort in the fact that every other weather service had been wrong about the weather. The temperature was dropping steadily. And no matter how many air currents floated over Manhattan, it seemed to make no difference. It was downright unnatural. Harry wouldn't be surprised if the city had a blizzard.

He combed his hair carefully, was made up, and went out to take his place on the set. He would give the audience a "teaser" at the beginning of the program, and then sit down out of sight until he was given his cue to stand in front of the weather map. It was too late for him to get anything about Joey Everson on the show tonight, but as soon as it was over he'd talk to one of the reporters. Maybe he'd even get to do the story himself if he applied a little pressure.

As he walked toward the hot, bright lights, a few of the people around waved and smiled and said, "Great party last night!" or, "Boy, what a hangover!"

The producer of the news, a heavy-set man named Jerry Withers, came over to Harry and slapped him merrily on the back. "Had a ball last night, kiddo. A real ball."

"Glad to hear it," Harry said.

"Say," Jerry whispered, "we all must have

been seeing things last night. It wasn't really snowing, was it?"

"I guess not," Harry said. What he really wanted to say was, "Yes, it was, and why the hell don't we get some meteorologists who know what the hell they're doing?!"

But he didn't.

Andrea Martin answered the doorbell and saw Steven Everson standing outside in the hallway.

"Steven!"

"Hi. I was at a restaurant around the corner. Thought I'd give you a call, but the line was busy. I knew you had to be home then, so I thought I might just as well walk over."

She stepped back to let him in. "Am I . . . intruding?" he asked. "When did you get back?"

"Uh, earlier today." She was lying. "I'm . . . expecting someone, a business associate, in a minute. But you can stay a while."

Steven noticed how she'd done herself up. Bright auburn hair freshly combed, sweeping down to her shoulders. Eye shadow, lipstick, the works. And that terrific dress. He sensed she didn't want him to kiss her. What was *happening* to them? They had been so *close* once.

The party dip and crackers were laid out on the table. A shaker of martinis. He *was* intruding. He wasn't jealous, though. She bought books for a major chain in New York and often entertained other people in the business; it was part of her job. Still . . .

"Steven, you look *awful*. Haven't you been getting any sleep?"

"Not much. Andrea—my brother's missing."

"What?" That look of concern came over her face, that look that he *cherished*. He knew she would care, that she wouldn't let him down.

"He's been gone for two days now, and I'm scared."

She softened toward him a bit, led him over to the couch. "Tell me about it."

When he was through she was nearly as upset as he was.

"The poor kid. What could have happened to him, Steven? I agree with you. I didn't know Joey very well, but he didn't seem suicidal to me. What are the police doing?"

"Not much. They've got so many other cases. Joey's *officially* a missing person, but so are a thousand other people. It looks pretty hopeless."

"Well," Andrea shrugged, "the cops don't put much effort into finding people unless they're relatives of VIPs or little children. Have you ever thought of hiring a private detective?"

"Yes. Yes, I have. Albright mentioned that. I guess that's what most people have to do if they want a thorough job done. You can't count on the cops, that's for sure."

"Can you afford one? They're not cheap."

"I know. But I haven't any choice. I could go into my savings—my father left me a lot of

122

money, thank goodness. But where do I find a good private eye?"

"My cousin," Andrea said. "Ralph."

"You never told me about *him.*"

"Yes. He's a big, burly, lovable guy and a good detective. His wife died about two years ago, and he's really thrown himself into his work to get over it. I think he's got a pretty good practice going. He doesn't work alone anymore, either. It's a regular *agency.*"

"What's it called?" Steven asked.

"The Andrews Detective Agency. Wait a minute and I'll get you the number." She got up and grabbed her purse from the kitchen. "Here it is. Why don't I give him a call now? I have his home number too, in case he's not in his office."

"Okay. Find out how much he charges."

"All right. When I tell him it's a friend of mine —" She stopped. "He's always been crazy about me." She picked up the phone and dialed.

Steven knew the end was coming. He was just a "friend" now, not her boyfriend any longer. Why did she torture him this way, why didn't she come right out and say that it was over?

Minutes later, Andrea came back into the living room looking very self-satisfied.

"$125 a day, plus expenses. I don't think you got a discount, but you can't win 'em all. Anyway, he *specializes* in missing-persons cases, and will give you 'preferential treatment' if you decide to drop by tomorrow morning. Any time will do. He can't see you before then. I asked."

"Thanks. $125 plus expenses? Well, I do have

a few thousand in the bank. And it's worth it. The longer I delay the more I'll regret it. Yeah, I'll do it!''

Andrea leaned over and patted Steven's hand. He was a German shepherd now. "If anything can be done, Ralph can do it. He's always been a very steady, meticulous sort of guy. His agency wouldn't have grown so much if he wasn't doing something right. And he'll handle your case personally. No more nonsense. He'll get to the bottom of it."

"I'm glad I talked to you about it," Steven said. "It's better than picking a name out of the phone book."

His spirits had risen, knowing that something positive was going to be done about Joey, knowing that someone was going to care, even if he was paid to care. It was better than nothing. Better than waiting and waiting for phone calls that might never come.

The doorbell rang. An impatient look came over Andrea's face. He *was* an intrusion.

Steven stood up awkwardly. "Uh, I'd better get going. Thanks."

She handed him a slip of paper as she went to answer the door. Ralph Andrew's card with address and phone number.

"Hi, Donald!"

Donald didn't look like a "business associate." He was tall and handsome. He was carrying flowers and a bottle of wine.

"I'll be in touch," Steven said, brushing past

the startled man in the hallway. He really did feel alone now.

Out of the corner of his eye he could swear he saw them kissing.

FIVE

ERIC THORNE STEPPED out of the taxi and walked over to the entrance of the Cafe Roja Casa. The big red awning of the restaurant stretched out to the curb, and a crimson rug covered the sidewalk. Eric straightened his tie, patted his hair, and nodded to the doorman. Eric was wearing a stylish blue outfit that made him look like a business executive—a business executive who was trying to look half his age. He had bought it on impulse a while ago, figuring it might come in handy. He didn't wear it often enough to wonder how he looked in it.

He stepped inside the outer lounge and approached the maitre d', a bald, saturnine fellow whose eyelids seemed caught in a permanent yawn. Eric gave the man his name and was escorted to a table in the corner where his friends, the Elians, were waiting. The place was half-filled: this was the in-between time, not as crowded as six or seven, when the cultural crowd ate hurriedly before departing for the theater, or ten or eleven, when the late-nighters decided to dine. Eight-thirty was the perfect time for relaxing with a good meal and nice conversation.

The Cafe Roja Casa had been open for five years and become a New York restaurant success story. Once you secured a reservation—no easy feat—you could sit and watch the "beautiful people" watch one another. Even they, however, had to work hard to compete with the sumptuous decor of the room. Long satin drapes, thick carpeting, pink and cerise paper on the walls. The tables were elegantly set, and even the menus looked as if someone had spent a fortune on them.

Eric said hello to his friends and ordered a cocktail. He had known the Elians since his married days, when they'd all been part of two close couples who shared everything from card parties to week-long vacations. They were two of his very favorite people. Beauford Elian was a good-looking forty-two year-old with neatly combed, slightly greased, greying black hair and a warm, tanned, and open face. His wife Sylvia was a very attractive and sophisticated blonde about her husband's age, but smaller and thinner. Tonight she wore her hair up and pulled into a small bun in the back of her head. She wore a low-cut blue evening gown and very little makeup. Together the Elians ran a successful travel agency. But what Eric really found interesting about them was that they were low-level psychics.

During the first two drinks, they spoke of business and work and other mundane matters. But it wasn't really small talk in the usual sense, since the three participants were absolutely comfortable with each other and genuinely interested in what each had to say.

127

The Elians had long since made their peace with the possibility that Eric might at times pick up thoughts from their minds. Since there were few secrets between them anyway, they had nothing to fear.

Finishing her daiquiri, Sylvia opened the menu and studied the contents. "Hmm. The duck sounds delicious. We were here after it first opened and I had the swordfish. I was disappointed then."

"I think I'll try the pork chops this time," Beau said with some finality.

"Pork chops? Darling, that's so unimaginative. Have something a little more daring."

"At these prices, who wants to be daring? What about you, Eric?"

"It's a tossup between the Chicken Cordon Bleu and the stuffed shrimp. I could eat just about anything and everything on this menu."

After ten minutes the waiter came by. They passed up another drink and ordered. While they waited for the food, Eric decided to tell them about the previous evening's ordeal.

When he had finished, Beau looked worried, and Sylvia, like Emily, tried to make light of it, for Eric's sake. "I wish something exciting like that would happen to me. All *I* can do is tell what playing card a person in another room is looking at."

"I guess it *is* silly of me to worry about it," Eric said.

"No, no," Beau disagreed. "You sounded very upset these past few minutes. I could tell that what happened really bothered you."

"But there's no guarantee that it will happen again," Sylvia said. "Anyway, can't you take any precautions?"

"There's no defense against something like that. Perhaps a strong sedative, I don't know. Whatever the case, I certainly can't afford to lose any more sleep."

"Yes, I thought you looked a bit peaked when you came in. But of course it could be all these damn red lights."

Sylvia giggled. "Do you suppose they're trying to remind us we're in the red-light district?"

The men laughed. The food came then, and they dug in hungrily.

Eric's chicken was juicy and succulent, and the sauce that covered it exceptional. Beau's perfectly grilled pork chops were thick and tender. Sylvia had the delicious Duck L'Orange with rice and breadcrumbs stuffed inside.

As they were finishing their dishes, the conversation came back to Eric's unusual psychic experience. Beau suggested that he might have determined the cause of Eric's harrowing nightmare.

"Big-city paranoia, Eric," he said grinding away what was left of the meat on a bone in his hand. "That's all it was. You felt claustrophobic. You felt lonely. You felt isolated. Who doesn't now and then? You were just a victim of the same disease that afflicts everyone else in this city. Especially when they live alone. And the reason it hit you so hard was because you are admittedly extra-sensitive to external stimuli."

The thought of it chilled Eric. He'd assumed he'd experienced something grotesque and unnatural. Could it really have been just the collective pain of this vibrant, terrible city? All that loneliness. *So much* loneliness.

"But it was like I tapped into someone else's *mind!*" he argued. "Someone who was experiencing the symptoms of the 'disease' you've described," he added.

"Maybe. Or maybe it was your *own* mind. Maybe the pressures have just gotten to be too much for you. Temporarily, I'm sure. It may not have been any kind of psychic monstrosity at all. But it's over and done with, so let's all just have a nice, big, fattening dessert—and I *insist* that you stop worrying."

"All right, I promise." His *own* mind? Was it possible? Was he more lonely than he realized? *That* lonely?

While the chocolate mousse melted on his tongue and went down into his stomach, it was all he could do to keep from asking the Elians if he could spend the night with them at their townhouse.

Lina Hobler woke up at 7:45 and threw the alarm clock on the floor. At least she hadn't overslept. Nervous, she was so damn nervous. Tonight—*tonight* she would find out what had happened to Brock.

She went into the bathroom and washed under her arms, too impatient to take a shower. She brushed her teeth and slipped into a warm blue dress. Then she did a sloppy job of applying her makeup. Her hair was such a mess she wrapped a scarf around her head and didn't even bother with the brush. She opened up the window to see how cold it was outside. Hard to tell with all the steam heat in her room—not that she was complaining. Didn't seem too bad. She put on a light coat, took the piece of paper out of her handbag just to check the address the man had given her on the phone the night before, and went hurriedly out the door.

She lived near the Flushing subway line, but it was useless to her tonight. If she took the train she would have to spend two hours in the subway system switching from line to line until she reached her destination. It would be much simpler just to take a bus to Jamaica Avenue. She could walk the rest of the way.

She arrived at the corner just as the bus pulled in. She stepped inside, paid her fare, and sat way in the rear where she could sit and watch the rest of the riders. She hated being up front where everyone could stare at her. She was afraid someone might recognize who she was—had been—and start an embarrassing fuss. As it was, she assumed every whisper she heard was some comment being made behind her back.

The bus was crowded and it took forever to make its way across Queens. She knew there had to be pretty residential neighborhoods in the borough, but they didn't pass through any. All she saw were flat brick buildings, garages, little brown children hanging out on stoops and in alleys. Every block seemed to have a small superette in which hungry people rushed about from shelf to shelf, anxious to get home before they missed their favorite TV shows. *Face it, Lina. You're one of them now. One of the little people.* She kept glancing at the slip of paper with the address, trying to memorize the words so she'd not have to look again. Too nervous. She couldn't do it.

She got off when the bus reached Jamaica Avenue and walked a few blocks beneath the elevated subway. This neighborhood was much like her own—both had train lines constantly thundering overhead, the crowded streets speckled during the day by the light coming through the tracks. The sky was releasing a light drizzle. Lina wished she had brought an umbrella.

Near the Cypress Hills stop on the J line, which ran above the avenue, she was to look for a bar called McGreeley's. So many taverns along the street—made her feel right at home. There were lots of pizza parlors too, as well as video-game arcades, real-estate offices, and tiny Chinese retaurants. And the usual squabbling children and their parents. She checked the address once more and stopped to make sure she was going in the right direction. Yes, she could see the lighted green sign in the distance. That was the bar. She was to go inside and order a beer—at nine o'clock someone would contact her. She was half hoping that this was all an elaborate joke that Brock had planned for her benefit, a "coming home" party at

McGreeley's Bar and Grill.

She saw through the window as she approached that few people were inside. The place was not as brightly lit as most of the old Irish bars, but wasn't nearly as dark as the places for singles some of them had turned into. Lina hated those joints. Youngsters, youngsters everywhere. Young bucks looking for pretty faces. Not for her, those joints.

No one turned to look at Lina as she entered. She saw with amused resignation that the bar was filthy. On one side was the counter, long and wooden, with chewed-up, red-cushioned stools for seats. There was a mirror behind the bar, exactly in the center, with row upon row of booze on either side of it. The other wall was lined with a lot of empty tables. The floor was grimy. No wonder they kept the lights down.

There were three people sitting at the bar. Two men and a woman. The men, both old and dissipated, were together, engrossed in a conversation about baseball. They looked as if they were ready to fall off their stools. A whole collection of beer bottles and shot glasses lined the bar in front of them. The woman, who was very old and heavy, was hardy more alert than the men were. Judging from all the butts in the ash tray, she was a heavy smoker, and appeared to be drinking straight scotch or bourbon. The lady was in another country.

The bartender was nowhere in sight.

Lina sat on the other end of the bar, close to the door, away from that awful harsh light that was always in the center of the counter near the register. She took a dollar bill from her purse, feeling very lonely and desperate. She only hoped that the man she was supposed to meet would show up before she got herself too stoned. According to the clock it was only eight-thirty. A cockroach crawled across the counter, its antennae quivering. It finally walked out of sight behind the bar.

A door slammed shut from somewhere in the darkened depths of the tavern and a man walked into the room and behind the counter. Rather young to be tending bar in this gin joint, Lina thought. Late teens, early twenties, good-looking Irish face. A good build softened by too much beer fat. The man walked over to her, dish rag in hand, and dispassionately wiped the counter as he approached.

"What can I get you?" he asked.

"A—a glass of beer, please."

"Okay." He went to the tap, grabbing a glass from underneath the counter. *Not the voice,* Lina mused, *not the voice I heard. And yet?*

He came back with the beer. "Thirty cents."

Lina handed him the dollar. "I'm Lina," she said, watching his face for a reaction.

"Dave," he replied. He rung up the cash register, came back with the change, and went down to the other end of the bar to wipe up. Obviously, her name had meant nothing to the man, so he couldn't be her "date." She doubted if either of the old sots talking sports were her mysterious callers, either.

She looked at the clock. 8:35. She would nurse this beer for as long as it took. Or she could have one more and then another and then yet another. But she wanted to be *sober* when she spoke to this man; she might *have* to be. If it did turn out to be a surprise planned by Brock, she'd certainly want to be sober, just so she could get drunk with *him*, soaking up the manly ecstasy of his company. They'd go home together, singing loud, obnoxious ditties, kissing messily, falling into bed for good, rough sex. Oh, she wished she hadn't thought of sex; she hadn't had it in so long. The bartender came by again, just to look out the window and watch passersby. Lina decided to go into the ladies room; the boy's nearness was unsettling.

The smell of piss hit her like a blast of hot air as soon as she entered the narrow corridor that led to the rest rooms. It even seemed to be sticking to the floor. She tried not to breathe through her nose. Opening the door marked Ladies, she discovered that the odor of urine was even stronger in there. It was as if the drunkards, entering the ladies room accidentally, pissed on the walls in the absence of urinals. She turned on the tap in the rusty, cracked sink and waited until the brownish liquid cleared. She splashed some water on her hands, and tried to see her reflection in the dusty, shattered mirror. The image was too distorted and dim to make out.

She looked up and saw the pitiful yellow lightbulb above her head, and the smattering of flies that clung to the small frosted window. The door to the toilet stall was open, and she was grateful she didn't have to use it. The seat was covered with brown stains, and a little puddle had collected around the base. She removed her compact, but was too overcome by the odor to stay in the bathroom, and couldn't see her reflection in the mirror in any case. Now that she knew what these crummy bathrooms were like when a person was sober, she'd need at least ten beers before she ever went in one again.

Walking back into the front room, she was surprised to see that a man was sitting on the stool next to hers. That must be her contact. Once Lina was back in her seat, she wondered why the man hadn't even bothered to look and see who had sat down beside him. He was around sixty, bald and heavy-set. He wore a pair of metal-frame glasses. She tapped him on the shoulder. "My name is Lina."

He looked her up and down drunkenly. "So what, Lina?" He was at least an hour past sobriety.

"I'm sorry. I was supposed to meet someone here. I made a mistake."

"Do I look like your friend, lady?"

"No. I've never met him."

He looked befuddled. "Whatever you say. Nice to meetcha Lina. M'name's Sol."

"Hello. Goodbye. I'm sorry I bothered you." Turning away, she could feel his eyes boring into the back of her head. She downed her whole glass of beer with one swallow.

"Hmmph. Had a cousin named Lina once. She was a bitch too."

Lina didn't answer him. She'd learned to

ignore comments like that a long time ago. She asked the bartender for another beer. She left a quarter and a nickel on the bar and went over to the jukebox in the corner. This place was so old and shitty she wouldn't have been surprised to find one of *her* old numbers on it.

She went back to the bar a moment later, grabbed the foamy glass of beer, and sat down two seats away from the fat man.

One false alarm. How many more? she wondered. It was barely 8:45. Her second glass. Hell, it took a lot more than that to put her away. But she didn't want to get *started*. Didn't want to be unprepared for what might be a *strange* encounter. She might need to have a clear head.

A man came through the front door then—a strapping Irish redhead about forty-five, with a big, taut smile on his round and homely face. He went straight to the bar and said hello to the bartender. "Dave. How's it going?"

"Fine, Jack. How's life treating you?"

"Okay, okay." The bartender brought the man a beer, and the two engaged in a spirited conversation about hockey scores and singles bars. Lina looked over the newcomer, but dismissed the possibility of his being the caller; the man she'd spoken to had not had a brogue.

Another man came in and set one seat away from Lina—next to the fat guy with the glasses. He was a loner, she could tell. Rather nicely dressed for this place. A worried face, sort of pinched, long and narrow. A heavy helping of proboscis. Neatly combed hair. Something sinister about him. Was this the one? Lina thought it might be. It was almost nine o'clock. Right on time, yet.

She studied him a while longer. He took quick looks about the bar now and then, darting his eyes into every corner. Didn't he see her? Near-sighted, maybe, but surely not blind!

Finally getting away from the verbose Irish redhead, the bartender made the new arrival a scotch and soda. The man took little rabbit sips, wiping his mouth after every swallow. *This must be him,* she thought. *Nervous. Nervous like me.* He wasn't bad-looking; younger than she was. She could easily match up the face with the voice on the phone. She decided to make the first move.

Waiting until the barman and his friend were again making loud conversation, she moved into the seat next to her quarry. She leaned over and said, "Are you looking for Lina?"

He didn't speak. Lost in thought, he was both frightened and annoyed by the interruption. Finally he said, "Excuse me?"

"Did you come here to meet someone named Lina? I'm Lina."

He stared at her as if she was crazy. "I didn't come here to meet anyone."

"Are you sure?"

"Yes."

"I'm very sorry." Mortified, Lina went back to her seat. The idiot had probably thought she'd been making a pass at him. She quickly downed the second glass of beer. It was now after nine.

She took out the piece of note paper again, just to make sure, but she was definitely in the right place at the right hour on the right night. Damn it! Where *was* the fool? If this was a joke, a cruel joke without rhyme or reason, she would find out whoever was responsible, whether it was Brock or one of his friends, and she would get them back no matter how long it took her. She ordered another glass of beer and decided to stay until nine-thirty and no later.

A middle-aged man and woman, both unattractive, walked in five minutes later and stood next to the two old sots at the end of the bar. Lina slowly sipped her beer. The woman went over to the jukebox and played a couple of country-and-western songs, pleasant melodies that Lina enjoyed listening to. They helped her mood a lot, helped ease her anxiety. When they were over, Lina put in fifty cents and played them again.

The music was still going when he arrived.

It was very sudden. One second the seat next to her was empty. The next it was taken. He was an unimpressive, mousy-looking man, small and nervous, with greasy black hair combed back from his forehead. He was given to quick, jerky movements and had a slight tic in his left eye. At times his leg would shake involuntarily. It was as if he was just home from World War Two.

It was hard to tell his age, but he wasn't young. In his forties probably. Not exactly bad-looking, if you liked the type. Cuddly. Probably very good in bed. Lina had no desire to find out. She hadn't had much time to wonder about his identity when he leaned over and said softly, "You're Lina, aren't you?"

"Yes."

"I'm sorry I'm late. Finish your beer and I'll buy you another one."

"Sounds good to me," she said. She liked him already.

The little man ordered the beer and got straight gin for himself. "Never drink anything else," he explained. He kept looking around, more nervous than the well-dressed guy she had "propositioned" earlier.

"Have you been here long?"

"A while. My fault. I got here early."

"I would have been here sooner, but I had to be careful."

As the bar was quite noisy now, their conversation was relatively private. The volume on the jukebox had been turned up by the man behind the bar. More people were arriving, and all of the stools were taken. The place was jumping. Lina would never have figured it.

"Well, what is this all about?" she asked. "You told me on the phone that you had information about Brock?"

Hearing the name had an affect on the fellow, something Lina couldn't quite pin down. "He *is* all right, isn't he?"

"I—I don't know," the man said, but Lina was sure he was lying. "Let's just finish our drinks and I'll show you something. Something that will explain what this is all about. We shouldn't talk here."

"All right," Lina said, rather excited by the

secrecy. "Say, what do they call you?"

"My name is George."

"Well, George. Thanks for the beer." Watching him out of the corner of her eye, she took a few healthy swallows. He gave her the creeps, yes, but she *felt* for him—there was an odd, helpless quality about him that made her feel sympathetic. She noticed all his assorted quirks—the tic in the eye, the shaking legs—and wanted him to know that she *liked* him, for what it was worth. Just then he started to scratch his crotch violently, particularly the area above the masculine bulge in his jeans. He looked over at Lina guiltily, but she pretended not to have noticed. Satisfied that she wasn't looking, George continued to scratch. Lina could hear the noise of his dirty nails clawing against the denim material even before the din of the tavern. *Must have "crabs,"* she thought, repulsed. She finished her beer quickly, hoping they could depart and that it would all be over as soon as possible. She saw with alarm that George had hardly touched his gin.

"Aren't you drinking?" she asked.

He stopped his manic scratching and grabbed the glass. Taking a swallow, he placed it back down on the counter. He noticed that her glass was empty.

"Do you want another?"

"No. Thank you."

"Well then, let's go. I've had enough."

Lina grabbed her bag and they went out into the street. The drizzle had stopped. George was busy looking around, up and down the sidewalk. Lina almost laughed. This silly little man acted as if the entire world was following him. She hadn't realized he was quite so short.

"Are you a jockey?" she said. *Oops.* The beer must have gone to her head for her to have asked such a *tacky* question.

"No, I'm not," he said, apparently unoffended.

"What do you do?"

He ignored the question and said curtly, "Cross the street with me. Walk over to that appliance store."

"Okay," Lina said. "Whatever you say."

George grabbed her elbow, pushed her across the street, and pulled her into an alleyway next to the store.

"Look here!" she protested.

"Shut up! I'm not going to hurt you. But *they* will, if we're not careful." He took something out of his pocket, another slip of paper, and pressed it into her hand. "Look, they can't control you the way they can me."

"What are you talking about, you little—"

"LISTEN! I try to tell people, to warn them—but something comes over me. I try to talk and —I can't finish. It's like something gets hold of my—my vocal cords—my speech. I start to stammer and shiver and—oh God! I'm so afraid."

He stood there quivering like a bowl of jello. Lina looked down at the paper in her hand. It was hard to make out in the dark, but it looked as if a name and address were scribbled on it. She put the paper into her pocketbook.

"*Don't lose it!* I want you to contact that guy—his address is on there. And tell him to meet me at this bar tomorrow night at the same time."

"But why should I?"

"Because I can't do it. His phone number's unlisted. And if I go to his house, somebody might see me, follow me there. He's got to come to *me*."

"What has this got to do with Brock? I want to know where Brock is!"

"No you don't, Lina. No you don't."

"Tell me what happened to him!"

He pulled her further into the shadows. "I've known your boyfriend for a long time. Him and me used to do jobs together. Both of us living high on the hog until the money ran out, and then starving until something else came up."

"I've always known that," Lina said wiping away the tears that had started to collect in the corners of her eyes. "It doesn't matter to me."

"We were buddies, you know. Then I got a job where my father used to work. They offered me a deal that was—" He gestured as if trying to depict something *grandiose*. "For the first time in my life I had—money. So much money."

"And Brock? What about Brock?"

"He wanted to know how come I was rich all of a sudden. He didn't understand why I didn't let him in on it. So I did him a 'favor'—ha!—got him a job with the company."

He looked so strange, this little man, as if he was about to sob.

"We had positions of importance. We were foreman over the project. There are a lot of foreman . . . all those people down there . . . need watchin' over.

"Brock and I got *treated* like the others did so that we couldn't talk. Nearly drove us both crazy. Brock fought against it, harder and harder all the time. I told him not to, told him not to, told him he'd be killed. But when he found out what they were gonna do to that kid, that Joey, what was gonna happen *because* of him, we had to do something."

George's face and clothes were soaked with sweat. His gesturing hands betrayed a constant trembling.

"Then one night something inside Brock just snapped. We were comin' home from a poker game, switching trains at Broadway Junction. The booze, I guess it must have made him lose his head. He slipped out of their control for a while. He started grabbin' people, anyone, just grabbin' them as they walked by, hollerin' and screamin'—*we're all gonna die, we're all gonna die*—started actually *tellin'* everyone what was happening. Everyone thought he was crazy."

I know how they felt, Lina thought. *This man has to be a psychopath.*

"And what happened then," she said hoarsely. "What happened?" She wanted to grab him and *shake* the truth out of him.

"I can't tell you."

"*What do you mean you can't tell me!* I have to know! I don't care about jobs or poker games or Broadway Junction—I just want to know where Brock is! Don't protect me, George. I couldn't bear to go on waiting and waiting for him to come home. Don't do this to me! I'm so *lonely*. Please. What is it—another woman? Did he skip town; is he in trouble? Did he kill somebody, George? Tell me. *Tell me!*"

In spite of his trembling, George was like stone. "Just get my message to the guy on that piece of paper. *Then* I'll tell you."

"*Why me?*"

"Because—because of what they did to Brock. I figured you'd want to help."

"*What* did they do to Brock?"

He turned away from her. "I need *somebody* to do it for me. I can't trust nobody else."

"Well, I won't do it. Not until you tell me where Brock is." She was furious and adamant, an unstoppable force.

George looked at her carefully, as if measuring her, trying to determine what she could take and what she couldn't. A few seconds later, he had made up his mind. "Okay, all right. I'll show you. But we have to go separately. I'm going to take the J train—toward Manhattan. But we'll get off long before then. You follow me—but don't make it obvious! Get on the same car I do and get off when I get off. Then I'll take you to Brock."

"God bless you," she said.

He gave her a look as disdainful as it was pitying.

"I'll go now. Remember, don't make it obvious that you're following me."

"All right. All right. I promise."

He took off. Lina waited until he was up the block, starting to climb the stairs to the Cypress

Hills station. She walked out of the alley and down the street. She climbed the staircase, bought a token, and went out onto the platform. She saw him way down at the other end. She sauntered down closer, careful never to look in his direction. The train was coming now.

He got into the last car, and she did too, entering through a different doorway. The metal panels slid into place, locking in the passengers, and the train pulled out of the station. She took a chance and glanced over at George; he was sitting way down in the corner. His head was shaking now, back and forth, rapidly. The tic in his eye was going. He looked as if he was terrified.

She was beginning to feel the same way.

The train maneuvered slowly through a curve in the track, the wheels squealing painfully under the weight of flesh and metal. They were practically standing still. Chugging along at a snail's pace. It seemed to take forever for the train to arrive at the next stop: Crescent Street.

The train moved much faster from then on. As it pulled into the large Broadway Junction station a short while later, George rose to his trembling feet and coughed. Lina followed suit. When the train came to a halt, they disembarked and waited for the platform to clear. The few other people who had exited the train went up the stairs to the left.

They were still above street level, on a narrow platform sliced in half by a central track, in addition to the two on the outside. Concrete beams supported a metal roof that protected waiting passengers from the elements. The wooden benches were painted light green, and big billboards advertising a variety of products were stuck on slates on the corrugated walls. The stop was a junction for several train lines; tracks, from a multitude of platforms, stretched out in all different directions around them. On the ground below them was a train yard, full of cars which were not in service, and beyond that, an overgrown field and warehouses.

They waited five minutes until there was no one about except for an elderly man sitting on one of the benches on the opposite platform facing away from them. George motioned for Lina to approach him.

"Down there." He pointed to a stairwell at the farthest end of the platform. It went down to street level. Lina looked at George quizzically. Even from where they were she could see that there was a metal chain strung across the top of stairs—the exit was closed at this hour. George grabbed her hand and pulled her after him.

"Now look," Lina said. She was tired of the rough stuff, scared of this strange man and his stranger behavior. She kept telling herself that there must be lots of people on the other levels even at ten o'clock; she need only open her mouth and scream.

When they reached the stairs, George looked about in every direction. His face was white with fear, his body was shaking, and the tic in his eye was more pronounced than ever. He lifted his legs one at a time over the chain, then turned around to help Lina do the same. Maneuvering her girth took a while longer. She could see that the token booth in the area below was unmanned, that there was no way out. They'd covered the turnstiles with movable grating and locked up the revolving contraptions—made up of iron bars—that were normally used for exiting the station. She looked apprehensively at George. He motioned for her to proceed down the steps.

"Why?" she said. "Why should I go down there? It's all locked up!"

"You wanted to see your lover, didn't you? You wanted to see Brock?"

"Yes. But I wonder if you really know where he is." She carefully watched every move the man made, hoping she could overpower him if necessary. "I wonder if I should ignore you and just go straight to the police."

He went rigid with horror. "No! NO! You can't go to the police! They'd kill me! You'd be responsible for my death—*and* yours! You mustn't see the police!"

"Why would the police harm us?"

"Not the police."

"Then *who?*"

"You mustn't go to the police, that's all."

"Then tell me what we're doing here. I don't see Brock. Where is he?"

"I'll show you. If you really want to see, I'll show you. It happened right here. A couple of weeks ago. I didn't care what they did until then, but Brock—he was my friend. Just about my only friend. But he wouldn't listen to me. He had to start talking at the top of his lungs." George began to sob from the memory, his whole face covered with moisture made of equal parts tears and perspiration. "It was the most horrible thing I ever saw. They had to punish him for what he did."

"Punish him? What did they do? *Where is he?*"

"He started shiverin' and couldn't talk no more. Most of the people were gone, and I grabbed him and led him to the stairs, these stairs." He stopped to swallow the mucus that had collected in his throat. "There was nobody around, no witnesses. It was late and the trains didn't come too often. I figured I could get him out of here and home before . . . Then I realized that this exit was closed. Brock broke away from me, hurdled the chain, drunk. When he collapsed halfway down the stairs I thought it was liquor—but it was the shiverin' that done it. I was so scared—there wasn't nothin' I could do. I just ran home and pretended it didn't happen. I was so scared!"

"Will you tell me what happened to Brock before *I kill you!*"

"They killed him, Lina. Murdered him. Just to shut him up. They killed him, Lina. Killed him."

"*No!*"

"He was on the stairs, sprawled out lengthwise, when it happened. His whole body . . . it just melted away, just *dissolved*, right there on the steps."

"Are you crazy? What are you talking about?" *Did someone throw acid at Brock?* she wondered. *What else could it be?*

"All that was left was a kind of jelly, a thick, sticky jelly on the stairs. Take a look—maybe there's some left. Down there. 'Bout halfway down."

Lina braced herself for the ghoulish task. *Might as well see it through—but keep one eye on George!* She told herself she would find nothing. What kind of acid could dissolve an *entire body?*

Disbelieving, she followed his pointing hand and started down the stairs.

Before she had gone two steps she could already see it.

It was hard to make out now, what with the thousands of people walking over it day after day, scraping the stuff away on their shoes . . . but it *was* there. The red outline had *soaked into* the wood, become a permanent part of the surface—unmistakably the outline of a man.

She continued down the stairs until she was standing right on top of it. She knelt, touched the underside of one of the steps—where feet could not reach. Her fingers came up bloody, a reddish viscous substance staining the tips.

She still refused to credit George's incredible story, *but* . . .

She stood up, turned to look at George, and saw that something had happened to him. His eyes were bulging from their sockets, his tongue sticking out like a tentacle. His entire body was shaking uncontrollably. It was such a terrifying sight that Lina recoiled, took a careless step backward, and lost her precarious footing.

The last thing she saw before she toppled down the stairs was the sight of George holding on desperately to the chain. As Lina rolled over and over the hard wooden steps, his blood-chilling cries were drowned out by the sound of a train.

PART III

Friday, October 18th

SIX

AFTER A RESTLESS night of constant tossing and turning, in impatience, he supposed, for the morrow's meeting, Steven got up early in the morning and ate a very light breakfast. As usual, he hadn't much of an appetite. He crunched his teeth into the toast and chewed listlessly, masticating each morsel until the bread was soft and gooey on his tongue. He washed it all down with yesterday's reheated coffee. He was not even in the mood to make a fresh pot.

He had been going to call Andrea's cousin before he went to see him, but then decided against it. He didn't want his first contact with the man—someone who might very well become responsible for his brother's welfare—to be so remote and impersonal. He changed from pajamas into a fresh white shirt and some new slacks he had only worn once. He wanted to feel as if he was starting out on a brand-new day, with new fortitude, new hope on the horizon. He was deliberately not thinking about Andrea and her "business associate," Donald. Time enough for that later.

He shaved and splashed on some rarely used aftershave, hoping it would help revive his deadened senses. He combed his hair; he'd need a haircut soon. He checked the thermometer outside his bedroom window and put on a warm, but light, winter jacket. He checked the address on the card he'd received from Andrea, and left the apartment. It was 8:55.

He hated rush hour subway traffic. Too many desperate people rushing to jobs they'd just as soon quit if they didn't need money for food and rent and entertainment. Steven wished he was self-employed. If only he could have afforded to drop the editor's job and concentrate solely on his free-lance efforts. Editing superficial pieces on New York nightlife, forgettable celebrities, and Broadway shows which might interest the visitor to Manhattan was becoming less and less of a thrill. He managed to get a taxi quickly, and told the driver where to go.

Fifteen minutes later the cab pulled up in front of a large office complex on the Avenue of the Americas in the Fifties. An impressive place for anyone to have their headquarters. He was relieved; he had been afraid that Andrea might have been giving dear cousin Ralph too big a buildup. Steven paid the driver, gave him a healthy tip, and walked into the lobby of the building. He headed for the elevator bank.

As the car rose to the nineteenth floor, Steven tried to swallow his apprehension. The last thing he wanted today was a shove-off; another creep telling him that his brother was simply off somewhere gallivanting with person or persons unknown. He wanted to be taken seriously. He wanted someone—someone with authority—to *care*.

The door to Room 1905 was a big, wooden affair with two sections. Opening it, he stepped into a small receiving area. The receptionist, a young woman with curly black hair and blue mascara, sat behind a small oval window to his right. "I'd like to see Ralph Andrews," he said.

"Do you have an appointment?" she asked.

"No. I didn't think I'd need one. Mr. Andrews' cousin spoke to him about my . . . situation yesterday on the telephone. I think he may be expecting me." He gave the lady his name.

She looked annoyed. "Just a minute, please." She lifted up the phone and "punched" a number with her pencil.

"Hello, Mr. Andrews? There's a gentleman here . . ." While she relayed the information, she traced the spaces between the buttons on her phone with the pencil's eraser. She looked up again. "You can see him now. Go through the door straight ahead, turn to the right, and walk down until you come to the third door. That's Mr. Andrews' office."

"Thank you." He followed her instructions. The main room behind the inner door was a large waiting area with couches and tables full of magazines. There were three desks at the far end, where secretaries were typing reports and filing papers. Behind them were three small offices. Steven caught only glimpses of the people inside them, talking on the phone or reading documents. He walked to the right, down a hall, counting the doors as he went. The third door was open. Though a large enough room, it was not enormous. Apparently Ralph Andrews was modest.

Sitting behind the desk, flipping through a magazine, was a brawny, pleasant-looking fellow around forty-five years of age. A rugged individual, he had broad shoulders and big hands. His hair was dark, cut short and parted on the side. His features weren't what you would call handsome, though he might have been quite good-looking in his youth. He was toughness merged with innocence, hardness softened by vulnerability. He had the look of a man who had fought hard to get what he wanted, yet someone who could be easily hurt and who cried at sad movies on the Late Show. His ruddy complexion was somewhat darkened by the thick stubble on his face, which gave him a permanent five-o'clock shadow.

The big man rose and grabbed Steven's hand in a firm but non-threatening grip. There was no macho challenge there, but a warmth and strength that Steven found appealing. He saw none of the weary detachment that character-ized the police officers he'd had occasion to speak to over the years. Even Detective Albright different as he was, had that same air about him. But not Ralph Andrews.

"So you're Andrea's friend?" he said.

"Uh, yes. Nice to meet you."

"Same here." He motioned Steven toward the chair next to the desk. "Have a seat, Mr—?"

"Everson. Steven Everson."

Andrews snapped his fingers. "Everson, that's right. Well, Mr. Everson, why don't you start from the beginning."

So he did. He mentioned every little detail. The park, jogging. Vivian Jessup's theory, her horrible death. His talks with Detective Albright. Everything. When he was finished, he was relieved to see that Ralph seemed confident in taking on the challenge.

"First of all, Mr. Everson—can I call you Steve?"

"Sure."

"Steve, we'd all like to think that we know everything there is to know about those that we love. But, of course, that isn't always the case. We often dig up truths that are hard to take, hard to understand. Last month a very distraught young woman came in—wanted us to find her husband. She was almost convinced he was dead. We found him, all right. New name, new city, new brunette. I think his wife would rather we had found him dead than have to face what she must have considered an impossible truth. All that I'm saying is that all of our clients must be ready to *accept* whatever facts we uncover, no matter how bizzare, how out of character, how impossible."

"I understand. I'm willing to admit that I don't know each and every thought that may be in my brother's head. Then you think Mrs. Jessup may have been right? That Joey's a— what do they call people who drown themselves —a 'floater'?"

"If he did drown himself, his body'll turn up eventually. But no, that's not what I meant. If anything, I was implying that your brother may very well be alive somewhere, keeping to himself for his own reasons. That might hurt. It always does. But it just might be the case. Let us do the legwork and I'll give you daily reports. I'll also check with your Detective Albright. Actually, it seems he's given you more time than usual. Funny."

"Must be my sad face."

Ralph chuckled. "Yeah."

"How are you going to go about this, if I might ask?"

"We take the police basics several steps further. I'm going to retrace your brother's steps, but more thoroughly. I'll also look into this Jessup woman's background. And then we track down every peripheral clue, no matter how minute, how seemingly irrelevant. It usually pays off. But it takes time."

"I understand."

"Meanwhile I want you to exercise your memory and try to write me up a list—day by day, as detailed as possible—of everything your brother did after he moved to New York. And maybe before that. And I mean everything. Everyone he spoke to and saw. Where he hung out. Where his one-night stands were. Any women besides Jessup.

"Where exactly did he go on interviews? Which firms? Which people did he speak to? Something might turn up. Maybe he saw something he shouldn't have."

Steven rubbed his forehead. "Pretty tall order." He didn't even remember what Joey had majored in in college. Had he paid so little attention to the boy?

"I know it's a tall order. But you want your brother back, right? The sooner I have all the information, the better. Whatever you forget now and remember later, I want you to write down and bring to me or my assistant's attention as soon as possible."

"Joey was with me for a couple of months. I don't know if I can recall all of his activities, but I'll try."

For the next hour Ralph took notes and Steven talked. By the time they had exhausted Steven's memory, Ralph had filled several pages in a small white pad. Ralph leaned back in his chair and said, "Well, this is enough for starters. By the way, she's not in this morning, but my assistant on this case will be Valerie Horton. Remember the name. She'll be in touch with you when I'm doing legwork. Or vice versa. One of us will keep you informed of everything."

They spent the next few minutes discussing payment of the daily fees and other expenses. Steven would definitely have to cancel his proposed trip to Europe in the summer. He was awfully glad he had that savings account.

Steven got up, shook Ralph's hand once more, and stepped out into the corridor. He walked past the big room with the secretaries and the offices behind them, busy, busy, busy. His brother's life was in their hands. Now he would go home and hope that he had paid enough attention to Joey's activities over the past few weeks to accurately record them.

Somewhere, somehow, he would find out what had happened.

Even if it killed him.

Johnny Albright hung up the phone and settled back in his padded green chair, the wheels propelling him slightly back toward the radiator behind him. He felt its heat and pushed himself closer to the desk. So, his Mr. Everson had hired a private detective. He was glad. Real glad. That was the only way any of these characters were ever going to be found. The only way. His workload was enormous. File after file was lying in one corner of his desk.

Why had he spent so much time mulling over the Everson case? Was it that the small, smiling picture of Joseph Philip Everson looked like what his little boy might look like in about fifteen years? That strong, handsome, but somehow sad and haunting face. Like his brother's face, only different, more hopeful and more tragic. What a shame to die so young. And he *was* dead. They all were. He was sure of it.

Knowing that, why had he taken such a personal interest in something that he knew would go nowhere? Every day he had his share of distraught relatives, angry husbands, and griefstricken parents. So why bother with Everson? Perhaps because he sensed that, unlike those neurotic relatives, disheveled husbands, shrewish wives, Steven Everson had not *driven* his brother away. Steven Everson was genuinely concerned for his brother's welfare, not worried over what people might think because, say, his child or his wife had left him. Was that it?

Every time he thought about it he got a headache. Or he got chills. Something kept nagging in the back of his mind, but he'd be damned if he could remember what it was.

Anything was better than the "nonchalants," as he called them, the people who came in calmly and dispassionately to report a missing person—two weeks after the fact—usually because the one who'd vanished owed them money. Those were the worst, he thought. The ones who didn't really care.

But it was this new wrinkle that bothered him the most. The increasing number of reports. The diminishing success rate. The number of MPs had always been incredible—the city's population was enormous, after all—but now it was really getting out of hand. It was enough to make you think some kind of mad conspiracy was going on. But who was it directed against? Everyone? Ah, his wife was right. He was exaggerating.

What was *it that he couldn't remember?*

Yes, he was glad that Everson had hired himself a private dick. Maybe he'd find something out. Maybe Everson could deal with the truth. Maybe he'd *rather* be called in to identify his brother's body than spend the rest of his life wondering where Joey had gone.

Sure he would.

Albright suddenly felt like calling his wife. On the third ring, knowing she always picked up by the fourth, he started to regret it. What did they have to say to one another anymore? Still, he needed comforting. Maybe she could help.

There was no answer.

When Steven got home, a strange woman was sitting on the outside steps of his brownstone. Her face was pale and puffy, and she had *suitcases* under her eyes. She wore a big, silly-looking hat which covered most of her hair. Judging from the strands of hair that struck out from underneath it, Steven assumed she was a peroxide blonde. It was hard to figure her age; pushing sixty perhaps. She looked so sad and lonely Steven had to look away from her pathetic face and quickly turn the key in the entrance lock. He could still feel her eyes upon him.

He stepped inside and went over to his own door. Suddenly he heard a rapping on the glass of the foyer. It was her, banging frantically on the pane. Against his better judgment, he opened the door and let her in.

"Do you live here?" she said, pointing to his apartment. "1-A?"

She must have read the number from the outside looking in. "Yes, I do."

"You're Steven Everson?"

"Yes. Can I help you?"

"I have to talk to you. Please, can I come in?"

He was wary, but she looked harmless enough. Ordinarily, he would have suspected a setup—thieves were very ingenious these days. But with his brother gone it was wise to talk to anyone who might have information. He took her into his apartment.

Lina Hobler looked around nervously, rubbing her hands together, seemingly afraid of everything around her. Steven saw that she was limping. She made her way to the sofa in the living room and collapsed onto the cushion. She looked and acted as if she hadn't slept for days.

"A man gave me this," she said, taking a slip of paper from her handbag.

"What is it?" He grabbed it and saw that his own name and address were written on it.

"*Who* gave you this?"

"A man named George. He said I should contact you and ask you to meet him. Tonight. He said he was afraid to come here on his own."

"And who are you?"

Lina was so upset that she dropped her usual pretense and didn't bother making up a name.

"Lina Hobler," she said.

Steven remembered there used to be a singer by that name, but of course this pitiful, bloated woman in front of him bore little resemblance to the beautiful entertainer of the Fifties. What had ever happened to *her?* he wondered.

"And what do you know about this George?"

"Nothing. He called me one night. And told me he had information about Brock. That's my boyfriend."

Boyfriend? Steven thought the term sounded

ludicrous when employed by someone her age.

"I met him in a bar on Jamaica Avenue. I guess he lives near there. He didn't say."

"Was Brock—uh—missing?"

"Yes. For days."

This is it, Steven thought. *The connection. Now I'll find Joey.*

"Did he tell you where Brock was?"

She looked up at him, threw her hands over her face and started to sob. "He was crazy. He told me Brock had been—eaten away. It was a cruel joke. Horrible. And then he started screaming—and—ran off. He just disappeared, like he'd never been there at all."

Steven sat down beside her and tried to comfort her. She threw her arms around him and continued to sob. "Oh, mister, mister, tell me I'm not crazy. Tell me I'm not."

"You'd better start over again. I can't help you until I know *exactly* what happened."

She moved away from him slightly and got a handkerchief from her handbag. She blew her nose noisily, then dabbed at her eyes. "Just give me a moment. I'll be all right."

"I'll get you some coffee."

"Please. That would be nice."

"Mister?" she asked as he started toward the kitchen.

"Yes," he said, turning to face her.

"You—you won't believe me."

Steven smiled. "Try me."

But her story *was* incredible. Not only that, it made no sense. Why would someone have gone to the trouble of smearing jam or jelly or fake blood all over the subway steps just to scare a pathetic and harmless woman like Lina? And that must have been the case. People just didn't "dissolve."

After tripping and falling down the subway stairs, Lina had landed at the bottom in a bloodied heap. There had been painful scrapes and contusions all over her body and her head had been bleeding, but she hadn't suffered any broken bones. She picked herself up, brushed herself off, pressed a handkerchief to her forehead to soak up the blood. It wasn't too bad. She then climbed the stairs, stopping only to stare again at the reddish outline that, according to a crazy man, had once been her lover.

At the top of the stairs she climbed over the chain and looked around for George. He wasn't there. He wasn't anywhere.

At that point in time she had wondered if he ever *had* been there. She was still wondering even as Steven's voice snapped her out of her reverie.

"I think someone must have been pulling your leg."

"You think it was some kind of practical joke?"

He nodded sympathetically. "I think so."

"Buy why? Brock wouldn't have done anything that awful to me."

Steven recalled Ralph's words about "impossible truths," but only said, "I'm sure he had nothing to do with it."

"Yes. He'll *kill* that George when he gets his hands on him, believe me. If *I* don't get to him first."

"I'd better keep my appointment with him

tonight, or else we'll be right back where we started from, with your Brock still gone and my brother missing too." He explained about Joey, giving only the barest details, still not sure if he should trust her. "You're sure he never mentioned my brother."

"No," Lina said, sipping her coffee. Steven handed her a photo of Joey. "Poor kid," she said. "Such a handsome boy."

She suddenly slapped her hand on her leg. "Wait a minute. I *do* remember. Something George said about a kid, some kid. Was it Joey? Jerry?" She shook her head and bit her lip, but the memory wouldn't come. "Damn—I can't remember." She looked at Steven helplessly. "I could be wrong."

But for Steven that was enough.

"Anyway, I don't want to go with you tonight," Lina added. "I can't. I'd like to kill the creep with my bare hands, but I'm still too upset over the whole business." Steven suspected there was still the smallest glimmer of doubt in her mind about the glob on the steps having been just a practical joke. "If I give you my number will you tell me if he mentions Brock again? I've got to find him. Got to find Brock."

Steve assured her that he would. He told her about his hiring a private detective. Lina agreed to speak to Ralph should he decide to call her. She gave Steven her address and phone number.

"Just in case your brother's and Brock's disappearances are connected. I guess they must be, huh?" She finished her coffee and put the cup down. "But if you don't know either Brock or George, and they don't know your brother, why does George want to see you? He won't try the same thing with you that he tried with me, will he?"

"I doubt it. But the only way I'll find out is to see him. None of this makes any sense. But we'll have to see it through. Ralph Andrews will know what to do."

"I'd hire him to look for Brock, but I can't afford it." She shrugged. "From what you say the police are no good. And," she lowered her voice, "just between you and me Brock may be in some kinda trouble, and the police are the last thing he'd need. Well," she stretched her arms and groaned, "it's a long ride home, so I'd better be going. I want to be there in case Brock comes back." She picked herself up and limped toward the door.

"You should see about that leg," Steven said. "It could be broken."

"I've had a broken leg. It would hurt a hell of a lot more than it does. But I'll see to it if I have to."

"Take care of yourself," he said. "And thanks for coming by."

"Thanks for listening," she said. She shook her hand, holding on to it longer than was necessary, as if hoping to absorb some of his warmth, his strength. "I hope you find your brother," she said. "I really do. Poor kid."

"Thanks."

Steven watched her walk out the door and

hobble down the sidewalk toward the subway. She was barely holding it together, a withered, emotional ruin.

She was the very personification of despair.

Ernest Hendon was intrigued. And when he was intrigued, he took action. He took off from the police lab during lunch and went to the Berkley Arms Hotel on the Upper West Side near Broadway. He'd made a few calls the day before and collected some interesting data. It was Room 919 that intrigued him. Room 919 that might have the answer.

He showed his police permit to the manager, who escorted him to the ninth floor and the apartment in question. The short, heavy-set, elderly man fitted the passkey into the lock and swung open the door. No one was inside.

Ernest paused out in the corridor. "And where does this Mrs. MacGruder live?"

"Right next door," the manager said. "917."

"And she's the one who reported that Mr. Peterson was missing?"

The manager seemed anxious to help. "That's right. She didn't so much report it as ask me if I had seen him. She said his door was unlocked, and that there was this strange goo on the wall; somebody smeared it there so that it was shaped just like a man."

"Will you show me where?"

"Sure. Follow me." As they walked in he continued talking. "I thought it might be best to call the police and find out if Peterson had been

170

hospitalized or something like that. We elderly are the easiest victims, y'know, and Mrs. MacGruder was terribly worried. Then I showed the police the glop on the wall, and one of them took a sample."

"And where was the smear?"

"Right here." The manager pointed to the far wall, which now was clean. "They said it was all right for me to have the maid wash it off, once they got their sample."

Stupid, Ernest thought. They should have left everything as it was. The other departments were full of incompetents.

"How big was it?"

"As big as a man, and shaped like one. The arms were spread out like this," he held his up in the air, "and the legs were far part. What a weird thing to do, huh?"

"Would you say that the pattern on the wall was the same size as Mr. Peterson had been?"

The manager took a while to answer. "Well, now that you mention it, I suppose so. It's hard to say. I didn't really think about it. Say, that was just some sticky shit on the wall. It couldn't have been a *body*." He laughed, nervously. "Could it?"

"Just checking," Ernest smiled. "What do *you* think the stuff on the wall was?"

"I haven't the slightest idea. I just told Mamie to clean it up. She wouldn't touch it until I told her it was just somebody's idea of a practical joke. Makes you wonder—what kind of mind would do that?"

Right now Ernest was more concerned with

how than who. "Yes. It does make you wonder."

"Say, what do you think happened to Mr. Peterson? Any more information about that?"

They'd find out nothing, he thought, until he told them. But how could he tell *this* simple-minded old fellow the truth? How could he tell him that Mr. Peterson *had* been found. According to the reports he and Judson had made, poor Mamie had wiped old Mr. Peterson off his own wall like so much dirt and dust.

Eric Thorne was having lunch with his friend Hammond Gratis, a middle-aged parapsychologist who had been with the Institute for seven years and had just returned from a week-long vacation in Bermuda. Gratis, a very intense man, was given to sudden bursts of temperament and frequent self-proclamations of genius. But despite his eccentricities, he was well-liked by both staff and volunteers. Eric was particularly fond of him.

Eric talked about his nightmare while they ate, largely at Hammond's insistence. The big man loved to discuss other people's problems, convinced he could solve them all with one bright flash of his incomparable brain. As he was very fond of Eric, he was especially eager to be of service.

Hammond was an unattractive man—despite his tan—but his strong, hyper personality and six-foot-two frame seemed to make up for what he lacked in looks. His nose was huge, almost overwhelming the rest of his face, with its craggy brow, jutting lower lip, and normally grayish complexion. He had very thick, stiff-looking hair that grew very fast and had to be cut every other week. He had been married and divorced *three* times.

"So Eric," he said as he stuffed a soft buttered role between his lips, "the nightmare was *not* repeated last evening?"

"No. I slept soundly. And we really should refer to it as my *trance,* since I was awake at the time."

"But it was a nightmarish experience."

"Absolutely."

"I rest my case. Pass me the salt." Hammond never lost an argument.

The restaurant in which they sat was a small coffeeshop on Lafayette Street which had an unappealing decor but reasonably good food and low prices. Eric would have preferred a nicer, more expensive place, but Hammond was always penny-pinching. Considering his alimony payments, it was understandable. He usually ate some kind of pasta with lots of bread, while Eric preferred sandwiches. Liverwurst today.

"Anyway," Eric said. "I guess I'm back to normal."

"Don't 'guess' anything," Hammond said with a quick shake of his large head. "What you described to me sounds like a very deliberate and deadly attack on your life, as surely as if someone had pulled a gun on you. So far all the bullet has done is *graze* you. But . . . *next* time?"

"How cheerful," Eric said. "Then you're

convinced that the same thing will happen again."

"Only it will be worse. The enemy has been testing your strength. He knows how far he has to go. Next time he will be prepared to go that far."

"How will he do it?"

"He will start out the same way as before. But this time, the despair will deepen, will, in fact, be too much to bear. Result: you lying in the bathroom with your wrists slit—by your own hand."

"Hammond, could you *please* be a little more optimistic?"

"I can't be. Because I value your life."

"So do I."

"And I can't pretend that you're not in serious danger. If I did that, you wouldn't take the proper precautions."

"What, may I ask, are they?"

Hammond leaned closer. "There is evil in the world, Eric. Great evil. There are forces men cannot understand."

Eric laughed. "Hammond! You're not going to start that 'good versus evil' crap with me again. We've gone over this a hundred times before. Your theories about eternal evil forces are based on your beliefs in a supreme being— a force for good—on one hand, and the devil, Satan, whatever you want to call him—the force for evil—on the other. I don't accept any of that. Don't you realize that not so long ago we both would have been burned at the stake as witches because of our special powers and interests? The very field we work in was—and still is—

misunderstood because of myths and religious superstitions. No, there's evil in the world, all right. But it's man's doing. Not the devil's."

When Hammond disagreed with someone, he simply "tuned" them out. "Eric, did you ever think you could have tapped into the mind of the *Anti-Christ?*"

"Hammond, haven't you even been *listening* to me. I—"

"I still say my theories aren't really in opposition to yours," Hammond insisted. "All right— so you're basically an atheist and I have faith. But there's more to it than that."

"Go on."

Hammond finished his soup and continued. "Well, isn't it possible that there might be— for lack of a better word—evil forces that have nothing whatsoever to do with God, the devil, or anything of a religious nature?"

"I believe that power such as mine could be dangerous in the wrong hands. If a bad individual had such power, or more power, it could be disastrous. I suppose you could say he or she would be an 'evil force.' "

Hammond smacked his lips. "And what about forces outside the mortal sphere. Spirits and bodies floating about in the astral plane. In alternate dimensions. The netherworld. Are *they* not possible?"

"Indeed. I believe they are. Although I'm primarily concerned with the power of the human mind, research has shown—"

"And if these forces were used for what you might consider negative ends?"

" 'Evil forces.' " Eric smiled. "Okay, I'll grant

you that. But you still haven't answered my question. Just *how* do I protect myself from this force, human or otherworldly."

"Well, since you will definitely not nail a cross over your bed . . ."

"—nor wear garlic around my neck."

" . . . I suppose you should make arrangements never to be alone until this is over and the evil force is discovered and dealt with. Assuming that it is within our power to do so."

"I can't do that!" Eric protested. "That would be such a bother that—"

"Eric, forget our differences in opinion. Face the facts. Something happened that scared the wits out of you. If it does happen again—and it might—you don't know *what* might occur. Now listen to me and take some precautions. Have a friend stay with you. Or move in with one. At least for awhile."

"Maybe I ought to."

"I'd offer to let you stay with me, but that might only delay the inevitable. I live on the other side of town—the force might be even stronger there, *or* too weak to reach you. Then it will simply *wait* until you return to your apartment. When your guard is down. No, someone must move in with you."

"But who?"

"I will. I snore, I'll eat you out of house and home, and—as my three ex-wives will tell you—I make abominable company. But—I just might save your life."

Eric shrugged. "Okay, Hammond. You're on."

* * *

Lina was already through three quarters of a quart of scotch—she'd started as soon as she'd gotten back from Everson's—when the knock came on the door. "Brock!" she screamed, knocking over her chair as she stumbled toward the door. Brushing her hair out of her face, she pulled the door open with a wrench.

"Oh, it's *you* again."

There before her were the two "friends" of Brock's who had shown up the day before. *Rat-Man* and *Pretty Blond Four-Eyes* she had called them under her breath every time she thought of them. "What do you want?"

"Christ, she's soused!" Rat-Man said.

"So, what's it to ya? Where's Brock?"

"That's what we'd like to know, *hag*," the bespectacled one remarked. "He owed us fifty dollars apiece."

"I suppose *George* sent you to bother me."

"Who the hell is George?" Rat-Man asked, looking quickly at his companion. He turned back to Lina. "Does *he* play cards too?"

Even through her alcoholic haze Lina could tell that the man's reaction was genuine. They didn't know who George was. "That's all you two want?" she said. "Money? You really don't know where Brock is?"

"And we couldn't care less. But Brock *owes* us."

"Well, he's not here. And I don't have that kinda money."

"Maybe we should take a look around," the little one snarled, giving Lina a shove.

"Nah, nah, come on!" the bigger one said,

pulling his partner away. "Brock wouldn't leave no dough with this piece of trash. He split for good."

"No. No, he didn't!" Lina screamed. "He'll be back. He just had to go away for awhile. That's all. You'll get your effin' money back! You wait and see!"

"Awww, go to hell, hag," the Rat-Man said, backing out into the hall. "What are *you* complaining about? We're the ones lost a hundred bucks."

Lina started laughing uncontrollably, almost involuntarily. "You want your money? You want Brock? Why don't you look for him at the subway. Look on the steps on the Broadway Junction. The steps, boys, that's where he is!"

"She's crazy!" the blond said, disgusted by her outburst. "It's paddy-wagon time."

"Looks more like AA time to me," his friend said as they walked to the elevator.

George spent the day huddled up in his room, shivering in the fear that he had been found out, that they knew what he was up to. Good thing he had these two days off, that was for sure. He had had only a cup of tea and a half a bagel for breakfast, lunch, *and* dinner. He had set the alarm so that the buzzer would alert him when it was quarter of eight, giving him enough time to make it to McGreeley's Bar and Grill. He hoped Steven Everson would be waiting there. More important, he hoped he could somehow be able to say what he had to say, that, if necessary, Everson would *beat* it out of him because of his brother.

Shit, that lady last night had nearly gone off her rocker. He had thought for sure *he* was a goner. Suddenly he felt pain, indescribable pain —just like he had felt that night when Brock died. It had hurt so much he had just started running, running to nowhere at all, trying to get away—as if there was anywhere safe. Somehow they knew almost every move he made. That had been his final warning.

Lord, it had hurt so bad he'd screamed out loud as the train came in. He was sure that what had happened to Brock was happening to him. But it had stopped as quickly as it started. He didn't know why. The train maybe? Maybe there would have been too many witnesses. He didn't wait to find out; he just saw that lady tumbling down the stairs and bolted out of there like greased lightning. He had run all the way home, back to his apartment a few blocks away. Everytime a train went by on the elevated track outside his window, he would start to shake, remembering what a close call he'd had. He had no idea whether Lina was dead or alive, if she'd managed to contact Steven Everson or not, but he would have to keep his appointment, just in case. If Everson showed up, George *had* to be there.

He realized now he should never have gotten involved in all this. It had seemed so great at first. What a mess it was now. Living in fear, watching his friends die a horrible death. It didn't seem worth the money—the extra booze, the richer food, the women whose company he graciously paid for when he went into Manhattan. Nothing seemed to matter but his threatened survival.

He didn't understand the whole business. There were times when the great fog was lifted and he could think more clearly and he questioned what was happening and why and how he fit into it. They'd explained it to him, of course. They'd needed people to keep the workers—the pitiful drunks and outcasts and mental defectives—in line, to make sure they stuck to their daily quota.

But in the morning, he just couldn't remember quite *what* it was he had done the night before. When he tried to think about it, something in his brain would click, and he'd start to think about something else. There were times when it was all he could do to remember when it had first started. Then other times he would recall the long, lonely periods of starvation, and he *knew* why he had accepted their offer. Funny, he could never remember who it was had first approached him, only that they'd been a member of what they called *the committee*. It was someone familiar. Someone his parents had once known well. He couldn't even remember when this person appeared to him. It was as if he had been working for them all his life.

His parents . . . sometimes he missed them. A lot. He'd never had his father's brains, his scientific acumen, never inherited his drive and ambition. Didn't have his mother's pretty looks either. A genetic mishap, he was. He didn't know which death had hit him harder—his father wasting away after his stroke, or his mother getting run over by a . . .

He came back into the present. They'd killed Brock. And he would be next. So he had tried to contact that Everson guy. Because now and then, when he was working, riding the rails and crackin' the whip in his midnight, nightmare task that paid so well, he would pick up things, little bits of information, from his superiors. A name here, a place there, things that stuck in his mind even though the larger picture eluded him. He had pieced together a great deal. Only, it usually all ended up to nothing.

He didn't like to think about the times when he felt someone, something, listening in on his thoughts, as if his brain was connected in some way to another mentality. He knew the others could explain it but they refused. "You know you were treated," *they'd tell him.*

But he'd been there the night the Everson kid was spirited away with the others. He couldn't remember now who the others were or where they were going, but they had entrusted him with valuable information about the boy—they must have, how else could he have *known?*—something they were going to use the kid for. Something horrible. That night when Brock had died right before his eyes, he had reached his breaking point. Filled with resolve, he knew he had to make an attempt to break out of their control, to contact the boy's brother. Took him all these days since then to take the first step.

He hadn't known whom to turn to. Normally it would have been Brock. But that was impossible . . . since he'd joined the company, since he'd died. So he'd called up Brock's number, hoping the dame he often spoke about would be on the other end. Now everything was up to her. *If* she was still alive. If she wasn't just a splotch on the stairs like Brock was. He would have to get a grip on himself and go to McGreeley's soon. Just in case. Just in case she had made it.

What was it exactly that was going to happen? Brock had been *screaming* about it. Why could he never recall in the morning what he did at night? It was always so dreamlike. He had finally realized just what he was *involved* in, realized that the horror would go on and on —would get *worse*, in fact—and that the Everson kid would somehow be responsible for it. Unless . . . unless someone could stop them.

Absently his fingers had been scratching on the denim material covering his pubic area. The itching was driving him crazy. Some bitch in the city must have given him crabs. Crabs—ugh!— how he hated them, those living creatures— lice, *bugs*—feeding off his blood and residing in his pores. Maybe it was something else, some other kind of rash. He hoped so.

The scratching brought no relief. He removed his trousers and underwear—where were they, the little buggers!—and poked and probed his pubic hair under the dim lamp of his night table. God, if he saw one he would *die*. Damn parasites!

It was only five o'clock, but it was dark out already.

His room was small—just a bed, a chest of drawers, a tiny refrigerator with the hot plate on top. The old wallpaper was peeling, and the musty closet in the corner held lots of new clothes that he hadn't even worn yet. He wondered if he'd ever get the chance. He'd never really been able to change his basic lifestyle, no matter how much money he'd made.

Damn—the itching was getting worse, but he still couldn't see anything. The lice were awfully hard to spot sometimes. His long, grimy fingernails dug into his flesh. Once or twice he *thought* he saw a flash of black peeking out from beside one of the tiny hairs.

He went up and took a piss in the john. He drank a few mouthfuls of lukewarm water from the faucet and splashed the wet stuff over his face. He went back to the bed, flopped into it, wriggling out of the rest of his clothes.

When he didn't dwell on it, the itching went away. There, there. Now it wasn't so bad. He relaxed, feeling sleepy, his head sinking comfortably into the pillow.

Outside it was getting darker. The clock ticked its way toward six.

George stretched out his arm to switch off the lamp. The alarm would wake him up later.

He slept peacefully, shifting his position now and then while he dreamed. He had nice dreams, soothing dreams. His mind was at peace.

Until his dreams took on a darker hue.

He dreamed that, inside his body, the lice were multiplying their bodies and numbers enlarging as he slept. Silently they fed off his flesh and blood. Silently they crawled along his bones . . .

"What?"

George woke up with a start. He felt funny—his whole body was wracked with horrible pain, and his head felt feverish. He had a bad case of the shakes too. The itching was more intense than ever.

He tipped his head forward onto his chest, and saw that something was *coming up out of* the skin above his penis, making its way through the jungle of pubic hair. It was growing even as it pulled itself out of his flesh. Then there was another and another, all of them coming out of his body, horrible black things as big as fists. They were swelling up, expanding, as if from contact with the air. He felt blood running down his legs and pouring over his chest as the creatures ripped out of his groin and fastened their mouth parts on his skin. They were crawling all over him, dozens of them, their pincers now as big as human fingers. They were eating him alive!

He knew it was only a hallucination. Somehow that just made it worse.

He started to scream. Several of them had worked their way up to his head, and he was thoroughly engulfed. It was as if his whole body was covered with black bugs, as if he were literally being eaten from *within*.

He closed his eyes and waited.

In his mind, his body had been almost

completely consumed when the alarm went off.

It was a quarter to nine.

"Wait a minute," George told himself. "This is just a hallucination. This isn't real. I have to get up and keep my appointment."

George opened his eyes.

True, there *were* no bugs.

But there was no *body*, either.

The last thing he saw before his head dissolved was the melting substance of his arms, legs, feet, and torso dribbling off the bed with a *sizzle*.

SEVEN

ERIC THORNE GOT back from the supermarket to find Hammond with his head in the refrigerator. Hammond pulled out—drumstick in hand —as he heard Eric approaching. Eric put the bag of groceries on the kitchen table and gently chided his guest. "Can't you wait until I have dinner ready?"

"You said I should help myself, so I did."

"Just teasing. Thanks for paying for half the groceries."

"It's only fair." He took a peek inside the bag. "Let's see what we have here. Ah, you got the sweet potatoes! My wife showed me a special way to prepare them. My second wife I think it was. Let me take care of them."

"What do you think of these steaks?" Eric said as he extracted two plastic packages from the shopping bag. "Nice, huh?"

"They look delicious. I'm starving. This drumstick will make a nice appetizer, but I'll be gnawing on the sofa if dinner isn't ready soon."

"How do you keep so fit?"

"I jog. I find it very useful in keeping my weight down."

"That's right. You've mentioned it before."

"What's *your* secret?"

Eric went to the oven, twisted the dial to the proper temperature. "I've never been an especially *big* eater, though I like good food. I guess I've always just naturally gravitated toward low-calorie foods. I ate yogurt before it was popular."

"Skim milk and that sort of thing?"

"Yes, only now they call it Low-Fat Milk and charge twice as much."

"I've noticed." Hammond headed for the living room. "I have a journal to flip through. Bake the potatoes and call me when they're done. I'll take care of the rest."

"Will you make the salad, or shall I?"

"I'm not that fond of salads. You can make some for yourself."

Hammond went into the next room. Eric took some lettuce, tomatoes, and cucumbers out of the refrigerator. He was washing the lettuce, tearing it into smaller pieces, when he felt a sudden weariness. His vision began to blur, while his hearing became conversely acute. The sound of the water pouring from the faucet was that of a thundering waterfall; the lettuce snapped in his hands with the crack of a gunshot. He stopped, wiped his sweating forehead, and leaned against the sink for a minute or two until it passed. He had to fight the urge to go into his bedroom and lie down. He couldn't understand why he was so tired. He had had an excellent night's sleep the evening before, even making up the hours he had lost the night of his frightful trance. His day had not been especially trying; no unforseen problems, arguments, or additional work. Why was he so exhausted?

He was about to give up, head for the bedroom, and ask Hammond to make his own dinner, when the spell suddenly passed. He could see clearly again, and the sounds in the room returned to their normal volume. What a strange experience! Still a bit woozy, he continued to wash the lettuce. At least his energy had returned. He didn't feel tired anymore. He must remember to tell Hammond all about it. Maybe not—he'd like to be spared the man's protestations of doom during the dinner hour, at least.

He cut up one tomato into several segments and put the other back for another time. He sliced up the cucumber, cutting off the dark green skin. He tossed it all into a small bowl and placed it on the little table by the window. He removed a large can of creamed corn from the cupboard, opened it, and poured the contents into a saucepan. He placed it on one of the burners.

He went into the living room and found Hammond fast asleep on the easy chair. Funny, now *he* felt tired again. He removed the journal from Hammond's lap and went back into the kitchen with it. He thumbed through it until the oven was hot enough to insert the potatoes. He did so, set the timer, and sat down by the table again. He must remember to put the steaks in the broiler in a little while. He shifted his concentration to an article on telepathy by Morris Urnheardt, that quack. Eric read it quickly, looking as usual for all the discrepancies in the man's arguments. As he read, the words became more indistinct with each line. He rubbed his eyes, but it did no good. The weariness was upon him again.

This time it was a dream. In the arms of slumber, his mind was free to drift, drift, out and over the walls of the buildings, high, higher, then down toward the ground. Then low, lower, down to a dark and secret place. He saw none of the things that he had seen that night of his frightening experience—but one. It was the door, that strange, gigantic door. Made of steel, he was sure. Eric murmured in his sleep. He wanted to get closer, much closer, so that he could read the writing on the door.

He could see it better now. Letters—an H? Yes, an H. Followed by a G. Then a C? All capital letters. H.G.C. HGC. What did that mean? The letters were not affixed to the door, but were part of its design, chiseled out of and into it. Eric wanted to open the door, but he saw no handle, no means to get beyond it. He heard voices, scuttling sounds like animals. More voices. Coming closer. Suddenly, he was very afraid. Then a high, screaming sound, an irritating, stabbing sound, like a buzzer . . .

The buzzer on the oven's timer had turned on, waking Eric up. He jumped out of the chair and shut it off.

While he went about fixing the dinner, he thought about what he had seen so vividly in the dream. He had gotten a sense of *place* this time, though he had actually seen nothing but the door itself, and had no idea where it might be located. And yet? And what about those sounds he'd heard? What could they be?

Hammond was still asleep. The apartment was very silent, except for the crackling noises from the oven. The smell that came from it, warm and delicious, had an identity of its own. Eric felt lonely. He was torn between turning on the television or waking up Hammond. He decided to do neither. Dinner would be ready soon anyway. Hammond would like that—his falling asleep in the middle of Urnheardt's article!

Eric prepared a drink for himself, and sat down on the sofa, his eyes on Hammond's chest as it slowly rose and fell. He would have to ask him if he remembered any dreams he might have had. Eric's dream had left him feeling slightly unsettled. What was the meaning of it all?

He set the table, brought out the dressing for his salad, and poured two glasses of tomato juice. As soon as the steaks were ready, he'd wake up Hammond. He was very hungry now.

But stronger even than his urge for food was his determination to find the door he had seen twice now inside his mind. He was filled with a compelling need to go *beyond* the portal, to discover the taunting secrets it was withholding. He sensed that the door had something to do with the tramp, that lonely, forsaken derelict who had briefly, but eternally, touched him.

Somewhere he would find that door. And that man.

It was only a matter of time.

Detective John Albright had stopped off for a beer before he went home to dinner. He had left the stationhouse early, without comment, sick of papers and disappearances, and gone to the nearest bar and grill. But one glass of beer led to another, which led to a bottle, and then another bottle, and then a third one. He was feeling pretty high at eight o'clock. He was about to order another beer when he glanced at his watch and got off the bar stool with a start. He dug into his pocket for change, left a sizable tip, and went out into the street.

It was quite dark outside, with a slight breeze that made the wind whistle as it went through the trees. He went into the coffeeshop across the street and ordered a strong cup of black coffee and one prune danish. After the man took his order, he went in back to where the phones were and dialed his number. No answer. No goddamned answer. What was the story? The phone at his house hadn't been answered all afternoon. He'd been trying and trying it, more out of curiosity as to where his wife had gone than out of a need to talk to her.

He let the phone ring for almost two minutes. Disgusted, he hung up, left the booth, and went back to the counter where his hot coffee was waiting. The first sip almost burned his tongue. He used the spoon to stir the liquid around and around, cooling it; then took a big bite of the danish. He felt lousy. He beer hadn't done much good for his stomach. But he loved beer. Loved being alone in the bar, surrounded by other people. Strangers. That's what he liked.

He paid the bill fifteen minutes later and walked outside again. It was colder now. Windier. There weren't many people on the street. He got into his car and drove home.

He lived in a quiet suburb in Brooklyn—with lots of trees and square, similarly shaped two-family houses. He parked the car, disembarked, and walked up the path to his front door. The lights were out and there was no noise whatsoever from within. Usually his son would be watching TV at this hour, getting ready for bed. Where were they?

He let himself in with his key and turned on the light in the foryer. He hung his coat in the closet and went into the living room, turning on the lamp via the switch on the wall. The room was small but comfortable, with well-worn but attractive furniture. Most of it had been given to them from her mother, hand-me-downs. He went into the kitchen and checked the bedroom and the bathroom. The house was empty.

He was starting to worry when he found a note stuck with tape to the refrigerator door:

Johnny—took Bobby to see Grandmama. Not sure when we'll be back. Will be gone at least a few days. Left fried chicken for your supper. Love, Gloria.

Albright didn't understand. Gloria's mother lived in Massachusetts. It was a long trip and she always hated to make it alone. Their visits to "Grandmama" were always well planned in advance—the three of them made a day of it, often meeting their other children up there as well. But Gloria hadn't mentioned it to him. He didn't remember their being invited. Why hadn't Gloria mentioned it?

Could it be something else? Was Gloria leaving him? *Not sure when we'll be back.* Was this the start of a trial separation? He knew their marriage wasn't the greatest, but surely things weren't *that* bad, were they?

Yes. Things were pretty bad. He'd noticed the signs but had been too preoccupied to respond to them. So that was it. She had taken their child and left him.

Had she told their other children yet? Should he call them now, tell them what their mother had done? To him? To them? Was he being too hasty? For a moment he hated her, he despised her, he never wanted to see her again. Then the next he felt like sobbing with despair.

Perhaps it was something else, he told himself. Perhaps her mother had suddenly taken ill. That must be it. An old lady, all by herself, would need a daughter to look after her. But why had she taken Bobby with her? She didn't want him to miss any school, did she? She could have dropped him off at the office before she'd left. He could have stayed with his Daddy all afternoon; they'd have gone out for hamburgers and milkshakes and had a lot of fun. Didn't Gloria think he was capable of taking care of his own son?

No matter. That was it. Her mother was sick. Should he call? No, Gloria would probably call him later in the evening to explain. He hoped he hadn't missed her if she'd called earlier. She'd try again anyway. He'd give her until eleven o'clock. She usually went to bed early. Especially tonight, after driving all the way alone. He hoped she had driven carefully—she was a timid driver, like a rabbit, all stops and starts, nervous and shy behind the wheel. He hoped she had driven slowly.

Ah, Gloria, he thought. Impulsive, dear, sweet Gloria. She hadn't left him—what a foolish thought. How ridiculous! Why did he jump to such absurd conclusions? He got out the fried chicken and turned on the oven so that he could reheat it. He poked inside the fridge looking for some left-over vegetables. He found plenty of succotash and a little creamed spinach. Little Bobby's chocolate soda was in the back, on the lower shelf. Albright could never understand how the kid could drink that stuff.

He ate quickly, still hungry in spite of the danish and the fattening beer he'd consumed not long ago. Gloria always made great chicken. He had another beer with the meal, then heated up a pot of coffee and had some store-bought apple pie for dessert. He put a slice of cheese on top and a big scoop of ice cream. Gloria always told him he was crazy to do that—to put both the cheese and the ice cream—but he had liked it just that way since he'd been a boy.

He watched TV, always the one ear listening for the phone in the kitchen. When it was eleven, he got up and went to the drawer where Gloria kept her address book—he could never remember her mother's phone number. The book was there. He flipped the pages, memorized the number, and dialed. The old woman answered promptly. He could hear her TV set in the background.

"Hello. Who is this?"

"It's 'Sonny.' "

"Who?"

"It's Sonny-Boy. *Johnny.*"

"Johnny? How are you?"

"Fine. Just fine." He could imagine her in her tattered old robe, hair in perennial curlers, her glasses falling halfway down her nose. "My back was acting up last week, but it's fine now."

"Good. I hope it stays that way."

"Me, too. Goodness, I haven't heard from you and Gloria for almost two months. How is my daughter, anyway?"

It took a few seconds for it to hit him.

He was momentarily speechless. All he could think to say was, "What's that, Mama?"

"I said, 'How's Gloria?' Is she there?"

"No. No, I just wanted to call you up, seein' as how I haven't seen you in so long."

"Well, that's sweet. It has been a while. When you coming up?"

"Thanksgiving for sure. Maybe sooner."

"Well, you're always welcome, you know that. How's my little grandchild?"

His mind was racing, unclear, unsure of what to do. "Bobby's fine. He's wonderful. His mom took him to a movie."

"My, he's up awfully late."

"Well, there's no school tomorrow."

"Oh, that's right. What did they go see?"

"Aww, some kiddie picture. I forget. Cinderella or somethin'."

"So you got lonely and decided to call your mother-in-law?"

"Yeah, that's right." *Where was Gloria? Did she have an accident? Wasn't her mother expecting her?*

"Well, that's sweet."

"I won't keep you too long. I know you go to bed early."

"Yes, I usually do. But tonight, I wasn't that tired. My, Bobby's going to be awfully sleepy tomorrow. It's after eleven. What was it, a double feature?"

"No. No, I think Gloria was going to drop in on one of her girlfriends on the way back. You know how she is, once she gets talking. Bobby's probably asleep over there somewhere on the couch."

Grandmama giggled. "Sure, Poor little thing. Your daughter sent me a lovely card last week. She can certainly write well. Loveliest letters I ever get."

"Yeah. She's got talent. Look, I won't keep ya. I didn't realize how late it was."

"Well, you probably want to call up and find out when your wife is coming home."

He laughed. "Yeah. That's right. My kibbitzing wife."

"Look, darling, take care of yourself. And give my love to Glo and to little Bobby, will you?"

"Of course, Mother. I'll do that."

"Fine. Goodnight now. And thanks for calling."

"Okay, Mother. Goodbye."

"Goodbye, Sonny."

He listened for the click on the other end of the line, then slowly placed the receiver in its cradle. He should have said something. But he couldn't. He didn't want to worry her. There were only two possibilities. Either Gloria hadn't told her mother about her plans, and had not yet arrived at her house for reasons unknown. Or else she had never planned to go to her mother's at all. John didn't know which idea was more repellent. No one had answered the phone at the house since early in the morning, which meant she must have left not long after he'd left for work. Surely she would have reached her destination by now? Unless she'd decided to stop at a motel. She tired easily when driving. But the trip wasn't *that* long, and she had left hours ago.

Who was he kidding? Her mother was obviously not sick. Gloria had only used the old lady for an excuse. She had never intended to go to see her. She was leaving him after all. She had gone somewhere where he wouldn't find her. He couldn't understand why she had even bothered writing that she'd gone home to Mother, since she must have realized how easily John could check it out. Maybe she *had* originally set out for her mother's, then decided it would be better to be off by herself. Alone with Bobby. That must be it. The other option was simply unthinkable. He would wait until the morning—if he didn't hear from her by then, he would start checking morgues and hospitals; hell, he would put out an APB on the bitch.

She had left him. He was sure of it. Left him. And like everyone else . . . she'd disappeared.

Four hours earlier Ralph Andrews and Steven Everson were standing on the steps of the exit from the Broadway Junction station. They had climbed down the stairs where Lina had fallen and were inspecting the reddish smear spread out over several of the steps beneath their feet.

Steven looked at Ralph. "What do you think?"

"I don't know. I suppose, if you used your imagination, you can roughly see it taking on the shape of a man. Especially when you stand at the top. But it's hard to tell, spread out over the steps that way. Most of the goo has been worn away anyhow."

Ralph extracted an envelope from his pocket and bent down to examine the stuff more closely. He took a pen from his shirt pocket. One end was a tiny flashlight—he shined it over the reddish material clinging to the underside of the steps where the thousands of feet that went up and down the stairs each day couldn't disturb it. He shut the light off, put it away, then pulled a book of matches out of his pants pocket. He used the matches to scrape some of the glob into the open envelope. After he had a sizable amount, he sealed the envelope, folded it, and placed it in his pocket. He got back up on his feet. "I can have a lab check this out. Should have the results pretty soon."

"Let's hope it's not what this George character claims it is."

"I wouldn't worry. Probably it's animal gunk. Or fake movie gore more likely. We'll find out."

"What time is it?" Steven asked him.

Ralph consulted his watch, its numbers glowing faintly in the dark. "Not quite eight-thirty. Let's go down to the car. We'll get to the bar early."

They went out through another exit and went down to street level. Ralph's car was parked two blocks away, near the end of the train yard by a grubby lot full of overgrown weeds and garbage stacks. They got into the car and drove off in the direction of McGreeley's.

Ralph told him about the afternoon's activities. "I've got someone digging into Vivian Jessup's background and the facts behind her death. Someone else is contacting people Joey was interviewed by. A young fellow is touring the singles bars tonight, asking questions. A couple of tireless trainees are scouring the more desolate sections of Central Park. And we've duplicated hundred of copies of that photo you gave me. And that's just the beginning."

Steven was gratified. Maybe, just maybe, this would work. "Thank God," he whispered.

"What's that?"

"Nothing. *Ralph!*—stop here. There's the bar."

McGreeley's was as empty as Lina had found

it the night before. They ordered two beers and stood by the counter. Steven's glass had brown stuff smeared on the top so he drank his beer from the bottle.

Ralph asked the bartender—the same young Irish guy—a few questions, but the fellow only had a vague recollection of Lina and no recollection of George whatsoever. "We got pretty busy last night," he said.

Ralph looked at his watch. "It's almost time. I'll go sit at one of the tables and look inconspicuous. Don't be nervous, now."

"I'm not," Steven said. "I wonder how he'll know what I look like."

Ralph took a pointed look around the bar. "The only other two people in this joint who are male look like they've been here since yesterday morning. So don't worry. If he doesn't come over to you, go over to him." Lina *had* given a pretty detailed description of George during her spirited rendition of what had happened.

"Okay."

Steven sipped his beer, his eyes on the clock. The young bartender came over and wiped the counter with a wet cloth. By the time Steven had finished his beer, it was five after nine. He ordered another one.

Looking through the front window from his table, Ralph was carefully studying anyone who even came near the bar. There weren't many people on the street now, as it was getting colder and windier. Even bar habitues were still at home digesting their meals, watching the idiot box. Most of the people he saw were kids, groups of boys looking for fun. McGreeley's was not a young-persons' bar. Without exception, they passed it by.

He checked his watch. They had planned to give George one full hour to show, though Steven had said he was willing to wait all night if need be—that's how desperate he was to see the guy. Though Ralph was also anxious to see how this all fit into Joseph Everson's disappearing act, if it did fit into it, he also knew that some jokers never intended to keep their appointments.

Soon it was nine-thirty. And then a quarter of ten.

At ten o'clock Steven walked over to Ralph's table and gave the detective a frantic look. "I don't want to leave," he said. "Maybe something detained the guy."

Ralph was hoping that this George character wouldn't walk in while they were talking together. If he saw them he might get awfully suspicious when he found out one of them was his quarry. "I don't think he's going to show, but it's up to you. Look, why not let *me* stay here. If he comes in, I can grab him easy enough."

"No. You look nothing like me. Joey and I have some familial resemblance, at least. Even if you grabbed him, he might not talk to you."

"Look, you hired me—have a little confidence."

"I do. Please—it's just that . . . He's my brother."

"Okay," Ralph sighed. "I understand."

"There's no need for you to stay here any longer. If he does come, I'll call you afterwards and tell you what happened."

"You might need me. I could tail him."

"Look, I'll only stick around a few minutes more. I just need some time by myself."

"Suit yourself." Ralph squeezed Steven's shoulder and grinned. "Okay. You stay here. I'm going to pursue a few angles of my own, as they say."

Steven nodded. "I'll be all right."

As Ralph walked out of the bar he knew that Steven would probably stay at McGreeley's until closing time. He could tell when clients wanted to handle things themselves and he knew better than to try and dissuade them.

Ralph drove around the block, then parked his car three streets down on Jamaica Avenue. There were plenty of bars in the neighborhood, and there was bound to be a bartender or patron somewhere who could give him more information on the mysterious "George."

He might even be lucky enough to find out where he lived.

Or *un*lucky enough . . .

While Steven nursed another bottle of beer, Ralph went into several nearby taverns and described George to the bartenders, asking if they knew who he was or where he resided. Nothing came up until the sixth bar, a dimly lit cocktail lounge with a black, polished, oval counter. A chubby barmaid in her forties, dressed in tight, black slacks, sauntered over to him with a winning smile.

"What'll it be?"

"A beer. And some information. I'm looking for a friend of mine, guy who used to hang out around here. Name's George. I'd like to pay him a visit but I don't remember where he lives."

"George?" the woman said. "Used to hang out here?"

"Maybe he still does. I haven't seen him in a while. Short guy, in his forties. Slick black hair. Kind of nervous."

The barmaid reacted instantaneously. "Oh him. *That* George. I know him. He comes in here a lot. He lives right around here. Porky could give you his address. They used to play cards together all the time."

"Porky?"

"That's his nickname. He usually comes in sometime after eleven. I'll get you your beer, and he'll probably be here in a few minutes. I'll ask him where George lives. All right?"

"Thanks a lot. I really appreciate it."

"Sure, honey."

Ralph smiled and watched her waddle to the middle of the bar, where she pulled a bottle from beneath the counter, snapped off the cap, and poured the beer into a freshly washed glass. The foamy head spilled over onto the bar. She wiped the bottom of the glass with a towel and brought it and the bottle back to Ralph. "Here you go," she said.

Ralph extracted a dollar bill from his wallet and handed it to her. "That'll be eighty-five cents," she said. She took the bill, rang up the price on the cash register, and brought him his change.

The door opened with a jingle, and in walked a balding, pot-bellied man of about forty-five. He was dressed in a sharp-looking suit and had a cigar stuck in the corner of his mouth. His features were broad and rubbery—he looked as if you could throw a ball at his face and it would stick there in the folds of his flesh before bouncing back out onto the floor. He was in a very happy mood.

"Dolly, Dolly, Dolly," he said cheerfully. "How are you today?"

"Fine, Porky. What did you do, win at the races today?"

"I sure did. Had a real lucky streak."

"Well, don't spend it all in one night. The usual?"

"Please. And don't worry. I'm holding onto *this* wad. I won't be doing any gambling for at least another day. Ha ha ha."

Dolly fixed a martini while she spoke. "This gentleman—" she indicated Ralph, "and you have a mutual acquaintance. George—y'know, the guy comes in here all the time? You play cards with him now and then, don't ya?"

"Ah, yes. My friend, George. Haven't seen him in a while. Nervous little fellow. Always looking around his shoulder. Comes and goes."

"But do you know where he lives?" Dolly asked.

"Yes. In that big, brown building on the corner, two blocks down. First building on the right. I don't know the address. It's right next to the dry-cleaning store," he waved his hand in the direction of the door, "on the other side of the street."

"Two blocks down, first building on the right," Ralph repeated.

"Yes, right next to the dry cleaners. His last name is—" he snapped his fingers, trying to remember, "Foran, Forrest, something like that." He looked at Ralph. "Well, you must know."

"Yeah." Ralph gave a noncommital grunt.

"He lives on the third floor in a crummy old furnished room. He's got roaches as big as mice."

Dolly grimaced playfully and Ralph smiled. "They grab the cards right out of your hands, eh?"

Porky laughed heartily. "That they do, yessir. Well, George isn't a bad sort of guy, especially after you know him for a while. He's a good loser and a good card player. And he pays up— right then and there. I like that. But he was odd —can't quite put my finger on it. A strange, quiet man. Never did figure out what he did for a living."

Ralph waited for the fat man to take another sip of beer. Porky had never even met Ralph before, yet there he was practically pouring out information about his "friend" George. Bar friends. They were like that. They existed for each other just to assuage the loneliness of otherwise friendless people. Ralph would have been like that, once his wife died, had it not been for his work. It kept him well occupied.

But not that occupied. He found himself wondering what Dolly would be like to sleep with, her body close to his, warm, comforting.

"Once he told me that he drove a cab—for Blue Dot here in Brooklyn—though I don't know when he gave it up. Can't blame him. Cabbies these days are in for trouble, what with the robberies. Too much crime in this city. Too much."

"What do you think he does for a living now?" Ralph asked.

"Beats me. Mechanic maybe. Seems to be good with his hands. Say, he did mention once that he used to work for the subway system. Could have been one of those guys that fix the tracks, walking around with the dirty clothes and the headlights. Yeah, that would have suited George to a tee."

"What was he doin' when *you* last saw him?" Dolly asked Ralph.

"Oh, it was so long ago, I can't quite recall," Ralph replied. "Driving a cab, I guess. George was never one to discuss his affairs."

"No sir," Porky said emphatically. "Not him."

Ralph finished his beer and left the bar. Enough talk—now it was time to find George.

He walked back up to McGreeley's. As he expected, Steven was still sitting there, and now it was way past eleven. The man was staring into his beer morosely, shutting out the world. Ralph eased noiselessly onto the stool next to him and said, "How ya doin', big guy?"

Steven looked up with a start. "Oh, it's you. You scared me."

"Didn't mean to."

"What are you doing here?"

"Come on, we're going to pay a call on George."

"Huh?"

"Last name begins with F. Third Floor. Just a few blocks down the street. Ready?"

"What are you talking about?"

"I know where George lives. While you were here, I did a little detective work. Do you want to come with me or not?"

Steven looked very excited. "I'm coming. I'm coming."

They were out of the bar before the bartender had time to rouse himself and go wait on Ralph. They walked down to the dry-cleaning store Porky had mentioned and briefly discussed what Steven would say if George was home. Ralph also explained where and how he had obtained the information.

The doorway next to the dry cleaners was a dirty, smelly alcove lit by a dim yellow light-bulb. The outer door had two small windows, both of which were shattered. The doors on the mailboxes—the ones that hadn't been torn off—were twisted and battered. Ralph looked up and down the list of names next to the buzzers. George *Forrance* was listed as being the occupant of 3C. As the inner door was ajar there was no need to use the buzzer. The bottom of the door scraped against the grimy, piss-stained floor as Steven struggled to open it. Finally they got through and started up the narrow stairs. There were no lights in the corridor.

They could hear sounds of activity from

behind the apartment doors. TV sets, radios, voices raised in contention, food sizzling on the stove. Someone on the second floor was cooking bacon. They paused on the stairwell between the second and third floors.

"You go up first," Ralph directed. "He may not talk if he sees us both. I'll be behind you. If there's any trouble, I'll be right nearby."

"Great. If it wasn't for the beers I had I'd be awfully nervous."

"Don't be."

Steven gave a reassuring nod. He continued up the stairs. Something small and brown skittered across the hallway as he reached the top.

The stairs continued at the end of the hall, which was only a few feet long. Apartment 3C was the farthest door on the left. Steven knocked on Forrance's door and waited for a reply.

He knocked again.

Nothing.

There was no doorbell. No knocker. Not even a little peephole.

"George? Mr. Forrance! Are you home? It's me, Steven Everson."

Nothing.

"Lina Hobler sent me to see you. She's all right, George, if that's what you're worried about. She's okay. Look, I just want to talk to you."

Steven looked over toward the stairs. Ralph was out of sight in the shadows.

"Mr. Forrance. Please let me in. I'd very much like to talk to you. I can make it worth your while. I'll even pay you for information, if that's what you want." Steven banged again, furiously. "Let me in, God damn it!" He couldn't have waited this long for nothing. He would not go home now. He would *not* go home. *"Please!"*

Suddenly Ralph was at his side, dangling a key chain. "Let me try one of these. I can get in almost anywhere with one of these babies." Steven stepped aside and let Ralph try the keys, one after another. "You didn't hear anything inside there, did you?"

"Nothing. What's the use of breaking in if he's not home?"

"So we can look around. See where this guy is coming from. You never can tell what we might find."

Both of them had the same thought: *We might find Joey.*

Another rat ran across the hallway like a furtive messenger.

Just then the key in Ralph's hand worked and the door was pushed open. They were both hit by the foul blast of an awful odor. Ralph reached in his hand and found the light switch.

A bunch of rats, a dozen or so that had been on the bed, ran into their crevices as the man advanced into the room.

"Yuchh," Ralph said. "I hate vermin."

Steven stood in the doorway as Ralph moved toward the bed to see what the rats had been chewing on. A few cockroaches that had gathered on top of the mattress in the brief time since the rats had relinquished it ran in instinctual flight from the vibrations of the private eye's footsteps. A few of the duller ones clung to the covers on the side of the bed. Ralph leaned over and looked down.

Bloodstained sheets. All Ralph saw were bloodstained sheets. And a pile of clothes lying next to the bed on the floor.

"Nothing," he said in disgust. "There's nothing here."

Steven didn't move from the doorway. "What do we do now?"

"*You* go home and get some rest. Killing yourself from lack of sleep won't do your brother any good. Besides, you may need your strength in the days to come."

Steven didn't ask what he meant by that. "Is that blood on the mattress? Or that stuff we found at the subway station?"

Ralph rubbed his chin. "I'm not sure." He grabbed the sheet in his big hands and ripped it, tearing off a piece to put in his pocket. "We'll find out. We might as well get out of here. I'll assign someone in the office to keep an eye on the place in case this Forrance guy comes back, assuming . . ."

Steven gave him a quizzical look.

"Assuming he's alive. That blood on the sheet, there's an awful lot of it. But no body."

Steven gulped. "The rats?"

"Nah. There'd be *something* left."

"You don't think *it* dissolved, do you?"

Ralph just looked at him.

"Are you going to tell the police about this?"

"What for? There's no body. What can they

do? I can find out the blood type—if that stuff on the sheet *is* blood, sure doesn't smell like it—and make sure it's not the same as your brother's."

"God," Steven groaned. He hadn't thought of *that*.

"Can you make it home by yourself? I've got a couple of calls to make. I want to stay here until one of my men shows up to watch the place. It'll give me a chance to look around."

"I'm staying."

"Steven, this is what you're *paying* me for."

"He's my brother, Ralph."

The private eye shrugged. "Okay."

"Besides," Steven added, "who wants to take the subway back to Manhattan at this hour?"

Long after most of the others had gone home for the day, a skeleton crew remained behind in the police lab for emergencies, routine tasks, and cleanup. Tonight, there were two new additions. Ernest Hendon, who often stayed late, as the head of the department is wont to do, and Henry Judson, his bright, spirited lab assistant.

They had had a lot of work to do during the daylight hours, and therefore had to hold off on re-examining the strange substance from Room 919 until the evening. They had gone through the day efficiently but automatically—their minds not on their work but on the possibilities of the discovery they might make once their normal routine was over.

So they subjected the splotch of blood, flesh,

211

bone, and cloth to a battery of exhaustive tests, trying to determine how part of a human being's body could have turned into a mush of jelly.

They stopped for coffee at ten.

"I didn't realize it was this late," Ernest said. "We'd better leave soon or we'll never get any sleep tonight."

"I keep thinking that we're so close, though."

"I know what you mean, Henry. All right. We'll stick it out to midnight. You can come in late tomorrow. Me, I better be here bright and early as usual. Wilminter wants the chemical analysis by noon." He ran his hands through his thick thatch of black hair and yawned. "I don't know how I can still keep my eyes open." He was a medium-sized man, with an olive complexion and pointed features. Now and then he wore wire-frame glasses, too vain to wear them outside of work. He had been head of the department for nine years, since he'd turned forty. He was good at his job and enjoyed it.

Henry Judson was a comparative newcomer, a "boy" of thirty-one, with a pleasantly homely countenance and longish brown hair that was fine and soft as silk. He had big, blue eyes magnified by thick-lensed spectacles. He seemed to be very industrious and was possessed of unusual curiosity. He wanted very badly to determine the process that had created the stuff he'd been assigned to classify earlier in the week.

Ernest drained his coffee cup and looked over a sheet of paper on the top of his clipboard.

"Well, let's see. We've ruled out explosions, implosion, artificial chemical means, acids, alkalines, erosion, natural decay," his hand went back through his hair again, "and exposure to the elements. I admit, I'm stumped."

"It's as if someone took the man and put him in a blender. Then turned it up to high speed and let it run for four hours."

"Short of securing a corpse from the morgue and testing your theory outright, I don't think we can determine if it has possibilities."

"I know it's not very realistic."

"What we have here isn't very realistic. We can't look anymore for realistic answers. A man's body does not wind up what way due to natural causes. A body is blown up—sure, you have a hell of a mess, but you don't get a human gelatin mold like this. A body is left for the wind and the rats and the rain to get at for weeks, but it still doesn't turn into *jello*. The flesh, blood, and bones of that man—and his clothes, considering the fibers we also found in the mixture— went through some extraordinary process, if indeed it was Mr. Peterson up there on the wall of room 919, and I'll be damned if I can figure out what happened to him. No, your blender theory may not be all that farfetched. Grotesque, certainly, but not farfetched."

"You mean," Henry said, his throat dry and scratchy, "someone might have cut up a body, inserted it in a blending machine, and smeared the contents on a wall in the shape of a man?"

"A disgusting, insane ritual killing. And an

awful lot of trouble for someone to go to. Some-one with a strong stomach."

"Do you really think that's the answer?"

"No. No, I don't. But I think you're on the right track. We have to find something, some process, something out of the ordinary, that would have a similar effect on a human body. Not a cuisinart. But something else."

"What, sir?"

"I don't know." Ernest went back to the hotplate. "I'm going to have another cup of coffee. One part of me wants to go home and sleep for the rest of the week."

"I could stay, sir. You *did* say I could come in late tomorrow."

"Yes, I did." Ernest thought for a moment. "All right, my intrepid young friend. You go on with the research. I'm going to bed." He went to the coat rack in the corner. "You can finish the coffee, I won't be needing it." He put on his jacket. "Much as I'd love to stay and help, I'm afraid I'd be of no help in this condition. Good night. And good luck."

"Good night, sir. Say hello to your wife for me."

"Will do. And uh, Henry?"

"Yes, sir."

"No blenders or bodies from the morgue, okay?"

Henry smiled. It looked so odd on him. "No, sir. Good night."

Ernest left the lab, turned to the right, and went out the front door. He headed toward the parking lot and his warm waterbed.

Henry waited until his superior's footsteps had faded, then went back to work. He looked at the small mass of reddish material lying in the white basin, wondering if a simple staring at it would be more successful than all the probing, magnifying, and poking about. He wondered if he should—could—touch it. Just once. Surely it could do no harm? If he washed his hands thoroughly both before and after? After all, it was only a glob of flesh, blood, bone, and fiber —nothing that could harm him. Just one touch? That's all. Just to see what it felt like?

He could feel the excitement rising within him. He went to the sink and washed up with soap and hot water. He dried his hands off with toweling—clean, unused towelling. Then he went back to the table, turned up the light shining on the goo, and studied it more carefully.

He lifted his hand, moved it toward the glob, touched the glob with his index finger.

A stab of excruciating pain entered his mind, scorching pain—searing into every nerve, every cell, every synapse. Henry cried out. It was as if a needle had punctured his brain. God, it hurt. It *hurt.*

Henry felt his mind being wrenched into an alternate continuum. The entire life of Peterson raced by in a matter of *seconds.* Then he saw *horrifying* images: people herded together like concentration-camp inmates, people working— *slaving,* really—on some terrible contraption.

He saw Peterson's death.

And then—most terrible of all—something hideous reached out and *touched* his brain.

"Arrggghhh!"

Henry's mind was no longer his own.

Deep down in a subconscious part that still belonged to him, Henry knew he had brought it on himself.

Henry lifted the mass of organic and inorganic matter up in his hands and brought it over to the sink. He turned on both faucets full blast and let the water run over the substance and start to wash it down the drain.

He tried to resist. This substance was too important—their only link. He pulled his hands away from the faucet—the substance was *safe* again!—and walked back over to the basin. *Must resist.*

He put the substance back in the basin where it belonged.

Before Henry's eyes the substance began to *grow.*

It overflowed the basin, poured across the table, and dripped onto the floor.

It's only in your mind, Henry told himself. But it didn't do any good.

Henry was a boy again at Orchard Beach. He'd nearly drowned that day, his small browned body buffeted by the gigantic waves—his father'd pulled him out just in time. He'd had a fear of the water ever since.

The substance was filling the room and Henry was drowning in it.

This time his father wasn't there.

Harry Faulkin came home early in the

morning, slightly plastered and amusingly disheveled. He gave the doorman a generous smile, walked unsteadily toward the elevator bank, and got into one of the cars.

He pressed his floor number and leaned against the mirrored wall. Getting a good look at himself, he started patting his hair into place. He hated the way it looked when the wind got at it. He tore off his tie and stuffed it into the pocket of his jacket.

He got off the elevator, whistling while he walked to his door, and got out his keys. Once inside he took off all of his clothes and scattered them along the floor on the path to the bedroom.

He headed for the bathroom, where he brushed his hair carefully and gargled with mouthwash. He simply could not stand the thought of a toothbrush in his mouth at this hour. He pinched both cheeks, smiled at himself, then ran over to his bed and jumped in with a war-whoop. Tonight he was glad to be alone. All he wanted to do was sleep, sleep, sleep.

Where the hell was Steven? he wondered for the fiftieth time. He'd called his apartment over and over again. He'd found out from a friendly source that Vivian Jessup's death had been classified a suicide, but one of the reporters at the station was still interested in exploring the "missing young lover" angle. He'd wanted to set up a meeting for the two of them. He'd finally given up calling Steven and called a blonde instead. They'd partied half the night away. Oh well, tomorrow was another day.

As for me, he thought, *it's been a perfect evening*. Even the weather had turned out just the way it was supposed to. Not a sign of snow anywhere. Something had been affecting the weather but he was damned if he knew what it was.

"Harry Faulkin," he said out loud. "You have it made."

He crouched on his knees in the bed and grabbed the curtains drawn across the big picture window which separated the bed from the cold night air and eternity. He liked to wake up and be able to see out across the city without even lifting his head up off the pillow. He threw open the curtains for one last look at his fabulous Big Apple.

Snow. Everywhere. As far as the eye could see. Millions of flakes sprinkling their whiteness down, down, down into the grimy city streets.

Harry groaned.

⚫

When Steven finally got home he was bone-tired and frustrated. Ralph had insisted he go home—he was too exhausted to argue with him —when his operative showed up to watch George's apartment. There was nothing more to be done that night and he simply had to face it.

It was too late to call Andrea, though he would have loved to have spoken to her, to have heard her voice, found out once and for all where he stood with her. He wanted to tell her how much he liked Ralph. How he'd try, try anything, to keep them from splitting up for good. He'd take his nose out of his books and papers and blue-pencilled manuscripts and listen more to what she had to say. Hadn't that been her major complaint? One of a dozen, he supposed.

He looked through the mail he'd retrieved from the box in the foyer on his way in from the street. A magazine he subscribed to. A bill from a book club, a phone bill, and a postcard from an acquaintance vacationing in Greece. And another envelope with his name scrawled in pen across the front, no return address. It had been postmarked somewhere out in Long Island. This he would have to open immediately.

He'd never seriously entertained the possibility that Joey had been kidnapped—he was not a particularly wealthy man—but suppose someone had intended that Vivian Jessup pay Joey's ransom? Then decided to contact Steven after reading of Vivian's death? His fingers were trembling as he opened the envelope.

Inside was a letter on plain white typing paper. Someone had used a manual typewriter with a worn ribbon. Some of the individual letters hadn't printed at all, and it looked as if whoever had typed it had been in a hurry.

Mr. Everson: While I can I must type this for you. You are in great danger, I fear. I know you must be worrying about your brother. I can not phone you as your number is not listed. Please come talk with me. I will explain when you come. If I told you in this note you would think I was crazy, you would tear it up. I can not take that chance. Do not tell anyone that you have received this letter, I beg you. No one must know or you may very well be responsible for my death. For my sake, for your brother's sake, do not tell a soul. Simply come. To the address below. The night of October 19th. Come after midnight and make sure you are not followed. Do not come to the house nearby, just drive into Lot 15 of the beach, and walk out to the lifeguard station that is there. I will meet you inside.

There was no signature, but an "address"— simply the name of a town and a road within it —was printed in the bottom righthand corner. A crude map and directions were scribbled in pencil underneath.

Steven sat down on the sofa and read the letter over and over again, until he was no longer reading but trying to see between the lines, trying to decide how seriously he should take it.

He knew he had to take it seriously. Obviously he had no choice. "For your brother's sake," he had read. That must mean that some-where, somehow, Joey might still be alive.

He wanted to tell Ralph about it, but was afraid to. Yes, the whole thing *could* be a trap. A deserted lifeguard station in the middle of nowhere, with no one around to help him. If he told Ralph, brought him along for security, *how* would anyone know, really?

Yet he was afraid to take that chance. When it came to his brother he simply couldn't afford to be too rational. If the note said tell no one, he would tell no one. Not Ralph. Not Harry. Not

Andrea. *No one.* He would rent a car and drive out there by himself tomorrow night.

He still had doubts. Walking foolishly into a potential ambush, getting himself killed without even letting anyone know where he was going would not only be suicidal—it wouldn't help Joey in the slightest.

But he had to take that chance. He *had* to.

He decided to compromise. He would write Ralph a note and mail it to him. That way if anything should happen to him at the beach, Ralph would get the letter a day or two later, and would be able to proceed with the investigation. Even if Ralph dropped the case, the police would have some information to go on. *Someone* would know where he had been. That was better than nothing.

The alternative was for him to also disappear without a trace.

Maybe his letter to Ralph wouldn't accomplish anything. But it was all he could do. He would not take a chance and jeopardize his brother's life if he could help it. Not in a million years.

He reread the letter one more time. Then he sat down and wrote his note to Ralph. There—that seemed satisfactory.

He was too tired to keep his eyes open any longer.

Twenty minutes later he was fast asleep in bed.

At first Steven wasn't sure what had

awakened him. His stomach growling again? Street noises? The crazy battling couple in the apartment above? No, it was something different this time. A noise from outside his bedroom window—a cough, or a footfall. Someone was out in the alleyway beside the building.

He looked over at the window, at the light that shone in through the pane. Someone had walked in front of it, partially blocking out the light. Steven gasped as a person's shadow filled up his bedroom. *It was like a huge, frightening darkness blotting out light and hope.*

Then he saw the face pressed up against the pane, looking into the bedroom. A frightful, tormented face that chilled Steven to his very bones. His body started to quiver with horror. He couldn't even speak.

The face went away. Steven got up, still shaking, and forced himself to walk over to the window. He lowered the blinds with a crash and turned the slats up tight so that he could never see that face again.

But it was too late. He knew that he was in for another sleepless night.

For he had recognized the face, had seen it for an instant with utter clarity.

The man who had looked through the window had been dead for almost three years.

Steven's *father*.

PART IV

Saturday, October 19th

EIGHT

STEVEN DIDN'T REMEMBER at what hour he had finally fallen asleep, but it was daylight now and he didn't feel like sleeping any longer. One of these days it would catch up with him, this lack of sleep, but for the time being he would just have to settle for whatever catnaps he could manage. He looked at the clock. It was ten-thirty.

He went over to the window with some trepidation, still wary after last night's vision. That was all he could possibly call it. He lifted up the blind, letting in warm, bright sunlight which filled the bedroom with its glow. Had he really seen what he had thought he'd seen? Now, in the daytime, it all seemed so unreal. Yes, someone had peeked in through his window, but it couldn't have been the man he had at first thought it to be. Yet Steven could still see the face in front of him now, the face of his father.

It was impossible, he knew that. His father had been incinerated in a fiery crash, buried over two years ago in the earth. The dead didn't come back except in nightmares. Even now

Steven wondered if he'd genuinely been awake at the time he'd seen that figure staring in at him from the alleyway. Perhaps not. Or perhaps it had only been someone who closely *resembled* his late father. That had to be the explanation! Perhaps it had been someone who had information about Joey. Or maybe Ralph had assigned someone to keep an eye on Steven. He'd appreciate it if the watchdog was a little less conspicuous.

Funny how the mind would rationalize. Last night there had been no question about the face in the window. He'd almost been convinced that his father had returned from the dead in his— in Joey's—hour of need, a ghostly specter come to offer comfort.

Today there were a million doubts.

As he made coffee, his thoughts kept returning to his late-night peeper, no matter how hard he tried to concentrate on something else. He could barely bring himself to suggest that his father might still be alive. It was an insane notion, nothing a rational, sensible man would give credence to. His imagination was much too vivid.

He went out to check the mailbox. Nothing. He retraced his steps, walked along the hallway past his door, and went out the back exit to where the trash was kept. He stepped into the alleyway at the side of the building and strode down to his bedroom window. A tall man—like his father had been—could have stretched up on his toes and looked in with relative ease. Standing there now, looking in, Steve tried to imagine what he must have looked like to that stranger—rising from his bed, his mouth wide open in horror, unable to speak. *Who* had stood here last night? Steven saw his bed, unmade, disheveled; his dresser, the top drawer open, socks spilling out. The bookshelf on the far wall, with its dog-eared paperbacks tumbling in disarray. Someone had invaded his privacy, seen him alone, terribly alone. Someone had dared to stare with impunity into his haven against the world.

And Steven dreaded the moment when that someone might *enter* it.

That morning Eric Thorne and Hammond Gratis rode down to work together on the subway. There had been no more dreams or incidents the evening before; both had slept peacefully and well. Hammond complained that the sofa wasn't the most comfortable mattress in the world, but Eric had no intention of turning his bed over to him—it had been Hammond's idea in the first place that they "bunk" together. Still, Hammond wasn't really bad company.

"Did you see the snow last night?" Hammond asked as the train stopped at West 4th Street.

"Snow? What snow?"

"Well, obviously it didn't stick. But it was snowing last night, believe me. I got up around three-thirty to get a snack, and I chanced to look out the window. There it was! Detestable stuff. I'm glad it all melted away."

The train started to move again, its passengers cramped and uncomfortable. While there was no actual rush hour on Saturdays, it did get crowded on some lines in the early morning. Making way for a very large woman with two shopping bags who was trying to squeeze through to the other side, Eric stepped back and went over toward the window in the front door of the car. Hammond tried to follow, but his way was blocked. He yelled out above the rumbling noise. "And to think I could be home sleeping in bed!"

Eric smiled and looked away, concentrating on the ads above his head. He didn't mind going into the Institute on Saturday—he had some paperwork to catch up on, and this was the best time to do it. At least Hammond would be there to talk to. Although Gratis himself was already caught up with his work, he'd agreed to accompany him.

Having glanced over the written spiels for coffee, soda, fresh chicken parts, and depositories, Eric checked to look out the front-door window. He hadn't realized that this car was the first one of the train. He liked to watch as the train moved forward, the tracks raced by underneath his feet, and the little yellow lightbulbs along the wall blurred together into one long yellow stripe. A distant station—at first just a mere hint of faraway light—would begin to take on form and substance as the train approached it.

They were coming toward Broadway and Lafeyette now, and from this distance the station ahead looked like little more than a white rectangle getting larger and larger as they advanced. *A white rectangle getting larger and larger as they advanced.* Eric stared out the window, his body rocking back and forth as the cars swayed uneasily from side to side. Swaying, *vibrating.*

"Oh my God!" Eric said it out loud, but softly, his words inaudible even to those nearest.

The white rectangle was coming closer and closer.

Eric's body swayed back and forth. He turned away from the window and looked around him, seeing the other people packed in the car, their pained faces, perfumed bodies, their tired, desperate looks. Swaying, swaying. Each of them holding on to the vertical bars above their heads, the horizontal bars which went from floor to ceiling, or the swinging metal "straps" which hung from the iron bar overhead. Not daring to touch one another. *Flashes of what he'd seen in the trance shot through Eric's head and he imagined his fellow passengers naked, writhing and twisting in agony.*

The rectangle of the station loomed larger now, until it enveloped the train. The train roared into the station and came to a halt as it approached the other end of the platform.

Some of the passengers began to exit.

"Eric. Eric? Are you coming?"

"Wha—" Eric turned and saw that Hammond was at the door, preventing it from closing with the bulk of his body.

"Come on now, I can't hold it forever."

Eric stepped outside. The door wheezed shut and the train pulled out of the station.

"Daydreaming?" Hammond asked.

Eric only smiled, snapped himself back to normal; and followed Hammond out of the subway.

The town of Tanton had once been a thriving community, a summer resort for the rich and the fashionable. But the rich and the fashionable had discovered other, more exciting places to go, like the Hamptons and Fire Island. There was no choice but for Tanton to open its beaches to the public. The location's primary appeal was that it was less crowded than the other, better-known bathing spots such as Jones Beach, which was further up the shore and closer to the city. Tanton made its money from parking fees and concession stands. Unappetizing hot dogs for $1.50. Soda for 85 cents.

There were few full-time residents in Tanton. Most of the houses near the shore were owned by upper-middle-class families which used them only for summer homes. The yellow house across from Lot 15 had been bought for that purpose by its owner, Gregory Olsen, but since his retirement he'd lived in the house year round. The house had two stories and both front and back porches. It was not especially appealing to the eye from the outside, but inside was tastefully furnished with attractive and expensive pieces.

On this cool, windy day in October, Olsen—an

elderly man with gray hair, a thin face, and pallid complexion—sat before the fireplace, a goblet of brandy in his hand. He stared continuously out the front window. He had been sitting in his easy chair since early morning, his eyes on the road outside, always watching—though for what he couldn't say.

The man was living in terror.

Olsen swallowed the rest of the brandy, feeling its delicious warmth, sadly realizing that it did nothing to take away the chill. Nothing would. Not the fire. Not the blanket which he'd draped over his body. Not the brandy. He should have felt safe, but he didn't.

He sat there and shivered, waiting for the hour of midnight. The witching hour.

How had he come to this? he wondered. Why had it happened? It was such a *strain*, but he tried hard to remember. Peterson, Jessup, all the others drafted into an unholy alliance with an inhuman master. All of them working together to make the master safe and sound, free from contamination, illness, all of them busily doing its bidding until the day that work on its great monstrous project—*submission, subservience*—could start.

As they grew old they were replaced by younger, stronger people in the firm, then—to their surprise—permitted to retire and live out the rest of their days in comparative freedom— just as they would have done had the master not appeared.

But there was a catch—the master was still *one* with them, still residing there, like a malignant cancer, in their minds. It knew always what they were doing and thinking, and *they* knew what *it* was doing too. Still, with some concentration—and while its "thoughts" were occupied elsewhere—they could act independently, do and think things that might be interpreted as dangerous and heretical.

In such a moment had Olsen typed the note to Steven Everson, mailed it to him at his New York address, and hoped and prayed it would reach him. He had known he wouldn't have time to type out the whole horrible story, to warn him about his brother—he could only hope that if Steven showed up at the appointed hour he, Olsen, would have the strength and fortitude to tell him everything he needed to know.

Lord, it was a nightmare.

Get Out Of My Brain! he would scream for hours at a time.

Olsen didn't live on the island of Manhattan. He was an old man, had lived his alloted lifespan—why did he care what happened, first to those in New York City and then elsewhere all over the world? Why couldn't he just put up with the occasional scanning in his head until it became a pleasant, comforting buzz in the background like the sound of his clock or refrigerator? Why didn't he sit back and enjoy his old-man pleasures and solitude until death—a *natural* death—came to claim him? Why tempt fate?

He had such a horror of messy deaths, bloody deaths, people killed in car wrecks, falling out of windows—*an absolute terror of mutilation*—

and falling in front of trains like Vivian Jessup . . .

Poor Vivian, he thought. *I thought I'd be safe out here on Long Island. Away from* the center *of it all. It thought I was just a harmless old man. But am I safe, will I be safe, if it finds out?*

Why couldn't I have stayed a harmless old man?

Why couldn't I have not *cared?*

Because I am not that way, he thought with some sadness and pride.

He sipped his brandy and waited for the night to come.

And for his appointment with Steven Everson.

His appointment with a terriby destiny.

Valerie Horton stepped into the office of the Blue Dot Taxi Center and looked around for someone who could help her. The room was of medium size, cramped with desks, a table, several wooden chairs, and pile upon pile of old newspapers and magazines. The only living things in the room with her were several cockroaches and two or three flies.

Someone stepped through the door behind her. "Can I help you?" asked a squat, ugly man with a face like kneaded dough. He had pockmarked cheeks and a cigarette clenched between thick lips. Before she could answer, he said, "If you're looking for work, forget it. We don't need no drivers."

Wonderful. Valerie said, "I'm not looking for

work. I'd simply like some information."

"What kind of information?"

"I'd like to know if a man named George Forrance was ever in your employ. You *are* the manager of the firm?"

"Yes, that's right."

"Good. Then you *would* know if Mr. Forrance had been employed here?"

"Yeah. He was here." He brushed past her on the way toward his cluttered, beer-stained desk. "But that was a long time ago. I don't know whatever became of him."

"Did you know him well?"

"He was a loner. No one really knew him. Except for Dave. They used to go out for a beer now and then. Me, I couldn't stand the fellow." He leered. "Was he a 'friend' of yours?"

"Sorry to disappoint you," Valerie smiled curtly, "but he wasn't."

"What's the story then? Why are you looking for him?"

"I just need information from him." Valerie toyed with the idea of showing him her I.D. card; often people were impressed with detectives, especially private eyes, and opened up in order to help. But she wasn't too sure about this turkey. "What about this Dave? Is he here now?"

"He's out on assignment."

"Could you contact him for me? If he came here and picked me up I could talk to him while we rode. I assure you, it will be a more than decent fare."

The manager left the office to speak to the dispatcher, who contacted Dave over his radio. Valerie sat down on a bench in the corner of the garage and waited. She resisted the urge to light a cigarette. She'd cut down if it killed her.

Valerie was an attractive thirty-five year-old with short black hair, hazel eyes, and a soft, feminine face that belied her unsentimental toughness. She'd worked with Ralph Andrews for several years, first as his secretary when it was a "hole in the wall" outfit, then as his assistant, and now as his most important operative.

Before that she'd had a brief turn as a police-woman—before it was fashionable—mostly because her late father had been one and the thought of being one herself was rather appeal-ling. Ten years ago the department had not been as tolerant of women officers as it was now—she'd quit early on as a reaction to the not-so-subtle patronization and condescension and when she realized her duties made her more of a babysitter and occasional decoy than an officer of the law. That was changing nowadays, but too late for her to take advantage of it.

Anyway, she liked working for Ralph. And just last week he'd told her he was going to make her his partner in the agency. Andrews and Horton. She liked the sound of it. Well, she deserved it. She'd worked hard.

But for now her *legs* were taking the strain, literally as well as figuratively. Ralph had previous commitments to take care of today, so that left her with the job of tracking down George Forrance's background, not to mention his current whereabouts. The Blue Dot Taxi

Company, where a guy named "Porky" said George had once worked, was the first stop. And if this didn't work she'd have to talk to this Lina person and find out more about her "boyfriend," Brock.

Fifteen minutes later her reverie was interrupted when one of the firm's ugly, unwashed taxis pulled up at the sidewalk. A door was flung open and Valerie got inside.

'Just drive around while we talk," she told the driver, a middle-aged man with red hair and a paunch, "and I can give you a destination later."

"Okay, lady. The boss told me you were interested in George Forrance. Friend of yours?"

"Not really. I'm a private investigator. To help out my client, I'll need as much information as I can gather on Forrance, his friends, any other places where he worked or lived. Spots where he used to hang out."

"When he worked for Blue Dot, he and I used to go across the street all the time to the Mayfair Cafe. It was a nice bar, until the neighborhood went rotten, if you know what I mean."

Valerie had almost lit a cigarette before she remembered her vow and shoved it back in the box. "Can you tell me anything about George's family or his close friends?" She watched the man ahead carefully, studying his crew cut and hard-looking face, realizing with some surprise that she found him attractive.

"I don't think he had any. He did mention his parents once or twice, come to think of it. They lived in Brooklyn too. To be honest with ya, babe, I don't remember where. George hardly ever said anything that was worth remembering."

"What did he talk about when you two went out for beers?"

"Girls. The job. How much he hated the boss. Stuff like that." He turned onto a sidestreet absently, one that was lined with lots of trees that were losing their leaves as the winter officially drew closer. "He and I weren't really friends, y'understand. It was just that we were the only two *single* guys. Everybody else would go home to the wife. We just had a beer or two and then, then we'd split. We never socialized any more than that. Once we'd planned on double-dating, but I don't think he could get a date. A loner type, y'know what I mean?"

"Yes. Did he talk with any of the other regulars at the Mayfair, or the bartender perhaps? Would it be worthwhile for me to talk to them?"

"The bartenders keep changing, babe. The whole place has a different crowd now. I wouldn't suggest it."

"Did you say earlier that he had *told* you where his parents lived?"

"He did mention it, but I can't remember, it was so long ago. Never really paid much attention to what the guy said—he was just, y'know, a drinking companion."

"I'd be appreciative if you could remember." Valerie noticed the complexion of the neighborhood was changing as they drove into the thick of the residential district. It didn't look quite so *hopeless* anymore. The children were less troubled, the lawns better kept, the sound of laughter less forced, hollow, and cruel than it often was elsewhere.

"Let's see," Dave was saying. "I remember one time . . . we were sitting in the Mayfair Bar. He had to leave early just so he could go to supper with his folks. Yeah, that was it. I asked him how far he had to go. I can see him right in front of me—"

"What did he say?"

"Hell. I just can't remember."

"Can you drive me back to the Mayfair? Maybe someone who works there can give me some information."

"Whatever you say, babe." Dave made a U-turn and they drove back in the direction from which they'd come.

They reached the bar in twenty minutes. "Care to have a beer with me?" she asked the man, telling herself she only wanted to try and get more information out of him.

He was startled. "Uh, *would* I? You're on, babe."

"The name's Val." She handed him the fare and a generous tip.

"Okay, Val. And thanks."

Valerie didn't know if Dave was *still* one of the only single guys at Blue Dot, and she wasn't sure she cared. There was something about the man that she liked—or was it simply that certain animal charm of the blue-collar worker? *Grow up!* she told herself. Yet couldn't a truly liberated woman have anything she wanted?

The Mayfair was a nice enough place—if you liked dumps—but had obviously seen better days. There was a semicircular bar and a small dining area in an adjoining room. A barmaid, young, pretty and half-asleep, came over to serve them as they slid onto two bar stools.

"Two beers, please," Valerie said. A few minutes later the barmaid came back with two bottles.

"Could we have glasses, please?" Valerie asked.

"Oh, sure, just a minute." The woman went away again and came back with two sopping-wet glasses. Then she filled them both up with beer from the same bottle.

"Kinda sleepy, isn't she?" Dave said.

Val smiled. "Is it coming back to you at all? What George said—about where his parents lived?"

"Give it a few minutes. Let me wet my whistle and I'll let you know."

Val watched him as he drained half the glass, wiped his mouth with the back of his hand, and turned about in his seat to study the place.

"Haven't changed the inside much," he said. "Still pretty much the same. I can remember that we were sitting down there at the end of the bar when he said that he was in a hurry, had to leave soon so he could make it to his folks' place on time for dinner. Right down there." He scrunched up his face and tried to remember George Forrance's exact words. He put his hand on his forehead again and tried to reconstruct the event; now and then he would mutter phrases which were hard for Valerie to make out, as if bits and pieces of the conversation were coming slowly back to mind.

"How's it coming?" she asked.

"I remember I asked him where they lived, and he told me the subway stop. What the hell was it. Wish I could remember." The darling was really trying, Val thought with some amusement.

"Dave, what are the subway lines that run through this area, or near it?" She'd taken a cab from Manhattan herself. Her firm's cars were all in use.

"Let's see. We got the IND lines and the BMT. The B train runs by a block away. He had to take that first, I remember. Wait a minute. He said he had to backtrack if he took the subway. He had to take the B going towards Manhattan, and then transfer to . . . to the F. That's it. The F to Macdonald Avenue. Funny I should remember that now. He said his folks lived on Macdonald Avenue near Church."

"Near a church, you said?"

"No. Church *Avenue*. It cuts across Macdonald. It's a stop on the F train. Macdonald and Church Avenues."

"And that's where he was heading that night? To his parents on Macdonald Avenue?"

"That's what he said."

"Why couldn't he just drive over in his cab?"

"You kiddin'? We don't own these things. And he didn't have no car of his own. Say, now I know why he talked so much about the subway and the long ride he'd have to take—he was hopin' I'd save him the trouble and drive him

240

over myself. Fat chance."

"Well, Dave, thank you very much." She took an extra five-dollar bill out of her wallet and handed it to him. "This is for your trouble."

"Keep it," he said. "Your company was all I needed." He leaned in closer and whispered, "Though if you wanted to give me your phone number I wouldn't complain."

Valarie smiled and handed him her card. "Give me a ring," she said. "Any time." Her mother had always called her a brassy girl.

Dave looked like a little boy who'd just been told he was getting a pony for Christmas. "Uh, don't you want me to drive you over there? It'll take less time. My treat, babe."

"Thanks, but I have other matters to attend to before I continue my investigation." Actually Val was afraid if she spent another minute with the guy she'd talk him into spending the afternoon with her. And she had *work* to do.

"Okay. Thanks for the beer." He put her card in his shirt pocket. "And for this. You'll be hearing from me, babe."

"I hope so, 'babe,' " She winked. "Goodbye, Dave."

She got up, put on her coat, and walked briskly out of the bar.

Ernest Hendon was sound asleep in his office when his secretary knocked on his door and accidentally woke him up.

"I'm sorry, sir. I—I didn't mean to—"

"Quite all right, Joan. How would it look if

241

someone else walked in and saw the head of the department snoozing in his office during work hours."

"You must be exhausted. I'll get you some coffee."

"No, Joan. No. I'm going home early today. I always hated working on Saturdays. I just have to accept the fact that I'm not going to get anything done. You have those reports typed up for me yet?"

"Yes, here they are." The middle-aged woman bent down and placed the papers on his desk.

"Thank you very much, Joan. I'll take these home with me."

"You poor thing," she clucked sympathetically. "I feel awful about Henry too. Such a young man."

"Yes, he was. And it was awful—is awful. I just can't understand it. Maybe I feel partly responsible. I left him alone because I was too tired to go on. Maybe if I'd stayed . . ."

"There's no use going on like that," she gently chided. "Who expected such a young man to get a heart attack? It could have happened at any time, I'm sure."

"I know that, but it doesn't help." He leaned back in his chair, tapping his fingers on the desk blotter in that way of his. "That'll be all, Joan," he said. "I'll be leaving in a few minutes. No more calls, okay?"

"All right, Mr. Hendon. Good night." She left the room.

At least someone else had notified Henry's parents, Ernest thought. He had met them once.

An elderly couple. Very sweet people. A small, friendly mother who was so proud of her son's new position. His father, also tiny, beaming as he looked around the important place where his Henry worked. What was left for them now?

Ernest couldn't help but think—insanely— that something Henry had seen, learned, last night while working on the stuff from Room 919 had given him his "heart attack." That look of horror still frozen on his face . . . nothing could have erased it. The boy had died of *fright*.

What had happened last night? What had Henry learned? There was nothing in his notes . . . .

Ernest got up, left his office and walked into the refrigeration room next to Laboratory A. He opened the door of the third metal locker and looked inside at the small mound of reddish material that someone had scraped off the wall of the Berkley Arms Hotel earlier in the week.

He couldn't take his eyes off it.

What, if anything, did it mean?

Telly's Tavern was pretty crowded for a Saturday afternoon. An old-style Irish pub, Telly's was frequented by lively middle-aged regulars, some of whom seemed to spend every waking hour within its confines. Lina Hobler sat at a table in the corner, half-blitzed, at a point where all the events of the preceding days had faded away into fantasy. She thought little, if at all, about Steven or George. Instead she sat and thought and thought about dear, departed

Brock. Departed from her bed and board, that is. She would never allow herself to think that he was dead, at least not while she was drunk and had money in her pocket for another scotch and soda. So much better than beer, she always said. Besides, Telly's beer was nothing but "piss-water."

Lina was still musing about Brock, minding her own business, when *they* came in, two of the neighborhood children—"brats," she called them. Actually the young man and the woman with him were both in their early twenties.

Lina had never been fond of young people. Even in her days of fame and triumph, her fans had always been grownups, serious, *learned* adults who could appreciate great art. She sneered at the two "brats" and went back to dreaming about Brock.

Booze and sex, Lina thought in her archaic manner, booze and sex made a woman bad. She raised her glass in a silent toast. *Let's hear it for booze and sex.*

Lina looked up and saw that the young couple was kissing, just smooching away at the bar, oblivious to the others around them. How Lina hated that girl. So young, so free, able to enjoy her private lusts in public without shame. What shame it had been for Lina when she was that age; what "shame" it still was. How dare that young brat have such fun!

The young man went over to the jukebox and put on some music. Telly, in an attempt to draw in a younger crowd, had put some of those new "punk rock" songs on the old nickelodeon. Lina hated them and grimaced as one of them started to play. The boy leaned against the bar and cheered the young woman on while she danced. She was dressed in tight pants and one of those blouses that ended at the navel and tied in front, barely covering her generous bosom. *What an outfit for winter!* Lina thought. Thrusting out her chest, wiggling her behind and twirling in small semicircles, the woman frolicked merrily to the music, innocent of the effect she was having on some of the patrons, though some of the leering male faces made obvious what they were thinking.

Lina watched. And waited.

Finally the song ended. The woman went back over to her boyfriend and gave him a quick kiss. During this pause Lina suddenly shouted at the top of her lungs: "We don't want to hear no more of that lousy boogie music in this bar, girlie!"

A few people looked up from their drinks or conversation. The young lady said nothing. Her boyfriend spoke as the second song started. It was a slower number.

"You talkin' to her?" he asked.

"Yes. I'm talking to the brat with her stupid punk music. We don't like it in this bar, girlie!"

"Shut up, you old gorilla!" the young woman hollered.

"She's drunk. Forget her," the boy said.

"I don't care if she's drunk. She doesn't have to talk to me that way, Eddie."

People turned away, disinterested. They'd seen enough arguments in Telly's already. The best fights—and the funniest—were between two drunks. Then a good battle between two sober guys belting each other all over the bar. But a fight between a drunk and somebody sober was nothing but a bore. The sober participant was too inhibited to start anything, making allowances for the other party's condition, and the drunk was too woozy to do much more than repeat the same obnoxious things indefinitely until someone took a swing at him. Generally, it ended with the drunk passing out or the sober one leaving the bar in disgust.

"Sally," the boyfriend said, "don't worry about it. Just dance."

"I don't want to see Sally dance," Lina bellowed. "This is *my* bar. I don't have to sit here and listen to that crap and watch your ugly girlfriend dance."

Sally, though not ugly, didn't like it even being implied that she was. She stepped up close to the table where Lina was. "Look you fat old whore, why don't you just keep your fuckin' mouth shut!"

Lina sat up straight in her chair. No little girl was going to talk to her that way. "Don't flap your tits in front of me you stupid little bitch," she hollered. "I'll hit you so hard you'll remember it when you're eighty."

"Is that how old *you* are?"

The next moment Lina picked up a half-full bottle of beer and chucked it in the woman's direction. It bounced painfully off of Sally's forehead, its contents spattering onto Eddie's white shirt. Two birds with one stone, Lina thought triumphantly.

When the bottle hit the floor, it shattered into pieces, alerting the patrons that a fight was indeed in progress. There was always that exception to the rule, after all. Telly, who had been switching channels on the TV set, turned around and screamed, "Hey! *Heyah!* Watch it down there!"

Enraged, Sally grabbed Lina by the hair and started pulling her out from behind the table. Wincing with pain, Lina flapped her arms above her head, trying to connect. She managed to land a solid blow on the young woman's neck. Holding onto her hair more tightly, Sally pummeled the older woman until Lina slumped down onto the floor in a heap.

Telly was both manager and owner and he disliked bar fights, if only because of the damage they caused. But in some cases, when everyone was enjoying a brawl, watching some creep get his comeuppance, he didn't step in unless it was absolutely necessary. He might have gone to Lina's aid had she not made the mistake of resisting his advances a few months before. As far as he was concerned, she could fend for herself. Besides, he was having a good time watching this one. So was everyone else.

Lina could feel the throbbing pain in her head even through the natural anesthetic of alcohol. She reached up and felt her scalp, wondering if the girl had torn any of the hair out by the routes. She looked up and saw that the bitch and her boyfriend were back at the bar, laughing uproariously at her plight. She picked herself up and pretended that she was going to head for the john. Instead, she quickly stepped over to the bar, lifted her right hand above her shoulder, and swung it viciously across Sally's face.

The sound of the slap was heard above the laughter, the talking, the music, and whoever it was who was puking in the bathroom.

The silence that followed served as vivid counterpoint. The music had stopped. Eddie acted first and thrust out his arm, shoving Lina backward, but she recovered her balance before she could topple to the floor again. Sally picked up her glass and threw its contents into Lina's face. Grabbing Eddie's empty beer bottle, she pounded Lina's body with it.

Lina twisted around, latched onto Sally's wrist, and shook it violently until the bottle crashed to the floor. This was only a delaying action. Lina was simply too giddy to adequately defend herself. Spurred on by the crowd, Sally bent Lina's arm behind her back, and pushed her toward the door. Eddie held it open for them.

Outside, Sally threw Lina down on the sidewalk and gave her a few kicks in the stomach. Eddie spit in Lina's face. "C'mon, let's get outa here," he said. Sally took his hand and they ran down the street, giggling and skipping like a couple of nine-year-olds.

Temporarily concerned, Telly came out just to see how Lina was. From her vantage point, Lina saw this big, upside-down, mustachioed

Teddy Bear hovering above her in the doorway. "Who is it?" she asked.

"Why don't you go home to Brock?" Telly said.

"Brock? Is that you?"

"Go on home, Lina. Sober up. Brock's waiting for you."

And she picked herself up and ran all the way home, for all the world believing that Telly had actually meant what he'd just said.

John Albright did not have to work on Saturday.

He stayed in bed the entire day, not wanting to get up and face the reality of his world. The phone did not ring, nor did the doorbell. It was as if Gloria and Bobby had ceased to exist.

He got out of bed at five-thirty to move his bowels.

Feeling hungry afterwards, he went into the kitchen and mechanically made himself some ham and eggs. He washed it down with chocolate milk. As he wiped his mouth with a napkin, his eyes went from the brown stain on the white cloth over to the note that Gloria had left him the day before. He studied it again.

How could this have happened to him?

He went to the phone, wondering if he should call his mother-in-law. He decided against it. He'd be damned if he'd track the woman down; Gloria would have to call *him*.

What if she wasn't able to? He hadn't considered that.

What if he started a search for her and she and Billy were found safe and sound in a motel room or with some other relative? How would he look then? Like a fool, that's how, an idiot who didn't even *know* that his wife had left him, a dope unable to accept the truth.

He went into the living room and lay down on the sofa. Hundreds of faces and names swam through his consciousness; he couldn't keep them away if he tried. Hundreds of missing wives and vanished husbands. Little boys who'd run away from home. Children who'd gone and disappeared. Where *were* they all? All the mommies and daddies, all the kids? Where had they gone?

Where was Gloria? Where was his son?

For the first time in a long time he started to weep, uncontrollably.

And then, somewhere in the center of his tears, like a natural cave hidden behind a foamy, cascading waterfall of brine, he saw a portal, a crevice, a tiny slice of knowledge revealed.

He *remembered*.

Those dreams he'd been having, those nightmares . . .

They weren't dreams.

It all came back to him in a rush:

He went into his superior's office with his files and data, went in to confront him with the alarming statistics about New York City's diminishing population—all those missing persons—and his boss just smiled at him, a strange haunted grin that said so much, said nothing.

250

"Come with me, John," his boss said.

They drove to a warehouse not far from the Bowery.

"I'm taking you to the committee," his boss said. "They'll explain everything."

The committee? Why didn't the man just explain? Why the secrecy? Why the drive?

Inside the warehouse they were waiting for John and his superior.

They led the two down a hole ... into a tunnel ... into a chamber. Fetid, furtive shapes ran through the shadows. How long the trip took John could not remember. There was something beyond a door they wanted John to see. Data banks. Computers. Hardware and software. And over in the corner, in the darkness, a living, breathing thing that seemed to command them all.

They hooked John up to cables and electrodes. They jabbed him in the arm with a hypodermic needle. What was spooky was that they all acted as if this was a normal, everyday occurrence, as if the thing watching from the corner was the most natural thing in the world.

In the middle of the process—John's treatment—the thing in the corner reached out an appendage and probed him. Then the thing's mind reached out and probed John's brain, made a mental link with him that nothing, that no one, could sever.

"You may not remember any of this," they told him later. "Some don't. Others—the more intelligent ones—remember everything or most of it at some point. Be smart. Don't fight it. Do

*what you're told. You'll know what to do. If you
fight it you'll get a warning—headaches, the
shakes—and if you* still *resist, you'll die.*

"Don't be a hero," they told him.

Now he knew why the Joey Everson case had
bothered him. Somehow Joey Everson's disappearance was connected to that thing under the
ground, to the tubes and computers and data
banks. He'd looked in Vivian Jessup's apartment that day after dismissing Joey's brother,
not even sure of why he was doing it—now he
knew the answer to that too. Vivian Jessup had
also been involved—his subconscious had
always been aware of that, linked as it was to
the computers and the thing . . .

He also knew why he'd had so many headaches, fevers, chills.

Even now his body was trembling—a vibrating hum ran all through him. *It* knew that *he*
knew; that he had achieved total awareness.
And it was *wary.*

Just as Albright reached the conclusion that
his problems with Gloria were as nothing
compared to *this,* he wondered:

Did it take Gloria too?

Did it take my wife and little boy?

And how on earth could *anyone* fight against
it?

NINE

VALERIE GOT OFF the B train at 9th Street and 4th Avenue and walked down the wide corridor that led to the F. She saw an unoccupied phone booth and stepped inside. Slipping a quarter into the slot and dialing, she studied herself in the mirrored surface beneath the buttons of the phone. A little haggard from lack of sleep, but acceptable.

The receptionist at the Andrew Agency answered, recognized Valerie's voice, and connected her immediately to her boss. "What's up, Val?" Ralph asked.

"Well, you sound jovial. You must have had a good lunch."

"Didn't you?"

"Just a half a beer with a taxi driver."

"Dig up anything?"

"Yes, I found out that his parents live somewhere on—"

"Macdonald Avenue."

She should have known he'd get it before she did. "Ah, all that work for nothing. They were listed with *some* agency, I suppose."

"Correct. They're also deceased. However—"

"I know, I know. I'll go talk to their neighbors about George."

"At least you won't have to go around knocking on doors just to find out where the Forrances lived."

"No, I'll just have to go around knocking on doors to find out if anybody's ever heard of them. Okay, what's the address?"

"Paper and pen ready?"

She rummaged through her purse. "Shoot."

"Mr. and Mrs. Elliot Forrance, wife's name Betsy." He gave her the complete street address.

"Great. Oops—here comes my train. Bye."

"Bye."

She got into the first car, which was quite crowded, and found a seat in the back.

Four stops later she got off at Church Avenue and climbed up to street level. She found herself next to a stationery store and newsstand. A gang of teenagers were loitering in the area, sipping bottles of soda pop. *At least it isn't whiskey,* she thought.

Crossing the street, she walked down the avenue toward Ditmas. In the distance she could see where the underground subway broke through the surface and became an elevated line. There were fences on both sides where the tracks sliced through the middle of the street and rose thirty feet in the air. One of the buildings on the right side of the avenue was the former home of the Forrances.

If the address Ralph had given her was the correct one, it was a certainty no one lived there

254

any more. It was an empty lot, just a space between two other buildings. The weeds were tall enough to scrape the windows of the houses they were sandwiched between. Rusty bicycles and old, gutted furniture were scattered throughout the overgrowth.

She rang the doorbell of the house on the left. A young woman came to the door, hair in curlers, a cigarette dangling from her mouth. She looked very busy. "Yes," she said, her voice surprisingly mellifluous.

"I'm sorry to bother you," Valerie said from the stoop. "I was looking for information about the people that used to live next door."

"Them? They moved out two months ago. The place is empty."

"No. No, I wasn't referring to the house across the lot, I was referring to the lot itself. There used to be a house there. The Forrance home."

"I think I remember hearing about them." A little boy came to the door and peeked out from behind his mother's knee. "But that house burned down even before we moved here."

"How long ago was that?"

"I'm not sure when the fire happened, but we moved here about five years ago. What is it, Tommy?" The boy did not reply, but stood transfixed, staring at Valerie with a cute, bewildered expression on his face.

"Well, thank you very much then. I'll try else-where." She gave the boy a wink, then smiled warmly at the woman. "Goodbye."

"So long." The mother grabbed the boy by the

arm, then pulled him in with her as she closed the door. From the back of the house, a baby was crying. An older man was hollering something about the TV.

There but for the grace of God go I, Valerie thought.

A train rumbled up from below the earth and sped past her, rushing up the tracks and fading into the distance. She heard the screech of its wheels as it stopped at the station at Ditmas Avenue.

She would talk to a few more neighbors. Though instinct told her they'd tell her nothing. Valerie had learned to trust her instinct.

And she couldn't shake the feeling that the disappearances of Joseph Everson, George Forrance, and Lina's boyfriend Brock were just the tip of a very large iceberg.

Eric finished up his extra work early in the afternoon and both he and Hammond were home by four o'clock. Eric didn't mind working on Saturdays occasionally, and when he did he usually made provisions for an interesting evening—except this weekend. As much as he liked the man, Eric could think of few people he'd rather not spend a Saturday night with besides Hammond. While he was an excellent, if at times overbearing, conversationalist, he was not exactly what one would call a "fun date." He was disinterested in both movies and the theater and seldom went out socializing. Eric thought of leaving him home alone, but felt that it might seem a bit rude. He resigned himself to an evening of rest and relaxation, hardly what he had been looking forward to.

Hammond prepared the dinner all by himself, mixing up an interesting chicken dish with an unusual array of vegetables. He sauteed an appetizing bunch of creamy brown mushrooms with onions and peppers, and prepared stuffed baked potatoes as if he had missed his calling. Pouring white wine liberally into the chicken, he developed a scrumptious sauce.

"Did one of your ex-wives teach you how to prepare all this?"

"I expect so. I picked up the recipe from somewhere, but I can't remember. I've always had a passion for chicken, no matter how it's prepared. If I saw a new recipe in a magazine, I would clip it out."

"Well, it's excellent. Congratulations. In fact, I think I'll appoint you head cook."

"And just what does that mean?"

"It means that you get to prepare all the meals, you lucky fellow you."

"Well then," Hammond said, a little smile playing at the edges of his mouth, "I think that I could do quite well without such a dubious honor."

"Suit yourself." Eric said as he placed some of the succulent chicken on his tongue. "But I must admit this is delicious."

"Well, don't enjoy it too much. You may not get these kind of meals for too long. If you don't have another psychic experience soon, I'm going to pack up my bags and go home."

"That a promise?"

"I am here to observe, not to cook. Seriously, though, I wonder if my presence has something to do with the *absence* of the psychic stimuli."

"Hammond, you've only been here two days. Not even that long."

"I know, I know. I should give it awhile, I suppose."

"Yes. And if I may be blunt, I am really not looking forward to having *another* experience like I had Wednesday night."

"Well, my presence here is just a precaution anyway. Hopefully nothing will happen and I can get back to my own bed and board."

"I know you better than that, Hammy. You're dying to get to the bottom of this."

"Not any more than you are. And not at your expense." He stuffed a forkful of mushrooms into his mouth. "Oh, I don't know." He waited until he could swallow the masticated vegetables. "I guess I've always wanted an opportunity to meet—to contact—to touch in some way the great force, that great mystic presence. It will only be perceived by a powerful mind, a mind like yours. You must be my intermediary, for I cannot speak the language, as it were. I haven't the advanced psychic abilities that you have."

"Hammond, I don't want to be an intermediary between you and God, thank you."

"Not God. I don't mean God, necessarily."

"Pardon me. You mean the Devil then?"

"No, not Satan either. I'm not sure. Why, if I knew, I wouldn't be here. No, what I'm talking

258

about is a power, a certain kind of—irresistible —power, a *feeling* almost. I can't quite describe it. But there is a barrier between us and it, a very sturdy barrier, and even when it penetrates that barrier, it can only communicate with a strong, extraordinary mind. Such as yours."

"Why Hammond, I do believe that's the first compliment you've ever given me." He spooned some vegetables onto his plate.

"It's not flattery, my friend. A mind like yours is capable of also breaching that barrier, of reaching out to the power, of stripping it of its secrets."

"Hammond, what if this 'power' of yours is one of the evil forces you were talking about the other day?"

"That's a chance you'd have to take, but wouldn't it be worth it? Aren't you willing to take the chance? To open yourself up to it? To allow yourself to receive the message?

Eric had to smile at Hammond's amusing histrionics. "If you're expecting me to willingly go through what I did on Wednesday night, the answer is no."

"We are scientists. We must take risks."

"Easy for you to say. A few minutes ago you said that you didn't want to get to the bottom of this if it was at my expense, correct?"

"But I'm not sure it would be. A little discomfort, a little fear perhaps. But what more? What really happened to you that night? Nothing! Besides, I'd be here to protect you, to keep you from harming yourself, to prevent that—loneliness—from closing in. That's the important thing."

Eric wiped his lips with a napkin and cleared his throat. "After what I told you about what I went through, why would you think that whoever or whatever you're talking about would be benevolent or not capable of affecting *both* of us?"

"But I'm not a sensitive. Just a researcher. How could I be affected?"

"Why not? You're not immune to a psychic suggestion or attack. If anything, you might be more defenseless than I. Maybe you can't communicate like I can, but you are still susceptible. You can still become a *victim*."

Hammond waved his arm in disdain. "Eric, you've been reading too many comic books."

"Comic books, nothing! Are you telling me that I don't know my own field?"

"Of course not. Now don't be angry."

"How could I be angry at anyone who makes chicken taste this good?"

"That's the spirit. Would you care for some wine?"

"Yes, thank you." Hammond poured a glass for Eric, then for himself. Neither of them were sippers.

"So, are you seriously suggesting that I try to make contact somehow with the force I tapped into on Wednesday?"

"Yes."

"It's not as easy as all that, you know."

"Perhaps not. But maybe you've been guarding against it all this time without even being aware of it. Let your guard down, Eric . . . relax . . . and it will come to *you*."

Eric used his napkin to sop up some droplets of spilled wine. "Hammond, why don't you explain to me exactly what this 'force' you keep talking about is supposed to *be*?"

"I only wish I could. I'm not sure."

"Well if I *had* to pick a name for it, I'd have to say that what affected me on Wednesday night was definitely one of your *evil* forces."

Hammond seemed excited by the prospect. "But can you be sure?"

"Hammond, I already told you how it made me feel. What happened to me was *not good*, let me tell you."

"Maybe you misunderstood it, or simply had a negative reaction. I—I—" He sputtered, trying to find the right words. "Maybe you were *too* susceptible, Eric. Just because the messages, the images, frightened you doesn't mean that the one who transmitted those images was evil. Can't you see that?"

Eric cocked his head and shrugged. "Maybe."

Hammond shifted in his seat and coughed. "Eric, what do *you* think was responsible for the experience you had?"

Eric could only shake his head. "I think it was someone . . . someone powerful. Not a demon. Not a devil. Certainly not God. But someone . . ." His fingertips pressed down on his lips. "I *did* feel . . . I sensed . . . the *human* presence somewhere. Or I should say, the human *factor*. It was there. Maybe what we're dealing with here isn't human itself, but it . . . *consorts* with us, works with us. Perhaps we work for it. The question is, Hammond, do we do so of or own free will?"

He'd lost Hammond. And when Hammond lost the drift he lost interest. "Whatever you say, Eric."

Eric smiled. "Want a cup of coffee, Ham?"

"Yes. And bring me one of those glazed donuts, will you?"

"Of course."

When Eric came back from the kitchen, Hammond was yawning, hand over mouth, eyes red and blurry. "Good thing I put the coffee on," Eric said. "You're about to fall asleep on me."

"Yes. I don't know what came over me. I suddenly feel so tired. I'll probably go to bed early."

"You didn't have your nap before dinner. That's why you're so tired."

"Possibly. I don't really need those naps. I'm not an infant. But they enable me to stay up later should I need to. I like to sit up late reading."

They had the coffee and dessert. Hammond was much too tired to engage in conversation, so they ate in silence. Hammond hadn't even finished his donut when he muttered something about being exhausted and went to the living room to lie down on the couch. Eric didn't protest, but this meant that he wouldn't be able to look at television. Then again . . . perhaps if he kept it low? Of course, now he was free to go out, but not having made any plans he decided against it.

He finished his coffee, collected the dishes and silverware, and placed them in the sink. Hammond would probably wash them in the morning. He threw the empty containers and wrappers in the garbage pail, washed his hands off, and looked through the newspaper for the TV section. He chose an old film, turned to the correct channel, and sat down in the easy chair to watch. Undisturbed on the sofa, Hammond was as still as a log, snoring like a saw. He must have fallen asleep as soon as his head touched the cushion. Eric had to raise the volume so as to hear over the noise of the air rushing through his "roommate's" nostrils.

At nine o'clock, Eric got up, shut off the TV, and went into the bathroom.

As he was washing his hands afterwards, it suddenly hit him:

Something was scanning his mind.

He was positive of it. Something was reaching out and touching his brain. And it was *because* of Eric's advanced psychic power, he was sure of that too. Otherwise, Eric would hardly have attracted the thing's attention.

Eric braced himself. This was it! The second attack! Where, oh where, was Hammond when he needed him? *Wake up, Gratis!* Well, at least he was prepared this time. No one would catch him off guard.

As the attack began, as Eric successfully warded it off, repelled it, negated it, Eric realized it was more of a *defensive* maneuver than an offensive one.

He'd been getting too close. His visions. His

263

dreams. HGC. The door. *Eric had seen too much*.

The thing was attacking for what it thought was its own protection!

But Eric was too much for it. *This* time. Eric beat it back, back, back to where it belonged. He wanted to shift to his *own* offensive maneuver, to probe and scan, to find out more about his opponent, but he dared not. It would be too easy to leave himself wide open to a third, devastating assault. He knew how easily your strength could be turned against you in psychic warfare, at least in theory. How often did he *have* psychic battles? So few consciousnesses were as strong as his own.

But *this* consciousness was stronger. Incredibly so. Eric had only managed to "defeat" it — for lack of a better word — because he'd been prepared and his opponent had *not* been. He sensed his opponent had never come into contact with a human mind *quite* so paranormally powerful before.

Eric's entire body was dripping with sweat. He looked in the mirror and saw a ghost staring back at him. He'd better go wake up Hammond and tell him what had happened.

When he returned to the living room, it struck him that something had been moved or changed, although at first he couldn't figure out what it was. Slowly he looked around the room.

Hammond! That was it. Hammond wasn't there. Boy, that experience in the bathroom had taken a lot out of him.

The sofa was empty. "Hammond? Where have you gone?"

There was no answer.

He went into the kitchen and found Hammond there. He was standing next to the range, staring straight ahead, his eyes going right through Eric's body. He had the strangest look on his face, like a somnabulist. Could it be that he was sleepwalking?

"Hammond?" Eric said, stepping closer.

The man didn't move.

"Hammond?" Eric was suddenly struck by a painful headache. It was as if all his nerve endings had been set on fire. He gritted his teeth, placed his hand on his brow, and began to tremble. Perspiration seeped out of his skin, coating his temples.

Hammond had also been affected. The big man was revolving his head, stretching his neck toward the ceiling, then pushing his head down onto his chest. All the while he moaned and made animal-like noises. All Eric could see were the whites of Hammond's eyes. Could this be a joke? he wondered. Had the circumstances not been so out of the ordinary, it would have seemed a comical exhibition.

Eric tried to block out the pain. He had just about succeeded when Hammond lunged at him.

The man's face was contorted with hatred; bubbly foam spilled out from between his lips. Within seconds he had his arms around Eric's throat, his hands shaking with frightening strength as they pushed down on Eric's windpipe. Eric's vision began to darken. He pulled at Hammond's shoulders and kicked him, hoping the blows would startle the man

265

and make him let go. Finally Eric was able to move his hands to the front of Hammond's chest. Pushing with all his might, he shoved the man away from him.

Hammond tottered on his feet for a second, then fell to the floor.

Eric used this opportunity to look around for a weapon, just in case he'd need one. Judging from the look on Hammond's face, he probably would. Eric didn't know what had come over his friend, and certainly didn't want to hurt him, but his sense of self-preservation was too strong for him to simply stand there and take a beating. In all probability, a fatal one.

He grabbed one of the kitchen chairs. Holding it in front of him, he hoped he'd be able to ward off any more attacks without doing serious harm to Hammond. He was sure his friend wasn't responsible for his actions. He would have to be very, very careful.

Hammond had risen to his feet. Apparently he was partially able to reason—he went to the drawer where the cutlery was held and pulled out a very large butcher knife. Still snarling, his face a study in fury, Hammond advanced once again on Eric.

They moved backward into the living room. Perhaps if he could maneuver him into the bathroom, Eric thought, lock him in, Hammond might eventually calm down. But even then, how could he be sure there wouldn't be a reoccurrence of this madness?

A stab of utter helplessness shot through Eric. Even if he could disable Hammond, what hope would they have against a foe who could set one friend against another? Like *this?*

"Hammond! It's me! Eric! You've got to stop this!"

"Got to—got to—*kill* you! It's *making* me—"

"No! You're not going to kill anybody," Eric shouted, not sure if he was addressing Gratis or their unseen opponent. What on *earth* were they dealing with here? Eric thrust out with the chair, aiming for Hammond's knife hand. It didn't work. Hammond grabbed one leg of the chair with his free hand and tried to pry it from Eric's grip. Eric was terribly afraid that Ham would succeed. Normally, Hammond was stronger than he was—and now, under this demonic influence, who could tell how *much* stronger he might be?

Eric stepped back very quickly, pulling the chair leg out of Hammond's hand. Hammond's *other* hand tightened on his knife. He advanced, fearlessly, twisting his body sideways so that his back could take the brunt of Eric's blows should he start hitting him with the chair. Whoever was controlling him was doing an excellent job.

Eric backed up too hastily. He bumped into the coffeetable—the chair started falling out of his hands.

Hammond rushed forward, plunging the knife directly at Eric's heart.

Eric pulled the chair back up again just in time. The knife hit *it* instead of him, becoming imbedded in the red vinyl seat cover and the wood underneath. Eric only had time for a quick glimpse. The blade was buried up to the hilt—an incredibly powerful blow! If that had punctured his *chest* . . .

Eric and Hammond wrestled for possession of the chair. Decidedly the stronger of the two, Hammond started jamming it into Eric's body. Eric decided not to rely on the protection of the chair anymore, as it had been too easily turned against him. He pushed aside the coffeetable with one arm, held the chair off with another— then sidestepped the table, getting out of Hammond's way.

Enraged, Hammond lifted the chair over his head. He let out with a cry that seemed as anguished as it was angry, and threw the chair at Eric. It went flying past him, crashing into the curtains and the window behind them. Amid a shattering collection of razor-sharp glass shards, the chair hurtled down to the pavement below.

Wearing the tormented look of an infected and dying animal, screeching at the top of his lungs, Hammond rushed past Eric toward the wall and the window. Tears of resignation and determination dripping down his face, Hammond followed the path of the chair and plummeted downward to an abrupt and hideous death.

For the second time in three days Steven stood in the hallway outside Andrea Martin's apartment. This time he had received an invitation.

Andrea let him in and gave him a noncommital peck. He didn't know if it was out of pity that she'd kissed him, but he'd have to be satisfied. She put his coat away and made him a drink.

"Thought you might need somebody to talk to," she said. "Sorry I was so abrupt on the phone this afternoon. I was calling from work, and it was *really* a hectic day."

"That's okay. I was just glad to hear from you."

They sat together on the couch while Steven sipped his bourbon. She drank nothing. Not a good sign. He had wanted to "have it all out" with her, but surely she knew that *this* was not the time?

"So how is everything? What did Ralph have to say?"

He chattered on for several minutes, updating her on the latest bizarre developments. "Remember old Harry Faulkin? He brought a reporter over to my place this afternoon. They're going to put Joey's picture on the news. Yeah, I thought it was great too. But it was awful—vulgar, stupid. They're trying to make Joey out as some kind of murdering gigolo. They say that's the only way he'll get any attention. So tell me, what can I do?"

Andrea was fidgeting uncomfortably on the couch, staring down at her twisting, intertwined fingers. She had news, he knew. She couldn't bring herself to look at him.

"Steven, perhaps this isn't the time to tell you . . ."

No, Andrea. Not now. For God's sake, not now.

"I don't know *how* to tell you. But I can't wait any longer."

She was going to tell him it was over. She was going to tell him she'd found someone new.

"Steven—I'm getting married!"

"What?"

"It's—you met him, *saw* him—Donald. We've been seeing—a lot of each other. He *insisted*—when he saw you—said it was *cruel* to delay any longer. . . ." She kept rattling on like a warped record skipping every other chorus.

Steven couldn't believe his ears. This woman beside him had once been his girlfriend, his *lover*, the person he went through life with, sharing and caring each moment. Now? *When* had they drifted apart?

"But *how*, Andrea? We were—seeing each other—going together—"

"It's been *months* since we were 'going together,' Steven. Really, how often have we seen each other in the past few weeks, *spoken* to each other? I didn't ask for it to happen, it just did.

"But we're still friends," she added.

Steven let out a humorless laugh. Could it be possible? Had he been so self-involved—in his books, his job, his assorted literary endeavors—that he'd failed to see what was happening? Had Andrea met and fallen in love with, agreed to marry, another man behind his back? Was she right—was this not a sudden thing, had the breakup started many months before? Could it be possible?

"I'm sorry, Steven. I—"

"This is quite a shock." He inhaled deeply, exhaled. "Donald, huh?"

"We met . . ."

"No. No, I don't want to know."

"We have to talk it out."

"Not now, Andrea." *Next she'll be inviting me to the wedding.*

"Steven, if I could have held off—till this thing with Joey—"

"This thing. Joey's disappeared, may be dead—"

"That doesn't change anything between us. I feel awfully sorry about Joey, but Donald—he insisted—"

"Does Donald tell you what to do now?"

"Steven!"

He got up, finished his drink. Seems he was always gulping his bourbon lately. "Look Andrea, I'd better go." In an instant of clarity he saw how right she'd been, how large the gulf between them had always been. Part of him felt relief. Had he really loved her, or had he only *needed* someone, needed someone to keep loneliness away?

"I have an appointment to keep."

"Steven, I—"

"I'll let myself out."

To hell with her. His brother was still missing, and somebody on Long Island had information.

He told himself *that* was all that mattered.

Vaguely Eric could hear the sirens screaming. Their horribly loud screeches were tearing through the night, coming closer and closer, then abruptly fading out. Then booming on again louder than before. Funny how sirens were that way. One minute it was as if they were right outside; then the next it seemed as if they were far away in the other side of town.

The cold air came through the shattered window. The drapes fluttered inwards, now and then brushing against his face. Their embrace was like that of frigid fingers, tracing a macabre outline upon his brow. He felt alone again; horribly alone. Hammond had left him, was lying even now in a bloody pool of flesh and blood seventeen stories below. Eric had chanced one look out the window after he'd recovered from the shock, had cried out in horror and disbelief, then fallen to the floor, waiting, just waiting for his body to stop quivering. It seemed as if it would take forever.

Then it hit him. That icy, numbing feeling of fear and despair. Of total submission. It was that force again, that uncanny power that had taken him on Wednesday evening, that had taken him again on Wednesday evening, that had taken him again on Friday night, and had tried to overcome him earlier. He tried to repel it again, but was unable to muster enough strength to prevent the outside force from overwhelming him, from taking control of both his body and his mind. He lost all desire to call the police, to pick himself up, to put his life back in order. He just let himself drift on and on into a netherworld of light and dark, shadow and fog.

He felt that vibrating sensation again—he was swaying to and fro, back and forth, gently, gently, swaying ever so slightly, back and forth. His whole body seemed to tingle. He was rushing forward through some sort of tube, suspended in mid-air, traveling onward and onward, without bearing, without any feeling of *destination*. Then he saw that rectangular door coming closer and closer. That huge steel door with the strange writing. H.G.C. H.G.C. HCGHGCHCGHCGHGCHGC

H.G.C.

What did it mean?

Then, through the mist of the darkness, Eric got a fix; a sudden, but perfect, unmistakable fix.

He knew where that door was!

If someone had asked him, had been able to ask him then, just *where* it was, he could not have told them—not in so many words. But he knew just the same. He knew that he would be guided there by an "instinct" planted in his mind. He had only to rise, put on his hat and coat, and take the elevator down to the lobby. He knew where to go! He *knew!*

The sirens had faded now, his head had cleared. He could hear doors opening, excited shouts, lots of talking and an occasional gasp. It was as if it was all taking place right outside the door instead of outside the window seventeen stories down. What were they doing? He tried to focus on the evening's events, but couldn't. He was obsessed with only one desire—to find the door, to reach it, before it was too late.

He had to be there when it *opened*.

Donning his jacket on the run, he went into the corridor and pressed for the elevator. It came quickly; empty. He did not get off at lobby level, but the second floor instead. He then walked down to the basement, and went out the exit through the laundry room. He wanted to avoid the crowd that was surely collecting out front—the morbid, manic horde of bloodthirsty vultures.

He went through what seemed to be a veritable maze of back alleys, laundry lines, and snow-spattered alcoves before he reached the street. It was cold out, and the city was filling up with the still-falling snow. Eric wished that he had remembered to bring his gloves. He thrust his hands into his pockets, glad for the warmth. In the back of his mind he knew that what he was doing was not rational—he should stay and wait for the police—but he was under the spell of a terrible compulsion that he simply could not dispel. He knew that Hammond's strange behavior and subsequent death had been *his* punishment for resisting, repelling his opponent's psychic assault. It had tried to use Hammond as a weapon. Hammond had killed himself rather than murder his friend. *Oh, God, Ham. Ham, you sacrified yourself for me*. He owed it to Hammond to see this through, to give in to the terrible compulsion running through him and let it take him where it may. He tried not to think about what would come later, how he would explain his absence and those signs of a struggle in his apartment. Would they accuse *him* of hurling Hammond out of the window? All the more reason to get to the bottom of this. But he mustn't think about that now. He must only think about the task at hand.

He was relieved to discover his wallet in his pocket. He hailed a cab, got into the back seat, and sat there flustered, the cabbie waiting impatiently, while he tried to put his destination into words. Finally he said: "Just drive downtown. Stick to the East Side. When we arrive, I'll let you know."

They had driven leisurely for about ten minutes when Eric directed the driver to get down to the Lower East Side as quickly as possible. The cabbie gave it an honest try, but the traffic was much thicker in midtown. He leaned on the horn, shouted a few curses, swerved this way and that, but they made only moderate headway. In the back Eric was quite distraught, constantly holding his hand to his brow, squeezing his eyes shut. The driver didn't know what to make of him.

Twenty minutes later they pulled up to the subway station at Delancey and Essex Streets. The area was crowded now, with shoppers, gangs of kids, people coming out of stores and restaurants. Eric pushed open the back door and threw several bills in the cabbie's lap through the open front window. The driver didn't have a chance to give him his change— Eric had disappeared into the crowd.

Eric climbed down the stairs and entered the station, a confusing miasma of people, small underground shops, and food stands with orange drink and hot dogs. He went to the change booth, bought a token, and walked down the platform to where the tunnel led to the BMT line. The presence was stronger than ever now; his head was throbbing from its force. Then he saw what he was looking for.

Over to one side, out off from the rest of the station by a gate, was some sort of abandoned access corridor. Eric looked around—people were walking briskly past him in either direction, no one paying him the slightest attention. There were no police in the vicinity, and the change booth was hidden from view.

He started to pull at the gate, watching as its whole structure shook back and forth from his efforts. It must have a weakness somewhere! The padlock was rusty—with time he could work it open, but he'd have to wait until it was late and the corridor was empty. He *couldn't* wait! He went to the right side of the gate, and saw that there it had been partially pried away from the wall. Kids, probably. It hardly mattered. There was just enough room for him to get through.

He pushed the metal fence away from the wall, gently squeezing his body through. A few people looked at him, curious, but no one made a move to stop him. It wasn't as if he was breaking into a store.

Part of the gate clipped him on the side of the nose. He winced, cried out, stifling it before he could alarm anyone. There were fewer people about now, most of *them* preoccupied in their own private worlds. He finally pushed himself all the way through, using his hands to keep the gate from snapping back on his left leg.

Success.

The dark, dank passageway loomed ahead of him. It looked impenetrable, unwilling to let anyone explore its inner recesses or fathom its grim and unknown secrets. The air was thick, foul. Eric cautiously advanced, holding up his lighter to provide illumination. The noises of the people and the trains gradually receded into the depths of his consciousness. Now and then he would hear the rumbling of a train, but eventually even that failed to register.

He was all alone. Just him and the darkness.

The passageway seemed to go on forever. He wondered why it was there and for what reason it had originally been built. As far as he knew there were no abandoned subway stops in the vicinity. Perhaps they'd started a platform for a different subway line at some point. Well, he'd find out what this was used for *now* when he got there.

The width of the passage stayed the same— always several yards across, like most tunnels which connected the subway lines to one another. The ceiling was quite high. Several times he would find himself stepping into puddles. His foot tripped on an old sneaker. And the tiny glow from the lighter revealed a copy of a torn and wet magazine lying in his path. He stepped over it and continued.

The passageway now seemed to be slowly descending to a level that was probably just below the one he had entered on. He had lost all sense of direction, though he was seemingly in control of his senses. He had never imagined that he could have been this brave. He looked back toward the entrance with its gate and shivered. It was no longer in sight. All he could perceive was a very dim splotch of light that seemed far, far away. He was surrounded by nothingness.

Still, that compelling feeling persisted. He was frightened, but not paralyzed. Something seemed to be assuring him, leading him on, *insisting* that he proceed. Nothing could have made him turn back now, didn't his opponent realize that? He *had* to see this through to its conclusion.

He went further and further into the passageway, walking steadily, both anxious and afraid to reach the end. Then just when he was planning to stop and rest, he saw it. The door. Huge. Formidable. Massive.

There were the letters, just as he had seen in his vision. H.G.C. What did they mean? He reached out to touch the door. It was made of metal. Steel. It glinted in the light from his hand. It stood at least eight feet high, six feet across. A line ran down its center, denoting where its two parts divided. Eric leaned against the door, resting. Then he played the light all over it, searching for some way to make it open.

He couldn't find any knob, any button, any way whatsoever to gain entry.

Then, just as he was pondering what to do next, the fluid was all burned up, and his light went out.

Utter darkness.

And then from the door came a *creak*.

Gregory Olsen was staring at his clock.

He watched the small metal hand count off the seconds, and tried to catch the nearly imperceptible movement of the minute hand as it made its slow, steady trek toward the bottom of the clock face. He sat there like that until nine-thirty. Then he rose, went into the bathroom, and washed the perspiration off his face with a wet wash cloth.

He looked at the haggard, pale complexion in the mirror. His hair, which had once been so flamingly crimson, was now gray and sparse. He'd managed to keep himself in shape by sticking to a proper diet. Still, the strain of his ordeal was stamped on his face and body. It seemed as if every nightmare was etched in lines on his face. The puffy collections of flesh beneath his eyes were grim reminders of the price he'd had to pay. Sleepless nights, days awake by the fire, just watching. Waiting and watching.

But tonight, Steven Everson would come. He was sure of it. All he had to do was wait patiently until midnight. Nothing more. He would go out to the beach and wait there until he came. It was only a matter of time.

Time. How much was left? How much before they got to *him* too? How much before there was no turning back? When would he ever feel safe again? He went back to the easy chair and listened to the wind as it howled outside, sure that his every breath brought him closer to death.

Could it reach him, even out here? That presence in his mind was less intense since he'd moved out of the city, but never entirely absent. Still, it had been quite preoccupied with other things these past few weeks. Little, if anything, escaped its notice—but perhaps Olsen, living way out here in Tanton, would manage it somehow. At least at midnight the creature would be at rest, if you could say it ever rested.

He shuddered. The clock's noise seemed so loud, cutting through the musty air inside. The fire was dying out. He decided not to rekindle it. Time enough for that later. If there *was* a later.

He wondered if some of the master's conscripts were watching him even now. Were they out there in the dark waiting like he was? No, he must not dwell on such things. He could not afford to stay shuttered inside tonight of all nights.

It was while he was watching the last sparks of the fire disappear that he first felt the sensation.

He felt queasy. Filled with alarm, he rose to his feet. Yes, this was it. He'd taken a chance in the crapshoot and lost. That pounding! The blood rushing through his circulatory system! Spots were forming before his eyes. He wondered for a moment if this was a natural seizure, a stroke, something normal and—*human*—but he knew with dread that that was simply not the case. Olsen tried to fight it off, but he only felt worse every second.

He must get away. Somehow. *He must reach Everson!* He looked at the clock but his vision was too hazy for him to make out the time. He knew there was no chance for him to get away from the sphere of influence—that much was being demonstrated—but if only he could reach the rendezvous point before he died. If only he could hold on until Everson arrived! If he collapsed, let it be where Everson would know where to find him! Yes. *Yes!* He must get out of the house now!

He was shivering so fearfully he couldn't get his arms into his jacket. He threw it in disgust on the floor.

Still fighting off the queasy feeling, he threw open the front door, stumbled across the porch, and ran down the steps. He crossed the road, darting through the empty parking lot opposite his house until his feet hit the cool, hard sand of the beach. In the distance, the ocean stretched out before him, its waves and smell and sound suddenly so tempting, so inviting., *To keep running, running. To let it finally* end.

He felt something on his arm as he ran, as if he had brushed against something. But there was nothing in his path that he could have hit. He stopped, pulled up sleeve, and saw a short, red scratch just below the elbow. Where had that come from? Still dizzy, he dropped the sleeve, and proceeded toward the lifeguard station, this time at a slower pace. He was already winded.

He felt another tickle on his other arm. This time there was a longer, deeper scratch, extending from his wrist to halfway up the arm. What the hell? He had no memory of injuring himself.

Then there was another sudden tingle along his belly. He tore open his shirt. The scratch was longer and redder than the others, extending from the ribs down toward the groin. And it was bleeding profusely.

"Oh my God!"

He ran even faster now, struggling to stay upright, crazed with fear. He must make it; he must not die before he spoke to Everson. He must not die!

The scratches came faster now, as if he was being clawed by an invisible creature which ran along beside him. On the neck. On the face. Along the sides of his body, his arms and legs. Some were short, some were long. They got progressively nastier. The cuts on his arms were also starting to bleed. God—when was it going to end?

He knew he was only hallucinating, but it didn't help.

He put his hand to his face and realized that his cheeks were swelling. His very flesh was crumbling, cracking, coming off in his fingers! Blood poured from his eyes and nostrils, blood seeped from his every orifice.

Tiny pinpricks of blood were coming through his skin, the pores of his flesh, as if by osmosis.

He finally reached the station. He grabbed onto the white wooden banister, and pulled himself up the incline toward the enclosed, raised room which housed the lifeguard's first-aid supplies during the summer. It was empty now. And unlocked.

He dived into the little room, crouched on bended legs, and pulled the door shut tightly behind him. He sat there, gripping the door handle, shivering and praying.

An eye fell out of its socket and fell onto his cheek.

Just your imagination, he told himself.

The bleeding continued. Blood was seeping through his clothes, dripping onto the floor and sinking through the slats. Olsen started to cry.

Sobbing, he put his face in his hands.

Something wrenched free of his shoulder. He felt a sudden weight on his fingers.

Olsen screamed.

He looked down and saw—impossibly—his own disembodied head staring up at him in horror.

TEN

ODD THINGS WERE happening in the city.

The weather was the first thing you noticed. It was never the way they said it would be. The freak heat spell that had been predicted was nowhere in evidence.

But there were other little things that nobody much talked about. How you could get electric shocks just by walking down the street at certain times of the day in certain neighborhoods. People blamed it on their shoes or on—of all things—the humidity!

Or that eerie haze that lit up the skyline very, very early in the morning, an aura or outline tracing the buildings. Only the drunks, the few who were left, ever noticed it, and they were way beyond caring.

In the past few weeks the city's transient, homeless population had all but disappeared. The shelters were practically empty and fewer people were picking up their welfare checks. The Mayor said the poor had migrated to other cities and better conditions—though everyone knew New York city spent millions of dollars on aid to the poor.

And the number of missing persons cases was staggering. Now it was not just the so-called dregs of society, but "decent," respectable, middle-class men and women who never came home from work, who never arrived at the office. Yet the papers made no connections, no observations even; they simply reported each case dispassionately, until there were so many they didn't report them at all.

It was as if someone had told them not to.

Lina Hobler lay in her bed, half asleep, struggling to overcome the effects of the alcohol she'd consumed. The bruises and contusions she had sustained during her scrap in the bar earlier that day were starting to hurt; a sure sign of an encroaching hangover. She knew that the only sensible thing to do was to lie there, get lots of rest, and wake up in the morning for a fresh start, but she felt too uneasy to sleep. She kept seeing Brock in her mind, calling to her, calling for help.

He's dead.

Suddenly, just like that, she accepted it. *Brock was dead.*

Suddenly she felt foolish sleeping and drinking away her life over a man who would never come home. If he wasn't dead, he had left her. For good this time. Forever. She could die, sure. She could kill herself over him. But she didn't *want* to die. She wanted to live.

Funny, she had never realized that before.

She knew, of course, that the alcohol, having

285

plunged her into a dismal depression, was now only snapping her back into a manic "feel-good." She should have been suicidal at the thought of Brock's passing; instead, her instinct for *survival* was welling up inside her.

Face it, she told herself. *You're old, ugly, running out of money. But you're* alive! She would have to get herself together, find a way to make it through life without Brock to guide and support her. It was going to be tough. But other women did it. Why couldn't she?

The good old days were gone forever.

She got up and wiped away the seeping discharge in the corners of her eyes. *Time to move on, Lina old girl.* She would just have to learn not to think about him so darn much. She had to. Not that she was giving up, no sir. She would stay in touch with that Steven Everson, just in case something turned up. Just in case Brock was alive and was in need of help. Just in case he'd been murdered. She'd want to help get the crumb that did him in. She'd want him to have a decent burial, not get dumped in a soggy plot of shit with no stone above to record his passing. Not her Brock.

She felt the tears coming on again. She held them back tightly. *Not now. Not when you're just learning how to be strong. Not now, Lina.* Oh, it was tough, tough, tough. But she had to go on. There was no other course. If she couldn't control her drinking she would join AA. She would get some kind of decent job. She would be proud that she was once *the* Lina Hobler. Her voice was gone, no use dreaming about that. But she could still do something, maybe find someone to share her life with. She didn't want to be alone forever.

She felt a sore spot on her back. How it hurt! That's what she got for starting fights. And for what? Because she couldn't control her jealousy over some woman who'd done nothing to her but dare to be younger and prettier. *Poor idiot*, Lina thought with bitter satisfaction. *She'll probably get herself knocked up, marry too early, spend her life washing diapers.* At least *she'd* been spared that. At least she'd been *somebody* for a while.

Lina sat down in the chair by the window. A nice, big overstuffed chair. Brock's favorite. *No —mustn't think about him. Not now.* She still loved him, would always love him, but she had to finally accept the obvious conclusion that he was never coming back. She would not even allow herself to think of his fate. He had not been reduced to some grotesque smear on the subway steps—no one would convince her of that. Not while she was sane, at least. But he *was* gone. Gone for good.

She wanted to run back to the bar for another drink, wanted to turn the place upside down looking for a bottle filled with any sort of booze, no matter how cheap or tasteless. For a second she almost did it, almost broke her silent promise to herself.

That's not the way, Lina. That's not the way.

She went to the sink and instead filled her mouth and stomach with water. It didn't taste so good, but she pretended it was cold and wonderful. She let it wash over her face, watched the water mix with the remains of her makeup, watched the brownish liquid that resulted flow down the drain. She gulped down more water, came up for air.

She dug into her pocketbook and got out her wallet. She counted the money in there, and added it to the amount she knew was hidden in the apartment in various places. She checked just to make sure it was all there. Every penny was accounted for. Formerly it had been her drunk money, now it was for survival of a different sort. She had enough to last a couple of weeks if she was frugal and didn't touch the hootch. She took out five dollars, and got her coat.

Tonight she would celebrate her independence by going out to a movie. Any movie. Where she could be with people while being alone. Then she'd come home, get a good rest, and look for a job in the morning.

Things were looking up for a change. Just as long as she didn't think about Brock. She could not stand it if she did. Everything would just fall apart.

She turned out the light and left the apartment. *What a performance!* she thought, as she walked down the street toward the cinema. *You're pretending that you're a happy, well-adjusted woman with a perfect job and a wonderful love life. Just like the ladies in the TV commercials.*

Damn it, she thought. Why not? She wasn't that old. She could make a new start, find happiness somehow. She'd give it her best shot.

Please don't let anything go wrong, she told her conscience.

But she couldn't shake her premonitions of doom.

She was scared she wouldn't make it.

"There's no answer."

Valerie Horton put down the phone and swiveled in her chair to look at Ralph, standing in the doorway to her office. "I've tried Miss Hobler's number a dozen times today, and there's never any answer. Can I go home now?"

Ralph smiled. "What's the matter, my soon-to-be-partner? Don't like putting in overtime?"

"It *is* Saturday night, but you know I really don't mind the work. I'm just worn out. Besides helping you with this Everson case, I had that Ferguson business—the missing jewelry—and the Paddington twin to take care of. I'm tempted to tell him if he hasn't seen his brother for fifty-three years, why the hell does he want to track him down now."

Ralph sat down on the edge of her desk. "Can I buy you some dinner?"

She reached for her purse and jacket. "You're on. Buy me a steak and I'll promise I'll be in bright and early tomorrow."

"No painting the town red on Saturday night?"

She rolled her eyes. "I'm so tired I couldn't hold the brush." She switched out the light. "Or anything else."

"Well, that's the private-eye business. Saturdays. Sundays. Late nights and early mornings. And paperwork, paperwork, paperwork."

She pressed the down button on the elevator. "You're telling me. Everyone thinks we're so *glamorous.*"

He went up and down on his toes. "The glamor is all in the feet."

Between yawns Valerie talked about the Everson case while they rode down to the lobby. "It really gets to me, Ralph. I mean, I know we *have* to sleep and all that. But I keep thinking. That young man is *out* there somewhere, and each day the trail gets foggier. It just . . . gets to me."

"Slow, methodical work always gets results," Ralph reminded her. "As long as we leave no stone unturned and track down every lead, we're doing the best we can." They stepped out of the elevator. "We're *going* to find Joey Everson."

"I know," Valerie said. "But will we find him *in time?*"

For that Ralph had no answer.

After he had forecasted clear skies on the six o'clock news, Harry Faulkin stepped out of the studio some hours later, and was immediately sprinkled with thousands of falling snowflakes.

"Damn!"

What he needed was a nice stiff drink at O'Malley's around the corner. Closing the top button on his jacket to keep out the chill, he walked in the direction of the bar.

It had been a busy day. He'd finally gotten Steven together with Job Foster, the reporter he'd interested in the connection between Joey Everson and the Jessup lady's death. Hadn't been the greatest meeting, that was true—Steven was so damn sensitive—but at least the kid's picture had been splashed all over the six-o'clock news.

Harry'd wanted to report the story himself, but the producer had nixed it. "Harry, stick to what you do best. Let Job cover the story." Harry had to face it. They'd let him anchor the news on weekends when the regular guy was sick, but actual reporting was out of the question. What did they think he was—just some pretty-boy dumbo?

Well, he had plans up his sleeve. Big plans. Like the story he was working on now . . . about the weather, about how it didn't behave the way the meteorologists said it should. *That* was a big story—and he'd devote his whole report to it some time next week whether they liked it or not. Nobody could argue that it wasn't about the weather . . . but it was a lot bigger than that.

Only no one had a clue as to what was going on. So what he planned to do was somehow hijack a camera crew and go interview the weather brain-boys and videotape them as they told him how baffled they all were. All that stuff about air currents, barometric pressure, and so on only bored and confused him anyway, and would only bore and confuse his audience—all anybody really wanted to hear was whether or not it'd rain tomorrow—so he'd just tell the guys to shake their heads ominously and keep it simple.

He could see it now. "And now with the weather, it's Harry Faulkin."

Hello, folks. Gotta strange one for you tonight. It's always been a big joke how weathermen never accurately predict the weather—but in point of fact, most of the time we guys are downright perfect. I haven't time to explain all the factors that go into predicting the weather. Let's just say our modern-day meteorologists can predict it pretty accurately. So how come every weather forecast—in print and on television— has been inaccurate for days now? Where's that freak heat spell we've been hearing so much about?

Good question, folks. You see— and this is pretty scary—something other than the usual everyday factors is affecting the weather. Only nobody knows what it is. At first, we thought it was simply a matter of human error, but now . . .

And then the videotapes of the meteorologists would come on.

If *that* didn't get him noticed, nothing would.

He started unbuttoning his jacket as he turned into the entrance of O'Malley's.

A singles hangout, O'Malley's was crowded from five o'clock on. It emptied slightly toward eight o'clock, as the martini crowd left for home or other restaurants—O'Malley's had good food, but was a bit noisy for some diners—and filled again to capacity about three hours later with the lonely late-night cruisers.

Harry walked into the bar section of the restaurant and went over to his crowd of regulars, mostly men in their thirties who also worked in the television industry. O'Malley's was a spacious wooden tavern modeled after an old-fashioned saloon. The big picture windows allowed the patrons to scrutinize each new arrival before he or she even walked in through the door. "Friends" of his were turning to greet Harry before he'd even spotted them.

"How goes it?" asked a blond chap who wrote the TV column for a local paper. "Still employed?"

Harry laughed. WNUC was known for the way they quickly and quietly removed key personnel before they'd even known what hit them. "No pink slip yet. I'm on their good side."

"Speaking of good sides," another man butted in, "are they still putting your ugly mug on the air?"

"Of course. WNUC needs all the sex appeal it can get."

The blond man laughed. "He doesn't suffer from an inferiority complex, now does he?" The other men agreed. Harry was about to counter the remark, but excused himself and went instead to the side of a young woman down near the end of the bar.

Her name was Adele Wanamer, and she had been dismissed from WNUC six months ago. She had long, straight hair that swerved down to her shoulders, and a kittenish expression that made her look as if she was always signaling for those around her to "come hither." She gave Harry one of her patented Cheshire-cat grins as he approached.

"Hello. Can I buy you a drink?" He didn't

293

wait for an answer. "Adele, isn't it? What are you drinking?"

"Club soda," she said, peering up from the delicate straw between her pursed lips. "I have quite a lot left."

"Then why don't we add something to it? Something with a bit more kick and bite."

"What would you suggest?"

"Some scotch perhaps?"

"But it does such terrible things to the breath, don't you think?"

For a moment Harry felt self-conscious, until he remembered that he had not yet had a drink. He would definitely not order a scotch.

"Then how about vodka? Vodka has no taste. No odor. Goes down real smooth. What do you think?"

"No, thank you. I think I'll just stick to my club soda."

"If you insist." He ordered a vodka-tonic and turned back to the woman. "Care for a cigarette?"

"No thanks." Harry thought quickly for something to say, something with which to segue into a bright and snappy conversation. She beat him to it, disastrously. She brought up the one subject he was in no mood to talk about. Not until he was sure he'd beat the competition.

"I saw your weather report tonight. While I was shopping. In an appliance store. They had the set turned to your channel."

"That's, uh, nice."

"You didn't say anything about snow."

"I know."

"In case you hadn't noticed, it's snowing."

"Nobody *else* mentioned snow either."

"I wouldn't know. I only watched *your* report."

He took a quick swallow of his drink. "Well, those are the breaks. What can I say? I only read what they tell me to."

"Better watch out," she said. "If you don't start getting it right, they're going to replace you."

Harry hated her. She was mocking him, laughing at him. The nerve of the little bitch.

"Like they did you," he said. Tit for tat.

"Oooohh," she purred. "You *are* upset. I'm not complaining. I got myself a better job, with more money. I'm sure *you* could name your price at other stations. In fact, according to what I've been hearing, you just might be able to write your own ticket."

"Where did you hear this?"

"I have my sources."

"Might I ask who they are?"

"Not here. Even the walls have ears, if you know what I mean. Why don't we go to my place, and I'll . . . fill you in on some things." She winked. "Why settle for reporting the weather when some anchor spots may be opening up elsewhere?"

She had him hooked. "Sounds good to me. Sure we can't have a drink or two first?"

"Uh, uh. We're taking a chance being seen together as it is. Besides, the snow may get even worse. I'll go to the powder room, and you leave first. I'll follow you in a minute or two. My car is just down the block, at the corner. A red Camaro. Wait for me."

Harry was excited. By her, by what she had to offer. Her body, her information. He thought about how exciting it would be to go to another station; more money, more prestige, not to mention all the publicity. He watched Adele walk to the ladies' room, then went out the door, avoiding the crowded bar by going through the restaurant. Someone yelled out a greeting, but he pretended not to hear.

She arrived at the car five minutes later, wearing a seductive smile and a lot of fresh makeup. They got into her car, pulled into traffic, and headed out of the city.

"Where do you live?" he asked. "Uptown?"

"Nope. Long Island. It's not that long a drive. You didn't have *plans* for the evening, did you?"

"Not any more. I'm not on at eleven on Saturdays unless the weekend guy is sick."

They drove on, the night arriving in full, darkening the sky until only the lights of approaching cars lit up the highway. Their polite conversation had come to a halt once they were on the expressway. The snow was thickening, making driving more hazardous than usual. Whatever brightness the snow created was dissipated by the fog-like swirling of windblown snowflakes. They had to go slowly.

Harry found himself fighting off feelings of claustrophobia, as well as his mounting desire for the woman sitting next to him. He could barely see the road, and wondered how she could manage it. He looked at her—the glare from outside was playing strange tricks. It highlighted the sculptured bone structure of her face, made her appear gaunt and unusually pale. She turned to face him, aware that he was staring.

For just a moment, Harry could have sworn he was looking at a death's-head.

Steven Everson was also in the process of driving to Long Island, but on a different highway. He was trying his best not to think about Andrea, concentrating only on the meeting at midnight. Driving was treacherous enough as it was. He had already seen two accidents back on the West Side Highway, and was determined not to make himself the third.

The snow was falling even heavier now, making use of the windshield wipers mandatory. He had hoped that conditions would improve once he'd left the city and the traffic behind. Instead they got worse. He was worried now about what it would be like driving home afterward.

He had thought about turning around, calling the whole thing off, but couldn't seriously consider it. He'd gone too far, been through too much, to give up now. The snow thickened and the wind howled, a haunting, indescribable melody that chilled his blood. A half an hour passed. He turned the heat up higher, and reached for the radio knob. The radio didn't work. Too bad, he could have used some cheerful music, some news about the weather. He hoped it would stop snowing soon.

Renting the car had been easy and fairly inexpensive—all he really cared about was that the engine worked and that it would get him where he had to go and back. So far, so good.

Several miles out of the city it was as if he had crossed some kind of invisible barrier. Just like that, the snow faded away into a few trickles dotting the windshield. He could see much more clearly.

The highway he was on was a thin, two-laned strip of road that sliced through the beach at the edge of the formidable Atlantic Ocean. Even over the noises of the auto, he could hear the pounding surf—relentless, icy cold—splashing over and over again onto the nearby shore. Now and then a house would light up the roadway. He saw no more cars. No wonder—who but an idiot or someone obsessed as he was would travel in such weather?

He chanced to see his reflection in the rear-view mirror. Lord, he looked like hell. Sunken eyes, uncombed hair. He must have looked a fright to Andrea—*No! Don't think about her.* A horrible thought: he looked like Joey might have looked had he been *dead* for a week. Never had the resemblance between the brothers been so striking in such an *unhealthy* manner.

He slowed down, dismissed his morbid thoughts, and looked again at the note he had received. It wasn't far now. He had only to follow directions. He started looking out for the sign.

It wasn't long in coming. His headlights illuminated the word *Tanton.* According to his correspondent's crude map, if he kept driving straight along this road he would bypass the town proper and arrive in minutes at the correct lot, 15. He started to feel tense again. His breathing was so loud and forced that it obliterated the sound of the roaring ocean. Just as well. Ever since he'd been a child he had been afraid of the sea. So large and fierce, without boundaries that one could perceive. He had felt so small against its vastness. Even today the feeling persisted, intensified by the night.

He wondered why this meeting had to occur so late, when it was so dark and cold.

This was it. His destination. The lot number on the sign corresponded to the one on the note. There was a house across the street from it. For a moment he wondered if he should go to the house, but there was no guarantee that whoever lived there had sent him the letter. He parked the car in the lot, got out, and looked around for the lifeguard station. It was a few minutes after twelve.

There it was. Way down almost at the edge of the water.

He made sure the car doors were locked securely, pocketed his keys, and started in a diagonal direction toward the station. There was no sound except for the wind. There was a small amount of snow covering the sand, enough for his feet to leave faint impressions. The sand was soft at first, hardening as he got closer to the water. No one seemed to be around.

He became aware of a new noise as the wind

grew stronger. A squeaking, grating kind of sound. Then a loud report which almost made him jump.

He was just regaining his composure when it happened.

The door. It was *the door*.

The wooden door that opened into the small room behind the lifeguard's lookout platform was flapping open and shut with the wind. As it squeaked back to a closed position, it would suddenly shut with a *bang*. As Steven approached, looking upward, he tried to see if anyone was inside. It was too dark to tell. There was no sign of life behind the window, and he could only catch a quick glimpse through the door each time it opened.

He stepped onto the inclined platform leading up to the little shelter.

The wind died down and the door stayed ajar about two inches. There was no movement from inside as Steven climbed upward. Was he the first to arrive? he wondered.

When he reached the door he called out timidly. "Is anyone there?"

There was no reply.

As he stepped inside the shelter, his foot came down on something squishy on the floor.

There was a reddish outline on the wooden planks. A reddish outline like the outstretched figure of a man.

Suddenly the events of the past few days came rushing up to him, slamming into Steven's mind and stomach. He couldn't take it anymore. He backed away and out of the room, spewing vomit all over the area outside the door. He leaned over the railing and continued throwing up on the sand. His body heaved with each new gush of bile.

It was bad enough his brother was missing, his own life falling apart. But now some maniac kept playing tricks on him. Crazy tricks. Or was that gruesome paste on the floor exactly what this maniac wanted him to think it was?

He ran down the wooden slope, across the beach, and back to his car.

Behind him the door banged open, shut, open, shut, over and over and over again until the wind stilled and all that was left was the calm, raging sound of the ocean.

After the engine had been sputtering away for several minutes, Adele's car finally conked out and came to a stop on the side of the highway.

Adele tried again and again to start the engine, but it was no use. At least she had been able to move the car into the slow lane as soon as she had realized what was going to happen—though there was hardly enough traffic to worry about. It was snowing harder than ever.

Adele cursed. "Now what do we do?"

"Beats me," Harry said. "I don't know shit about cars."

Adele opened the door, letting in the frigid air. "I'll have to go out and look at the engine." She put on her gloves and trudged off toward the front of the car. Harry stayed inside where it was warm.

After fifteen minutes went by, during which not a single car appeared in either direction, Harry exited the vehicle and went up front to ask Adele what was going on.

"Have you spotted the trouble yet, sweetheart?"

"No. It looks like we're stranded here until a car comes along."

Harry looked down at the engine. "Well, there must be *something* wrong. Cars don't just stop working for no reason. Must be your engine froze up."

"I've checked everything else. We'll just have to wait."

"We have enough gas?"

"Yes. Yes, I checked that. I'm not an idiot."

"Sorry, sweetheart. I didn't mean anything. Damn—it's cold."

"I've noticed. Let's face it—neither one of us knows enough about cars to get this thing started, or to figure out what we're doing wrong. I know it's hard to start a car in cold weather, but once it goes there shouldn't be any problem."

"Let's see what it says in the manual. You have one in the dashboard?"

"Yes." She touched his shoulder. "Go get it, please."

Harry found the booklet easily. He poked out of the open door and yelled for Adele to join him inside. "No reason to freeze your ass off out there while we read it, is there?"

After closing the hood, she climbed in to snuggle up next to him and they scanned the booklet. They needed a push to the nearest service station was what it finally turned out to be.

"I haven't seen a gas station for miles," Adele moaned, burying her head in his shoulder. "I don't want to walk that far in this weather."

Neither did Harry. "You don't have to. Someone will come along soon. Until then, why don't we take *advantage* of this sudden intimacy, hmmm?"

"It *would* help us keep warm."

"Too bad we can't turn up the heat. I'd rather undress when it's nice and warm."

"Undress? You mean—here? On the highway? What if somebody comes?"

"It's late. No one will be coming for hours." He hugged her fiercely. "Except you and me, that is."

"Harry, I haven't fucked around in an automobile since high school, and I'm not about to start again at this late date."

"Can you think of something better to do?"

"That's beside the point."

She moved away from him, her mind clearly on the discomfort, the possible embarrassment their lovemaking might entail. She watched the snow outside as it piled up higher and higher, as it began to obliterate the view around them. Terrifying! This was a real *blizzard*. She leaned against Harry again for warmth and closeness. He smiled and said, "Maybe now is the time to talk about that better job. Y'know, the one with more money and prestige? And where you got this interesting information."

"Oh, later, Harry," she said. Adele had been lying about the job, hoping to screw him both literally and figuratively. She was not fond of Harry Faulkin, never had been, and she certainly had no desire to help him with his career. He was a *pig* and nothing else. He had fucked over enough careers and lives in his process of moving to the top; some of those careers had belonged to friends of hers. All she had wanted to do was involve herself in some sort of intimate relationship with the man so that whatever information she gleaned could be used against him. She would *use* him, like he had used others; especially women. It had been so simple, her deception. So easy. Now everything was quite effectively grounded for the duration. Until whenever they would get out of this car, off of this road.

But she was tired of watching and waiting. Watching the snowfall, waiting for another car to come along—an unlikely prospect at this point. She decided to use this man to appease her desire, to make him perform for *her*. He was an attractive bastard, she could not deny it. It would please her too in the long run.

But when it started, when they were both half-naked, entangled in each other's arms, she knew that he could not even deign to satisfy her in this smallest of ways. Like other men of his kind, he was a selfish lover, unable or unwilling to move her to the point of orgasm. He experienced—relished—his ejaculation, but left her unfulfilled, forcing her to masturbate. When it was over he looked at her and smiled.

She stared at him disdainfully. They began to put their clothes back on.

"Liked it, didn't ya? Had a good time, huh?"

"It was nothing to write home to mother about. Sorry, Harry."

"Huh?" The verbal blow hit him like a punch in the solar plexus. "What are you *talking* about?"

"Forget it, Harry. The cold is just putting me in a bad mood." She mustn't lose him now. She wanted to humiliate him a lot more than *that*. It was too early to lose his interest.

"You did enjoy it, didn't you?"

"Oh, yes. Yes, I did," she said politely. What a juvenile ego the man had!

"I *know* I'm a good lay," he said with pride.

That did it. Adele decided to tell the bitter truth. "Whoever told you that?"

"Lots of chicks."

" 'Chicks' ?"

"Dames. A lotta women like it when I do it."

"I guess they have nothing much to compare it to. What do you specialize in, nuns?"

"Look here, what the hell is your problem?"

"You're only a fair-to-middling lover at best, and it's time somebody told you. That's the only way you're ever going to improve."

"Look, girl, you weren't so hot yourself."

"Oh really? *Mr. Hot-Shot Weatherman is a lousy lay.* That's what it will say on the ladies' room walls at WNUC next week.'"

"You do that and I'll kill you. I swear it!"

"Oh, you're so hung up it's pathetic. Haven't you ever even tried to please a woman? To concern yourself with *her* enjoyment? One-two-three. Bam-zoom, it's over. That's a great lay? Come off it, Faulkin. You stink!"

He slapped her across the face viciously. The strength and pain of the assault left her face stinging for moments afterward.

"Get out! Get out of here! Get the hell OUT!"

He panicked. "Look, I'm sorry!"

"Get the hell out of here, and I mean it!"

"Where will I go?" Alarmed, he reached out to placate her. She pushed him away, her fingernails scratching against his cheeks, digging for the eyes.

"Cut it out, damn it!"

"I said *get out of here* and I meant it!"

"All right!" He clapped his hands down over her face, covering it, and pushed her head away with a violent shove. "All right. I'll get out! So stay here by yourself, bitch. You can stay here till you rot. And don't expect *me* to tell anyone where you are."

He got out, slammed the door, and shimmied into his jacket. It wasn't as cold now, but he was knee deep in white powder. It was *still* snowing, though not quite as bad as before. He realized that he wasn't really dressed for this kind of weather.

He stormed off in the direction they had come from, his feet already soaked from the moisture seeping in through his shoes. He hadn't expected to be in a situation like this or he would have worn boots. He gave one last look at the car when he was several yards away, spitting savagely and swearing. Then he started out again.

Looking to either side of the highway, he saw no lights, houses, or signs. He might as well walk back toward Manhattan until he came to someplace where he could find shelter or transportation. Even a warm cup of coffee would be enough for now. Leave the bitch to stay there until the summer thaw, or to get so covered up in snow that she'd be crushed to death by the first approaching snowplow. Yeah—that'd be a scream. Squashed in the snow. Would serve her right.

It was slow going. There was no wind, no sound, except for his feet struggling their way through the mounds and drifts of powder. Everything was still and eerie. At least the snow was now down to a light trickle.

He passed the time thinking about the special report he planned to do. *That* wold show everyone. He'd make this town sit up and pay attention to Harry Faulkin. Hell, he'd make 'em sit up and *beg*.

Harry's pants were all wet and covered with the white stuff. Expensive slacks too. Everything was warm except his legs. They were beginning to *feel* funny—the effects of the cold, he figured. They were tingling, hurting the way his fingers did when he placed them under extremely cold tap water. He had to stifle an urge to run off the highway, to run toward some area—any area—where the snow was not quite so high and he could free his legs from its wet and stinging embrace. His leg muscles were so terribly tired too. He wanted to rest, but was afraid to. The journey ahead seemed endless. What's worse, he had the damnedest headache and a queasy feeling in his stomach.

He must have been a quarter of a mile away from Adele when he happened to look down and saw that his trouser legs were torn and matted with blood.

"What the hell—!"

His pants legs were literally torn to shreds. Blood was dripping down them, thin rivulets of red from the knees to the ankles. He tried to balance on one leg so that he could inspect the other.

He tottered, tried to regain control, but slipped and fell down into the snow. He saw movement all around him. Quick flashes of red were disappearing into the piles of snow that this falling body had displaced. Blood? His blood? No, the spots of crimson were moving on their own volition. Moving!

The snow was alive with some sort of small grotesqueries, little red things that had been *feeding* on his legs. His calves were covered with dozens of puncture marks!

Fighting to control his anxiety, Harry thrust his gloved hand into the nearest mound of snow, and felt around, not sure what he might discover. There! He touched something. It tried to squirm out of his grip. He wrapped his fingers around it and pulled it out where he could see.

At first he thought it looked like some hideous internal organ pulled from a human's insides. A pulsating liver or heart. It was covered with blood; his blood. It was about six inches long and four inches wide, so thick he could barely hold it tight inside his fist. It squished around inside his palm, trying to wriggle free.

It looked like nothing so much as an overgrown kind of worm or larvae. Its middle was the thickest part of the body, tapering off to two points at either end. On one of those points, the mouth parts were working. Harry could even see teeth somewhere inside the almost colorless membrances.

The snow worms! The snow worms his grandma had told him about. They were real!

And, if it weren't for the blood consumed—*his* blood—one might not be able to see the things at all!

He got up and started running back in the direction of Adele's Camaro. She would have to let him in; he would have to convince her of the danger. He threw the "worm" out of his hand and saw it flop into a snowbank some yards distant. He could sense the movement in the snow all around him. They were *everywhere!*

He was in sight of the car when his foot hit something lying unseen in the road. He sprawled into the powder covering the highway.

Harry let out a sceam as he felt mouth parts converging on his body, the little teeth tearing into his flesh.

Adele had seen him running toward the car, had seen him fall headlong into the snow, scream, and disappear.

Thinking it was a trick, but afraid that it might not be, she opened the door to investigate.

Harry Faulkin was dead, sprawled out on the road like a hit-and-run victim.

It must have been a heart attack, thought Adele, staring at the still figure in disbelief.

For Harry Faulkin's body was *untouched*.

Silence reigned in the decrepit Berkley Arms Hotel. The old drunks who congregated in the halls had long since passed into sweet oblivion. Tomorrow was soon enough for them to once more face the harsh reality of daytime. The crazy lady in the lobby had stopped her swearing and complaining and finally gone to bed. The oldsters who could not sleep, the aging night people, lay in their cots and stared into space, read yellow-stained books, or prayed. Mrs. MacGruder, however, had turned off her light, put her face to the pillow, and dozed off peacefully. It was still night when she awoke, blinking and rubbing her eyes so that they would adjust to the darkness.

She often woke up early initially, drifting back to sleep for an hour or two more until she rose for her morning coffee and hot, buttered bun. But it was *way* before her usual wakeup time. Something had disturbed her sleep. Some uncanny sound, like distant wailing, but close, too close to come from outside. The noise was coming from inside the building. Near. She got up and turned on the light.

She stood by her door and listened.

The sound seemed to be coming from out in the hall, although it was muffled. That must mean that it was coming from one of the rooms! Mr. Peterson's room? The old woman opened the door carefully and stepped out into the corridor. She walked down to room 919 and listened at the doorway.

Yes. The moaning was definitely coming from inside Room 919. *What could it be?*

Peterson? Had her dear friend Mr. Peterson returned at last?

She knocked on the door. Two small, inoffensive taps.

Nothing. The sound inside had stopped.

She rapped again, louder. "Mr. Peterson—are you there? It's me. Mrs. MacGruder."

Nothing.

She was scared. Perhaps he was injured, unable to cry for help. Perhaps he needed a doctor!

Her fingers closed over the knob. As she gave it a twist, she noticed that it felt funny, as if someone had forced the door open and in so doing had snapped the lock. It swung open faster than she had anticipated. She stepped back with a start.

As the door completed its arc toward the wall, the scene inside was revealed. A black-haired man was crouching near the spot where the stain had been scraped off of the wall. Mrs. MacGruder did not recognize him as Ernest Hendon; she only knew he looked pathetic and deranged.

Ernest was pounding the wall, licking it, trying to *gnaw* his way through. Foam was gathering at the sides of his mouth. Now and

311

then he would look up at the elderly woman, but her presence had no effect on him. He started moaning as he had been doing before Mrs. MacGruder had seen it all—crazy people, loonies, drug-crazed maniacs, blitzed and bellicose winos and alkies. But never, *never* had she seen anything like this. The man seemed more animal than human.

Finally, his voice rising to a high-pitched scream, Ernest stood up and began banging his head against the wall, over and over again, harder and harder and harder.

Mrs. MacGruder was repulsed, but her compassion took over. She ran forward and tried to constrain him. It didn't work. He was too strong. She ran out again to call the police.

"I touched it," Hendon whispered to no one. "I touched it . . . it told me to come here. I must get out . . . the *walls* . . ."

When the police finally arrived, Ernest Hendon was dead. He was on the floor, arms spread out, his head in the center of a grisly, widening lake of blood.

It was dark and it was cold and it was wet.

Eric Thorne wondered how long he'd been there, crouching in the darkness. He was in some kind of conduit, an underground tunnel, one of the miles of tunnels that were part of New York's subway and sewer system. He had no idea where he was exactly. He'd been running from them, it seemed, for hours.

It started when his light had gone out and the

heavy door opened. Suddenly he was being examined by hordes of unseen fingers. He smelled sour breath on his face. He felt like an H.G. Wells hero surrounded by *morlocks* as an outpour of slimy, furry half-men streamed out of the opened portal.

These abominable creatures grabbed him and pulled him through the door, which was then shut firmly behind him. He felt that *presence* in his brain relinquishing some of its hold. Apparently it felt that since Eric had been captured he was now beneath its notice.

On the other side of the door it was lighter. The light was low, but enough for him to see by. His captors were humans like himself—dirty, dressed in rags, covered in filth and soot, smelling of excrement. Humans! Tramps, bums, male and female. He even noticed a middle-aged lady in a torn Givenchy gown. Who *were* these people?

He had to get away from them.

His eyes locked into the eyes of one of these samples of human debris. A short white man with pasty, unshaven skin and hollow pits for eyes. He caught a name, the man's name: *Ronnie*. He'd been a friend of . . . Haupster, was that it?—Haupster, the man Eric had talked to at the subway stop on Wednesday, the derelict whose psychic powers had started it *all*. Eric's part in it anyway.

From Eric to Haupster to Johnny to . . . "the master," they called it. That's how the master had come to know of Eric's existence. Everyone who served it was part of a gigantic, unnatural chain of information that was passed along the currents of the brain.

Some of these people were normal people from normal homes. Missing Persons. All of them. Snatched in subways and streets by Ronnie and others of his ilk. Ronnie had snatched Haupster—but the experience had been too much for the man; Haupster had died. That very night that Eric had talked to him, looked for him—he'd died.

Eric broke free and ran past steaming pipes and overstuffed trash cans, through one conduit after another, wading through muddy odorous liquid and ducking under metal obstructions. He dashed from one chamber to another—resisting *its* control—successfully eluding his mentally subjugated pursuers.

He was inside a little maintenance tunnel that was barely large enough for a man to stand comfortably. The odor was almost unbearable. His feet were soaked with all manner of slime. He hugged the wall, shivering from the cold. The padding footsteps of those horrible creatures had finally faded away into the distance. He had time to rest, time to plan his escape. Time to decipher the bits and pieces of data he'd picked up from the minds of his almost-captors.

He and Hammond had been completely wrong. True, the master, the force, they were dealing with *was* inhuman, was—as far as he was concerned—evil, was from a world other than their own. But it was not from an astral plane, a mystical dimension, the supernatural ether.

It was from another world.

It was not demon or devil. It was simply a sentient lifeform from *another planet!* An alien! An extraterrestrial with mental powers and abilities that made its mastery over humans almost a matter of course.

How did it get here and what was it doing?

What *form* did it take?

Eric finally understood the significance of the "white rectangle growing larger," the swaying, the naked people herded together. It *was* a subway car they were in, as he had suspected that morning when he had traveled to work with Hammond. For some ungodly purpose those derelicts and drunks were transported from spot to spot beneath the city in abandoned subway cars. Why? Were they *building* something? What could it be?

The white rectangle . . . one of the chambers these people were transported to as seen from the front of a subway car. Just as he had seen it that morning with Hammond. But where exactly was this chamber, and did it have special significance?

He'd also seen that door, the entrance to the underworld, in his mind. HGC—what did the letters mean? He had to find out as much as he could before he got out and went to the authorities. Assuming they could help. How many people of prominence were already under "the master's" control?

He heard scuttling sounds in the distance. He had more to fear from his subjugated fellow humans than he did from the alien itself. At least for now—while he sensed its attention was elsewhere, gathering its strength for some supreme final act that would insure the end of humankind's domination of Earth for centuries to come.

What was going to happen?

An image flashed through Eric's mind.

A young man. Blond. Handsome. About twenty or twenty-one. Who was he? How did he figure into it?

As long as the alien's monstrous mentality was directed elsewhere, as long as Eric could resist its subsequently weakened mental suggestions, he would have a chance. If only he could continue to elude its frenzied slaves.

He got up from his crouch, prepared to look for his way out of the tunnels. It was now or never. The path seemed clear.

A dirt-stained hand reached out from the darkness and grabbed Eric's wrist.

PART V

October 20th
Sabbath Day

ELEVEN

By TEN O'CLOCK Sunday morning it had stopped snowing. The trucks and snowplows were out, trying to clean the streets and avenues, but as it was not a work day—for most people—things proceeded slowly. It was slow going on sidewalks too—rush-hour pedestrians hadn't stomped down the snows as they would have had it been a weekday.

The snow had reached almost six inches in certain parts of the suburbs, and rescue teams had spent the night extricating those luckless enough to get caught in the storm. Steven had had to leave his rented car at a train station and take the Long Island Railroad back to the city. He didn't get home until early in the morning.

Steven sat in the back of the cab and listened to the radio blaring from the front seat as the driver drove up snow-covered Sixth Avenue at a snail's pace. The city was a winter wonderland, all right, all of its dirt and grime hidden underneath a pretty sheath of white. Yet there was something bleak about it too. Children making snowmen and flinging snowballs at each other were exotic counterpoint to the somber churchgoers on their way to worship.

On Sundays the city was dead.

The taxi pulled up in front of the office building where the Andrews Agency was located. Steven paid the driver and walked briskly into the lobby. Ralph had said on the phone that he had a lot of things to tell him. While he'd offered to give his report over the telephone, Steven had suggested they meet at the office, seeing how Ralph had already gone in in spite of the weather—"I spend more Sundays in the office than anyone should have to." Besides, Steven wanted to get out of the house before the silence drove him to distraction.

The receptionist and the secretaries and most of the other employees were not there, but Ralph had left the front door to the suite open. He was in his office, looking through a stack of papers. He smiled when he saw Steven and motioned him to sit down. "How are you holding up?" he asked as he lit a cigarette.

Steven shrugged. "Okay, I guess. Any news?"

Ralph gave him a quick update. So far a lot of interviewing, bar canvassing, etc. had led to nothing. "That news report last night might bring us a few leads. Too bad it had to be so—"

Steven nodded. "—lipsmacking. Yes, they made it all seem so . . . *sleazy*. They practically implied that Joey was responsible for Vivian's death."

"Well, at least we got your brother's picture in front of the public," Ralph said. "Trouble is, a lot of weirdos will come out of the woodwork saying they have information. It always happens."

320

Steven was very hopeful. "But maybe one of the weirdos will really have something to say."

"Maybe. I already spoke to the station, and the police—"

Steven interrupted. "Albright?"

"No, he wasn't around. Everyone's promised to pass along information to me if that news story gets results." He stopped to take a few puffs of his cigarette. "I wouldn't count on that reporter, Job Whats-his-name, coming up with anything on his own. He's strictly from the tabloids. A hack who does minimal work and sensationalizes it on the air so it sounds better."

Steven agreed. "I noticed."

"I did uncover something interesting," Ralph said, stubbing out the cigarette in his ashtray as an afterthought. "But I'm not sure what it means."

"Before we get to that," Steven said, "I'd better tell you what happened last night." Steven had been dreading this. He had been wondering exactly how he would tell Ralph about the letter and the trip to Tanton. What he'd found—or rather *not* found. He handed Ralph the letter he'd received and gave him a chance to read it.

"You went out there last night? By yourself?" Ralph asked increduously. "Steven, why didn't you tell me about this?"

Steven didn't know what to say.

Ralph put the letter on his desk and shook his head. "Well, you'd better tell me everything."

Steven gave him the whole story, what there was of it. "So you see, the guy didn't even show up. I didn't wait around. Seeing that gunk all over the floor—I was sick of the whole thing."

Ralph leaned back in his chair and patted one hand with the other. "Steven, one of the most important aspects of a client-detective relationship is trust. It's essential. If you don't trust me, if you don't let me handle things my own way, how can I possibly be of service? I've been in this business for many, many years. I've seen everything, handled every kind of case imaginable. I know how you feel. I can imagine what goes on in your mind. You're no different from anyone else, Steven, believe me. You want your brother back. You'd do anything to make sure that he's safe and sound. But that's *my* job. You've got to be willing to let me handle things my own way. You can't keep secrets from me any more. It just won't work that way. Do you understand?"

"Yes, I do." Steven felt like a little boy in front of the principal.

"Maybe no harm was done. But it could have turned out badly. We're not sure *what* we're dealing with here. Until we find out, we've got to handle this very, very carefully."

"I was just *afraid* to tell you, afraid *not* to go."

"Believe me, I understand. But from now on don't keep *anything* from me. I'm not the police. *I* know how to be subtle and discreet. And I know how to handle things."

"Okay."

"All right then. Let's get back to business. This has got to be one of the strangest cases . . . I don't know what you've gotten me into, but I'm hooked."

Just then a young woman walked into the office. She dropped a pile of folders onto Ralph's desk. "Here's the files you wanted." She looked at Steven. "Hello there."

"Steven, this is my assistant Valerie Horton."

Steven stood up and took her hand. Lovely woman, he thought. He offered her his seat, but she refused, standing instead to one side of Ralph's desk. She wore a green jacket and skirt. An emerald scarf was tied around her neck.

Ralph set the folders aside for the moment and continued. "Steven, have you ever heard of Hawthorne Greater Chemicals, Incorporated?"

"It sounds familiar. I'm not sure."

"You should have. Your father worked for them."

"He did? I knew so little about my father's work. It seemed to me that he worked for Ruftins Laboratories."

"Well, Hawthorne is the parent company of Ruftins Laboratories. They're really the same outfit, more or less."

"Ah, yes. I think I remember, now that you mention it." He paused, puzzled. "Does this have any bearing on Joey's—"

"We think so," Valerie interjected. "At one time Vivian Jessup and her husband were also employees at HGC."

"HGC?"

"Hawthorne Greater Chemicals."

"Of course," Steven laughed. "I'm still a bit sleepy." Then he reacted to Valerie's information. *"Really?"*

"Hold onto your hat," Ralph added. "It gets better. Three additional employees of HGC were Mr. and Mrs. Eliot Forrance. *George's* folks. And George too! In fact, he still works for them."

"And what about—"

"Brock Madison, Lina's lover? We finally got her on the phone this morning," Valerie said. "Yep, he works—or *worked*—for them too."

Ralph explained. "HGC has chemical plants and other kinds of laboratories all over the world. Their main plant is over in New Jersey. It was like pulling teeth—they're very uptight out there—but we got this information from them finally. It started when we dug into Vivian Jessup's background, and looked for a link between her and the other parties in this case. *Voila*—we found one."

Valerie cut in. "They have a New York office, a warehouse really, down in Tribeca. They don't keep regular office hours, that's for sure."

Steven leaned forward in his seat. "This is remarkable. Do you think this HGC has something to do with my brother's disappearance? There's got to be a connection. Vivian, Forrance, Brock. My late father."

"All of whom are dead or missing," Ralph said. "Which means that it's especially dangerous for you to go running off by yourself without me. This whole thing is beginning to stink to high heaven."

"But why would my father's old firm be involved—"

Valerie smirked. "A lot of laboratories and chemical firms make lots of extra money manufacturing *illegal* drugs. These people, your brother, might have found out too much." She stopped and looked apologetically at Ralph. She had always had trouble keeping the feelings of their clients in mind.

What was she implying? Steven wondered. That Joey had sold drugs for Vivian? That they'd killed Joey? "My brother wasn't mixed up in it," he said. "I know it. A little grass, a little booze. Nothing more." But all of this *was* putting a new complexion on things. "Hell, I don't know what to think anymore."

"Relax," Ralph said. "Let's not jump to conclusions. None of this may have anything to do with Joey."

"Damn it!" Steven fought hard to hold back tears.

"Now, now. It will be all right." He felt Valerie's soft fingers on his shoulder, comforting, warm.

"What could have happened to him?" he asked them. "He must be dead . . . or in trouble. People just don't disappear, unless . . . What could have happened? I feel like a court jester dancing for somebody's amusement. Like someone's playing games with me."

"Look," Ralph said. "Let us get back to work and get to the bottom of all this. It's no use telling you not to worry—but don't let it kill you. Don't let your imagination run away with you."

"All—all right."

Valerie gave him a sympathetic look.

"I'm going to go home now," Steven said. "I think I'll sleep for twenty-four hours. Friends and co-workers were calling me early in the morning because they saw that news story on TV. I'm *exhausted.*"

"We'll be in touch," Ralph said. "And don't give up hope."

Steven held out his hand when it looked like Ralph was going to get out of his chair. "I'll let myself out. I want you, both of you, to know . . . I appreciate what you're doing."

He said goodbye and walked out to the elevator.

Val sat on the edge of Ralph's desk. He handed her the letter Steven had received. "Shall we try and get out to Tanton this afternoon, look around?" she asked. She handed the letter back.

"Yes. I wish I knew who sent him that letter."

Val picked at a fingernail. "You didn't tell him about . . ."

"The lab report? No way. Not in his condition. He doesn't need it."

"It's pretty scary, Ralph. I'm beginning to think—"

"I know. I know. Imagine! That George guy was right! That stuff on the subway steps was *actually* comprised primarily of human tissue. We'll have to see if we can get a sample from that lifeguard station too."

Valerie shuddered.

She was beginning to wish she'd never heard of Steven Everson.

Steven had walked all the way down to the

Lower East Side before he'd realized it. In spite of his fatigue he hadn't felt like going home after leaving Ralph's office. He couldn't stand being cooped up in his apartment, unable to do anything but worry, unable to concentrate on any of life's essentials. And he wouldn't be able to until this whole business was over.

He needed time to think, time to ponder. A good long walk was just what the doctor ordered. The sky was clear; much of the snow had been cleared away or was melting.

He'd been rather startled to look up and see how far he'd walked from midtown. He had had his first apartment in this area many years ago. Hadn't much money then, couldn't afford any better.

He walked up Essex until he reached Grand Street, then turned to the left. The neighborhood had not changed much. Jews and Hispanics, kids on the prowl and strolling oldsters. The moviehouse, the bookstore, the Chicken Delight. Once you got away from the shopping area there were fewer people on the street. He saw that the old abandoned tenement he had passed by every day was still there, still deserted except for the occasional vagrant, he assumed, still crumbling into the sidewalk.

The children on the street were wearing their hunger and poverty, their faces haunted by despair, most of them doomed to always live their lives in the same squalid conditions, the same overcrowded, unheated apartments. The faces of the elderly were harder to read, already having shriveled up from bitterness and pain.

Always there was that inescapable *thirsty* look, a product of need for the basics of life which were denied them. Good clothes, good food— and most important, dignity and pride.

In the distance he saw the towering co-ops, large apartment buildings which had been meant for the lower classes, but which had somehow been appropriated by middle-income families. Further down there was a smaller housing project—the buildings were only three stories high, with little gardens and play-grounds between them. He decided to walk through the project and make his way toward the East River. He and Joey had spent many afternoons by the river when Joey had come to visit and the weather was warm.

He walked across the little footbridge that went over the F.D.R. Drive, heading for Jackson Park. His ankles sunk into the mushy snow on the footpath. He leaned against the railing and watched the cars speeding by below. He imagined his brother, his red cheeks shining beneath the tousled, wind-blown hair, standing beside him as he had done so many times back then. The river had been Joey's favorite place.

Across the bridge he continued until he reached the water's edge, walking past the trees and the outdoor auditorium. A wide pathway stretched up and down along the river. He used to sit for hours watching the boats chugging slowly through the water.

There was no one about on this cold day. He wiped some snow off a bench and sat down. He wondered where his brother was now, if he was alive, how he was feeling. Vivian—that poor woman—had been right. He did feel like a father who had done his job poorly, who had lost someone it had been his *duty* to protect. All the horrors of the past few days melted away— he could think only of his brother, out there alone somewhere. Not knowing what had happened was unbearable.

He realized that it had been stupid for him to come here to this spot. It had only released a flood of painful memories. And yet he *wanted* to think about his brother. Wanted to remember him when he was at his best. So young, so idealistic, not yet corrupted by the world. Too young to have been defeated by the heartbreak, the unfulfilled dreams, the struggle of day-to-day life. With nothing but the future ahead, a glorious future full of promise. Except for their parents' untimely deaths, he had been untouched by the cruelties of the world. Those cruelties had not left him embittered or broken. Rather Joey had been filled with a resolve to right the world's wrongs.

Or was that a mythical Joey? A Joey he only *hoped* existed?

Steven started to cry, almost glad for the warmth of the tears on his face, glad that he could let it out now, once and for all. If Joey had been involved in some kind of nasty business, he told himself, someone had *dragged* him into it. *They* had destroyed Joey. He wanted to kill anyone who had taken away Joey's future. He wanted to find out their names and track them down. Why had they destroyed a beautiful young man who had done no harm to anyone? No matter what anyone said to the contrary.

He realized with some surprise that he had always looked up to Joey instead of the other way around. Deep down in his subconscious, Joey was the man he most wanted to be. It was almost as if their parents had missed the boat with their first child, but gotten a perfect score with their second. Joey was more athletic and better-looking. Joey had a more outgoing personality. Joey was at ease in all social situations, and never failed to impress the opposite sex. Joey was the one who would really amount to something.

And part of Steven had always resented it. Perhaps the *strongest* emotion he felt right now was guilt. With Joey out of the picture . . .

No, he had to stop thinking like that. Sibling rivalry had never been a major factor in their relationship. Joey was all that was left of his family and he loved him.

Whoever had taken him, Steven would not let them get away with it.

But what could he do? he asked himself. What could he possibly do?

He wished his father was here. Wished he really was alive as he had imagined that night. He wondered what Ralph and Ms. Horton would have said had he told them he'd thought a man who'd peeked into his bedroom window was a corpse come back from the grave. At least he'd spared them that.

He got up off the bench, wiping away the moisture on his cheeks and under his eyes. He walked over to the metal railing that separated the pathway from the river and stared out into the water.

The city, his city, had never seemed so bleak.

John Albright had been in bed for hours.

He had no intention of going into work on Monday. He'd tell them he was sick and unable to report. He'd tell them he'd be out for a few more days. He knew that he would be out at least until his problems with Gloria were resolved. And that was the *least* of it.

Still no word. It was as if his wife and child had ceased to exist. He had finally called his other children to inquire indirectly if they knew of their mother's whereabouts, but always the answer was negative. He knew that he was not acting rationally about the entire matter, but somehow he couldn't muster the strength to do anything about it. What was the point? If *the master* wanted his wife and son, what could he possibly do to get them back? He felt so depressed, so *tired*, a ruined and deserted creature.

Why had she done this to him? What had gone wrong with their marriage? He didn't know which frightened him more—that Gloria had been taken by the master, or that she had left of her own free will.

What an irony! It had gotten to him. It had finally gotten round to him. His job had dared to reach beyond the nine-to-five routine to invade his home and personal life. The statistics had

*faces now: one the face of a woman he had loved
and lived with for years, and the other that of a
little boy he had barely had time to know. It was
a living, breathing nightmare. There he was—
unable to help even himself, unable, in effect, to
do his job when it was most important that he
did so.*

More and more his thoughts were of death.
Fast death, slow death, voluptuous death, and
messy death. Death in all its forms. The
ultimate destination: sweet, soft oblivion. Every
last one of them. The missing husbands, fathers,
brothers, son. The daughters, wives, and
mothers. All of them. Oblivion. Gloria too. And
Bobby. All dead.

Why not he?

All the departed lovers had *truly* departed,
had sincerely left this veil of tears; all of them.
They had gone into rivers and basements, abandoned buildings. That's where they were. Not
hiding. No, not hiding. Dead. Each and every
one of them.

Why not he?

Those who weren't dead *the master* had
claimed. A fate *worse* than death. Living constantly with that thing a part of his brain,
always listening, monitoring his thoughts. He'd
rather be dead than live that way. *Why* had he
remembered what had happened that awful day
when he'd been *treated?* It was true, he knew:
ignorance *was* bliss.

How should he kill himself? he wondered.
Not messy. He couldn't stand the thought of
doing it messy. He wanted to be in one piece, for

all that that was worth, when it was over. Nothing too grotesque. But fast, yes. How could he do it fast without doing it messy? There was no way. What to do. How to do it.

Pills? Slow perhaps, but peaceful. Yet vestiges of machismo still clung to him: a *man* wouldn't kill himself that way. Did he really care any longer? He could not live anymore. There was simply no choice, was there?

He'd lost all stamina and initiative. Gloria and Bobby were lost. The world was lost. He didn't care what that creature was up to anymore. Didn't care what happened to Joey Everson. There was no way he could save them. He went into the bathroom and opened the medicine chest.

He didn't know how many pills he'd consumed when it finally hit him what he was doing.

No!

I will not give up. I will not give in this easily.

In his mind's eye he saw his wife as she had looked when they had both been younger. He saw his children, his little boy at birth. He felt an ache, a disturbing desire to find out what would happen to the boy when he was grown, a need to see how he'd turn out. *There had to be something he could do!*

It was too soon to join his missing persons in their blank, purposeless purgatory, to join the nameless, numberless others that had disappeared before him. Too early. He still had things to do. He would not give up so soon.

The pills he'd already taken were making him

sleepy. That terrified him. He'd never really thought about death before. He saw an image of himself lying dead and naked in his bedroom—a *worse* image—his wife and son, his associates, seeing him lying there like that, vulnerable and pitiful, nothing but cold meat. And it chilled him. To think that that was all he'd leave behind him after all these years, just his flesh and blood, the cold meat of his body.

He got up and stumbled into the bathroom. A cold shower, that's what he needed. A cold shower would set him right. He didn't think he'd taken enough pills to kill him, but he was afraid if he fell asleep he'd never wake up again. *That must not happen.*

He was going to fight back! He was going to storm into the precinct and tell everyone the truth, look for people who weren't under the master's influence to help him. Regardless of the consequences, John Albright would not give up without a fight.

He stepped under the cold spray of the shower. It felt good—the sharp chill of the gushing stream was beginning to revive him. Then he'd make a good strong pot of coffee . . .

He was getting the shakes. Was it the pills? It had to be the pills.

It wasn't the pills. The master had heard, judged, and passed sentence.

Albright leaned against the shower wall for support. The *pounding!* He could hear his own heartbeat as if it were amplified over a million-watt system. The blood seemed to be rushing and rushing and rushing through his circulatory system, through each vein and artery, tearing its way around his body and its hundreds of miles of vessels.

He couldn't breathe. The pain was indescribable. His eyes started to bulge, almost popping from their sockets.

Albright knew what was happening. They'd warned him it might. Even while it was happening he couldn't quite believe it. He sobbed in the little time it took, partially in pity for Gloria— she'd undoubtedly walk into his office and have to go through the torment of begging someone —anyone—to care that someone she loved had disappeared. *Like Everson had. Like they all had. They had all begged for someone to be concerned over a dead person whom no one had noticed when alive. Didn't they know the spaces they left were much too easily filled?*

Albright's flesh began running down the drain with the water, a horrible, swirling whirlpool of white and red and gray.

The skin was gone from his arms and legs, exposing muscles and ligaments. His head was a hollow skull. He slid down the wall and plopped into a puddle at the bottom of the tub.

The sum and substance of John Mortimer Albright was completely washed away by the water.

Gloria Albright put the key in the lock, entered the foyer, and looked around nervously, almost shamefully, for her husband. She'd finally returned from her brief vacation, having found herself at the last moment without the courage she needed to *stay* away. She called out her husband's name.

How would she explain? Surely he must have checked with her mother by now and knew the truth. She *had* planned on going to her mother's, but hadn't wanted to deal with the questions, the hurt look that would surely have been there in her mother's old-fashioned eyes. She and Bobby had gone about like widow and child, suddenly free. It had been so . . . so strange, but peaceful. But how could she have let John worry so? What had possessed her to do such a thing? She *loved* the man for all his faults, that much was certain.

Bobby ran into his room to change out of his good clothes.

Gloria heard the sound of the shower running. She opened the bathroom door. "John. John?" she called.

Funny. The shower was on but John wasn't in it. He wasn't anywhere. His wife didn't know it, but John Albright had become a statistic.

Ralph dug a candy bar out of his jacket pocket and offered it to Valerie. "Want a piece?"

She leaned back in the passenger seat of the company Chevy and smiled. "No thanks. I'm still full from the lunch we had."

Ralph turned the wheel and they pulled out into traffic. "I think we'll take a look at HGC's New York office before we head out to Long Island."

"But why? I've been there. It appears to be just a tiny office in a big warehouse. Spare parts, I guess. That sort of thing."

"I wonder what *kind* of spare parts. Look, it won't take long to check it out. If the place isn't manned on a weekday, you can be sure nobody'll be there on a Sunday."

"I hope so." She shifted in her seat. "Ralph, we're not going to break in, are we?"

"If this *is* a drug case, I want to know. I want to see exactly what they've got in that warehouse anyway. We may not find any drugs but there's bound to be some evidence of some kind. Though evidence of *what*, I'm not sure."

"Well, if you think we ought to . . ."

Ralph drove down toward Tribeca instead of heading out of the city as had been his original intention. Tribeca was a small area on the west side of Manhattan between Greenwich Village and the Financial District. Once dominated by warehouses and small factories, it had recently become a fashionable place to live. Expensive lofts full of upwardly mobile urbanites shared space with art-deco restaurants and discos.

HGC's office, however, turned out to be on one of the lesser blocks of Tribeca, a narrow, dirty street of large, gray buildings and parking lots. Ralph parked the car around the corner under a large tree and turned off the ignition. They got out of the auto, locked it, and walked around to the other side of the block.

Aside from one man who was patiently waiting for his dog to relieve himself near where they had parked, they saw absolutely no one on the street. This was not at all a residential block. There was no traffic either.

The HGC building was still several yards distant. As they walked past the lot of an auto-parts dealership, Valerie's gloved fingers played along the grill of the metal fence across the driveway.

Suddenly something jumped up out of the shadows and lunged at her hand. She stepped back quickly, withdrawing the hand from the gate, and turned to see a pair of snarling German shepherds.

"God, they scared me!"

Ralph chuckled. "Good watchdogs, eh?"

"I'll say!"

The dogs continued to bark and growl until Ralph and Valerie were down the street. "I hope they don't alarm the neighborhood," Valerie said.

"I'm sure if anyone lives on this street they must be used to the noise by now. Those animals are trained to bark at *everything*."

There was no fence around the HGC warehouse, and no guard dogs either. They walked past the large garage door at one end of the building and approached the smaller entrance to the right of it. It led into a small foyer and hallway. Ralph looked around and got out his key chain.

Val giggled. "Don't bother, Ralph," she said, holding open the door for him. "It isn't locked. It never has been."

Ralph motioned for her to go inside. The actual office was behind another door to the right, and this door was locked securely. A door on the left led directly into the warehouse. This was also locked.

Ralph tried several different keys until he found one which would open up the latter. "Bingo."

"Well, at least we aren't exactly *breaking in,*" Valerie said. "You first this time."

Valerie followed Ralph into the warehouse and closed the door behind them. The room was dark and cavernous. Ralph pulled his flashlight out of his pocket and shined it around the enclosure. The floor, as well as pile upon pile of wooden crates, were coated with a layer of dust. Many of the crates were stamped HGC in red; any other writing was difficult to make out under the covering sheath of gray matter. Ralph cupped his hands in front of his face and tried not to cough as his advancing steps stirred up the "blanket." Valerie pulled out a handkerchief and clamped it over her nose.

"Ralph, no one's been here in *decades,*" she said. "And it smells awful."

"Well, let's look around anyway."

"I suppose you'll want to open one of those boxes."

"Hadn't thought of that, but it might be a good idea. See a crowbar anywhere?"

"Fine. It's my time to get an asthma attack."

They traversed the large room and discovered two smaller offices in the back. Another door led back into the hallway from which they'd come in. "Look how the dust is disturbed here. See the footprints," Ralph said. "People have been in here. And fairly recently."

Ralph opened yet another door and found that it led into a small garage—empty except for a rusty old truck—that opened out onto the street around the corner.

Valerie prevented him from closing the door. "Not so hasty. Let me check the dashboard. You never know."

"Okay. I'll be back inside the warehouse."

She went over to the truck and pulled open the door, half expecting a body to fall out of the seat. She was so jumpy lately. Still holding the handkerchief over her nose, she climbed in and looked around.

Back in the storage area, Ralph had looked up and noticed that the ceiling was surprisingly low. Judging from the height of the building, there had to be a second story. Where were the stairs? he wondered. He went back into the small offices in the rear.

Sure enough there was another tiny area behind the offices that one could reach through a door which he had at first assumed led only to the bathroom. There was a small bathroom, all right, but there was also a staircase which led to the upper level. He took that first dusty step and made his way to the top of the stairs.

It was much darker up here than it had been below—it would be safe to turn the lights on, he figured—but when he found the switch he discovered it didn't work. They must have turned the electricity off. He held the flashlight in front of him and proceeded down the corridor, not even sure of what he was looking for. Here too the dust was voluminous.

The narrow hall was lined with several doorways. He stopped now and then to shine his light into the small rooms they led into. All of the rooms were empty, as he had expected. There was nothing up here, that much was certain. He was just wasting his time. He had just decided to go downstairs again when something caught his eye at the end of the hallway: a large open space—doorless, black, like an empty eye socket. He *had* to walk toward it. He was drawn to it, compelled to investigate.

It appeared to be some sort of open shaft—an abandoned freight elevator perhaps? The dimensions were about right. Webs clung to the sides of the opening and a musty, dank smell issued from below. Ralph aimed his light down into the abyss and saw that there was a floor several feet beneath him. Metal rungs were attached to the front side of the shaft. Ralph would use them to descend.

The rungs were strong and firm, easily supporting his weight. Balancing the flashlight in the crook of his arm, he started to make his way down. He assumed that he would find himself in a closet or storage space adjacent to the room with all the boxes. He reached the last rung and placed his right foot on the floor. Then brought his left foot down beside it.

His full weight was on the wooden floor. He had at first thought that the floor was secure, but he now felt it beginning to yield. There was a creaking noise, the sound of groaning, twisting metal, and the platform caved in under him. His body shot through the remnants of splintered wood and hurtled down into the darkness.

Ralph's scream echoed throughout the building.

He was in free fall, in utter darkness. He tried to grab on to something but he was traveling too fast, a bulky piece of meat caught helplessly by gravity.

His body hit bottom like a sack of water thrown against a wall. There was a brief jolt of agonizing pain—then nothing.

Valerie had heard the scream but had no idea where it came from. She ran from the garage into the main room and looked around frantically, pointing her own flashlight in a dozen directions. She was beside herself—there was no doubt in her mind that it had been Ralph who'd screamed. She called his name and ran back into the small offices that she'd just come through a moment ago.

She finally discovered the stairway that Ralph had used to go up to the second floor. She followed literally in his footsteps, having noticed his shoe prints in the dust. She had to find him quickly; he might have been badly injured.

As Ralph had done, as she passed each room she stopped to make sure they were unoccupied. She was halfway down the hall when she noticed the beckoning shaft. A suspicion was building in her mind. Fearing what might have happened to her associate, Valerie started running toward the hole.

She was only a few feet away when she heard

noises—odd, bloodchilling *scratches* that came from the shaft. It was as if some long-clawed monstrosity was climbing up slowly from the cellar. Valerie stopped in her tracks, petrified.

Ralph's face suddenly popped up into the open space, causing her to gasp. His head was lolling at an unnatural angle. She watched with amazement as his entire body rose out of the shaft, his arms hanging limply at his sides, seemingly suspended by invisible wires. He simply *levitated* upward without support— until Valerie looked at his legs, and saw the several stained hands that were holding him up by the thighs.

Another moment and the faces—the faces that went with those gnarled, sooty fingers— would come into view. Valerie started to run back towards the stairs.

Her instinct told her that this had something to do with the Everson case. When they had connected it with HGC they had been right on target. This was indirectly the result of their meddling into the affairs of Hawthorne Greater Chemicals. That day when they'd contacted them had been the beginning of the end. The end of Andrews and Horton. The end of Ralph Andrews. The end of Valerie Horton.

Before she could reach the stairs she was brought down by something heavy, a bulky shape that hit her from behind. Valerie went crashing to the floor. She tried to extricate herself from the bulk that held her pinned to the ground but it was too large and leaden.

Her flashlight, which had dropped from her

hand and rolled down the corridor, grimly illuminated the horrible tableau. Valerie looked up and saw Ralph's dead eyes staring into hers —those things from the shaft had thrown his *body* on top of hers! She and Ralph alike were soaking in his blood.

The things from the shaft were now walking toward her. *People.* Human beings. Maniacs and murderers. *She could not know that these were renegades—mentally defective hordes too unstable to obey the master's commands. Instead they wandered the subterranean passageways, killing, fighting, eating garbage and each other for survival. They smelled the warm fresh blood of this woman—and wanted her. They were going to feast on her flesh.*

Valerie's scream was cut off as Ralph's hairy arm flopped down across her mouth.

When Steven got home from Jackson Park he took a quick shower and ate a small brunch of eggs and coffee. The largest thing in his life now seemed to be the phone—and he would wait forever if need be until it rang and brought forth some news, any news, about his brother. There had to be some explanation for the hideous occurrences, deaths, and disappearances of the past few days.

He came across an old, weatherbeaten magazine published by the Ruftin Laboratories. *A subsidiary of Hawthorne Greater Chemicals, Inc.* it read in small print at the bottom. Apparently Ruftin Labs was their research division. The magazine seemed to be a company publication distributed to their many employees in what appeared to be over a dozen different sections. He flipped quickly through the pages. It was a thin but oversized booklet, with glossy paper stock and good printing. On one page there were pictures of all the section heads.

Seeing a picture of his father—head of New Product Development—Steven knew that the person who'd stared into his bedroom that night had been the man's virtual double.

He flipped further on and came across a picture wherein a bespectacled, gray-haired man was receiving a commendation. Mr. Herbert Peterson. Steven remembered meeting the man once, many years ago, at one of his parents' cocktail parties. And there, in the background, was a much younger Vivian Jessup, standing beside a man whom he assumed to be her late husband.

The total picture he was receiving was frightening and suspicious. What could it mean? Why, Vivian had *known* his father, might have even met himself and Joey when they were children. Why the secrecy?

What was going on?

He had just finished putting away the newsletter when the phone rang.

It was Andrea.

"How's it going?" she asked cheerfully, as if nothing had happened between them.

He wanted to tell her everything, to confide in her and beg for her comfort, but remembered that she was no longer what she had once been to him. Was she calling to say it had been a big joke, a mistake, the other evening? Were she and Donald through? Did he care any longer?

"Everything's all right, Andrea. No news on Joey. But I'm feeling optimistic," he lied. He was tired of feeling vulnerable in front of a woman who no longer loved him.

"That's good. I was worried. Steven, believe me, I *do* care, you know that. A person's feelings —just because—a person's feelings can't change that easily."

Oh Andrea. You're only making it worse. A clean break, that's what we needed. Still, he was grateful for her concern.

"I know, Andrea. Neither of us . . . asked for this to happen. I guess I . . . wish you and your friend," he couldn't bring himself to say his name, "the best of luck, I mean it."

"Are we still friends?"

Damn, she was pushing it. "Andrea, I don't— I suppose so—only I can't *deal* with this right now. Joey's—this business has me so I don't know my right from my left anymore."

"I understand, Steven. I do. I just want you to know I understand."

"Okay."

"Okay," she repeated.

"Look, Andrea, I have to keep the line open."

"All right. Call me if you need someone to talk to."

"I will."

"I'll check back tomorrow."

"Okay. Bye and thanks."

"Bye."

Was it possible? Steven wondered, as he hung up the phone. Was Andrea like one of the women in old romantic movies, doomed to marry one man while pining all her life for another, one that she *really* loved but simply couldn't live with? Probably not. If anyone would do the pining, *he* would.

He went to bed for the rest of the afternoon but could only sleep fitfully. He got up a few hours later and started making dinner. He had to get back into a regular daily pattern again. He'd have to go back to work, get himself together. Falling apart wouldn't do his brother any good.

While he fried a couple of hamburger patties, he thought about all the things that had happened in the past few days. Vivian's grisly death. Lina Hobler's story. The goo on the steps. That awful midnight visit to Tanton, Long Island. That dreadful room with the rats and the roaches.

That spooky face he had seen in the window.

And that's when all the lights went out.

Steven stood there for a moment in the darkness, waiting to see if the lights would come back on. His eyes had trouble adjusting—he could barely make out the outlines of the kitchen appliances. He made his way slowly into the living room, where he knew he could find some candles.

Judging from the noises in the building, the doors opening, footsteps in the hallway, he figured the blackout had affected the entire apartment house. Nothing to worry about—it had happened before. The super would have it fixed in no time.

Just to make sure he stumbled over to the window, pulled up the shade and looked out.

It *wasn't* just the building. The whole city was affected!

Suddenly he knew that he was no longer alone in his apartment.

He had not heard the door open, not heard a window being forced or a lock jimmied, yet he *knew* someone was standing there with him in the blackness. Steven could hear the intruder's *breathing*. He looked around, trying to spot *anything* that he could use as a weapon.

Then a hand reached out and touched him, and a voice said:

"Steven. It's your father."

"How long have you been working as a secretary, Miss Hobler?" the personnel manager asked suspiciously.

Lina sat demurely in the cushioned chair before the oaken desk. She was wearing a bulky brown winter coat and played absently with its buttons. "Well, I've never actually held a secretarial position—not exactly. I—I am qualified, it's just that I—I've been doing other things."

"According to this application, you've never been employed anywhere as a secretary. How can you be a secretary in a Burger Bun?"

"Well, I was actually a waitress, but I did a lot of bookkeeping, and I was answering the phone all the time."

*"Then you were a bookkeeper or a reception-
ist. That's not the same thing as a secretary."*

"Well, I did some secretarial duties."

"Which were?"

"Uh, I just told you."

*The interviewer was exasperated. She shifted
in her seat impatiently and touched the bony
bridge of her nose. "Miss Hobler, how fast do
you type?"*

"I don't know for sure."

"Do you do light typing?"

"I'd say so."

"Under forty words a minute?"

"Yes."

*The interviewer scribbled something in a
small, square box on the white application form.*

"Do you have any other skills?"

"Pardon me?"

*"Is there anything else you're skilled in?
Office machines? Adding machines? Anything
like that?"*

"I've used an adding machine. A little one."

She scribbled again. "Anything else?"

"No. Nothing."

*The manager looked over the white sheet and
then stared blankly into Lina's bloodshot eyes.
"Well, Miss Hobler. We don't have any openings
now, but we'll put this on file. We don't think
you're experienced enough for a secretarial
position at this time, but we often get clerical
openings. Would you be interested in one of
those?"*

"Yes, I think so."

*"Okay. Then we'll be in touch." She dismissed
Lina with a sudden averting of the eyes . . .*

It all came back to Lina as she walked. The last time she'd gone on an interview. The last time . . . before Brock had saved her from all that: She'd always been trying to get a higher-paying job.

It was because of Brock that she was here at the Broadway Junction station. For one last look. She reached the top of the stairs and looked down. The outline was nearly invisible now unless you knew where to look. It would be completely gone some day. Now, before she started out on her new life, she wanted to see it again . . . not because she gave that loony George's story any credence, but . . . just in case. It was a symbolic gesture.

"Oh, Brock," she said, tears dripping into her handkerchief. "Why did you leave me? It's gonna be so hard."

Steeling herself, she dried her eyes, put the kerchief in her purse, and walked down to the street. She had to catch the bus back to her place.

She was so distraught and confused she had forgotten she still had to take the train back to Cypress Hills before transferring to the bus. Should she go back up to the token booth, pay another fare? No. She decided to walk. It was quite a distance, but in her mood it didn't matter.

Every time she thought of her resolution to start a new life—without Brock, without her baby, the love of her life—she felt Reality with a capital R hitting her in the face. Memories of what the job search had been like back then—

before Brock—kept coming back to her.

She walked down the hall past the young, pretty receptionist, the girl who sat chewing gum and filing her nails. Don't look at me that way, Lina thought as she stared back at the woman. I'm Lina Hobler, do you know that? Miss Lina Hobler. Who the hell are you? You nobody! You nothing! I was somebody once. Can you say the same?

It was so discouraging. She'd been to five places that day. She was either too old or too inexperienced. One old buzzard had even implied that her appearance wasn't attractive enough. Could she help it if she had no money for decent clothes or makeup? No money for a face-lift like the other hags got? She should have said that to her, the old biddy, yeah, she should have. She could have just seen that old buzzard's face when she said, "I can't afford a dozen face-lifts like you can." Yeah, she should have said that.

Cursing under her breath, determined to contain the anger and heartache she was experiencing, she looked once more at the list of places she had copied from the help-wanted section of the paper. Noting the address of number six, she strode off purposefully in that direction.

Damn if she'd let them get to her.

But they had gotten to her, all right. And they would again if she went back to pounding the pavement for a job. What was the use? Who was she kidding? Who was ever going to hire *her*?

No! she told herself. *You've got to stop*

thinking like that. Brock loved you, he did. He wouldn't want you to fall apart. Keep yourself together for his sake. So that you can avenge him some day.

Her mind was made up. She'd do it *for Brock's sake.* She was entering a new phase of her life, and she was determined to blot out the past so that she could meet each new challenge successfully.

Twenty minutes later she realized she had somehow turned a wrong corner at some point and lost her way. *Great start, Lina darling.* She must have been going in the wrong direction for the *longest* time. Not only was she no longer under the elevated subway—the darn thing was nowhere in sight. She now stood on the right side of a lonely road in an isolated warehouse district. Worse—directly ahead of her was a cemetery. The road she was walking on divided the cemetery into two equally ominous sections.

A cemetery. What an omen!

She had always hated cemeteries. Hated those little cubicles of death that people were placed in upon expiration. She wrapped her arms around herself to keep out the cold and slapped her wrists to keep warm. She checked her watch for the time. It was barely eight P.M. but it was so dark it might as well have been midnight. The watch was the nicest present Brock had ever given her. Expensive too. It lit up in the dark when she pressed the tiny botton on the side. Instead of hands, the time was told in numbers with the day and date in smaller

352

numerals above. This was the only nice thing she owned that she'd never, ever hock. No matter how hungry she got.

There was no point in retracing her steps since she'd no idea where she'd gone off the track in the first place. She'd continue on until she reached a residential district and found some friendly stranger who could give her directions.

She walked briskly past the silent rows of tombstones. *Brrr.* She looked ahead and tried to see how long the block was, wanting to estimate the time it would take her to reach more pleasant surroundings. This was a big cemetery, but something about its vastness and peacefulness was almost comforting.

She had walked a distance about equal to half a block when she heard what she first assumed was music—a strange, plaintive melody with vaguely sinister undertones. Where had she heard it before? She turned around and saw figures in the background, hidden in the darkness behind the streetlight. When had they snuck up behind her? She stopped, suddenly feeling a chill which came not from the dark, and waited to see who or what they were. She prayed they weren't gang members. As she stood there she realized it was voices—not music—that she had heard.

It seemed to be a bunch of people, singing, chanting rather, as they walked up from the corner where the cemetery began. They must have come from around the block. The group of darkened figures walked directly into the path of the streetlight, and Lina gasped when she saw what they were.

Strange shapes, hideous visages, all decked out in gruesome colors and macabre costumes.

Then she laughed.

Of course! The high-pitched, child-like voices. The devilish outfits. Children! Children out trick-or-treating. She could see now that the distant figures were all quite short, that they were carrying little orange and black shopping bags, waving their tiny arms up and down with frenzied anticipation. How silly she was, getting frightened by a bunch of schoolchildren! She laughed again, and continued on her way. Children. Just children!

Funny, she hadn't realized it was Halloween.

She walked along the cemetery at a slower pace, her dislike of children at war with the hope that they would overtake her and provide company as she traversed this lonely and isolated area. The headstones had been replaced by large, gray vaults which contained, she imagined, many different piles of dust and bones. Whole families gone to ashes.

Remembering something, she stopped and turned around again. What was it she wanted to check? How odd that there were no adults accompanying the children. How could their parents let them walk alone in this neighborhood at this time of night? Unfit as she might have been had she been a mother, she'd never have let a small child out of her sight in *this* city. There were enough lunatics on the streets on a regular night. *Tonight* every nutcase that could walk, crawl, or wiggle would be on the loose.

Wait a minute! *Now* she remembered. She pressed the button on her watch again. The tiny red numbers lit up obligingly and she checked the date. She was certain it was correct. According to the timepiece, tonight *couldn't* be Halloween. It was only October 20th! Halloween was over a week away!

Then what were those children doing?

They were not chanting trick-or-treat any longer, but something else, something obscene and repulsive, something deranged. She remembered where she had heard that "melody" before.

It had been on another Halloween many years ago. She'd been a child, a young girl still in grade school. She'd wanted to go trick-or-treating, but her mother wouldn't let her go out on her own. She'd had a fight with her friends in school—those jealous nitwits—and didn't want to go with them. Her mother couldn't be bothered dragging her around the neighborhood. She had a party to go to. She left Lina home alone.

The kids had come to the house and stood outside on the lawn. Wearing their gaily colored costumes and fright masks; they started to sing instead of ringing the bell and shouting trick or treat. They sang:

Lina Hobler is a freak
Her mother picks up men on the street
Lina Hobler is ugly and poor
The whole town knows her mother's a whore
It had been something like that—not exactly

the same, Lina's memory was so bad—but similar.

The children had scrawled dirty words on the walls of the house with crayons. Lina had screamed from the window for them to stop—and they'd threatened to come into the house and beat her up.

Her mother had come home and found her hiding in a closet, sobbing in misery.

Lina turned about and saw that the "trick-or-treaters" were less than one half block away and gaining, their tiny bodies dangerously close to catching up to her. Lina was seized by a feeling of icy terror—children had always been her enemies; why hadn't she remembered that? She started running up the street as fast as she could go.

Even before she heard the louder patter of their feet on the pavement, the sick, giggling noises coming from their mouths, she knew that they had started running after her.

A few yards ahead to her right she saw the gate across the entrance to the cemetery. It was closed at this hour, but perhaps someone was working inside. She darted over to the gate, wrapped her hands around the bars, and tugged. The chain that held its two sections together rattled noisily.

"Help me! Help me!" she screamed. She pulled frantically at the gate, but at best it would yield only a few inches. "Help, please! Please help me!"

There was no one there to help her. No one walking amidst the gravesites, no one on the street, no cars passing by. As the children approached from behind, they began to extract long, sharp cutlery from inside their shopping bags. From behind the monstrous masks came demented, delighted laughter.

Lina started screaming, her hands still pulling on the iron bars of the gate.

The first thick blade was thrust up into the space between her shoulders.

As Lina cried out, slipping down messily toward the ground, a flood of crimson liquid poured out from the wound. More of the phantom knives in her mind slashed out, cutting into her back, her ribs, her neck.

"Help! Help me! Please help . . . help . . . he . . ."

She tried to get up, tried to shield her face from the attack, but they were surrounding her, were all over her, those little hideous faces laughing and chanting while they hacked away at her body. *They'd come into the house as they threatened to and were beating her up as she always knew they would. Mommy—where are you?*

As they sliced her face to ribbons, the blood welled up in her eyes.

A delirious bloodstained Cinderella holding a carving knife in her hands was cackling.

Lina reached up her hand and pulled off the Cinderella's mask. She wanted to see its face.

As her heart stopped, as the mask that had never been there dematerialized in her hands, she saw that the little Cinderella's face was *her own.*

TWELVE

THE HAND WAS still on his shoulder.

Even before he turned around, he knew who it was.

He recognized the smell of him, that certain way he would breath, that strong, unmistakable grip that had held him so fast in childhood.

"Father?" Steven said, still not turning around.

This was crazy. Some mugger or thief, some junkie, had climbed in through a window and was trying to freak him out. That was all it was. Or else it was a ghost—or was he going out of his mind?

"Steven. You must believe it's me."

No! His father was dead! He had seen the burned wreckage of the car he'd been trapped in. He had gone to his funeral.

"Steven, it's your father!"

Steven was afraid to turn around and look. He wasn't sure which scared him more—that it wasn't his father or that it *was*.

"Steven. Turn around and face me. *Look at me!*"

He did.

It was his father, all right. Steven's eyes had adjusted enough to the comparative darkness to be sure of it. He saw the high forehead, the wide brow, the brownish gray mustache, the prominent cheekbones. He saw the full, determined lips, the worn wrinkled face of a handsome sixty-eight-year-old man.

Steven felt as if his whole world had gone topsy-turvy. Suddenly he could no longer believe in anything or anyone. Nothing made sense. There was no up or down. No right or wrong. Just a horrible feeling of utter help-lessness in the pit of his stomach.

He longed for the security of a womb.

"Yes, Steven. It's me."

Steven reached out his arms and held onto him, on some primitive level not knowing or caring where he had come from or why he had been gone so long. His life had been so miser-able lately—his father was here to set things right.

Then he drew back. "You're dead. I don't understand." He could scarcely believe the evidence of his own eyes. "It *was* you that night. Looking in through the window."

"Yes. I only wanted to look at you, maybe tell you that everything was all right. But I hadn't time. I felt my . . . independence weakening."

Steven stepped away from his father and leaned back against the wall. The momentary euphoria he'd initially felt had dissipated. He had to struggle to fight back the fear. Surely he was seeing a ghost, a phantom of his imagina-tion. He went to the china cabinet and withdrew some candles and holders, lit them. In the dim light his father's face was ghastly, but Steven was even more certain he was who he said he was.

"I—I don't understand, I—" Steven couldn't think of anything else to say. "How did you get in here?"

"The door was ajar, Steven. I simply came in. I wanted to make sure you were all right."

Steven looked over at the entrance foyer but the door itself was beyond his sightline. Well, it figured—he was so distraught and nervous and sleepy he *would* have forgotten to close and lock it.

"Look, Dad. I want some answers. You owe me that. I thought I had *buried* you."

Something suddenly broke inside Steven and he grabbed the man by his collar, almost wrenching him off his feet. His loving response had been replaced by doubt and curiosity.

"Steven! Please!"

"I want to know what you're doing here. You're supposed to be *dead*. What sort of joke is this? Why have you come back now, after all this time? Why did you let me go on thinking you were dead? You *are* dead. Burned to a crisp and buried. Why did you come back?" Steven was sobbing now, unable to hold it in. "*Why?*" He let go of his father and started wiping his eyes.

"I had no choice but to deceive you. I didn't *want* to. I didn't have any choice."

"I want answers—whoever you are. I want to know the truth!" How could he be sure that this apparition, this—this doppelganger—was really his father? It could be a trick. Another part of the lousy game.

"You'll get answers, Steven, if you calm down. I'm taking an extreme risk just by being here, you must understand that. I'll explain everything to the best of my ability. A lot of it you'll refuse to believe, but you have to believe, if we're to save your brother."

"Then Joey's *alive!* Your coming back has something to do with him!"

"Yes. Now sit down, Steven. And I'll tell you what happened."

Steven did as he was told, the little boy in him responding to the paternal command. His father looked out the window. "There isn't much time. It's already blacked out the city. It needs the power."

"What are you talking about?"

"We call it 'the master.' It's responsible for Joey's kidnapping, the deaths of Vivian Jessup, George Forrance—all the others."

"*It's* responsible. You talk as if you're referring to some kind of *thing.*"

"In a way, I am. The master is not a human being, Steven. The master is an alien entity, neither male nor female, a bio-mechanical, computerized horror. We've come to refer to it as a *biocomp.*"

Steven's father walked over to him, bent down before the chair, and struggled for a few moments to transform his thoughts into words.

"It all started not long before my 'death'— which, as you must realize by now, was a fabrication."

So Bradford Everson told his son the story,

361

the whole incredible story. How a futuristic capsule dating back to primeval times had been unearthed during the foundation-laying of one of Hawthorne's chemical plants in the Midwest. How the company had greedily locked away the capsule in their main labs in New Jersey. How an assemblage of scientists in the employ of the firm—who were later to come to be called "the committee"—were gathered together to open the capsule and examine the life-form inside it.

He told Steven of their remarkable finding: The lifeform was practically indistinguishable from the technological innards of the capsule—it was a living computer, in fact, half tissue, half alloy. None of the scientists had ever imagined the *possibility* of such a life-form, let alone seen one. The capsule—of extraterrestrial origin, that much was apparent—had landed on earth centuries ago. Something had gone wrong, and the alien had remained in suspended animation —so the terrible task for which it had been created and sent to Earth had been *postponed* for ages.

"Our tampering . . . woke it up," Mr. Everson said.

The creature wasted no time taking over. While physcially immobile for the most part, its mental powers were frighteningly acute. It could control minds. Before long the members of the committee—Peterson, Everson, Jessup, all experts in their various fields—were completely under its domination.

"On the surface everything was normal, more or less. But underneath . . ."

The creature's mental influence was extended day by day, reaching out to capture each and every employee. The major efforts of HGC and Ruftins Labs went to carrying out the creature's plans—anything else became obsolete.

"Worse, many of us were subjected to what we call 'treatment'—a permanent mental bonding to the alien. It prohibits us from rebelling, from betraying it."

Mr. Everson paused, holding his forehead. He looked terribly weak.

Steven felt a pang of fear. How was his father managing to resist this thing's control, assuming his fantastic story was true? Yet he believed—as awful, as terrible, as outlandish as it was, he *believed* it. His father was *alive* in front of him—what more proof did he need?

Mr. Everson continued: "I was forced to engineer my own death so that I would be free from contact with any human beings outside the project. Believe me, I didn't want to do it. But I had no choice."

"Why you?" Steven asked. "Why not the other members of the committee?"

"The alien knew it might be a little *too* suspicious if so many were 'to die' at once. It has a fairly logical mind. After all, it is a computer—biological, alive—but a computer nonetheless. As for why me? It sensed I had psychic abilities, low-grade but potentially disruptive. It wanted to keep its eye on me. It was intrigued. Also, it wanted at least one of us to be at its beck and call at all times. I wouldn't be free to carry on with my personal life as the others were. So I had to die."

Steven shuddered. To think his father had been alive all this time, conscript of and consort to an extraterrestrial being, his mind not his own. It was beyond belief, and yet he believed it. What choice did he have?

Things moved slowly at first. There were a lot of things to do and much preparation required. The alien was moved to a new location. Everson and the others were finally permitted to learn what its mission entailed. They were appalled, but unable to do anything to stop it.

The biocomp had been created by a race of beings on a world a trillion light years away; the natural habitat of the race was under the planet's surface, in caverns and tunnels. The biocomp also preferred such a habitat—the man-made caverns below the surface of Manhattan. And there its work would begin.

"The master's purpose is colonization. It has come to prepare our world for *its* master, the star-spanning race that spawned it. There are thousands of these capsules traveling through space, or that have already landed on other worlds and remade them in their image. The race that created them is an ancient one, predating mankind by a million millennia. In our language, the closest word for the alien race would be *Marikai*.

"Each biocomp functions in the same way. First it dominates every life-form it comes into contact with—it needs mobile drones to do its work for it. It builds itself a 'nest'—a war room, so to speak—and commands its slaves from there. Then it . . ." Everson stopped suddenly, held his stomach.

"Father, are you all right?"

"I just need to rest, Steven. I have so little time. Tonight, tonight . . ."

Steven had to ask. "How does Joey fit into all this?"

Mr. Everson looked at his son helplessly, then turned his head away. "Later. I'll tell you later."

"Does it know what you're doing now? That you're here talking to me?"

"No." He explained: "Steven, have you ever read crime stories in which masterminds rob a bank vault or museum under the noses of security guards by placing photographs over the closed-circuit camera lens—a *picture* of the vault or room that the guards see on their monitor while they steal the money or treasures out of the real room without even being seen?"

"Yes."

"Well, that's what I've done, in a way. The alien, as I've said, is part computer. It has pre-programmed commands. But it can be . . . tampered with, if you're quick and careful. Through this careful tampering, I've been able to fool it into thinking I am where I'm not, freeing me for hours at a time to do as I wish. Friday I waited across the street for you most of the night. You must have come home while I was having coffee. I peeked into the window . . . but I had to get back, my time was almost up. It would have known that I was gone. I've also managed to hide *your* existence from the creature by tampering with its system."

Steven could hardly digest all of this information. "Where have you been living all this time?"

"In the barracks under the streets with all the other slaves. All these months. Waiting and planning. Hoping the day would come when I could finally fight back. That day has come. But it's right down to the wire. If we don't act now, Steven, everything is lost. Joey's life. All our lives."

"Something's going to happen tonight, isn't it? Something that involves Joey?"

"Something that involves Joey *and* the entire city. The borough of Manhattan, at least."

"What?"

"That's the . . . hardest part to explain. I guess I'll just come right out with it. The alien has chosen Joey . . . for its mate."

"Mate? Is it a female?"

"No. As I said, it has no sex, as we know it. It reproduces in a very different way—"

"But how could it be *compatible* with a human being?"

"That's just it. This isn't a question of fornication. It *absorbs* the entire body of its 'mate,' reduces it to its basic chromosomal elements, and creates, spits out to put it crudely, a new life-form. Half-alien, and, in this case, half-human."

"Why, for God's sake?"

"Since the purpose of each biocomp is to subjugate a planet's dominant life-form so that it will serve as drones to make the environment fit for the colonizers when they arrive, it figures that the task will be easier if the dominant life-forms are led by a ruler that is at least, in this instance, half-human. The other half, the alien half, will always be faithful to the biocomp, who will supervise, as always, from behind the scenes. The power behind the throne.

"Normally the biocomp would mate with me, or my counterpart on other planets—the human it has chosen to lead its slaves in the pre-offspring period. Unfortunately, all mates *die* during the process of 'reproduction.'"

"In other words," Steven said, "you aren't expendable."

"No, I'm afraid there's more to it than that. Once this 'messiah' is created, I *will* be expendable, so *my* sacrifice isn't of relevance. The problem is that many mates, especially if they're old and weak as I am, die even *before* the process is completed. And that won't do. When that happens, very often the alien dies too. It's very complicated. The master's biological system is completely different from our own."

"Why can't it simply use some of Joey's sperm, a tissue sample, a few cells from his skin? Why does it have to consume him?"

"It won't work otherwise. Joey is young and strong. Joey shares my genetic heritage. He was the beast's first choice."

A bizarre thought flashed through Steven's mind. *I was spared this fate because I, the first-born, was second best.*

"How can we stop it, Father?"

"That's going to be my job. The reason I came to you tonight is because there's something you must do while I try to save your brother."

"Name it."

"This alien culture, the *Marikai*, has its own 'god' to which it prays and makes sacrifices, as does the biocomp. Remember, Steven, to this alien being we are less than nothing. Tonight, so that its god will bless the union and its mission, it intends to make a sacrificial *offering*. That offering consists of every man, woman, and child on this island, Steven. Millions are going to die!"

It took a few seconds for the full impact of his father's words to hit him.

"During the past few months it's been commanding its human drones to build a complicated power grid under the city streets. The grid was completed a few days ago. There have been a few advance tests which have affected the weather and caused other odd phenomena. As work proceeded on the grid, we needed more and more workers. We got them by snatching people—first Bowery bums and derelicts, later anyone and everyone—right off the street. There is a conspiracy of silence in this city. You people up here live your lives, never even dreaming of what goes on beneath your feet. The whole city is dying and no one even knows it. No one is even missed. Even people in positions of authority are under the biocomp's influence."

The whole business was getting more petrifying and outrageous by the second. "Let me guess," Steven said. "You want me to do something to destroy this grid, while you rescue Joey."

"Yes. You're the perfect choice. You see, you're literally the 'invisible man.' When I surreptitiously managed to program the alien not to know of your existence any longer, I cut you off from all of its senses, and hence from the senses of all its slaves. No one will even be able to *see* you, even if you're standing right in front of them. No one will be able to stop you."

Steven would never understand how such a thing could be, but it sounded good to him. *I'm going to wake up,* he told himself. *Any second I'll wake up and this will all be a dream.*

"Remember, a chain is only as strong as its weakest link. I managed to build a weak link into the power grid. If it is destroyed, the entire system goes down. All you have to do is get to that link and throw a switch—one simple switch—and your part is over."

"What exactly will this power grid do? How will it destroy the city?"

"The same way the biocomp destroys anyone who rebels. It dissolves them, literally. It does something to their molecules. The science of this alien culture is so advanced that it seems like *sorcery* to us."

Had Steven heard correctly. "Everyone in Manhattan will dissolve?"

"Everyone. Destroyed. Every last living soul. But it needs tremendous power to pull it off. Power which it has siphoned from the city's electrical system."

"So that's why there's a blackout."

"Yes. The grid is *warming up* now."

Steven had absorbed the full implications. "Then that means—Brock; that man in the lifeguard station. God, it's true. They really were *dissolved!*"

"We'd better get going. At midnight—that's when Joey will die and the city will be sacrificed. Twelve o'clock. Coincidentally, on the night of our Sabbath. This will not be a day of rest for us, I'm afraid."

"But I have so many other questions . . ."

"On the way, Steven. I have a car outside. Get your hat and coat and *let's go!*"

In a car that was marked *Ruftins Laboratories,* Mr. Everson drove down the silent streets past rows of blacked-out buildings. It was eerie and unreal. The whole *thing* was unreal. Steven—to keep himself from getting scared shitless—rattled off one question after another while his father drove downtown.

"How did Vivian Jessup figure in all this? Was she really Joey's lover?"

"Yes. Though that had not been her original intention. She only wanted to warn him, to protect him. A noble effort. It failed. She was punished. She lied to you only to protect you. She figured the less you knew the better."

"Brock Madison. George Forrance? What were their parts in it?"

"Both of them were foreman—two of several —overseeing the construction of the power grid. At first our workers consisted only of tramps and mental patients, people who wouldn't be missed. They needed constant guidance. Some were driven mad by the alien's

370

insensitive mental persuasion. A whole slew of them run about through the subways causing mischief and making a nuisance of themselves. We call them 'renegades.' Others committed suicide.

"Anyway, George's parents had both been lower-echelon employees of HGC many years ago. Both died before this ghastly business started, lucky them. But we thought it a good idea to bring George 'into the fold.' He'd once worked on subway maintenance, and his experience and knowledge of the system were invaluable."

"I suppose he's dead too."

"I'm afraid so. The biocomp won't tolerate betrayal or rebellion of any sort."

"It can only kill people that have been 'treated', right?"

"If only that was true. No, I'm afraid it can kill anyone . . . whose existence it is aware of, at least. It can dissolve, erase from existence, only those who have been treated, true. But it can literally stop the hearts of anyone it sees as an enemy, anyone who even suspects what it may be up to. In *either* case, it can cause frightening, realistic hallucinations—that depends, however, on the mental state and suseptibility of the victim. It can also *control* the actions of people who have not been treated."

"This thing prays to a god? It *is* a god."

"Compared to us—yes!"

Mr. Everson turned the corner and headed downtown. Some people were out on the street, drunk and carousing, reveling in the blackout, any change in the dull status quo. *If only they knew*, Steven thought.

"As the time of the 'union' draws near," Mr. Everson continued, "the biocomp is, for lack of a better word, becoming paranoid. In other words, it's killing more and warning less. It sees everyone as a threat. After Friday night I erased all knowledge of your existence from its memory—believe me, I would have killed it if I could, but that's a nearly impossible task—but I'm afraid it still retains knowledge of your friends and associates. Everything I see, *it* sees. It links up with, locks onto—on a psychic level —one mind after another after another. The question is: will it see any of your friends, anyone you've talked to, as a threat to its survival?"

"I can't imagine why it would."

"I'm afraid it has already. Harry Faulkin, Lina Hobler, and John Albright are dead. Albright had been treated, of course. The other two died of 'natural causes.' And that man who tried to see you—Gregory Olsen—he was killed too."

Steven was thunderstruck. Harry dead! And the others. And his father had recited their names so coldly and mechanically. And to think that Albright had been one of the master's "drones" all along.

"No time for sorrow, Steven. Every war has casualties. And make no mistake about it. This is a war. Our entire planet is at stake."

Steven felt his blood pressure rising. "Even if we stop this damned biocomp, what's to prevent it from trying again?"

"I have plans. Once Joey is safe, I'll have nothing to lose. Trust me. If I fail—"

"Then I'll take over. I'll still be invisible to it? If anything—happens to you?"

His father paused. "Hopefully."

That was not encouraging.

"Who were the members of this 'committee' you spoke of earlier?" Steven asked him.

"Myself, Jessup. Herbert Peterson. Others you don't know. Jessup tried to get his wife to help us, but all he did was get her *involved*. Jessup was responsible for immunizing the biocomp to earth mico-organisms. We all had our jobs. Peterson and Olsen prepared its food supply of nutrients and proteins."

"Why didn't Vivian take her husband's place after he passed away?"

"Somebody else was judged more qualified. Besides, she had washed her hands of the company. It would have looked suspicious. At times the biocomp allowed us—or so we believed—to make day-to-day decisions ourselves."

The car was slowing down. Steven looked out the window and saw row upon row of dark, neglected warehouses. They were on the edges of Tribeca. Now and then, beyond the metal fences that surrounded the warehouses, Steven could see small four-legged shapes growling and barking, scrambling up against the barriers, shouting at the car as it went by. The whole area was bleak and forbidding.

Steven had lost track of time. He had no idea how long they'd spent talking, traveling. The pitch-blackness outside wasn't even relieved by

an occasional streetlamp. There were no pedestrians. He wanted to ask exactly where they
were, but his father—if it truly was his father—
seemed so distant and preoccupied that he
found it impossible to disturb him.

For some strange reason, Steven was no
longer frightened. *Living computers, cities sacrificed, invaders from the stars; how could he take
it seriously until he saw it for himself?* Perhaps
he was letting his subconscious take over,
reverting back to childhood, letting him become
once again the small boy in his father's loving
care. *Daddy will take care of it. Daddy can take
care of everything.* Or could he? He didn't know
any longer. He didn't remember when it was
that he'd first realized parents weren't
infallible; not invincible. That they were just as
frightened and alone in the world as he was.

Mr. Everson pulled over to the curb and
parked.

"There are several special entrances to the
underground complex HGC built for the
biocomp—all clearly marked—as well as
several other ways to gain entry. Of course, you
could enter the subway or sewer system at any
point and eventually make your way to the
complex, but you'd have to know which way to
go. This is HGC's New York office, by the way."

Steven remembered that this was the
building Ralph and Valerie Horton had been
talking about. He was afraid to ask his father
about *them.*

They locked up the car and went over to the
entrance to the warehouse. As they stepped into

the foyer, Mr. Everson pulled out a key, which he fitted into the lock of the office door.

He went over to the cluttered desk and pulled out the side drawer. There was a piece of equipment inside, a small box like a geiger counter with a small screen filled with lines and dots. "Though the regular subway system has come to a halt due to the blackout, *our* trains are still running." He pointed to the lines and dots. "I can tell where each of the work trains are located from this." He studied the screen. "Good. One should be arriving at our platform downstairs in a few minutes. The HGC built a whole new line, its own stations, for its own purposes."

He led his son down the corridor to another doorway at the far end. He opened it, motioned for Steven to follow him inside. They were in a small office. Footprints in the dust on the floor indicated that people had been here before. Mr. Everson pushed a desk to one side and pulled open a trapdoor. Steel rungs led down to another narrow hallway.

As they walked down the lower corridor to a dimly lighted platform several yards distant, Mr. Everson told his son what he would have to do. "Remember, you're invisible. *No one* can see you. All you have to do is throw the switch. And your part is over. Leave the rest to me."

The platform was no different from the ones in the normal subway system. A train was even now pulling in. Wordlessly, his father motioned Steven toward the back end, while he went in the opposite direction. Steven hid behind a pillar and waited for the train to come to a halt. His father had said no one would be able to see him, but until he was sure of that he intended to stay out of sight.

The train jarred to a stop. The doors slid open, and several greasy types got out. Mr. Everson had already disappeared into another passageway down the platform. A very last car of the train was an open flatcar full of garbage cans and other maintenance equipment. Making sure no one was looking in his direction, Steven scrambled over the rusting side of the car and ducked down out of sight. Still crouching, he made his way toward the next car, which was a regular one. No one was inside.

He stepped up and over the connecting brace and entered the car, relieved to find the back door open. The door to the little engineer's room was also unlocked and ajar. He found the compartment empty and went inside, pulling the door closed behind him. Now all he could do was wait. He kept repeating his father's further instructions over and over in his mind, wondering if this was a trap or a fantasy—but not caring. He suspected his father had "done" something to him to make him more pliable, to cut through the layers of fear, disbelief, and incredulity and help him relax and *accept*.

About five minutes went by and the train finally started to move. It was not going to be a smooth ride. His father had explained that this and other special HGC trains were going to pick up drones from various points in the system to prevent them from inadvertantly going up to street level at midnight. Afterwards, after the city had been murdered, the master would still need its workers. Tonight they would sleep safe and sound in the barracks. The master's control of its slaves was spotty due to its preoccupation with more important matters.

Steven wondered how the biocomp intended to follow up this massacre. Surely the slaughter of the entire population of Manhattan would attract the attention of authorities. How would the creature hope to fight off the Army, the National Guard?

But it would and it could, he knew. Anyone who came to investigate, it would dominate. *One after another after another,* his father had said. Government officials, soldiers, reporters —all under its spell, all working with its "offspring" to prepare the world for colonization. It was staggering; in theory the biocomp could spread its consciousness across the entire planet; every single organism would have the same mentality!

Minutes later the train was still heading in a downward direction. Steven chanced to look out the window, but could see nothing but the narrow tunnel and the progression of dim, yellowed lightbulbs along the wall. He was about to sit back down on the grimy floor, when he heard a sort of *squealing.* The train had slowed to maneuver a curve, and something had jumped up over the side of the flatcar. A man. Two men. Several men . . . and women.

Steven smelled an odor of sewage and chlorine. The people—if they could still be called that—began to burrow into the uncovered cans and stuff refuse into their mouths.

Steven pulled back out of sight. These must be the hungry "renegades" his father had mentioned, unmanageable workers driven crazy by the master's mental probing. But if they were not under its control, did that mean that they could *see* him? He lowered his head. This was no time to find out, not while they were gobbling up that garbage. Not while they were *feeding*.

A few minutes later when it was silent outside he took a cautious look. The renegades were gone. All of the garbage on the back car had been consumed. The train had resumed its former speed. Clearly the renegades knew precisely at which points the trains were forced to slow down.

The men on the train hadn't bothered to corral those starving semi-animals. They were of no use to the master anymore.

The train continued to wind its way through the catacombs of New York, traveling along special tunnels the HGC had constructed in the bedrock. Steven felt like he was trapped in somebody else's nightmare.

He could see now that there was another track next to the one he was traveling on. Through the pillars that separated his track from the one adjacent to it, he could see that another train was approaching from the opposite direction. It looked exactly like the one he was in, the kind of train that went daily through the regular subway system. Steven looked through the dirty, spray-painted windows of the other train and saw that the cars were packed tight with writhing figures.

People! Then that must mean that they were traveling the regular byways of the system. That the power had gone back on!

No.

He realized that he had been wrong, terribly wrong. That was no normal passenger train passing by. It was packed to capacity with people, yes, but the people were screaming, crying, tearing at each other in a desperate attempt to get out. And each one of those terrified human beings was almost completely naked.

No wonder so many workers went crazy. No wonder there was such a rapid turnover. They were treated like concentration-camp prisoners. That garbage had been meant for them. They were dragged around from place to place and forced to work until they dropped or died, given only enough food to keep them breathing. But if the power grid—and the bio-comp's complex—were already finished, what were these bedraggled drones working on?

Hundreds of men and women were crammed together in those small cars, reeking of urine and vomit, their bodies covered with blood and sweat, their faces wet with tears. Steven was utterly sickened. A full five cars were filled to the brim. So many people, stuffed into those sweltering metal containers. Some of the windows were open, and he could see arms flailing out of them, people struggling to jump out and onto the tracks. Anything to get out, get out, *get out!*

Some of the people were still aware of what was happening, still aware of friends and family, of the life they had been taken from. They knew what had been done to them.

Now the two trains were directly opposite each other. Although he wanted to look away, Steven found himself unable to shut out the horrible sight before him. The screams were unbearable to listen to. Stuffed together so tightly they could barely move, the people still managed to bang against the walls of the car or at each other. They were all crazed beyond reason, tomorrow's "renegades." The biocomp simply *dumped* them when it was through with them.

He saw a woman, her naked body covered with dirt and a multitude of dripping scratches, banging with her fists against one of the windows. She struck at it repeatedly until it cracked. She continued to beat at the shattered glass, causing blood to gush from her wrists and run down along her arm. She was oblivious to the pain and the danger. It took Steven a moment to understand the significance of her distended, sagging belly. *She was pregnant!* Putting on a burst of speed, the train shot forward, pulling away the woman and all the others.

Steven sunk back to the floor of the tiny compartment. He wished that he had never seen it, that it had never been there. All a trick. A figment of his imagination. That's what it must have been. *But it wasn't.*

The train was slowing down. *The first stop,* his father had said. This was it. He got up and stepped out of the compartment. Everything was up to him now.

He made his way back to the flat car and again crouched low behind some garbage cans. The track ahead was getting lighter—they were coming into a work station. The train stopped and the men he'd seen before disembarked, directing several drones who were milling about to get into one of the cars. They walked around the enclosure making sure no more slaves were in the area.

Steven waited several minutes until he was certain the men had gone back into the train, then climbed out and stepped onto the platform.

He heard footsteps.

Too late! Two other HGC maintenance workers were coming out of a corridor to the left. He was right out in the open with nowhere to hide.

The two men walked right past him.

It was true. They couldn't see him. *No one could see him.*

Down here Steven Everson didn't exist.

The two men boarded the train and it started to move. Steven checked his watch. A quarter to eleven. He had better hurry.

He saw part of the power grid over his head as he walked down the hallway—a large circular tube of silver blue metal. The drones had been making last-minute maintenance checks. In several strategic points under the city, according to his father, those tubes converged into huge transformers. It was to one of those transformers that he now headed.

There was no way he could have missed it. It was the size of a boiler, a cylindrical black object that hummed and hissed. Steven bent over and looked for the lever that was hidden on the far side of it. *There!*

It seems incredible. All I have to do is pull this lever and I'll save several million people!

He was about to reach out and pull it down when he heard funny scrabbling sounds behind him.

Renegades! A whole group of slavering human rejects. There were about a dozen of them, filthy, gibbering, advancing on him with devious intensity.

And they could see him!

At least he had an answer to his question.

Quick! Pull the switch!

The renegades were too fast. Before he could make a move, one had jumped on top of him and brought him to his knees. He tried to get up, tried to fight back, but his arms and legs were pinned.

The switch was just above his head . . .

He felt the renegades surrounding him, breathing down his neck, their eyes mad and hungry, their mouths open wide to taste his flesh.

. . .a million miles away.

* * *

His time was nearly up.

Brad Everson saw by his watch that he would not be able to fool the master much longer. He had to be present at the ceremony—the damned emotionless creature was going to make him watch! It was not programmed in any natural or mechanical, real or artificial, way to feel guilt or remorse, love or sorrow or sympathy. It just coldly did what it had to do. It was a machine, that was all. A monstrous organic machine.

But Everson had still managed to build up a resistance to it. And he had a plan. If Steven could defeat the beast on that larger level, *he* would defeat it on the more personal one. He would save his son. It would take every inch of will power that he had, but he could do it. He'd wait until the very last second. And then it would be too late for the biocomp to stop him.

He started to walk back toward the complex. He always spent some time during his "free" periods in the natural cavern at the edge of the barracks—or one of the others they'd unearthed—giving food, comfort (and medical assistance, which was otherwise never provided) to the drones building the various chambers of the underground city. The biocomp had them working right up until the appointed hour—when it would grant them rest because of the "ceremony." Hundreds of hungry, tormented men and women were digging out and streamlining three separate caverns which would one day—*never!*—be home to the first *Marikai* settlers. Miserable moles!

Groundslugs!—for all their advancement, that's all they were, burrowing into the earth and shunning the sunlight. And if the buildings of Manhattan were to tumble to the ground, what did they care?

He found the current members of the committee in the complex's operations room. They gave each other silent greetings. The others walked about checking dials and levers, computing energy levels, making ready for *the moment*. The moment when the grid would reach full power and the city would die. The beautiful thing was he'd *doctored* the system so that if Steven was successful no one would know it until it was too late to do anything about it.

The biocomp was expecting him. He walked down the hall that led into what he had come to call the creature's lair. They had attached Earth computers and data banks to the machinery which in part made up the biocomp's super-structure so that they could more easily deal with it on a human level. They spoke to it in *fortran*.

His son Joey had been kept from him, secured somewhere in the barracks adjacent to the complex.

The afternoon the drones had snatched him from the park had been the worst day of Bradford Everson's life.

Tonight he would see his son for the first and final time.

Steven thought he was drowning when the waves suddenly receded. He opened his clouded eyes and wondered what was wrong with the movie. The picture was running in reverse. The ogres, the goblins, were moving away from him instead of toward him. The ogres, the goblins, were going the wrong way.

He could still feel the pressure from the fingers that had been around his throat, still feel their tongues and teeth upon him.

He shuddered, pulled himself up to a sitting position.

Yes, it was true. The renegades were moving backwards. Why hadn't they finished him off, devoured him?

One of them detached himself from the others and came stumbling back.

Steven looked around for something to defend himself with.

"Are you all right?" the man asked.

He *spoke*. He was disheveled, but apparently sane.

"My name's Eric Thorne. Another moment and they would have had you, I'm afraid."

Eric Thorne was about Steven's age, shorter, mustachioed. Cakes of clotted blood were sticking to his face and his clothes were torn in several places. He held out his hand and pulled Steven to his feet.

"How did you—?"

"Oh, them? They almost got me too. Yesterday. At least I think it was yesterday. I've lost all track of time. What day is this anyway?"

Steven brushed himself off and checked for

wounds. Finding none, he replied, "Sunday night."

"Sunday night. It *has* been over a day."

"Who are you? What are you doing here?"

Steven felt the fabric of his mind being wrenched ninety degrees.

"The same thing you are, I imagine. Yes—I did read your mind just then. Being down here in close proximity to our alien friend has done that to me." He tapped his head. "Expanded my consciousness. Opened up some of that other ninety percent of the brain. Increased my paranormal abilities. I'm even more adept at reading thoughts *and* transmitting them too.

"That's how I escaped from our friends . . . and saved you. I filled their feeble minds with fear and panic. Fear of me, panic over what I might do to them. I discovered I could do that quite accidentally yesterday—when they were about to do to me what they were about to do to *you*. The first group of people I ran into down here were only drones who wanted to capture me. The renegades snuck up on me later while I was hiding and resting in a tunnel."

Steven didn't understand all of it but he thanked Eric anyway. During that brief moment when their minds had touched, all information, everything, had passed between them. All Steven had to do was sort it out gradually as they went along.

His rescuer looked over at the transformer. "It's lucky I ran into you. Well, actually it wasn't luck as I've been trying to find my way out of here for hours. But anyway, if what I picked up in your mind is true, I can do what I've been wishing I could do—shut down this whole operation—just by pullling that lever. Or do you want the honors?"

Steven checked the time. "*Yes!*"

He pulled the lever.

At first there was no reaction. Then the transformer stopped humming. Steven looked up at the silver blue tubing and saw that it had turned a solid black in color.

"I think we did it, buddy," Eric said. " 'Cept what's to prevent them from turning it back on?"

They got their answer in the next second. The transformer began to smoke and whistle. The black tubing was crystalizing and crumbling onto the floor of the passage. They stepped back. There was a loud whine and the whole trembling contraption collapsed into itself, turning into a heap of molten slag.

His father had told him: *The destruction of this unit will knock out the whole system for an indefinite period. It will take hours to repair it. Long before then I hope to have put the biocomp out of action for good.*

His father had not told him just how he was going to do that.

But Steven had a pretty good idea.

"Now what?" Eric said. "Is it over?"

"My brother. My father," he reminded him. "I've got to save them, got to destroy that alien once and for all."

"That's impossible. You have no idea how powerful it is."

"But like this system, it has a weakness. Two weaknesses to be exact."

Eric looked at him.

"You—who can resist it. And me—whose existence it can't perceive. *We're* going to kill it."

As his father had predicted, the work train came back to the station a half an hour after it had departed. The plan was for him to go to the complex in case his presence was needed. It was now eleven-thirty. They were cutting it close.

Eric and Steven waited until the train was pulling out of the station before they climbed into the garbage car. The workers could not see Steven, but they *could* see Eric, and his newfound psychic prowess might not work against the comparatively normal drones.

The other cars were now half-full with more of the pitiful workers. Steven tried his best not to think about them. Soon they would all be free. But for how many of them would it be *too late?*

The train wound its way back to the platform where Steven had last stood with his father and came to a stop. Steven knew which way to go from here. The complex was only a short distance through the tunnel on the right. As Steven followed Eric out of the car he grabbed a large flashlight—a power lamp, it was called—and a wrench as an afterthought. They might come in handy.

Eric and Steven waited an appropriate time

until the train had gone on, and until those who'd disembarked had left the station, before they came out from behind the pillars at the end of the platform. They walked into the tunnel that Steven's father had gone into earlier.

The walls were made of white tiles. The fluorescent lighting made them shine. Everything was as bright and medicinal as a hospital. To think an alien consciousness had brought all this into being.

They reached the end of the corridor and came to a double door. The letters HGC and the words *For Authorized Personnel Only* were written across it. This was where they had to go. This was where Steven's brother and father were. Behind the door was a short flight of stairs.

At the bottom of the stairs was another narrow corridor lined with doorways. His father had told Steven to walk the entire length of this hall. If anyone came upon them and saw Eric, Steven could always use the tools in his hands as weapons. They literally wouldn't know who had hit them.

They heard someone coming around a bend in the corridor. Steven—his invisibility providing courage—was ready to fight if need be, but Eric insisted they duck into one of the rooms. Steven figured his companion was right. Why not avoid a confrontation if at all possible . . . save your strength for when you really needed it?

They were in a darkened laboratory. Tubes, vials, and machinery glittered in the light from the hall. The complex was certainly well stocked.

The footsteps went by. They felt it was safe to reenter the corridor.

They rounded the corner and approached a new set of double doors.

Steven held Eric back. "Let me go first. At least they can't see me." Eric didn't argue; he was not as calm, as cocky, as he had been before.

Steven prepared himself. He had no idea what he was going to find behind this door. *Or how many of them.*

He tightened his grip on the wrench with one hand, and placed one finger on his other hand above the switch on the power lamp. Using his four remaining fingers, he gripped the door handle and pulled it. He immediately smelled a strange and pungent odor, and his eyes began to tear. It was as if the room behind the door was full of ammonia. His eyes blinked involuntarily. He pulled the door open completely and was hit with a spell of nausea. He was afraid he might pass out.

The lighting was dimmer in this chamber. The walls looked red and sticky, but they were only covered with shiny pink paint. Eric and Steven advanced into the room.

A group of men and women in white smocks appeared out of nowhere.

At least two of the people were holding guns. The weapons were not aimed only at Eric.

A woman stepped foward and spoke. "Hello, Steven. Yes, we can see you. We could always see you. Except when the master didn't want us to. Your father underestimated the biocomp. It *wanted* you down here. It wanted your father to bring you."

"In case something goes wrong," one of the men said. "*Then you will be the backup.*"

Steven felt the bottom drop out of his stomach.

At least they didn't know that the power grid had been destroyed, did they?

"As for your father, the traitor," the woman continued, "he will pay for his transgressions. After he has watched his son become one with the master. The fool—he was doing the master's bidding even when he thought he was 'rebelling.' "

Steven wasn't about to be intimidated by these zombies. "Where *is* my father? Where's Joey?"

"You'll see later. *If* you're needed."

Eric could no longer keep silent. "Why don't you fight it, you people? Why don't you fight back? You're human beings, not slaves. Why don't you resist while its attention is diverted!"

"We don't want to die," one of them said.

"The whole *city* will die. The whole world—"

"*Except us.*"

So that was it. It was safer to go along, to play their part and follow the leader. Life was so precious to them they were willing to live it in constant subservience.

"Wait here," the first man said. "It will all be over shortly." He pointed toward a corridor behind them. "Even now they are taking your brother to the biocomp."

Steven knew he had to act. Flicking the switch

on the power lamp, he held it up to the nearest gunman's eyes and blinded him. The gun suddenly sprang to life, but Steven dodged the projectile. He lashed out with the wrench and knocked the weapon from the gunman's hand. He heard Eric cry out.

The psychic had managed to disarm the other gun-carrying committee member, but had taken a bullet in the shoulder for his trouble. "It's not serious," he assured his companion. "Go after your brother before it's too late!"

The others tried to stop him, but Steven would have none of it. He swung out with the wrench, enraged, slamming the heavy instrument into tender flesh and yielding bone. He ran away from the startled, injured group and darted into the hallway ahead, following the stench, fighting back the waves of nausea and the stinging tears that filled his eyes. His whole face was burning.

Eric held his bleeding shoulder and followed as best he could.

It was almost impossible for Steven or Eric to see anything ahead of them. Steven could just barely make out three figures. Two large ones, carrying a third, struggling, smaller shape between them.

"Joey!"

The young man answered. Steven would have known that voice anywhere. "Steven? Help me! *Help me!"*

Back in the operations room the members of the committee were over at a console adjusting dials and pressing buttons. "The system is *down!"* the first woman yelled. Staring past the running figures of Steven and Eric she tried in vain to catch sight of the three forms they were pursuing. Referring to the latter, she said, "We've got to stop them!" But it was too late. The biocomp was *aroused* and could not wait even if it would incur the wrath of its god.

Steven put on a burst of speed and tried to catch up to his brother. It was no use. One of the bodyguards knocked Steven to the ground with such force he had all the wind knocked out of him. As he tried to rise and clear his head, a huge door began to open, and a white hot stab of brilliant light illuminated the hallway. He saw Joey thrown into that room, where the stench was so overpowering, the air so acrid and thick. He heard Joey screaming. And, as the door began to close, he caught a glimpse of some enormous living thing, a throbbing mass of tissue, and he saw an eye, a gigantic eye, and it was *looking* right at him with disdain. *The firstborn, but the second best.* Steven screamed out loud to keep from fainting. Drawing upon a well of bravery he never knew he had, he jumped up, brushed away one of the guards as he tried to grab him again, and slipped into the lair of the biocomp just as the wide, massive door thudded shut behind him.

The stench was unbearable. Steven's eyes stung so badly he could only keep them open for moments at a time. He heard his brother squealing with pain, saw him being pulled toward the throbbing semi-mechanical orifice of the monstrosity. He ran in the direction of his brother's voice, hit something soft and squishy, yet firm and unyielding. He saw his brother at his side, grabbed him, and tried to pull him out, tried to get him away from the creature's consuming embrace, but couldn't.

Steven felt something tight surround his waist, then his chest and neck. Tentacles—if that's what they were—were pulling him away from Joey and from the beast. He was flung up in the air, his whole body going up and over, twirling furiously until he hit the hard concrete of the wall. He fell to the ground in a heap, covered in blood, his own blood. Something wet and heavy slammed into Steven's forehead. He had to fight to stay conscious.

Through the haze Steven saw that another figure was in the room with them. Their father. *He knew what he was going to do.* No. *No!* He wanted to save his brother, but not at that price! He didn't want to lose his father just as he'd found him again. There had to be another way!

Steven was too weak to stop his father, and really didn't know what he would have done had he been able to rise to his feet. Would he have taken his father's place, sacrified.himself? But would that have done any good?

He'd never know.

Bradford Everson pushed Joey to one side and took the boy's place in "the ceremony."

In a moment the man was being sucked into the thing, being devoured by the very "sexual act" he was forced to take part in. He was being engulfed by the viscous substance that made up the creature's reproductive region.

Dad! No! I still need you!

The biocomp ingested the man, made love to him.

But then something happened.

Bradford Everson's heart stopped. Bradford Everson died . . . before the biocomp had a chance to complete its task.

And when Bradford Everson died . . .

The creature squealed in agony. Its flesh, its mechanical fibers and organic tissues began to quiver.

Steven thought: *My father died a hero and no one will even know it.*

Huge appendages slapped against the walls in defiance. A jelly-like substance flowed across the floor. The biocomp's tremendous "eye" revolved and bulged in its socket. The hulking, nightmarish monstrosity was in its death throes.

Harry. Poor Lina. All of you. You have been avenged.

Steven saw that the door was opening. Eric and the others—at last free from the alien's control—were entering, dragging him and Joey to safety while the creature dissolved into an odorous stew of lifeless limbs and metallic organs. There was a final spasm . . . and the beast succumbed.

The beast succumbed and died.

EPILOGUE

WHEN STEVEN WOKE up he was in a hospital bed.

Had it all be a dream? No—it had happened. His father had come back from the dead, only to die again. An alien invader had landed on Earth and been defeated. It had enslaved, driven crazy, and murdered hundreds of people, but the human race had prevailed. *But would anyone believe it?*

They would have to believe it. Even now liberated slaves were making their way back to their homes and their loved ones. One person might not be believed; two, a dozen, two dozen. But a hundred, two hundred? *The world would have to believe.*

Something from the stars had come and nearly conquered the earth. Something devious and merciless. Something dead. Yet how could they hate a thing that had only been doing what it had been bred and programmed to do? Better to hate the *Marikai*, who had sent it.

Would they ever send another? Another biocomp? He assumed the colonizers would never arrive because of the biocomp's failure. Was there already *another* biocomp on earth somewhere, waiting to awaken, or already working its wiles? Steven's head hurt—he was too tired to think, too weary to worry. *Let the police round up the renegades, I'm too busy.*

Steven heard a rustle to one side. Someone was standing beside the bed.

"Andrea! Is that you?"

She bent down and kissed him.

It just came out. "Shouldn't you be with Donald?" There was no rancor in his voice; it was just a question.

" 'If all you can do is worry about that Steven Everson,' " she quoted, " 'you can't build a life with me.' And that's that. It's over with Donald." She leaned down and whispered with all her heart, "I want to try with you again."

Steven smiled. He could hardly contain his joy. "You're not just feeling sorry for me?"

Andrea shook her head. "Uh uh. You're not getting out of this *that* easily."

"How did you know I was here?" *How much she she know, period?*

"I got a call from an Eric Thorne. Nice man."

When Eric Thorne read your mind, Steven thought, *he didn't kid around.*

"Said he was there when you got hit by the car. Really Steven," she jokingly chided, "you *must* watch where you're going in a blackout. At least your injuries aren't serious. You'll be out of here soon."

She didn't "know" anything yet, but soon . . . soon everyone would know.

"Mr. Thorne said to tell you his shoulder was okay. Also . . . I didn't get it, but he said, 'If there's any more trouble, I can take care of it.' And he told me to tap my head when I said it. Does it mean anything to you?''

Good old Eric Thorne. The paranormal wonder had a swelled head, but that was all right. His services *might* be needed some day.

Steven would have something to say to the members of ''the committee'' who had refused to help his father. Yet, if he had been in their place . . . ?

''The lights are back on,'' Steven said.

''Yes, the blackout is over.''

''Good.''

''Somebody *else* is here to see you. He finally came home, the bad boy. And *you* were so worried.''

Yes. Yes—there had to be someone else. After all they had gone through he had to be all right.

Andrea made room for someone tall and familiar who was smiling down at Steven. Someone who had haunted his thoughts for days. Someone he had gone through hell for.

A blond-haired, freckled-face young man was grinning. ''How are you, Stevie?''

Steven couldn't control the tears. He reached up and held his brother close.

''Joey!''